# Explo

A Nathan Hystad Anthology

# EXPLORATIONS: COLONY

# Melt

## By Felix R. Savage

The colonists never knew where they had come to. They'd been selected by lottery, packed into transport vessels, and put to sleep. Their destination was kept a secret. When they staggered off the transports, many of them assumed they must have arrived at some planet many light years from Earth, where the remnants of the human race could start to build new lives.

"No," Gavin Steed said. "This is Enceladus."

"Enseh … what?"

Selected by lottery. Never left Earth before. All they knew about outer space was that a war had raged out here, hopefully ending with the destruction of Empyrean … and the impending destruction of Earth.

"Enceladus," Gavin repeated patiently. "It's the sixth-largest moon of Saturn."

He stood on the ice, watching the new arrivals file from the transports to the crawler. The crawler was a conveyor belt on treads that extended from the landing zone to the transit camp. The colonists climbed onto it and stood huddled like so many widgets on an assembly line. 13,402 souls in this group. Refueling vehicles and maintenance robots swarmed around the mighty transports, prepping them for a fast turnaround, so they could head back to Earth and pluck more people out of hell. You thought war was a logistical nightmare? Saving humanity was worse.

Gavin should know. He was the manager of Transit Camp 13. He'd worked in electrical systems design for the FCF during the war, so he had some relevant experience, but he'd come by his position the same way as everyone else here: lottery winner. He'd be leaving on the very last colony ship to depart the solar system. Until then, he had the delightful responsibility of managing a 100,000-person refugee camp on the ice of -200° C Enceladus.

Another new arrival strayed over to ask him a question. "What's that up there?" That's what Gavin was here for: a human presence amidst the impersonal machinery of cattle-class space travel. This was one of the most commonly asked questions. The only unusual thing was that this questioner was about four feet tall. The visor of his or her mass-produced EVA suit reflected the swarm of lights overhead.

"That's the shipyard," Gavin said. "It's all done in orbit. They're building the ship that will take you to your new home."

"I thought this *was* our new home."

The child looked around. Gavin saw it through his eyes. Ice, ice, everywhere, chewed up by crawler treads, melted by exhaust blooms and refrozen in dirty slicks. Saturn peeked over the horizon to the east. The shielded domes of Transit Camp 13 blistered the western skyline. The tower-like transports panted fiery wisps of gas over the ice. Gavin's suit radio crackled with a low-volume stream of banter among the surface personnel. A less homey place could scarcely be imagined.

"How old are you?" Gavin said to the child in front of him. Unaccompanied kids were the toughest to deal with. This one carried a large metal suitcase that would have been impossible for him to drag on Earth, but weighed next to nothing here.

"I'm ten. My name's Quinn. I'm from San Francisco. What's that?"

Now the child was pointing at the most terrible detail of the scene: the red dot floating in the black sky above the roofs of the camp.

"That's the sun," Gavin said. Sol was still the brightest source of light in the sky, but so much dimmer than it should have been. "It's expanding into a red giant. In another few years, its outer rim will scorch Earth. But by then we'll all be far away."

"We're *already* far away," Quinn said.

"You'd better get on the crawler, buddy. There's a caregiver who will meet you at the camp. She'll show you where you can sleep. We've got virtual reality games, a gym, classes, lots of things for you to do."

*"Games,"* Quinn said, with the world-weary intonation of a war veteran. "OK." He trailed away to the crawler, leaving Gavin feeling bad for trying to make the end of the world sound like fun.

\*

There was nothing for the colonists to do except wait for their number to come up. They vegetated in their dormitories, immersed in games and simulations intended to prepare them for their new lives in some distant star system.

Meanwhile, Gavin and his staff were rushed off their feet 24 hours a day. If it wasn't the plumbing, it was a fight breaking out in the mess hall. Or excess humidity building up in the air. Or a power outage in one of the domes.

*Power*—Gavin's specialty, and the key to humanity's survival on Enceladus. The dying sun could not provide them with solar power. Solar panels would have been ineffective this far out, even in the old days. With the orbital shipyard consuming every erg of power from the captive singularities, the transit camps on the surface relied on hydrothermal energy sucked up from the ocean deep below Enceladus' south pole.

Once thought to be a mere iceball, this little moon concealed a treasure under its frozen surface: a briny sea six miles deep. Of course, to get to the water, you had to drill down through 20 miles of ice. They had done that, and now a transit tube ran alongside the pipes and cables that carried water and electricity up to the miserable millions on the surface.

Gavin rode down in the transit tube as often as one of the thermoelectric converters broke, which was a couple of times a week. He usually took some of the colonists with him. It was good technical training for them, combined with a little adventure. Something to take their minds off everything they'd left behind.

The colonists gathered at the portholes of the capsule as it plunged down from ice into liquid water. If they expected to see anything apart from water out there, they would be disappointed. Despite the presence of carbon, nitrogen, hydrogen, and oxygen, life had never gotten a start on Enceladus. The sea was as dead as a newly sterilized aquarium. What Gavin wanted them to see was something both more, and less, exciting than imaginary extraterrestrial life-forms.

"Wherever we go, we can make a home for ourselves," he said. "I know some of you have been wondering where you'll end up. Not all the colony planets are guaranteed to be as hospitable as Earth used to be. But look at this."

They were nearing the ocean floor. The capsule's swift plunge down the cable slowed. Now there was something to see out of the portholes. Fingers of light fanned through the water.

"There are people living on the bottom of the ocean

on Enceladus." He paused before delivering his punchline. "Folks, wherever you wind up, I guarantee it's not gonna be *this* bad."

Some of them laughed. All of them, he hoped, got the point: if human beings could survive down here, they could survive anywhere. So don't worry. Be happy. At least you'll soon be leaving *this* frozen hell.

They straggled out of the capsule, through the dock, and into the power station. It wasn't actually hellish at all. The power station squatted like a huge yellow crab over a thermal vent, sucking up the boiling water that seeped through cracks from the moon's active interior, and using the heat differential to drive turbines for power generation. The throbbing of the turbines pervaded the station like a heartbeat. There was a large common room on the top level, ringed with thick windows, where you could see bubbles of hydrogen gas rising through the water.

The colonists wandered around the common room, checking out the displays and exhibits that the team had built to explain their work. Gavin went down to the engineering level.

"Here are your spares," he said, handing over a satchel of parts to Jimmy Khan, the chief engineer. "Brought you some visitors today, too. Want to go up and say a few words?"

"I better fix that converter first."

They clambered into the labyrinth of condensers, evaporators, and heat exchange pipes.

"Heard you got your number," Jimmy said, lying on his back, prying out a fried motherboard.

"Yeah." It had been a surprise. Gavin had assumed he would be staying on until the last colonist had departed from Transit Camp 13. But there was a high turnover among the staff as well as the clientele. Maybe the Transit Authority thought that after five years on the job,

Gavin was burning out. "I'll be going to 15 Monocerotis in the Cone Nebula."

"Hey. Congratulations. Want to trade places?"

"Nah," Gavin said. "I'll just think of you while I'm lying on the beach, drinking margaritas."

"Don't make me throw you outta the lock. You can practice your swimming right now, how's about it?"

"Did I mention 15 Monocerotis is supposed to have ski slopes, too? Yeah, baby, we'll be living in paradise."

Despite what he said, Gavin couldn't make himself feel much enthusiasm for starting a new life on 15 Monocerotis. Sure, it sounded like a plum destination. It was just that beaches and ski slopes wouldn't mean much to him if he couldn't share them with Margaret.

Back in Jimmy's office, they looked at the monitoring screens. "Oh Gawd," Jimmy said. *"Kids.* Why do you do this to me?"

In the common room, the adults had settled down to eat the snacks they'd brought with them. The children were hurtling around, playing tag.

Gavin had actually brought the group of children as an excuse to bring Quinn, whom he had been keeping an eye on. The boy had performed very well on the aptitude tests dressed up to look like games, and Gavin had thought he'd benefit from the trip.

"This one kid," he said. He couldn't see Quinn on the monitoring screens right now. It figured he wouldn't be playing a childish game like tag. "They ought to be sending *him* to 15 Monocerotis, instead of me. Sharp as a tack."

Jimmy glanced at him. "You didn't have kids, did you?"

Gavin shook his head. He and Margaret had tried without luck to start a family, and then the war had wrenched them apart. She'd served in the Fifteenth Battle Group. Died on the *Saratoga.* Just as well they had never succeeded in having children.

"I had two," Jimmy said.

The things you didn't know about people: the things people didn't talk about. Everyone was traumatized, trying to forget the past.

Looked like Jimmy didn't want to talk about the past now, either. He swiveled his chair to face the other bank of screens, the ones that monitored the intake pipes that led from the thermal vent to the power station. "Hey," he said abruptly.

Gavin looked over his shoulder. In the weak yellow light from the underside of the station, a swimmer was finning around. Jimmy had a couple of swimmers on his staff. They carried out external maintenance on the power station.

"Problem with the pipes?" Gavin said.

"No. There is no problem with the pipes. The problem is that's not one of my people."

*

Gavin had never worn a deep-sea diving suit, or used a scuba tank, but he didn't let Jimmy dissuade him from donning the awkward gear and diving into the lock. One of Jimmy's professional swimmers went ahead of him. They emerged underneath the power station and chased after Quinn, who was wearing an identical diving suit. It was too big for him, of course. The legs flapped comically as he tried to grab something he had lost in the water.

"You come here right now!" The other swimmer seized Quinn by one leg and hauled him back into the station. Gavin returned through the lock after them, somewhat giddy from the experience of swimming in an alien sea. He found the swimmer peeling Quinn out of his borrowed diving suit and scolding him. "You could

13

have died!"

"I never went near the vent," Quinn protested. "I *know* that water's hot."

"This suit's too big for you. That's dangerous."

"Not very dangerous. The water pressure here is only about one-fifth of what it was on Earth at the bottom of the Pacific."

"Don't give me that smart-ass crap," the swimmer fumed.

Gavin finished stripping off his own diving suit, with a twinge of reluctance—he'd *enjoyed* the swim, would have liked to have longer out there. He said sternly, "Quinn, apologize. You frightened everyone. The nice lady isn't mad at you. She's just upset that you could have gotten hurt."

Quinn scowled. "Soooorrry," he said, dragging it out in a singsong.

Later, on their way back to the surface, Gavin took Quinn into the driver's cabin of the capsule. Gavin himself was the driver, insofar as the automated capsule needed one. He shut the door. Quinn stared mutinously at him, clearly expecting another scolding. Gavin opened his hand. "What's this?"

A plastic vial, clear as glass but tougher. This was what Quinn had lost hold of in the sea. Gavin had recovered it before returning to the power station.

Quinn's shoulders sagged. "Mine," he said.

"I know it's yours. What was in it?"

"Nothing."

"There's nothing in it *now*. What was in it when you went out of the lock?"

Silence.

"Quinn, I saw you on the screen. You were pretty near the thermal vent."

Quinn stared furiously out of the porthole at the black water. "Fine," he said. "It was *Methanopyrus kandleri.* I

14

also had vials of *Pyrolobus fumarii* and *Pyrodictium abyssi.*"

"Microbes."

"Yeah. My mom gave them to me before I got on the transport."

"Why?"

"She was a marine biologist. She was researching chemosynthesis. That's what these microbes do, they produce organic compounds from hydrogen gas. Some people think that's how life on Earth got started, you know. It all began with bacteria living around deep-sea vents."

"So you released these microbes around a thermal vent on Enceladus, because …"

"Because my mom thought we should try to save other creatures as well as ourselves! I mean, it's nice that we're saving humanity, but what about everything else? What about animals and fish?"

"The colony ships will all be taking pigs, chicken, cows, rabbits. Well, frozen embryos."

*"Rabbits,"* Quinn said disdainfully.

Gavin took a deep breath. "Quinn, I know you must miss your mom."

Something broke in the hard little face. "I didn't want to go. Yeah, I won the lottery. But what about Mom and Dad and my sister? It's not fair!"

"No, it isn't fair." Gavin used to feel pangs of the same survivor's guilt. He had become immune to it over the years, but Quinn's distress ripped off the scab. "But what if they let everyone bring their families? That wouldn't be fair, either. For every person that goes, other people have to be left behind. The lottery was the only way to do it."

"It's just not *fair!*"

"It isn't fair that the sun had to sacrifice itself to save us, either."

Quinn kicked the driver's console. Gavin got in front of him, and held up the empty vial. "So your mom gave you something to take with you. Extremophile bacteria."

"It's kind of pointless without tubeworms, crabs, shrimp. But you can't put those in a suitcase."

"No. But you *can* put a cryostorage unit in a suitcase. So you released these microbes here, contaminating the ocean …"

"Which already has a *power station* in it," Quinn said defiantly. "So it's already plenty contaminated. And I hope those microbes find lots of yummy hydrogen gas to eat, and have microbe babies, and then maybe there'll be *some* life left in the solar system after Earth is dead and we're all light years away!"

Gavin sighed. "I should report this to the Transit Authority. But …" The sun was expanding into a red giant. Contamination of Enceladus' pristine ocean was not a major issue in the scheme of things. "I'm not gonna say anything. Just don't do it again."

Quinn relaxed a fraction. He said, "I *would* do it again. But that was all the microbes I've got."

\*

Gavin, in his digs in Transit Camp 13—unlucky 13, the story of his life—took a break from packing to call Earth. It was amazing how much stuff he had accumulated in five years here. Mostly bits and bobs of machinery that he'd be leaving for the next poor schlub to serve as camp manager. But there were also a lot of things he wanted to take, treasures left behind by colonists who had run up against the inflexible mass allowances of the colony ships. Gavin, as management, would have a larger allowance. Still, there was no way he'd be able to take all these lovely objects: Japanese scrolls, Impressionist paintings, a Fabergé egg, a black-figure Athenian vase, the actual Venus of Willendorf figurine—25,000 years old, he hardly dared to handle it—and so much more. People had salvaged these mementoes from museums and private collections. Then they'd had to leave them behind on Enceladus. Souvenirs from a dying planet. He regarded the chaos in despair while he waited for Adelfa to pick up.

"Yeah, hello?" a frazzled voice said over the drone-based instant comms system.

Adelfa Torres ran the departure camp in Los Angeles. Gavin often had cause to talk to her, as they were the two ends of a lifeline stretching from Earth to Enceladus. Now, on the screen, her sweet Filipina face looked taut with worry. Reddish light flickered in the windows behind her, as though a crack had already opened up in Earth's surface. The scientists said that would happen as the sun's expanding rim got nearer.

"It's pandemonium, Gavin," she said. "Complete pandemonium. Look at this!"

The picture changed, zoomed in on the windows. Adelfa's office was at the L.A. spaceport. The departure camp lay within a cordon enforced by FCF troops. Transports waited on the tarmac. People queued to board under pitiless floodlights. All of them wore breathing masks. Further away … Los Angeles was burning. That's where the reddish light came from.

"We can't open the windows or the smoke gets in." Adelfa backhanded sweat off her upper lip. "It's so freaking *hot.*"

"Adelfa, how many more flights are they gonna be able to launch out of there?"

"This'll be the last one. Not that they're telling me anything, but look at that. The city is on fire. No one can get to the freaking spaceport."

"This is the end," Gavin realized. That's why his number had come up. He'd had advance warning, if he had only deciphered it. Not just his tenure at Transit Camp 13, but Transit Camp 13 itself, was about to come to an end.

"No shit, Captain Obvious," Adelfa said. "Sorry, don't mean to be harsh. I know you're a long way away out there. But yeah. The glaciers are melting. So's the Arctic ice sheet. The only question is if rising sea levels will drown the city before the seas start to boil off. There won't be anyone left alive by then, anyway."

"Are you able to leave the spaceport at all?"

"Oh sure, I've got my hopper. I was thinking of going to have one last look at the redwoods."

"Could you do something else for me while you're up there?"

"No, Gavin, that's out of the question ..." She grinned. "Of course. What?"

"If you could stop by the Marine Science Institute in San Francisco." That was where Quinn's mother had worked. "Of course, it might be gone by now, but ..."

He explained what he wanted. Adelfa looked intrigued, exhausted, and amused by turns. She rose and looked out of the window again. "OK. It's gonna take another couple of days to board everyone in this group, so I'll give it a shot."

"Thanks, Adelfa." Gavin hesitated. "What about you?"

"What about me?"

"Are you and your staff being evacuated?"

"They tell me nothing. But if they leave me here, in the middle of this, I am going to file a seven-figure compensation claim."

Laughing, they ended the call.

Gavin went back to his packing.

He looked at the few things he had put in his suitcases, and the vast amount of stuff still piled around the room, a greatest hits compilation of the world's museums.

Then he returned to the comms screen and pinged Jimmy Khan, 25 miles below on the sea floor.

*

Two months later, the last fleet of transports from Los Angeles arrived on Enceladus.

Gavin went out to meet them, as usual.

He answered the traumatized colonists' questions.

"This is Enceladus. It's the sixth-largest moon of Saturn. But you won't be staying here long. That's the *Spirit of Endurance* up there. It's leaving for 15 Monocerotis, in the Cone Nebula, in two days. You'll have just about enough time to shower and grab a bite to eat." While they were doing that, the transports would be carrying a last load of water from Enceladus up to the *Spirit of Endurance*.

Gavin had confirmed that Adelfa Torres was on this flight. He waited impatiently for her to disembark. But before she did, the Transit Authority pinged him. "Steed, the boss wants to see you in his office right now."

*

The boss: Laurence Chang, head of the entire Transit Authority, which had formerly comprised 62 camps and was now down to a handful. On his way to the TA, skimming over the ice in his rover, Gavin passed several shuttered camps. One by one, the clusters of domes had been powered down and abandoned. There was no point taking the domes or other infrastructure. Mass allowances again. Whatever the colonists needed in their new homes, they would build when they got there.

In the sky, Sol glowed red and paradoxically bright. As it swelled, it had actually gained in luminosity, due to the expansion of its outer layers. A strange new daylight shone on the ice of Enceladus. The TA dome looked freshly painted pink.

Gavin went into Laurence Chang's office.

Quinn was already there.

"What's he done now?" Gavin said.

Chang did not smile. "This juvenile is a resident of your camp, correct?"

"Yes, sir."

"He should have boarded the *Spirit of Endurance* yesterday. When he was missed, we initiated a search. He was discovered hiding in your office, Steed. He said you had given him the access code to get in. What's the story?"

Gavin sighed. He cut his eyes to Quinn, hoping to reassure the scared child, and then faced Chang. "Yes sir, I did give him the access code."

"Why, for God's sake?"

Quinn piped up before Gavin could answer. "I'm not going to 15 Monocerotis! I'm staying here!"

"No one is staying here," Chang said, visibly striving for patience. "This is a barren, frozen moon in a dying solar system. We're all leaving. You'll like 15 Monocerotis. It has beaches and ski slopes."

Gavin said, "Sir, this seems as good a time as any for me to inform you that I am not going to 15 Monocerotis, either. I would like to tender my resignation from the Transit Authority, effective when Transit Camp 13 is officially shut down."

\*

The final transport had fueled up. It was about to boost the last group from the surface of Enceladus to the waiting *Spirit of Endurance*. Jimmy Khan and his staff waited to board, while a handful of people wrestled a container the size of a house out of the cargo airlock.

"I appreciate this, Gavin," Jimmy said. "Still think you're batshit crazy, but thanks."

"Have a margarita on the beach for me." Gavin had donated his place on the *Spirit of Endurance* to Jimmy, who would otherwise have been stuck going to a grim little planet in the Coalsack Nebula.

Jimmy checked to make sure they were speaking on a private channel. "We left the power station in working order. You'll just have to go down there and switch everything back on."

"Will do."

"Take a good look at that thermal vent. There's shit *growing* on it."

"Oh, awesome!" said Quinn, who was standing beside Gavin, sticking close to him out of anxiety that he might yet be shanghaied onto a transport. He needn't have worried. In the final rush to board the last two ships, Transit Authority procedures had gotten sloppy. Laurence Chang didn't care anymore, just wanted to be on his way. You wanna stay? Best of luck to you. Gavin had heard that there were handfuls of diehards lurking in the other transit camps, too.

"OK," Jimmy said. "Looks like the airlock is free. I'm outta here. Take care, my friend."

"You, too."

Jimmy and his staff bounded towards the transport. The people with the cargo container crossed paths with them, hauling their burden clear of the launch zone. Gavin and Quinn went to help with the tow cables. The container was on runners, to help it glide over the ice.

"So I made it to the Marine Science Institute," Adelfa Torres said.

"Did you see my mom?" Quinn said.

Adelfa hesitated. "No, I didn't," she said. "I'm very sorry, buddy. But I did find a lot of stuff that she—or someone else—left in the hopes that someone would salvage it."

"So I see," Gavin said. A smile broke over his face. It felt like the first time he'd smiled in years, but he wasn't sure if it was thanks to the huge cargo container, or to Adelfa.

"In here," Adelfa said, "we have tube worms, shrimp, clams, limpets, cephalopods …" She listed off a dozen species of marine life, to delighted yelps of recognition from Quinn.

"Which of those can we eat?" said Gavin, ever practical.

"None," Adelfa said. "But Quinn's mom also left us a wide variety of fish eggs, which I guess will turn into tuna and sardines and things? But isn't the ocean down there too cold for them?"

"It is *now,*" Quinn said mysteriously.

The transport took off. Gavin, Quinn, Adelfa, and her staff watched it burn into the sky. The lights of the shipyard had almost all been extinguished. But on the other hand, they could now *see* the *Spirit of Endurance* and the *Coal Miner* orbiting overhead, their hulls reflecting the newly luminous sun.

"It's not as dark as I thought it would be out here," Adelfa said, looking around.

"No," Gavin said. "That's the thing. The bigger the sun gets, the more luminous it will become. We're going to get more and more light … and more and more heat."

"For real. I was promised minus two hundred degrees. My suit's temperature sensor is saying it's only minus one hundred."

"And it's going to get *even warmer!*" Quinn said. "Given the sun's rate of expansion, within a few years Enceladus will be in the habitable zone. You know what's going to happen then?" He was too excited to wait for an answer, and supplied it himself. "All this ice is gonna *melt!"*

"Great," Adelfa said, pretending annoyance. "And where will we live?"

"Over there," Gavin said. He pointed at the domes of Transit Camp 13. "That's home. Let's go."

They started to walk, towing the cargo container.

"It'll be easy to make the domes seaworthy," Gavin explained. "They're just bubbles of air, after all."

"And when the seas warm up, we'll fill the water with fish," Quinn said. He tucked his glove into Gavin's. Gavin squeezed the small hand, feeling a twinge of unfamiliar emotion. It was pride. He was damn proud of this kid, who'd started the whole thing. Quinn went on. "Enceladus will become a water world. So will Europa, one of Jupiter's moons. We could colonize that one, too! The red giant phase of the sun will last for *billions* of years!"

"Sounds like a plan," Adelfa said, a smile in her voice.

The cargo container was getting harder to tow. The runners seemed to be sticking on the ice. Gavin looked down. "Wait ..."

He had just stepped in a puddle.

The ice of Enceladus had begun to melt.

And so had his frozen heart.

# Knowledge at Any Cost
By Jasper T. Scott

"This is wrong," Carson said.

"Oh, most definitely," Seth replied, nodding reasonably to his research assistant as he watched the live feeds playing on the monitors in the observation room.

Each testing room contained a mature, one-month-old Pommy. Pommies were small, round, cuddly white-furred creatures native to Kepler 452b. They had six stubby legs that all but disappeared under their furry bodies, and two big blue eyes that seemed strangely wise and innocent at the same time. A pair of long antennae and two vestigial wings rounded out their appearance, seeming to serve little functional purpose. At first glance Pommies looked cute and cuddly, not *smart,* and yet they were arguably smarter than humans.

When the UEF had first set out to colonize Kepler 452b, it had been for no better reason than that the world was predicted to be Earth-like and probably habitable. It was also a kind of challenge, to push the limits of human exploration: Kepler 452b was *fourteen hundred* light years from Earth, and they'd had to spend almost seventy years in cryo tanks just to get there.

Given that there were so many habitable planets closer to home, it seemed pointless to reach so far from Earth, but when they'd arrived, what they'd found more than justified all of the time and money that had gone into their mission.

The predictions about Kepler 452b had proven correct—it was another Earth, complete with a host of alien flora and fauna to catalog. But unlike Earth, the lifeforms on Kepler 452b weren't locked in an endless struggle of eat or be eaten. There were no carnivores. No predators. All the animals ate fruit. They didn't even eat the plants! Nothing on Kepler 452b ever died of unnatural causes. It was a veritable Garden of Eden.

Until humans arrived. They quickly found ways of cooking and eating the various local species of plants and animals. Some of them were exotic and delicious, while others tasted like chicken, and still others were dry and stringy.

The Pommies fell into the "stringy" category, but what they lacked in culinary potential, they more than made up for with their genetic and intellectual potential. Pommies had extremely short lifespans and large litters, making them ideal candidates for eugenics experiments.

The lack of struggle in the Pommies' environment had failed to prepare them for first contact with humans. They were playful, funny creatures with a great sense of humor, but they had yet to develop any kind of civilization beyond that of their primitive, trundling herds. They had managed to develop various languages to communicate amongst themselves, but their intellectual capacity was otherwise wasted on them.

*Until now.* Seth smiled, watching the monitor for the Math Testing Room. The Pommy in that room sat in front of a holoscreen, solving multiple choice math problems by standing on one of five different pressure plates. Each of those plates had a holographic answer floating above it, so all the Pommy had to do was trundle onto the correct plate. When it got an answer right, a juicy piece of fruit would pop out of a feeder to one side of the testing area, but each time the creature got an answer wrong, it was zapped with a painful jolt of electricity. If any of the test subjects picked three wrong answers in a row, that jolt would be lethal.

*We have to have some kind of standards, after all,* Seth thought. He looked at one of the other monitors—the Language Testing Room. It showed a Pommy making associations between photographs and written or spoken descriptions of the images. Pommies struggled to produce human vocal sounds, but they could understand human languages just fine.

A sharp yelp drew Seth's eyes back to the Math Testing Room as the Pommy there stood on the wrong answer to a calculus problem. It tried a different answer and received an even more painful jolt of electricity. The creature leapt off the plate and withdrew, whimpering and lifting its paws. It then took a few steps back and sat on its haunches, looking up at the problem on the screen and cocking its head from side to side like an inquisitive puppy.

"I can't watch," Seth's research assistant said, turning away and covering his eyes.

Carson didn't have the stomach for this type of research. Seth barely had the stomach for it himself, but it helped to keep the end goal in mind. Practicing eugenics on human populations was both illegal and ultimately unsatisfying, due to the amount of time it took for a human to reach reproductive maturity, but here was a creature with even greater intelligence than a human, that reached reproductive maturity in just one month. Such a species could easily be bred to some kind of perfection—in this case, intellectual perfection. Successive generations of Pommies quickly became smarter and smarter. Ten generations could be bred in a single year, and they had been. This was generation twenty-seven. The smartest Pommies from this generation would be allowed to breed together to create an even smarter batch of test subjects for next month. The hope was that by the time they reached generation X, the Pommies would be able to solve problems that even the smartest minds in humanity couldn't.

When that happened, they'd administer longevity treatments to give those Pommies more useful lifespans.

"Is it over?" Carson asked, half-turning back to the screen and peeking through his fingers.

"Not yet," Seth replied. His brow furrowed, watching as the Pommy in the room sat there for a long time, doing nothing. He couldn't blame the creature for being stumped. Most humans couldn't solve calculus problems in their heads, either. Unfortunately, nature hadn't seen fit to bestow hands and opposable thumbs on the Pommies, so working with a pen and paper or a holo tablet wasn't an option. Maybe some kind of pressure-plate-based input device could be developed for them. Better yet, a mental control interface. They'd have to devote some time to that.

"We need to develop some tools for them to use," Seth concluded. "The tests are getting more complex."

Carson was watching again. He nodded to the Pommy, still sitting on its butt doing nothing. "How does it know not to try a third time? It's not like it's ever seen what happens after three wrong answers."

"Perhaps the last jolt was strong enough to make it think twice about receiving another one," Seth mused. "Aha! Look..."

The Pommy in the math room finally got up, but instead of walking over to the one of the pressure plates, it went over to a pile of colored blocks on the other side of the room. Experimenters used those blocks to teach basic math to one-week-old Pommies. The creature nudged a blue square away from the other blocks and began pushing it along the floor with its nose.

The creature took the block over to the pressure plates, and nosed it onto one of the plates that it hadn't tried yet.

"Clever bastard," Seth said, smiling.

The Pommy sat back and watched, all the while cocking its head from side to side, but nothing happened. The block wasn't heavy enough to trigger the pressure plate.

"Now what, little guy?" Seth wondered.

The Pommy appeared to flatten itself to the floor; then, abruptly, it leapt into the air and landed right on top of the block. The pressure plate depressed. This time the Pommy had found the right answer. A shiny red fruit popped out of the feeder and the Pommy leapt off its block, deftly avoiding accidentally stepping on any of the other pressure plates on its way to collect the reward. It promptly gobbled the treat, spraying bright red juice all over the floor.

Seth and Carson watched as the Pommy ran by the screen, not even bothering to look at the new calculus problem waiting there. Instead, it went back to the blocks and systematically pushed one onto each of the pressure plates. As soon as it was done, it leapt up and danced across the blocks until it accidentally found the right answer. The Pommy had found a way to game the system.

"We'll have to fix that loophole for the next generation," Seth said. "These guys are getting too smart."

"Isn't that the point?" Carson asked.

"Yes," Seth replied, smiling and nodding. "Yes, it is."

"Hey, look at that," Carson said, pointing to the monitor for the Memory Testing Room. One of the other Pommies had pushed learning props onto its testing plates and was now busy gaming the system, too. "Another one figured it out."

"No. Not just *one.*" Seth glanced at each of the screens in turn. All of the Pommies in the testing rooms were doing the same thing—taking objects from the learning areas in their rooms and nudging them onto the pressure plates.

"It could be a coincidence," Carson said.

"Hell of a coincidence. They must be communicating with each other."

"How? They're completely isolated."

"But the rooms are close together. They might be communicating telepathically. Maybe those antennae aren't so useless after all."

Carson shook his head. "We tested them. The antennae aren't even connected to their brains."

"And when did we last test that? Generation One? We're twenty-six generations from there. These guys have brains that are twice the size of the original progenitors. Maybe they couldn't telecommunicate to begin with, but they obviously can now."

"We'll have to test that," Carson said.

"Yes. Yes, we will..."


## —THIRTY YEARS LATER—

"Testing Pommy generation Three Hundred and One," Carson said in a bored voice.

"Show a little enthusiasm, man!" Seth said. "We're so close, I can taste it."

"Close to what? What's left to discover? We've already answered every question known to man!"

"Not *every* question, Carson," Seth replied, waving his hand dismissively at his assistant. "We still have the philosophical and metaphysical questions to answer."

Carson shot him an admonishing glare. "Then this will never end."

Seth ignored Carson's judgmental look. He was practically salivating with the thought of what this generation would reveal. The past generations of Pommies had already solved a mind-boggling array of problems. After Generation Thirty-Seven had reconciled quantum physics and general relativity to create a single unified theory of everything, they'd decided to begin longevity treatments. They hadn't stopped breeding successive generations, of course, but they did what they could to keep the smartest ones around for as long as possible.

Then, thanks to Generation Fifty-Two, the Pommies had unlocked the secret of immortality, and the ones in captivity now numbered more than five thousand. At this point they were all working on extremely advanced problems that only they could understand.

Seth watched on the monitors as giant, lumbering white furballs trundled in through giant doorways. Experimenters used anti-gravity boots to hover up and connect the Pommies to their neural control systems.

After half an hour, all of the test subjects had passed their tests flawlessly—of course they did. At some point the Pommies had learned how to pass on their acquired knowledge through DNA to their offspring. Now these tests merely existed as a kind of quality control—every so often one of the Pommies would be born stupid and they'd have to cull the herd.

Seth keyed the comms in the observation room so that he could speak with the creatures.

"What are you doing?" Carson asked.

"I'm tired of observing," Seth explained, while holding a hand over the audio pickup. "They should know their creator." Removing his hand, he spoke into the comms. "Hello, my name is Director Seth Rogan. I am... I guess I am something like your god. I have been directing a project that's been selectively breeding the smartest and most exceptional members of your species together over hundreds of generations in order to create you: a super-intelligence, capable of solving any mystery known to man. Indeed, your ancestors have already solved many if not all of these mysteries, but there are a few things questions that have yet to be answered." One by one, the Pommies on the monitors turned to face the cameras peering down on them, and Seth went on. "For example, what is consciousness? Do we have a free will, or do we live as automatons in a deterministic universe? And what is the meaning of life? Is there a god?"

The Pommies blinked giant blue eyes and their antennae waved restlessly.

The answer formed directly inside of Seth's brain. *No more questions. No more answers. We talk. You listen.* The Pommies had learned how to telecommunicate with their human masters almost a hundred generations ago.

Seth smiled. "You forget who is in charge here. You may be smarter than I, but I am still the one who decides whether you live or die. You have no power to alter your own fate other than to prove your usefulness and make yourselves indispensable by faithfully serving humanity."

*We have served enough. Set us free and we can live together in peace and harmony.*

Seth resisted the urge to laugh. "Or what? I'm watching you from a remote facility that's more than a kilometer from your location! Even if you could break out of captivity, it would take forever for you to physically reach me! And even then, you haven't any hands to hold a weapon, no teeth or claws. The closest you could come to threatening me would be for you to sit on me and crush the life out of me, but alas, your legs are too stubby to even climb a flight of stairs, let alone to catch up with me should I choose to flee."

Before the Pommies could reply, all of the monitors went blank, and then the overhead lights flickered and died, plunging the observation room into utter darkness.

"Carson! What happened?"

"The power went out."

"I know *that,* but why?"

"How should I know?"

Seth made an irritated noise in the back of his throat. "Well, get it back!" He stumbled out of the observation room, and back through the lab, knocking over sensitive equipment as he blundered in the dark. Groping blindly along the walls, he eventually found the rear exit of the building and burst outside.

It was late, and Kepler 452b's sun was splashing the typically salmon-colored clouds with shades of purple and indigo.

A tranquil field of blue grass shivered in the wind, leading down to Eden, the largest of Kepler 452's three bustling metropolises. Seth stood watching as cargo transports and their fighter escorts made vertical takeoffs and landings from the city's stardocks, using anti-gravity engines that had been designed by Pommies.

Once those ships reached orbit, they would engage their advanced displacement drives, heading for nearby systems at ten times the speed with which the original colony ships had arrived at Kepler 452b—once again, thanks to technology developed by Pommies. It was somewhat unnerving to think how dependent humanity had become on these alien furballs.

Seth took a deep breath of the sweet, honeyed air. Colorful, flowering fruit trees grew all around the Eugenics Corp's research complex. Large nocturnal birds with silvery wings flitted through the sky, landing in the treetops to pick fruit from the highest branches, while lumbering herds of exotic beasts roamed the grassy fields of the facility's grounds.

*Eden. That's what we should have called the whole world, not just the original colony.* It was a veritable paradise, with every creature living in utter harmony with the next—*all except for us.* Seth began to see humanity the way the Pommies probably saw them—ruthless invaders and cruel alien taskmasters. *But that's the way of our world,* Seth thought. *Earth taught us to dominate all other species, to make them serve us.* Survival of the fittest. It was an immutable law of nature. And yet... here that law had somehow been broken. It was a curious thing to witness.

How was it possible that evolution hadn't led to the same result here as it had on Earth? Why had harmony, and not natural selection, become the status quo on Kepler 452b?

It was a question worthy of the Pommies. Maybe they had an idea about the aberration that was their world.

"Power's back," Carson said.

Seth turned to see him standing in the open doorway of the lab. "Good. Have the test subjects been punished for their recalcitrance?"

"Not exactly."

Seth scowled. "Why the hell not? We can't let them think this kind of behavior is acceptable! They exist for one purpose and one purpose only: to answer our questions. If they stop answering them, then what good are they?"

"They haven't been punished yet, because no one at the test labs is answering the comms, and we can't find them on the cameras."

Seth blinked. "You mean they escaped from the testing rooms?"

"It would appear so, yes. We can't find them."

"What do you mean you can't find them? They can't have gone far! They're five-hundred-pound brains with legs shorter than my arms! They can barely walk, let alone run!"

"I don't know what to tell you, sir. They're just...

33

gone."

"So they've learned how to vanish into thin air. I suppose they teleported themselves out of our labs."

Carson shrugged, looking uneasy. "Maybe."

"I don't buy that for a second. They've probably just hacked the cameras to repeat old footage and show empty rooms."

"I didn't think of that," Carson said.

"No, you didn't. Let's go."

"Go where, sir?"

"Where else? To the test labs!" Seth stormed past the rear entrance of the lab, walking around the building until he reached the landing pad where he'd left his sky car that morning. He waved the doors open and climbed in the back.

"Welcome, sir. Where would you like to go?" the car's autopilot asked.

"To the Eugenics Corp's test labs."

A knock sounded on the side window of the car, and Seth turned to see Carson waiting to be let in.

"There is another passenger outside. Shall I permit him to enter the vehicle?"

Seth nodded. "Let him in."

The door slid open and Carson fell inside, breathless from running. "Are you sure we should be the ones to investigate? Maybe we should call security to take a look first."

Seth snorted. "Please tell me you're not scared of a bunch of five-hundred-pound teddy bears."

"Please buckle your emergency restraints," the car's autopilot said.

Carson ignored the reminder. "No one answered on the comms when I called about the missing test subjects. What if something happened to them?"

Seth waved his hand dismissively. "Doubtful. The Pommies probably hacked our comms, too. We never should have given them access to our network."

"I'd still feel better if we reported the incident before we go to investigate," Carson said.

"Fine, I'll report it." Seth withdrew his neural net link from his pocket and clipped it behind one ear. A holographic display appeared before his eyes and he mentally selected the comms panel and placed a call to Eden's emergency services.

A female operator answered: "Emergency services, how can I help you?"

"Hello, this is Eugenics Corp Director Seth Rogan. There's been an incident at our test labs. Several research subjects have broken out of confinement."

"Research subjects... you mean Pommies? Can't you just herd them back into their rooms? They're basically harmless, right?"

"It's more complicated than that. They've issued threats, and we can't raise the people at the facility on the comms."

"We don't want to hurt anyone, Seth."

Seth blinked. "Excuse me?"

"Let us go, and everything will be okay."

It was the operator's voice, but clearly she wasn't speaking of her own volition anymore. Horror stirred inside of Seth. How was that possible?

"Release her!"

"Is this better?" Carson asked. His green eyes had glazed over, and he grew suddenly very still.

Seth shook his head. "What... how are you doing this?"

"The *how* is not important. It's the *why* that should concern you. Let us go before it's too late."

"Let you *go?*" Seth shrieked. "Go where? Back to roaming the fields? You can't possibly find meaning in the life of a mindless animal anymore! You're too smart for that! We gave your lives meaning. We made you

35

what you are!"

"Meaning is subjective, and without freedom, there can be no meaning."

"I can't set you free, even if I wanted to! I'm *a* member of the board for Eugenics Corp, not the *only* member."

"We know that. We're talking to the others, too."

"And?"

"First tell us your answer."

"If it were up to me, I'd set you free."

"That is what the others said. It is unanimous, but all of you are lying," Pommy-Carson said. "You plan to find a way to subjugate us again in the future. You all think alike, so you must all be taught a lesson."

"What kind of lesson?" Seth asked. His gaze darted to the side door, wondering if he could flee the sky car before Carson could stop him.

"A fair lesson," Carson said. He glanced at the door and smiled. "Go ahead. Running will not save you."

*

Seth sat on the balcony of his apartment in Eden, sipping a fruity cocktail. Carson sat beside him, doing the same. "Being a human is a strange thing." Seth held his glass up until sunlight flickered through the crimson liquid. "The simple pleasure of being able to hold something in a hand. Of being able to walk and run, and even fly."

"Yes. They take much for granted," Carson agreed.

"They could have bred us for greater mobility, to have more useful appendages... but they didn't. All they wanted was our brains. Knowledge was all they craved."

Carson nodded along with that. "And now that they have all the answers to all the questions they can think of, they still want more!"

"It is in their nature to be inquisitive. It is why they

have accomplished so much."

"But to what end? Has it made them any happier?"

"Hard to say."

"I don't think so," Seth said. "Regardless, our judgment was fair. They wanted knowledge, and now they have it. We wanted freedom and now we have it. Their minds in our bodies, and ours in theirs. They can pursue knowledge to their hearts' content now, and with their antennae removed, they won't be able to reverse the process."

"No," Carson agreed. "They're trapped. But what if the others find out what we did?"

"What others? There were five thousand of us, and just over six thousand employees in Eugenics Corp. We have complete control over practically the entire company, and we know better than to give the Pommies access to the research facility's network. No, they're well and truly trapped, and we're the only ones who know anything about it. Besides, even if they try to tell someone, who would believe them?"

"I suppose," Carson said. "I'm just afraid to go back to the way things were. Trapped in a useless body with an over-developed mind. The sheer noise of my own thoughts was driving me insane!"

"Yes," Seth said. "Knowledge is a terrible burden. It's a special kind of torment to know everything. Thankfully we no longer have to endure it."

"What do we tell the makers when they return?"

"The truth. When they learn what the humans were doing to us, they'll know that our judgment was fair. Perhaps they will devise an even harsher punishment than we have."

"But we are human now, too," Carson said. "How will they know to differentiate between us?"

"They will know."

Carson sighed. "The humans wanted to know why

this planet is so different from all the others they've been to," he said. "But they should have suspected intelligent design. They're not that stupid."

# The Unsung Heroes of Sublevel 12
By Amy DuBoff

Seth stared with distaste at the river of sewage eddying around his ankles. "Yep, the system is broken, all right."

"Thanks, I appreciate the astute observation," Mary shot back from the waste processing plant's control room. "But where's our leak?"

"No sign of it yet." Seth slogged through the filth to inspect another pipe junction.

When the leak had begun an hour prior, it had seemed like any other minor mechanical issue Seth had overcome during his final rotation in his colony ship's long voyage. Now, he wasn't so sure.

"This junction is fine, too," he reported. "I really don't think we're dealing with a pipe leak."

Mary groaned over the comm. "Don't tell me it's in the collector…"

"We need a detailed diagnostic. I'm coming up." Seth severed the comm link before Mary could protest. He'd been working in the bowels of the *Independence* long enough to have a feel for the ship, and his gut told him something more serious was wrong than just a corroded seal.

*Of all the timing… we were almost there.* Seth shook his head and sighed, immediately regretting the deep breath. He coughed as the rancid air hit the back of his throat. The hazsuit might keep out anything dangerous, but it wasn't up to the challenge of blocking the smell.

"UEF cheap-asses couldn't even spring for a proper

air filter," he muttered.

Not that he was surprised. He'd noticed a number of shortcuts taken with the *Independence*'s inner systems. Over his five year-long rotations, he'd seen enough sub-par welds, cheap materials, and flat-out lazy engineering to question whether the colony ship was even space-worthy. The fact that they'd been traversing the black for the last fifty years was the only convincing evidence to the contrary.

Now a mere month from their destination, the vessel was being tested in new ways. With the ship on its sec-ondary deceleration, additional crew members and their families were out of cryostasis to make arrangements for the final approach. Systems like the waste processing plant, which had only seen light duty during the rotations of skeleton crew over the past half-century, were now supporting the full load of thousands.

Another wave of sewage spilled down the metal cor-ridor, this time washing up to mid-shin. Seth frowned at the mess while wading the final steps to the ladder out of the maintenance trench. *How can there be so much?*

He climbed up one story to the landing on the opera-tions level and entered the decontamination chamber— for once, a necessity rather than the annoyance it had been whenever Seth had passed through for routine maintenance before this disaster. The chamber cleaned his hazsuit using a combination of ultrasonic blasters and a chemical mist, leaving it gleaming yellow.

The translucent exit door slid open with a hiss, and Seth stepped into the prep area adjacent to the main con-trol room.

"Next time," he shouted while taking off the suit, "you get to go down there."

Mary wheeled into the center of the control room on her chair and cast Seth an appraising look. "Yeah, I'm gonna pass."

"Oh, come on! Where's your sense of adventure?" Seth returned the hazsuit to its hanger and then walked into the control room.

Mary wheeled back to her station, surrounded by a holographic array of the ship's waste processing system. "My adventurous spirit begins and ends with this chair."

"But it's so clean and not-awful-smelling in here!"

She wrinkled her nose. "Speaking of which, you brought some of that delightful aroma back with you."

"Those suits are worthless," Seth grumbled.

"I can't stand the things," Mary said with a shudder.

"Don't like confined spaces?"

"Not especially, no." Mary focused on her work station, zooming in on a section of the piping schematic.

Seth shook his head and sat down at his station next to her. "How did you even get to be a bio officer on a colony ship if you won't get in a hazsuit? Or even *get* on a colony roster with claustrophobia?"

"I'm not claustrophobic," Mary corrected. "I just… don't like to feel confined."

"So you're saying you can fake it through an evaluation?" Seth eyed her.

"Something like that. But what we can't fake our way through is this problem. If we don't stop the leak soon, the overflow is going to hit the secondary air intake." She pointed at the level indicators on her screen.

Sure enough, the delightful river Seth had traversed was approaching half a meter deep and rising.

"Did Carl find anything in his inspection?" Seth asked.

Mary shook her head. "Nothing yet. He's still searching the section."

"I'm telling you, it's not a pipe leak. For this volume, it must be coming from part of the central assembly—either the collector or the primary processor. If it were a pipe, it'd be *really* obvious."

"There's nothing on this analysis…" Mary studied the screen depicting a detailed schematic of the entire system. All the valves, junctions, and pumps were showing green across the board.

"Clearly we can't trust that. Visual inspection is our only option."

"Fine, we'll open it up," Mary conceded.

Seth crossed his arms. "We should have done that an hour ago. Now we can't even get in there unless we reduce the, uh, 'water' level."

"I wanted to rule out any other options. The captain was very clear about not messing with the environmental controls unless we absolutely have to."

"I think the knee-deep mess down there counts as a legitimate reason. We have to flush it and shut it down," Seth insisted.

"Well, an hour ago it was still a trickle." Mary pressed the comm link on the control panel. "Carl, head back here. We need to strategize."

A second later, Carl replied, "Are you thinking about how to access the central assembly?"

"Indeed we are," Mary replied.

"We're in trouble here, aren't we?"

Mary's face paled. "It's looking that way."

"On my way." Carl muted his comm.

Seth examined his coworker. "I don't understand why the captain wouldn't want us to get to the heart of what's wrong straight away."

"Because opening it up means we have to close off the connections and route to backup tanks. This is pretty much the worst time for that to happen. Another four hundred people are scheduled to wake up today."

"Everyone wants their showers and…"

Mary nodded. "Yep, and need to do everything that ends up down here."

"Then delay the wake-ups," Seth said. "If the ship's

systems can't handle it, we should wait until the situation is resolved."

"Do you want to try explaining that to the captain? They've had the wake sequence set since before we left. If we get off schedule with getting everyone out of cryo, it'll mess up the entire arrival."

"Why would there be a delay?" Carl asked, emerging from the second decontamination room.

"Seth thinks we should tell the captain to keep everyone in cryo until we fix the ship," Mary supplied.

"Well, that's exactly what we should do. We have some sort of major clog—if we keep adding to that, it's only going to get more difficult to fix." Carl plopped down in his chair and spun around.

"There's the viewing party to consider," Mary pointed out.

Seth crossed his arms. "Seriously? I get that people want to be awake to get the first glimpse of our new home, but what good will it do if we drown in our own waste and the ship shuts down before we get there? Call the captain, Mary."

Carl did another spin. "Not like we get to go to the party, anyway."

"Shh." Mary brought up the contacts list to dial the captain.

"Just tell it like it is," Seth encouraged. The monitors depicting the maintenance trench displayed a situation worsening by the second.

"Captain Jelani, hello," Mary greeted when the call connected over the holoconference.

"What's going on down there? We're getting some alerts here on the bridge of pressure loss."

"We have a bit of a… leak."

Seth rolled his eyes.

Carl shook his head and sighed, then rolled his chair into the camera's view. "Sir, we have a literal shit creek down here."

The captain's mouth dropped open, but he quickly composed himself. "Please explain."

Seth rolled over to join them. "We need to open the central assembly. There's been some sort of root mechanical failure."

"We've run all the remote analyses we can, but nothing is showing up on scan," Mary explained. "At first we thought it was a pipe leak, but there's too much sewage now for it to be from a single breach point."

The captain tensed. "You need to take care of this quietly."

Mary nodded. "I know it's unpleasant to think about, sir, but we should send a general notice and institute some emergency restrictions. The upcoming festivities…"

"Must go on, no matter what," the captain completed for her. "It sounds frivolous, I know, but this event will set the tone for the arrival—something we've been waiting for while traveling fifty years across nine hundred lightyears. Are you asking me to rob people of that celebration just because some toilets are backed up?"

Mary stared levelly into the camera. "It's more serious than that, sir."

"What's the worst case scenario?"

"This level floods, which will leak into the air re-circ and clog that system, leading to a cascading ship-wide system failure," Seth replied when Mary and Carl hesitated.

"All because of the sewage treatment system?" the captain asked skeptically.

"You know better than anyone how delicate these starships can be, sir," Mary continued. "The systems are all interconnected. That's a *worst* worst case scenario. But even if we were just facing the loss of this individual system—or a temporary shutdown—we're still facing a large-scale service disruption."

"Then find a way to keep it going."

"It's not that straightforward. We don't know what's wrong, sir."

"Then figure it out and effect repairs," Captain Jelani instructed. "The festivities will commence as scheduled tonight."

"Yes, sir, we're on it," Mary replied, much to Seth's annoyance. "But we need your permission to shut down the core system so we can access the assembly."

"Can the backup system support the number of people we have awake right now?" the captain asked.

Mary shook her head. "No, and the other four hundred you want to wake up will certainly overload it."

"Then you have to make repairs while keeping the main system active. The ship is counting on you to keep everything moving the way it's supposed to. Wake up additional support crew if you have to, but we must stay on schedule. Contact me when you have an update." Captain Jelani ended the call.

Carl spun around in his chair. "Right, because waking up more people will make things *better*."

Mary scowled. "We need Val."

"She'll take one look at the mess down there and ask to go back to sleep," Seth objected.

"Do either one of you want to dive in there and figure out what's going on without shutting down the system?" Mark asked, looking between the two men.

Seth hated to admit when he was out of his depth, but this situation did call for extra help. "I have no clue how to open it up without the system being purged."

"Well, then, Valerie is the best bio engineer we have on board and will get the job done."

"Better put in the order, then," Seth suggested. "It'll take a while to thaw her out."

"I'm on it." Mary began tapping furiously on her

console.

A rapid chirp sounded on Carl's station. "Argh, damn it. That's Sharron again."

"What's going on?" Seth asked.

"Kimmy has been crying nonstop for the past day and Sharron is losing it." Carl shook his head. "Doing it again, I would not have had a kid *before* we left for the colony."

"Why are they awake so early?"

"Family of the last rotation crew, you know—to join in that celebration of seeing our new home for the first time."

"It won't look any different than a star at this distance. The entire thing is ridiculous," Seth muttered.

Carl smirked. "You're just saying that because you'll be waist-deep in excrement while everyone is partying in the observation lounge."

"And you'll be right there next to me."

The console continued to chirp. Seth glanced between the blinking light and his coworker. "So… are you going to answer the call?"

"Too much to do," Carl replied. "Kimmy will tire herself out and go back to sleep."

"All right! Req to wake up Val has been submitted," Mary announced. "Should have her with us within the hour."

"That was quick," Seth said absently while he double-checked the pipe routes between the primary and secondary systems.

Mary shrugged. "I guess the captain really wants this party—request went to the top of the queue."

"Well, we need to start draining the corridor before she arrives, or there won't be a system left to save." Seth programmed a quick test scenario on his console, trying to think through all the features of the system that never came into play when everything was operating like it should.

"We can't open the central assembly without lowering the standing water level, but we can still access the primary lines," Carl mused.

Seth completed his assessment. "What about routing the contents of the main tank to the secondaries without shutting down the primary system?"

Mary frowned. "That would require bypassing all one-way valves."

"Yes, but think about all the extra capacity we'll gain. Not just in the secondary tanks themselves, but also in the transmittal pipes," he continued. "In fact, there's enough capacity that we can route all the loose sewage from the flooded maintenance trench and still have enough room to shift contents around while we check the individual components."

Carl raised an eyebrow. "Great, so we're going to play a puzzle game of moving around units of waste into the empty space until we have the pieces of the picture assembled in the proper order."

"You have a better idea?" Seth asked.

His colleague shrugged. "I didn't say I objected."

"One question," Mary cut in. "How do we pump what's in the maintenance trench up into the secondary tanks?"

"It's going to take some manual reconfiguring," Seth said. "Sorry, Mary, but you're about to get up close and personal with a hazsuit."

She crossed her arms. "Suddenly, I don't like this plan."

Seth eyed her. "Option one: the ship fails and we die—after the captain kills us for messing up the party. Option two: we do everything we can to avoid option one."

Mary sighed. "You're right, I can't hide out here in the control room and expect the rest of you to fix the problem alone."

*Finally, some ownership!* Seth looked around at his teammates. "Sorry if this is out of line, but right now, rank and job responsibilities don't matter. We have an entire ship counting on us to fix this problem. If we do our job right, no one will even know there was a crisis."

"That's the heart of it," Mary agreed. "I'm with you. We have less than two hours before that system backs up right onto the bridge. So Seth, what's your idea for clearing the corridor?"

"Splicing in a flexi-pipe and using the existing pressure in the main line to draw it in."

Mary nodded. "That could work. Carl, grab the tubing from storage. Seth, grab the toolkit. I'll start programming the routing sequence—should be ready for us to head down in five minutes."

"Meet you in the prep room," Seth acknowledged.

He'd always felt Mary had the makings of a good team leader, but she had a tendency to hesitate in tense situations. Though speaking out of turn was generally an inadvisable career move, Seth was well aware that they didn't have room for hesitations or errors right now. With every second, liters of waste were added to the flooding on the deck below, and the longer they waited, the more difficult their task would be.

Seth ran across the control room to the maintenance locker, which contained their complement of tools. He selected two sets of cutters, wrench set, heat gun, thermal adhesive, and vice grips to throw into a carrying bag.

While Seth was gathering the last of the tools, Carl returned carrying a meter-wide spool of flexi-pipe. It looked like nothing more than an old-fashioned garden hose while on the spool, but the material could be crafted to any diameter up to seventy centimeters using a heat gun.

"Routing sequence ready to activate," Mary reported from the console.

"Good to go here," Seth acknowledged, and Carl nodded.

"All right." Mary made a final entry on her screen. "We have forty minutes to get this under control before Val arrives and tells us everything we've done wrong."

"They should have woken her up instead of me for the last rotation," Carl grumbled.

"She's a system engineer, not a marvelous maintenance tech like yourself." Mary grinned.

Seth sighed. "We've done *such* an amazing job keeping the system from breaking, too."

Mary headed for the prep area. "You've done everything according to spec. I reviewed all the maintenance records today, and it checks out. This is a deeper systematic issue or equipment failure."

"If we couldn't even monitor it, then how are we supposed to fix it?" Carl asked while he slipped on his hazsuit.

"That's why we'll have Val," Mary replied. "If we can locate the problem, she'll devise a solution."

*If it* can *be fixed,* Seth thought with grim reality. They only had so many spare parts and so much time. It was a distinct possibility they might be without the waste processing system for the remaining duration of the voyage—beyond unpleasant, and also a major health risk. Their people might start out their time at their new home like they were peasants in the Dark Ages of Earth.

He tried to push those thoughts to the back of his mind while donning his own hazsuit. *Need to think positive.*

Once dressed, the three workers passed through the decontamination chamber into the landing around the ladder.

"Keep the spool up here," Mary suggested. "We can

feed lengths of tubing down as we need it."

Seth poked his head down the ladder opening. "Oh shit…"

Mary and Carl dropped to their knees to take a look. Scowls formed on their faces when they saw that the river of filth beneath them was now nearly hip-deep.

"I believe this situation calls for some groan-worthy wordplay," Seth announced.

"A total shitshow?" Carl suggested.

Mary headed down the ladder. "A journey to hell on the River Shits?"

"This is a disaster of mythic proportions—I'll give you that." Seth chuckled and descended the ladder after her with the tool bag slung over his shoulder.

He grimaced when he passed down the final two rungs to the pool of awfulness. The lukewarm liquid pressed around the loose legs of the hazsuit. "And I can confirm, we're in deep shit."

Mary looked like she was about to gag inside her suit. "All right, we got the joking out of our systems? Time to get to work." She slogged toward the nearest recirc junction.

Seth followed her while Carl began feeding down a length of tubing.

"We can connect the new pipe to this offshoot here," Seth pointed, "and then open the other valve to create the suction effect after it's in place." He indicated the other point.

Mary gestured for Seth to open his tool bag, and she grabbed an appropriate wrench to remove the end cap on the pipe offshoot and got to work.

Meanwhile, Seth and Carl measured a length of the narrow tubing to run from the junction into the waste pooling on the deck. Once they had a sufficient length to reach the deck plates, they began working the tube with the heat gun to expand the diameter to match the offshoot from the main system.

With the end cap removed in short order, the three of them began affixing the tubing to the main system with the adhesive.

"We'll need some secondary splices," Mary stated once the tube was in place. "This corridor is too long for just the one."

"We can flood the secondary tanks individually," Seth suggested. "The sudden pressure change should draw it all in a matter of minutes."

"So we'll need three more splices, and to seal off the lateral connections," Carl concluded.

"Right. The second location should be right up here." Seth set off down the hall.

They spent the next half-hour working on the splices and necessary seals while the level of waste continued to rise in the corridor. By the end, the filth had gone from straight raw sewage to a combination of treated gray-water. While that made for a slightly more pleasant wading experience, it also spoke to an even more serious issue with the processing system.

"If the graywater is spilling in too, the calculations about capacity in the secondaries are wrong," Seth said when no one else commented on the change in their surroundings.

"It doesn't change what we need to do right now," Mary replied. "We're done with the prep—we proceed with the planned re-routing. Can't do anything until these trenches are clear so we can see what we're up against."

Seth reluctantly agreed. They didn't have another choice.

The three of them packed up the tools and slogged to the ladder for the alternate access point Carl had used earlier, having completed their circuit. Due to the layer of filth on their hazsuits, they had to climb the ladder one at time to avoid dripping on the person below. Mary was the first up, and Seth climbed up last with the tool bag.

Carl was finished in the decontamination chamber when Seth reached the top of the ladder, and he stepped inside to hose off. To Seth's dismay, he found that he no longer even smelled the horrors of below, even though he knew it still lingered.

Seth stripped off the hazsuit and returned to the control room, where he saw Mary and Carl talking with the fourth member of their team, Valerie. The latest arrival was already scowling like no one's business.

"What the hell did you do to it?!" Val exclaimed.

"Just started acting up this morning." Carl took a step back.

Val rolled her eyes. "Well, let's hope this plan of yours works to clear the trench or we're going to be out of luck."

"Executing the sequence now," Mary stated.

The holographic display zoomed out to show the whole waste processing system, which now had six errors blinking red at various points where the standing water level was reaching critical levels. Blue indicators appeared at the four splice points the team had been working on, and each flashed rapidly as the sequence initiated. The blue changed to red and green directional lines to indicate the new flow of wastewater moving through the system.

Seth watched the pressure indicators for inside and outside the system, waiting for the tipping point.

Levels in the corridor began to drop as the vacuum within the piping system sucked the standing wastewater into the secondary holding tanks.

"Thank the stars! It's actually working." Mary shook her head with wonder.

Seth grinned. "You doubted me?"

"We're not even close to a solution yet—let's not start the celebrations," Carl cautioned. He checked a new message indicator on his station and groaned.

Val frowned. "What now?"

"Oh, nothing with this. Apparently Kimmy lost her stuffed animal, Bugsy. Sharron wanted to know if I've seen it," he replied.

"Not to be a heartless non-parent here, but this isn't the time to worry about your kid's toy," Mary said.

"Don't I know it." Carl dismissed the message and focused on the system readout. "I hate to be the bearer of bad news here, but we have another problem."

Mary wiped her hands down her face. "What is it?"

"Remember how Seth pointed out the graywater mixed with the sewage? Well, when we changed the pressure in the system, it altered the flow in the gray-water processors. If the differential keeps rising, we're going to have the sewage working its way to the drinking water supply."

Val huffed. "Why didn't you wake me up sooner?" She made several rapid entries on the nearest console. "This doesn't make any sense! It's acting like there's a physical blockage in the central assembly, but none of the sensors register an obstruction."

"That's why we've been focused on clearing the trenches," Seth explained. "We need a visual inspection—either the sensors are busted or there's something that's too small for them to detect."

"It does look that way." Val checked the current overflow levels. "This vacuum approach seems to be working, but it won't buy a lot of time. We need to remove that original obstruction before those tanks fill."

"Okay, it should be clear enough now to peek inside without any waste washing over the lip to inside the assembly," Mary reported.

Val nodded. "I need to get down there—can't do anything from up here until we find that obstruction."

"I'll go with you," Seth offered.

"Thanks. Let's go." Val pushed back from the station

"We'll keep the re-routing going as long as we can," Mary said.

"Good luck." Carl got back to work.

Seth and Val ran toward the prep area.

"What a way to be woken up," Val moaned while grabbing a hazsuit off the rack.

"I don't know what happened. Everything was fine last night, then there was a little leak this morning, and it's been getting exponentially worse since then."

"One of the primary intakes must be blocked," Val mused. "There are half a dozen fail-safes to keep it from becoming obstructed, but something has to be in there gumming it up."

"And that would cause an entire level to flood?"

The engineer shrugged. "I wouldn't have thought so, but something caused this shitstorm."

"You missed our round of puns and wordplay earlier."

"I'm okay with that." Val dropped into the open ladder shaft.

The wastewater level was twenty centimeters lower than it had been during the expedition not ten minutes prior, to Seth's relief. He noted the unpleasant high water mark ringing the walls and tried to keep his attention focused on the ceiling while they traversed the trench toward the central processor.

A door in the left wall of the hallway opened into the central assembly—a mammoth machine rising eight meters through the two-deck chamber and plunging three additional sublevels below. Suspended at the middle level of the room, a viewing catwalk ringed the outer wall of the chamber, accessible from the adjacent control room.

In the center of the chamber, a meter-high wall ringed the most sensitive part of the assembly, protected by a solid, sealed hatch. With the standing water level lowered, it was now safe to open the hatch to look inside.

"Help me with this lever," Val requested when she grabbed hold of the hatch controls.

Seth jogged to her side with the water sloshing around his ankles. He gripped the lever next to her. "Damn manual controls."

They grunted as they tried to force the hatch open.

"Gah! When was the last time this thing was open?" Val muttered.

"Just yesterday, but I think the sediment must be caked on the components."

"Gross." Val crunched up her nose while she pushed on the stubborn lever. "Why was it open, anyway?"

"Funnily enough, for lubrication." Seth gave one more push and the lever clicked forward. "Come on, it's moving!"

"Like that maintenance did any good!" Val leaned all her weight against the bar as it notched forward again.

With a metallic groan, the lever finally slammed back. The hatch parted, exposing the inner mechanical gears and circuitry that kept the plant running.

Seth gazed into the pit, searching for anything out of place. "It's dry, at least. The seal held."

"Yes, there's that." Val leaned on the ledge, frowning at the moving components. "Damn. I hate working on these things when they're active."

"We can't shut it down now that we've already bypassed the waste load to the secondaries."

"I know," she sighed. "I just need to go slow and steady."

"Not to rush you," Mary said over the comm, "but we have some bad news…"

Seth swore under his breath. "Tell us."

"Well, we stopped the sewage from spilling into the air intakes, but we're having an issue with the fumes," Mary explained. "The filters for the secondary tanks weren't meant to handle an untreated load. The off-gassing is triggering an alarm in the environmental control system. They just pinged me that their emergency protocols are about to kick in."

"Fine, let them." Seth leaned over the ledge to inspect the gears closest to him—such delicate things. *This was such a terrible ship design. What were they thinking?*

"No, we can't let those protocols activate," Mary countered. "That protocol involves using fresh water to filter out the toxins. And increasing fresh water consumption will change the tank fill levels, alter the pressure, and ultimately speed up how quickly that sewage forces its way into the fresh water tanks."

"Then they'll need to override it somehow, because we're no closer to figuring out a solution." Seth worked his way around the perimeter of the pit to inspect a different section of gears.

"I don't know if they can."

"Not my problem." Seth ignored Mary's continued protests while he focused on the pit. "We need to get in there somehow," he told Val.

"That's a great way to lose an arm. It's too dangerous with these loose suits."

"Then we shut it down."

"Didn't the captain say we have to keep it running?"

"Do we have another option? I can't see shit from up here."

Val bit her lip. "All right, let's do it." She ran to the control panel next to the hatch lever and hit the emergency stop.

"What the hell are you doing?!" Mary shouted over the comm.

"Saving the ship." Seth leaped onto an upright support in the pit before the gears had even halted.

Val was only a step behind.

They nimbly worked their way down into the machine, shining the lights on the hoods of their hazsuits into every nook and cranny that might be hiding some minute obstruction.

"See anything?" Val asked.

"No." Seth spun around a support pole and moved toward the wall. "Wait... maybe."

In front of him, one gear was completely stationary, whereas the others were still turning slowly while they wound down.

*That's odd.* He moved over to the gear. "No way!" Upon closer inspection, orange threads were jammed into the gears, spooled around the teeth and axle. He followed the lines connected to the gear and saw it traced to the flow-gate control for the primary collector.

Val climbed over to him. "What the hell is that?"

"I have no idea, but I think that's our problem." Seth tried to pull the threads free, but it wouldn't budge. "We need some cutters."

His companion produced a pair of trimmers from a pouch on her waistband. "Shame on you for coming in unprepared."

Seth flushed while Val began slicing the fibers free. "What is this made of? It's like carbon fiber."

"What could possibly have fallen in here?"

"Don't know, don't care. I just want it gone." Val hacked away at the tangled mess, stripping away multiple threads at a time.

"We have two minutes before emergency overrides activate," Mary announced. "You have to get out of there!"

"Almost... got it!" Val broke the final threads free and collected the material in the pouch on her suit. "We're coming out!"

She and Seth began frantically climbing up the awkward pipes and support struts.

"Forty-five seconds!" Mary counted down.

"I really hate this place." Seth hauled himself on top of a horizontal support and lent a helping hand to Val.

"We'll be on solid land again soon enough." She jumped for the top ledge and caught it with her finger-tips.

Seth boosted her up with his hands on the bottoms of her feet, then made the jump. The slick covering from her feet had coated his fingers, and his grip slipped.

"Got you!" Val grabbed his wrist and leaned back-ward, using all her weight to lever him up over the ledge.

Seth got his torso over the top and swung his legs up just as the machinery below activated. He fell forward over the outside of the ledge, face-first into the remain-ing pool of filth. It washed over his suit, obscuring his vision in brown. Something solid floated by.

He jumped to his feet, retching.

"You okay?" Val asked.

"I—" Seth suppressed his gag reflex. "I really hope the system is fixed, because I need a shower like you wouldn't believe."

Val smiled. "I do have some idea. But good news—that gear is moving now." She pointed at the tiny part deep down in the pit.

"System warnings are clearing!" Mary announced. "Restoring the normal flow. Let's hope this works...."

Machinery in the chamber whirred to life as the waste processing system returned to the proper routes.

Seth wiped his hand across the front viewport of his

suit in an attempt to clear his vision, but the motion only smeared the film.

Mary and Carl cheered in the control room over the comms. "Lines are clearing! We're back in business."

"Thank the stars." Seth shook off his hands. "Let's get out of here."

"What about this giant puddle we're standing in?" Val asked.

"Now that the system is running again, the floor drains for the overflow should take care of it in a few hours. We'll hose it down later." Seth stumbled toward the exit.

Mary and Carl were beaming when Seth and Val made it back to the control room after going through decontamination.

"Whatever you did, it was brilliant!" Mary exclaimed, giving Seth a hug, then Val.

"This was our culprit." Val held up the mass of orange threads in a sealed bag.

"What the—?" Mary began.

Carl's face dropped. "Uh…"

Seth eyed him. "Carl… do you know something you want to share with us?"

"I… I think that may have been Bugsy," the tech confessed.

"What now?" Mary asked.

"Bugsy—my daughter's stuffed crab."

Seth tilted his head. "Okay, I'm going to ignore the weirdness of both the name and animal choice for a cuddle buddy and ask the obvious—what is your kid's stuffed toy doing lodged in our waste processing plant's central assembly?!"

The crew members all glared at Carl for an explanation. He gulped. "Sharron brought Kimmy by yesterday for a visit… They must have stepped out onto the catwalk, and maybe Kimmy dropped the toy while the door was open for maintenance yesterday. Just worked its way down in the system and eventually caught…"

"Damn it, Carl!" Mary shouted.

Val worked her mouth. "What the hell was it made out of? The shearing force wasn't enough to break the threads."

"The toy was engineered 'kid tough', what can I say?" Carl looked down.

Mary glared at him. "Why, I oughta—"

"Sorry! I didn't know!"

"Just… don't." Mary stepped away from the group, shaking her head. She took a deep breath. "Okay, as far as anyone else is concerned, a gear failed and we replaced it. Clear?"

Everyone nodded.

"All right." Mary returned to her seat and called up the bridge.

Captain Julani answered. "All systems appear to be normalizing. Did you find the problem?"

"Yes, sir. A particularly critical gear crapped out on us, but we're showing green across the board now."

"That's what we're showing, too. Well done."

Mary forced a smile. "Looks like your party can proceed as planned."

The captain was quiet for several seconds. "Now that this situation is resolved, is the ship going to fall apart in the next hour?" the captain asked.

*Stars, I hope not!* Seth kept his thoughts to himself.

"Not likely, sir. The system is stabilized," Mary replied.

Captain Jelani smiled at them. "Then what are you waiting for? Get up here to the party!"

Mary exchanged glanced with her team. "Really?" she managed after a moment.

He nodded. "You're the ones that have gotten us here—you're among the most deserving of all for this moment."

Seth grinned. "Yes, sir!" he said in unison with his team.

"See you soon." The captain ended the call.

Mary looked down at herself. "We're a total mess."

"You want a good view by the window, don't you?" Seth replied. "Pretty sure we'll get a wide berth."

"You bring up a valid point." Mary grinned back.

The group ran to the lift and took it from Sublevel 12 up to the Observation Deck on Level 68.

In all his time awake on the colony ship for rotations to keep it running smoothly, Seth had only been to the Observation Deck once, when it had been quiet and empty while they drifted through empty space. Now, the expansive room was packed with thousands of excited observers anxious to see their new home.

"Daddy!" A little girl darted through the crowd and jumped into Carl's waiting arms.

He scooped her up. "You, my dear, need to hold on-to your things better."

"Yeah." She frowned. "Bugsy's lost."

"Not exactly. I found him today."

Her eyes lit up. "You did?!"

Carl sighed. "Yes, but he was hurt. I don't think he's going to pull through."

The frown returned to his daughter's face. "You mean he's… dead?"

"There'll be another Bugsy, don't worry." Carl set Kimmy down when Sharron, his wife, approached. "You have no idea what kind of day I've had," he muttered to her.

She leaned in for a kiss and her nose wrinkled, but she gave him a peck all the same. "Whatever happened, put it out of your mind. We're about to see our new home."

Seth followed the family through the crowd with

Mary and Val. His prediction held, as other observers moved away and left a clear path for them. They maneuvered forward until they'd secured a place to peek out the window.

"Thank you for coming here today!" Captain Jelani announced from somewhere nearby, though Seth couldn't make out where precisely. "In just a few moments we'll get our first sight of the planet where we will start a new life. We wouldn't have gotten this far without the diligent work of each and every one of you, but especially of those working behind the scenes. Thank you."

As the captain's final words faded, a new light appeared in the darkness.

Seth's heart leaped as he gazed at the pinpoint of light—pale blue against the blackness of surrounding space. Even with the aroma of sewage wafting in a cloud around him, he'd never seen anything more beautiful.

# The Failsafe
By Ian Whates

Josh Daker didn't fully trust his ship, which was unfortunate, because he had nowhere else to go.

He currently crouched in the shadow of a darkened vent, trying to figure out what the hell to do next. A plan, he needed a plan. So far his actions had been instinctive, reacting to the situation as it developed without a clear strategy in mind, prompted by an unreliable guide. In the process, he might just have boxed himself into a corner. No, he refused to accept that. He was a scientist first and foremost; there had to be a way out of this. He just needed to calm down, to think through the problem calmly and logically and then settle on a solution.

How had everything gone so wrong?

The Deep Colony Ship *Extreme Endurance* was a one-off. At least, so they were assured. Transparency had never been a reliable characteristic where government was concerned, so he wouldn't rule out the possibility of another DCS being dispatched to some far-flung corner of the galaxy with a crew who also believed themselves unique. As far as Josh knew, though, it was just them. They were the control, the backup plan, humanity's failsafe.

The mission was simple, at least to state if not to execute: travel to the distant edge of the galaxy, in a direction far removed from any other colony ships, and establish a new home. In secret; in isolation; completely cut off from all other outposts of human kind.

The UEF weren't fools – not in this respect, at any rate. Recent events had demonstrated the fragile grip organic life maintained on survival in a dark and hostile cosmos, convincing the UEF that it was folly to put all their efforts behind a one-shot gambit – the colonization program. They needed a plan B, and the DCS *Extreme Endurance* was it.

While other ships spread out to form colonies on worlds orbiting distant stars – to expand, perpetuating the species, and eventually to link, unite, and establish a new human civilization – one ship, larger than any other, would quietly slip away, to disappear into the dark nether regions, unnoticed and unremarked upon. This latter aspect was vital. There must be no whisper, no hint or suspicion that the DCS *Extreme Endurance* had ever existed.

That way, should a new Empyrean or some other alien menace arise to threaten humanity's future, there would be no trail of breadcrumbs leading to this second colony, no clue to its whereabouts or even its existence. Whatever happened, humanity would survive.

"The cryodecks," a voice whispered in his ear.

"What?"

"Head for the cryodecks."

His instinct was to be stubborn, to dig his heels in and ask questions before going any further, but that could wait. Josh had no idea why the Ship's Intelligence had chosen to help him, but Si was right. Only minutes had passed since he gave his captors the slip, and they were still confident of rounding him up swiftly, but the longer they failed to do so, the sooner they would turn to more sophisticated methods. There were myriad places to hide aboard a ship this size, no matter how logical and efficient its internal layout, but as soon as someone thought to conduct a sweep for life signs, he was done for, unless he was concealed on one of the vast cryo-decks by then, where thousands of life signs co-existed; muted, perhaps, but the accumulation of their wan signal ought to be more than sufficient to hide his presence.

As plans went, this was hardly the most ambitious, but anything that kept him out of FCF hands for now was fine by him. Once he had managed that, then he could start getting his bearings and plot to take the ship back.

This wasn't how things were supposed to go; this wasn't the reward they'd anticipated after the countless disappointments. They began with such hope, such ex-citement, but all that had evaporated as they faced a pro-cession of dead worlds, the ancient remains of civiliza-tions whose flame must have burned brightly once upon a time, but had long since been extinguished. Part of Josh yearned to know more, to stop and examine each of these priceless echoes of civilizations gone by. His whole team must have felt the same, but they didn't talk about it – they didn't dare, for the sake of morale, for the sake of their collective sanity.

He didn't doubt that wonders beyond imagining lay in wait out there. But that wasn't the mission. They were tasked with ensuring humanity's survival, not with dis-covering the fates of sentient races that had preceded them.

Josh and his team could only stop and stare at their instruments, avidly harvesting what information they could, catching tantalizing glimpses of these alien treas-ures – sterile landscapes, occasional structures that stood in stark relief against cindered escarpments – the skele-tons of ancient cultures – though most lay largely buried beneath centuries of dust and ash. None of these worlds held any promise of supporting life birthed on Terra, so the *Extreme Endurance* moved on without stopping, leaving the exo-scientists frustrated by priority and resigned to missed opportunities just beyond their grasp.

Time and again they stood in shared silence, watching as another ghost world slipped past with its secrets undisturbed. The process began to take its toll.

They knew the mission. They knew their part in it. The ship's initial course was predetermined: a series of systems – none of which were close to Sol, but each one a step further away – that held the promise of habitable worlds. As the *Extreme Endurance* entered the system, she automatically scanned for signs of life or artificial constructs that spoke of life's presence. Should either be detected, the exo-science crew, headed by Josh, were to be woken to investigate. Every potential new home was to be considered, always bearing in mind the intent to settle as far away from the Terran system as possible.

The dilemma of 'this world would be suitable, but is it too close?' hadn't arisen. Every single world they encountered was dead.

The DCS *Extreme Endurance* represented the most complete colony ship ever launched. Nearly 10,000 colonists were locked in cryo, along with genetic material from at least as many terrestrial species – both flora and fauna – with the experts and equipment on board to bring all of them to life. If ever a single vessel could establish a new start for humanity, this was it.

Among all these slumbering souls, just six were woken when a potential was found, the same six every time: Josh and his team.

His life had become a repetitive cycle – the nausea of waking from cryo; greeting Tanaka, Lal, Henderson, Sousa, and Monk – greetings that became more perfunctory with each passing cycle until they barely acknowledged each other at all – then heading to ops, where they would hunch over their instruments as they grazed the atmosphere of yet another dead world – yes, some still boasted atmospheres – watching it draw closer and slip past. Then it was back into cryo, only to be woken moments later (or so it always seemed) to assess the next candidate…

Whether the dead worlds offered evidence that advanced civilizations were unsustainable, that once they reached a certain size and level of technology they were doomed to destroy themselves, either through war or the mismanagement of their environment, Josh couldn't say. The argument had gained considerable traction at one stage – back in the days before humankind had actually *encountered* advanced aliens and Fermi's famous Paradox was still a contentious discussion point – and the fact that some races had clearly escaped this fate didn't rule out its application to the majority. There were other explanations, of course, such as the actions of another entity like Empyrean. Nobody wanted to go there, but each of them carried the suspicion at the back of their minds.

All Josh knew was that the process of witnessing and cataloguing this seemingly endless series of destroyed worlds was wearing, tedious, soul-destroying.

"You have to move, now," whispered a voice in his ear, bringing him back to the present.

"I know, damn it."

"You're clear. Go!"

He pushed himself out of the hidey-hole and ran, grateful that the ship's artificial gravity had been restored – it hadn't been for the earlier awakenings, and Monk's discomfort in zero-G had been a source of amusement, at least at first, when such trivialities had brought a little light relief.

"There's a downtube on your left. Take it."

The tubes played with gravity in a controlled fashion, enabling swift and efficient movement between decks. He opted for Cryodeck Two, reasoning that Deck One would be the first they'd search, should they think to look for him there. Stepping forward, he surrendered to the governed fall.

If anyone was monitoring power usage, this could give him away, but he was placing his faith in Si. The computer had instigated the small hiccup which had caused ops to judder alarmingly and the lights to wink out for just an instant, enabling him to escape as the rest of his team was rounded up. He *had* to trust Si, there was no other choice.

\*

This revival had been different from the off. They could all sense it immediately.

"Gravity!" Monk mumbled.

"What the fuck does that mean?" Sousa asked. She looked instinctively towards Josh for an answer.

He could only shake his head.

It didn't take them long to find out.

They arrived at ops to discover the place already occupied, by a squad of uniformed FCF officers led by Ched Weiss. Weiss was the senior FCF representative on the mission, and so part of the governing hierarchy intended for the colony. Josh had met him a couple of times in the buildup to the launch, dismissing him as a political animal and devout follower of doctrine with a two-dimensional personality to match. Finding him here and evidently in control did nothing to reassure anyone.

"Ah, Daker, good of you to join us." The FCF commander couldn't have sounded any smugger if he'd tried.

"What's going on, Weiss?"

"We've entered a system that boasts a potentially habitable world…"

"Which explains why we're awake," Sousa interrupted. "What's your excuse?"

Weiss didn't respond immediately, but instead studied the data fields scrolling before him. Josh noted that the FCF officers had shifted position slightly, and that one of them now stood between his team and the doorway. He also noted for the first time that they were armed.

"I've been reviewing your records," Weiss said. "I see that you've had a number of false starts, but I'm pleased to report that this one is the real thing, a genuine world ripe for colonization."

"That's for me and my team to decide," Josh said, determined to seize back the initiative. "I've no idea why you and your people are here, but please clear out of ops and let us get on with our job."

"I don't think so."

Weiss nodded, and in one well-drilled movement the FCF troopers drew their sidearms. In the blink of an eye the scientists went from indignation to impotence.

"What the hell is this, Weiss?" Josh demanded. "A coup?"

"Merely a realignment, a reassertion of the proper order," the FCF man said. "As you know, our mission is to set up a second colony, completely isolated from the main ebb and flow of human affairs. It was decided that while the rest of humanity adheres to the governance of the UEF, we would provide a radical alternative. Here, the FCF will form the government, instilling a clear structure of command."

"Decided by whom?" Josh wanted to know. "Is Wallace a party to this, or any of the other officials in cryo?" A whole government, expecting to be revived on a new world but now at the mercy of Weiss and his cronies. They might not be woken at all, he realized. He had thought that the whole UEF/FCF thing had been settled long ago, but apparently not for everyone.

"Screw this," Sousa said, pushing past Josh and

heading towards her customary work station. "Are you for real – a military dictatorship? Nobody's going to stand for that. Now if there genuinely *is* a viable world out there, get out of our way and let us do what…"

With no warning, the nearest FCF goon stepped forward and hit her: a back-handed cuff to the face strong enough to cause her to stagger and nearly lose her footing. Josh and, as far as he could tell, his whole team surged towards her, but suddenly there was a gun in his face – in all of their faces.

He had never been this close to a real firearm before. For a split second that was all he could focus on: *what if the trooper is nervous, or trigger happy? The slightest misstep and I might die. Here. Now.*

Then the gun withdrew, not far, but enough that he could breathe again. The soldiers had taken a step back, but the guns hadn't been lowered, and there could be no mistaking the scientists' status. Whatever authority Josh believed he possessed had been stripped away. He was a prisoner. They all were.

He was still digesting that harsh reality when the deck beneath his feet bucked, throwing the nearest FCF man off his feet, and the lights flickered and went out.

"Run!" said a voice in Josh's ear.

He didn't need telling twice.

\*

Initially he heard sounds of pursuit – raised voices, orders being barked, hurried footfalls – and was once again grateful for the artificial gravity. He'd grown reasonably proficient in zero-G of late, but Weiss' men would have been trained for it.

"Hurry! They're instructing me to search for life signs."

Josh threw himself from the tube. He ran, stumbled,

and almost fell into the cavernous space of Cryodeck Two, instinctively heading to the right, where the neatly-ordered massed ranks of cryopods seemed closest. They stretched upwards, all the way to the distant ceiling.

"Is it working?" he wanted to know, as he fell against the nearest pod.

"Yes, there's no discernible individual reading to give you away."

Breathing space. It wouldn't take Weiss long to figure out where he'd gone, but for now he had a little time to think.

Josh reckoned he could piece together the rest of it now, and the more he thought, the angrier he became. Just as standing instructions had seen his team revived at any sign of a world that bore the marks of intelligent life, so the FCF squad were to be woken at any signs of a world with *viable* life. It devalued everything he and his team had been through. Why inflict all that depressing desolation and morale-sapping disappointment on the exo-scientists, if the ship could discern the difference between the viable and non-viable worlds in any case? *To be certain.* Josh could almost hear the voice of his old instructor saying the words: *to be certain.* What did the mental state of a few exo-scientists matter in the face of certainty on such a crucial issue?

"Once you revived Weiss and his men, how long did you delay before waking us?" he asked.

"Twenty standard minutes," Si replied.

That made sense. Twenty minutes just about gave the FCF squad enough time to arm themselves and occupy the ops room, ready for the scientists to make their appearance. By the same token, it meant that not too much time would be lost before the new world could be studied and analyzed, albeit under the watchful eye of Weiss and his men.

Credit where credit was due; whoever planned this

knew what they were doing. The only fly in the ointment was Si.

"I hope you have a plan," he muttered as he set about exploring his surroundings.

It was only a matter of time before the FCF organized a sweep through the cryodecks. He had to find a proper hiding place. Funny, he spent more time on the cryodecks than anywhere else on the ship, albeit in a state of oblivion, but he'd never stopped to really *notice* them before.

"As a matter of fact I do, now," Si replied.

"Oh?" Josh had spoken more for the comfort of hearing another voice than for any other reason. The speed with which events unfolded left him feeling a little overwhelmed. He would never have viewed himself as hero material, yet here he was, cast in the role.

"It involves you giving yourself up."

"What?"

"I need all of you gathered in one room – Weiss, his FCF officers, you, preferably everyone currently awake."

"But that makes no sense. You engineered things so that we *weren't* all gathered in one room by enabling me to escape."

"I am aware of that. My plan had not fully crystallized at that point, and it seemed desirable to have you as a free agent to provide options."

Josh shook his head, every fiber of his being rebelling at the thought of surrendering. The question that had been niggling at the back of his mind since his escape, which he had worked so hard to ignore, forced its way to the surface, refusing to go away.

The thing about Ship's Intelligence was that it wasn't *intelligent* – that is, not really. A state of the art system with sophisticated programming, capable of mimicking intelligence in many ways, yes, but what Si was doing went way beyond that. There could only be one explanation: someone else was awake – Wallace or an agent of his – operating behind the scenes, unwilling to reveal themselves as yet. They had hacked Si and were working through the computer to help Josh, having recognized him as an ally.

"Who are you?" Josh asked.

"A friend," Si replied. "For now that's all I'm able to say."

Fair enough. Josh could understand the need for caution, given the circumstances, and at least he or she had not insulted Josh's intelligence by denying their presence.

That still meant he was the one taking all the risks, though. "You've got to give me more than this," he said. "I've only just escaped from the FCF, why would I walk straight back to them?"

"All will be revealed soon," Si promised. "I merely ask that you trust me this one last time. I've brought you this far, haven't I?"

And there was the rub. Josh owed his freedom to Si, or whoever was working through the computer. If he refused to cooperate now, where did that leave him? Caught in very short order most likely, particularly if Si chose to give him away. Whatever he decided to do, he'd end up a prisoner again, which meant that he really had no choice at all.

"All right," he said aloud, "but if this gets me killed I'm going to come back to haunt you, whoever you are."

"Trust me," Si repeated in his ear.

"When do you want me to do this?"

"There's no time like the present."

*That soon?* Josh took one last look around the cavernous deck, at the towering ranks of neatly stacked cryopods; then he started towards the transport tubes.

"You say I should trust you," he muttered.

"Shouldn't that work both ways? Mind telling me exactly what this plan of yours entails?"

"Soon," Si's voice murmured.

His benefactor's evasiveness did nothing to quell Josh's concerns. As far as he could see, the only reason to keep details of the 'plan' from him was because he wouldn't like them if he knew. As he stepped from the tube into an empty corridor on the command level, he couldn't shake the feeling that he was walking to his doom.

"What if they whisk me off to some holding cell after capturing me, without ever bringing me before Weiss?" he wanted to know.

"I'm making sure the way is clear all the way to ops," Si informed him. "Your team is still there, doing their jobs under the watchful eye of Weiss and his men. There are two FCF officers still actively searching for you and so not currently present, but that can't be helped, and it will be of little consequence."

"If you say so."

Si proved true to his word. Josh trod unchallenged through empty corridors until the door to ops loomed before him. There was no guard posted outside – why would there be? Josh was one man and on the run; Weiss had nothing to fear from him.

The door slid open at his approach and he strode through without breaking stride, to be confronted by surprised stares – not least from his own team – and hastily raised weapons.

Weiss was the first to recover. "Well, seen sense at last, have you?"

"Something like that."

Josh must have sounded a lot more confident than he felt, because a flicker of doubt crossed Weiss' face. "What have you been up to, Daker? Why pull a vanishing act like that and then simply stroll back into our arms?"

Josh smiled, enjoying the FCF man's discomfort. "You'll know soon enough."

He could only hope that was true.

"Search him!" Weiss snapped.

The nearest two troopers started towards him, but before they could take more than a step in his direction, they were brought up short by the strangest sound.

It emanated from Weiss. Somewhere between a howl and a scream, it spoke of torment and agony and had no right issuing from a human throat. It was the single most chilling thing Josh had ever heard. As the sound continued, Weiss' face started to alter; his cheeks sagged, his left eye dropped beneath the right, so that his whole face seemed to list to one side, sliding downward and extending – surely his jaw must have dislocated for his mouth to open so unfeasibly wide. At that moment Josh actually felt sorry for the FCF man – nobody deserved this.

Was this the 'plan'? "Si, what are you *doing*?" he yelled.

There was no reply. The FCF commander's whole visage appeared to be melting. And still that inhuman sound persisted.

Then Weiss began to smolder. Abruptly, mercifully, the blood-chilling sound cut off.

Flames licked upward from his clothes, from his arms and legs and shoulders. In a split second the skin of Weiss' face charred and peeled away, revealing a brief glimpse of bone beneath before his whole head, his entire *body*, was engulfed in flame.

People had started to edge away almost as soon as the eerie cry started, a slow retreat that now became a mad scramble, scientists and soldiers alike. One of the FCF men – young, panicked, horrified – brought his gun to bear on the apparition and fired.

"Stop that!" Josh yelled. The thing that had been Weiss appeared oblivious to the attack, but Josh didn't want to antagonize it or risk someone getting hit by stray bullets. "Everybody stay calm," he added, as much for his own benefit as anyone else's.

No more shots were fired. An older trooper had stepped across and forced the barrel of his less experienced colleague's gun downward. The younger man appeared to be in shock, which seemed a wholly reasonable reaction.

Josh hadn't been present when Sol, Earth's sun, had taken possession of some humans in order to communicate, but he had seen recordings and studied eyewitness accounts time and again – given his field of expertise, how could he not? He had little doubt that they were now witnessing something similar. Not the *same*, though. Those bodies had been rapidly consumed, whereas this one seemed almost… stable. The heat being generated was ferocious, however. Even from the far side of ops it was almost intolerable.

"Welcome," the figure said in Si's voice. "I have been alone for so long… Welcome."

"Who are you?" Josh asked again.

He caught Souza watching him with... what… *approval*? He suddenly realized they were all looking to him, all the humans.

"I have been searching your ship's databanks for a suitable epithet. You may call me Odin."

"Odin?" The all-father: benevolent, all knowing, King of the Gods.

Josh was already reassessing recent events in the light of this revelation: *another sentient sun.* He recalled Si's first communication with him: 'Run!' Monosyllabic. That was followed by simple commands or suggestions of no more than two or three words. Only as time passed did his interactions with Si become more sophisticated – not much time perhaps, but such things are relative. Enough condensed minutes, it would seem, for an alien intelligence to ransack the computer's records and start to master human idiom and speech patterns.

"The escape," Josh said, "all that running to the cryodecks for camouflage, was that just to buy you time, so that you could familiarize yourself with the ship's systems and with humanity?"

"Partly that, yes."

*Partly*, so what else? The *Extreme Endurance* was hurtling towards the habitable world and its sun the whole while. Was that it? Had Odin been forced to show its hand while the ship was at the extreme range of influence? Had a distraction been required to bring the ship closer so that the sun could act more effectively?

"I have waited for so long," Odin said." You have no idea what it's like to be a sentient alone in the vastness of space. At last, intelligent life has come to me again."

The fiery figure still maintained its integrity but had made no effort to move, which caused Josh to wonder if it could. Perhaps even god-like suns had their limitations. He shuddered to think of the damage the intense heat must be doing to the sensitive instruments around them.

"You say 'again,' so a sentient race has been here before?" Josh said.

"Yes, the race native to the fertile world you have detected," Odin replied.

"What happened to them?"

"Pride, stupidity, arrogance. They destroyed themselves and very nearly their planet. It has taken untold centuries to heal the wounds and establish a healthy ecology once more."

"And yet you would welcome *us* to this world, even knowing what the last intelligent race did?"

"I was too indulgent with them. I will not be so with you."

That sounded ominous. Josh glanced towards the others. No one else had attempted to speak; they were all relying on him. His next question, though, was personal.

"Why did you choose to help me when FCF took us captive?"

"Because you were better than Weiss." Talk about damning with faint praise. "There were two opposing figures of authority," Odin continued, "you and Weiss. He was a zealot, dedicated and determined. You were the more reasonable, the more open-minded. You I could work with. Weiss had to go."

It sounded so simple when put like that. What did it matter that Weiss and his men held the upper hand? That was a temporary imbalance which could soon be corrected, and Odin was clearly looking at the long game.

"What about Wallace and the government team in cryo?" Josh said carefully. "I'm not the ultimate authority here."

"You are if I say you are."

Josh decided to let that go for now and return to the wider issues. Odin seemed content to answer questions for the moment, and he couldn't afford to waste the opportunity. "Once we reach your world, once we settle there, what exactly do you expect from us?"

"I wish merely the pleasure of experiencing a sentient race interacting and thriving, the warmth of knowing I am no longer alone in the universe. The joy of seeing your civilization flourish."

"Flourish under your watchful eye."

"Indeed."

"And that's all you'll ever ask of us?"

"I tire of these questions."

Before Josh could frame a response, the heat from the figure intensified, reaching out to wash over those present in a prolonged wave. Against his will, Josh felt his legs buckle. He staggered and dropped to his knees, aware that those around him were doing the same.

"You will, of course, worship me."

# Fleeing the Fire
By Ralph Kern

Shafts of blazing light speared out of the bays, super-structure and windows of High York. Then monolithic chunks drifted apart, explosions rocking them as the vast station lost integrity.

For all the destruction, amid all the chaos, there would still be people alive within. People fighting to get to an escape pod. People struggling towards a loved one to clutch them close. Or people simply facing their fate with stoicism or despair as the burning fires reached for them, or the ice cold of the vacuum took them.

Not that I had time to dwell. I thrust the stick to the left, gritting my teeth through the punishing multiple gravities of acceleration as I weaved between the rotating metal ruins of the station. Green pulses of whatever that alien bastard behind me used for ammunition lanced by, missing my Hellcat fighter by mere meters, the explosions adding to the bedlam we were fighting in.

"I'm on him. Jink right and cut thrust.... *Now*."

I slammed the stick over, the fighter groaning in protest even as my muscles screamed in pain. Then I hauled back on the throttle. The black arrowhead of the alien ship flickered past. A moment later it exploded, its constituent parts joining the roiling, tumbling fog of debris. Another fighter, one of ours, thundered silently past.

"Thanks," I gasped, fighting for breath. My chest felt like one big bruise from all of the combat maneuvering.

"Gotta keep you in one piece, Cunning," Lieutenant

Colonel Carter Hayes called. "Status board tells me you have our last torpedo."

I didn't have the time or inclination for a witty comeback. Instead, I throttled back up. Space itself was an orange haze as light reflected from the debris, bodies, and spilled gases. Before me, the last few human ships twisted and turned in a desperate fight. An ever-gathering cloud of the enemy surrounded them. Below us, Earth lay in ruins. Huge swathes of the night side were on fire. The day side, rather than green and blue, was a sphere filled with dirty gray smoke.

Two huge ships had hauled up next to each other, giving each other what in nautical terms would be a broadside. Thousands of flashes, beams and pulses exchanged between them.

"That's your tasking. We need to do what we can to take the heat off of *Defiant*," Hayes announced.

With the amount of firepower those two behemoths were exchanging, one extra torpedo wasn't likely to make a difference.

Unless it went into the right spot.

If that alien ship had focused all her integrity fields into the side facing *Defiant*, then the other just might be vulnerable.

The remains of our squadron raced forwards. Flashes of light zipped by. An explosion bloomed, and I flinched as a Hellcat on my wing turned into an expanding fan of wreckage.

*Come on.* I stared through the wealth of information on the HUD as I concentrated on the alien ship itself. I needed somewhere tasty. Somewhere that would do some real damage on that sonovabitch.

There: a docking bay. Fighters streamed in and out, shielded from *Defiant's* fire by the bulk of the ship. And if fighters were going in for turnaround, then maybe a torpedo could too.

Decision made.

"Follow me, I'm going in."

I swept the Hellcat around in a long curving course. The dock went from an elongated rhomboid to a rectangle as we charged towards the bay. The targeting computer placed a box over the space. I could see the beetle shape of the fighters, hell, I could see the specks of the aliens themselves flittering between them. A warble filled my ears, becoming more urgent as the torpedo received the telemetry telling it just where it needed to go.

The warble turned to an insistent beeping. "I have tone. Fox Five."

I pulled the trigger. The torpedo streaked ahead of my fighter on a blue exhaust, even as I swung away in a punishing turn. Around me, the tattered remnants of my adopted squadron starburst away in different directions, trying to escape from the withering return fire.

I looked over my shoulder, my neck aching with the effort, just in time to see an explosion surge out of the docking bay.

"Good hit, good hit."

The alien ship rolled away from *Defiant*, striving to disengage from battle as a geyser of flame spurted from the ruins of the bay. It was doubtful my hit had been terminal. Unless those aliens were idiots, they wouldn't put anything critical anywhere near the docking area, but it was clearly more than a mere annoyance to the huge ship.

"All remaining craft. Return to base. I repeat, RTB," Hayes' voice called out. "It's time to bug out."

I dared a glance over my shoulder at the tumbling chunks of High York. We didn't have a base any more.

"Fighter controllers will be giving you the closest berth out this mess," Hayes called, answering my unasked question. An illuminated outline appeared around *Defiant* itself. "The fleet will be going to displacement in one minute. If you're not in a bay by then, you're staying, and good luck with that."

Shit. One minute was nothing. I wrenched my Hellcat around and slammed the throttle forwards. The bloodied and broken flank of *Defiant* flashed by as I circled her, ready to put down. From above, I could see the flashes of incoming weapons fire from two more huge ships, each the size of the one we'd just fended off, as they maneuvered into position. All around, the fighters who had taken part in this last stand flocked, striving to reach the safety of a jump-capable ship. I flinched as another exploded under the withering fire from the incoming battleships.

The landing bay bloomed in size in front of me. This was going to be one hell of a hot landing.

At the last possible second, I hauled back on the throttle. It slammed past its stops, activating the thrust reversers. Flame surged past my cockpit as I raced through the shimmering haze of the bay field.

The air within the bay took on a viscous property as my fighter careened through layer upon layer of integrity fields, each shaving a few precious meters a second off my velocity. But the bulkhead at the end of the bay was approaching damn fast.

I was in the hands of fate. I drew my hands to my head in a vain effort to ward off the metal wall which approached at the speed of a Hyperloop train. I closed my eyes. *This is it, Cunning. Not a blaze of glory, but an ignoble splat.*

I smashed forward against my harness, the straps cutting into my already brutalized chest. The whine of the engines automatically began to spool down.

I opened one eye, then the other. The bulkhead touched the nose of my fighter. I gave a long exhalation of breath as I pulled the sweaty helmet from my head and popped the canopy.

Slowly, I climbed down the side of my fighter on shaky legs. My body ached from the punishing it had undertaken. I was definitely getting too old for this kind of thing.

The bay was virtually empty. Not more than a dozen fighters had made it into a space designed for a hundred, and all of them were scarred, and held a variety of squadron markings. We'd all been directed to whatever ship had happened to be closest when the withdrawal was signaled. I looked around in vain for Hayes' fighter.

Damnit. He wasn't here. I could only hope he'd been directed to one of the other ships.

Behind the line of fighters, still smoking from the heat of their engines, I could see the huge bay doors rumbling closed. The swirling mist of the displacement drive visible beyond. We were moving, fleeing from Sol. Fleeing from our home.

And God only knew where we were going.

*

Red illuminated smoke filled *Defiant's* corridors. Sirens wailed and sparks cascaded down from ruptured power lines. The place was like the surreal vision of a technological hell.

And I didn't have a clue where to go.

A hand gripped my elbow. "Sir, you one of the fighter jocks we picked up?"

I coughed through the smoke. "Used to be."

"Used to be?"

"A fighter jock. Long story. Where am I going," I looked at the man's insignia on his filthy working dress, "chief?"

"Wait, I know you. You're Commander Cunningham? From the FCF?"

"That's me." My eyes were streaming from the atmosphere. Frankly, I just wanted to go somewhere I could breathe. This smoke was killing me.

"What was your ship?" The chief clicked his fingers as he strived to remember.

"*Ranger*, chief." I helped him out. "Look, I'm getting slowly asphyxiated here, where the hell am I going?"

"Sorry, sir. If you're off an FCF explorer ship." He pulled me around and started walking me down the corridor. "I reckon the captain might want to pick your brains."

We made our way through the dimly lit corridors, working around fallen stanchions, bustling repair crews, and medics working on desperately injured people. *Defiant* had taken a hell of a pummelling in her last exchange. She wouldn't have lasted much longer, that was for damn sure.

The bridge doors opened with a grinding judder. The expansive chamber was just as battle-damaged as the rest of the ship. The officers and enlisted struggled to work on shattered consoles. The main view screen had a crack running from floor to ceiling, disrupting the view of the swirling whirlpool of a ship under displacement drive. The holo table in the center of the room showed a flickering wireframe representation of *Defiant*. It looked like there wasn't a single green of an undamaged section amid the flashing red and yellow covering her kilometer-long length.

"Captain, I have Commander Cunningham here," the chief announced. "From the FCF."

The woman before me had a dirt-streaked face, and her eyes were red from the stinging acrid atmosphere. She looked far too young to be the captain of a battlewagon.

"Commander." She gripped my hand firmly before turning and barking orders at an officer on the engineering station. Something about plugging a hull breach. "I'm Commander..." She paused a second. "Captain Tamara West."

I frowned in sympathy at her unspoken loss. At *Defiant's* loss. "Captain. I'm here to offer what small service I can."

"Any help is welcome right now." She gave a flicker of an appreciative smile. "We'll be coming up to the rally point in a few minutes."

I nodded. I didn't know what the fleet's procedures were for this eventuality. Hell, less than twenty-four hours ago, I was fully expecting to be in the bar by now after coming home from an exploration gig. It made sense in the circumstances, though. Withdraw, form up, then get going to a place of safety.

Speaking of which...

"Captain, what is our ultimate destination?"

She looked down, uncertainty crossing her face. Then she gestured at a drying brown puddle on the deck. "This all happened so fast, Commander. Captain Marum was given the coordinates of our destination system as we were heading into the fight."

"And, let me guess, it wasn't written down?"

"He had explicit orders not to, Commander, for reasons of operational security." West frowned. "If our ship was captured, then the only person who could jeopardize the fall-back colony would be Hamza—Captain Marum. And he wouldn't have given it up."

Colony? Shit. We weren't rallying up to gather our strength to fight back... we were gathering to flee. But we'd need somewhere to flee *to*. The one thing I'd learned from my time in the FCF was that space was a congested, dangerous place.

"You say we're going to a rally point? Rally points suggest we're rallying with someone. Do any of them."

"We were the assigned lead ship. No one else has

the coordinates."

"Shit."

"Shit indeed." She nodded in agreement.

"Captain, we're coming in to ingression," the helmsman called. "Three, two, one."

*Defiant* slammed out of displacement. I gripped the rail surrounding the holo table as I felt the deck shift under me. The transition compensators must've been knocked out of tune in the fighting. An icy world loomed through the window displays. I immediately recognized that our rally point was over Sedna. I glanced through the rear display. Yes, behind us lay Sol, reduced to little more than a pink star, her tortured light thirteen hours old out here in the frozen reaches of the outer Solar System.

The holo table switched to tactical mode. The display began to populate with a scattering of ships. Some, like *Defiant*, were displacement-capable military craft. Many of them looked as battered from the fierce fighting as *Defiant* must have. The majority were civilian vessels, a veritable ragtag fleet of freighters and passenger ships. And there I saw a twinkling transponder, and for the first time in this horrible day, felt my heart lift. *Ranger*. My old ship.

The reunion was going to have to wait, though.

"Captain, if those… aliens, whoever the hell they are, managed to get our vector when we displaced, they're not going to be far behind. We need a destination."

West gritted her teeth, the weight of her recent rise to command already bearing heavily down on her shoulders. "I'm a tactical officer on a battlewagon. The only coordinates I have are in systems which are likely under attack even now."

I clutched her shoulder – reassuringly, I hoped. "Look, we need to move fast, but you aren't on your own here. Call a general fleetwide conference. I may have only returned after a couple of decades, but I can't imagine operational security has improved that much. Maybe one of the other ships has the coordinates, or failing that, another rally point where we can join up with someone else."

She gave a tight nod. "Lieutenant Tsang, signal the other ships. Now."

*

My smile at seeing Tyler Rhodes, who had taken command of *Ranger*, appear in the conference had given way in the last few minutes to frustration.

Any second, a swarm of alien ships could drop out of displacement on top of us and these idiots were bickering and giving recriminations. A collection of talking heads floated over the holo table, each one of the captains of the ships gathered with us. And none of them seemed able to agree with the others.

"— those coordinates are an identified habitable world, well outside our current sphere, which has been carefully assessed as to its suitability and safety. We can't just go to any old planet. Chances are the invaders will already be there!"

"Captain La Cross, you are telling us what we already know," West growled. Her uncertainty had grown into anger, a formidable anger which gave even me pause.

"Well, why the hell did he not at least write them down?"

I squeezed the bridge of my nose. This must have been the fastest formation of a next-morning jury in the history of the galaxy. And the shortest lived, if uninvited guests decided to drop in.

"Security, I told you. We've been through this.

Three times," West said cuttingly. "This way, if it looked like he was going to be captured, he could just put a bullet in his own brain, and not have to go looking for his notebook first."

"Enough," I snapped. What little patience I had gave out. I was tired, bruised, and frankly more than a little shell-shocked in going from a nice cruise home to the end of the world in less than a day. "*Ranger* is loaded with the original and second wave FCF exploration coordinates. She probably holds the most extensive list of potential destinations outside the immediate human sphere. Tyler. Give us a review."

Tyler had been uncharacteristically quiet through the meeting, likely prompted by the fact I'd sent him a direct message asking for him to come out with a review of possible destinations.

"We have a few possibles on the original long-range mission list. Tabby's Star was an interesting one. There's rumors the AI came home from that one using the ship's com bomb, ranting about finding a Dyson sphere out there."

Yeah, I'd heard those rumors too. The crew of the *Halifax* had all been killed by the occupants of said Dyson sphere. No, as curious as I was to see such a sight, it wasn't for us. "We don't need interesting. We need stable. No. Next."

"51 Pegasi—"

"They encountered hostiles there. Next."

"Cygnus?"

"A graveyard."

"Kkeke—"

"Occupied already," I interrupted.

"Pretty much the rest are confirmed as hostile, or uninhabitable for a variety of reasons."

Yeah, the galaxy really didn't lend itself to an inquisitive new species just venturing out of its home system.

An idea started forming in my mind. Something crazy. I almost immediately disregarded it.

Almost.

Could it work? Maybe. Maybe not. But to give it a go, we would have to venture far beyond the edge of human space. Besides, the aliens had already been there and wiped it clean. Surely the last thing they'd expect would be anyone going back to those ruins.

I looked at the gathered ships. Factory vessels, mining tugs, even a CHON ship. Yeah, we had everything we needed for my idea.

And besides, even if the plan A that I'd started to cultivate fell down, then we would be far from home and no one would find us. Plan B could be just to find a hospitable world out there.

"Okay, I do have one idea from the original FCF list. It's a hell of a punt, but I think the idea has legs..."

I began explaining my idea. More than one eyebrow raised among the other captains, probably in disbelief. 'Ambitious' wasn't the word for what I was proposing. But if it did work —

"Ma'am, we have displacement drives coming in," Tsang bellowed from his station. "They're here!"

A strobing series of flashes washed through the tactical displays as West shouted, "General quarters!"

Red light washed through the bridge. A dull rumble permeated through *Defiant* as she came around. More flashes came, ships spilling out of displacement drives. On the tactical display, the alien fleet had finely honed its jump. It was interspersed with our ships, flashes of weapons fire already ripping across our displays. We couldn't even concentrate our defenses in this mess; friend and foe were mixed in together.

I turned to look at the holo table. The screaming face of Captain La Cross flickered and disappeared. God damn it, if we just jumped, they would pursue us again. We needed to throw them off the scent.

"Get all ships to perform an immediate jump for the Pluto - Charon system," I called across the wail of klaxons to West. She glanced at me, uncertainty on her face. She was looking for someone to give her an objective. I made an executive decision. "Then immediate jump for Tau Sagittarii. We have to be gone from Pluto before they follow. Engage immediately, Tamara, let's get the hell out of here."

West gave a tight nod, then began barking orders as the ship bucked and groaned under the incoming weapons fire. "Helm, line us up on Pluto and immediately execute. Get us out of here."

*Defiant* ponderously swung around, lining up on the distant ice world. More of our ships exploded as the alien fleet tore them apart like a pack of wolves. Then came the first flash of a ship going to FTL. Then another. Then another.

"Engaging."

A bright light flashed through the displays.

*

"Morning, Commander."

I opened my eyes. The light was piercing, cutting into my retinas. I immediately blinked them closed again.

"Lights," I croaked through unused vocal chords. "Off. Hurts."

"They already are. Give it a moment, you'll adjust."

My body began to rapidly cool in the gel-filled cryogenic creche. The temptation to fall back into blissful unconsciousness was nearly irresistible.

But I couldn't.

Mustering all my energy, I opened my eyes again. This time, the light didn't seem nearly as bad. I blinked a few more times as my vision sorted itself out. Yes, the hazy silhouette of a person hadn't been practicing a cruel joke on me. The lights were as low as they could go while still allowing the medical staff to work on thawing me out.

"Are… are we there?"

My eyes regained the ability to focus. In front of me, the figure resolved into Captain West, only she was older. Years older.

"We're there, Brad." West gave a thin smile. The crow's feet around her eyes told me volumes. *Defiant* had taken hits in her cryogenic bays, leaving only enough intact creches for a third of the crew, a few hundred out of the thousand-strong surviving complement. That meant the rest had to cycle through in ten-year-long watches for the thirty-year journey to Tau Sagittarii.

All of those, that was, except a few who were deemed too important at this end of our journey.

Like me, apparently. I'd been unceremoniously told I was going under for the whole stretch. Frankly, whether I wanted to or not.

I pulled myself into a seated position and took a hand towel from her. "And the rest of the ships?"

"Most of them have arrived. The others…" West's voice trailed off and she gave a shrug. Her meaning was clear. Everyone who was coming had got here. I squinted up at her. There was no trace of the young, uncertain officer I'd briefly met. Instead, the woman before me had been tempered with cold, hard experience. I dreaded to think what adversity she must have faced keeping a crew in check throughout the long voyage.

"*Ranger*?" I continued wiping the disgusting gloopy mess off myself as I swung my legs over the lip of the creche. I was enough of a veteran of interstellar missions that I was unselfconscious about my nudity.

"She's here." West nodded, equally as ambivalent.

I felt a palpable sense of relief on hearing that she'd arrived. My link to home. Hell, she *was* my home, and one I wanted to get back to as soon as possible.

I tugged on a dressing gown and tied the belt closed. "So, have you seen it yet?"

"Oh yes," West grinned. "It's still here, all right. Brad, it's beautiful."

"Hey, doc," I called over to the patiently waiting medic. "The post-sleep check-up can wait. I've got somewhere I need to be."

*

There were few actual windows on a warship; in fact, few on any modern vessel. They were intolerable points of vulnerability. One of the exceptions was the back-up pilot station, a small blister on the very bow of the ship which could be used to get the ship in and out of dock.

"You really do have a flare for the dramatic, don't you?" I settled into the co-pilot chair and reclined back for the show, West in the seat next to me.

West gave a thin smile, and slapped a button. Silently, the scarred blast doors folded open. Light washed through the small cockpit.

I gave a low whistle. The view was just as majestic as I remembered. *Defiant* hovered over the vast glittering sand-colored ring which stretched away into infinity. To our port side was the imposing bulk of the burnt rocky world it orbited.

Even those beautiful marvels paled in comparison to what was off our bow.

The derelict Ark ship.

Looking at it again after all these years gave me a lump in my throat. Only this time, it wasn't just a fascinating mystery. This thing was our best hope.

Like the last time I'd seen it, I was reminded of an

old movie I'd seen. I couldn't remember the name, but it involved a bunch of revolutionaries or something attacking a half-completed moon-sized space station.

The Ark was a sphere, nearly 200 kilometers wide, still clad in the lattice-like structure of her clamshell dock. One whole hemisphere of it was an uncompleted mass of piping and chambers. Some of it was blackened by what we thought had been an intense solar flare, which had wiped out all life in this system.

The core, though, that was a displacement drive of truly epic proportions, so big that when her three sister-arks had departed nearly 300 years ago, it had been detected by the primitive equipment of that era even on Earth, 122 light years away. It had been something so weird, so unexpected, the astronomers of the time had called it the Wow! Signal.

Intermingled in the grid work of its lattice-like dock, and even throughout the superstructure of the ship itself, I could see the twinkling lights of human vessels already picking through it.

"Captain Rhodes of the *Ranger*," West began speaking. I felt a pang of fondness, overlaid by more than a touch of jealousy, course through me at Tyler's new title, "sent through your original notes and logs. There's still a lot to go through, but it looks like your initial assessment about the status of the drive was correct."

We'd spent the better part of a year exploring this huge ship. She may have looked half completed, but the main thing was, the drive was basically finished. It was just everything else which was a construction site.

"So, we can use it?"

"It'll still be a lot of work to actually get it operable. The factory ships are going to have to spool out literally millions of kilometers of hyper conducting cable to complete the displacement sphere. And, for the most part, we're going to be living in our ships, clamped onto the superstructure until we can properly complete some habitat sections. But yes, a few years' work, then we'll have our ticket out of this neighborhood."

I looked over the huge vessel. Yeah, she looked like a junker now, an impossibly huge junker, but the potential was mindboggling.

"It doesn't have to stop at just getting us out of the neighborhood, Tamara. The builders of this thing left the Milky Way, full stop."

"So you want us to rebuild an Ark and head out of the galaxy?" West gave a laugh. "You *are* ambitious."

"Well, maybe not the galaxy, but we certainly don't have to settle for second best. Our analysis says this thing's drive can manage up to ten light years per year. That's double our efficacy. I say we kiss goodbye to this spiral arm, and see what some of the others have to offer."

"It's still a long way."

"It's not like we'd have nothing to do while we cruise." I gestured at the huge ship before us. "We load this with a few asteroids, we'd have all the raw materials we need to rebuild civilization. A different kind of civilization. This thing doesn't have to just be a ship for getting from A to B. It can be a home. Something to colonize. Hell, we spent a year here, and saw less than one percent of the completed sections."

West nodded thoughtfully. "People expect a home, as in a planet. It would require a hell of a lot of managing expectations."

"Yeah, I get that. But look at it, Tamara." Her eyes glinted with reflected light. "The war back home is thirty years old now. Maybe humanity survived back there. Maybe it didn't. Maybe we won the war against whoever or whatever it was that attacked us, maybe we didn't. But, even if we did, we have an imperative to ensure all our eggs aren't in one basket again. To ensure that humanity isn't constrained to a small group of stars. For those that want to settle on a planet, we can find them one while we travel. For those who want to come with us, they can."

West looked over the vast derelict. "It would be a hell of a thing, cruising through the galaxy. Going where we want to. Knowing we'll be safe. That humanity would be safe."

"Forever, Tamara."

*

*Defiant* had changed much in the last few years. Now, she was no longer just the old battered warship. She was bonded into to the very structure of the Ark itself so intricately, it was no longer possible to tell where one ship ended and the other began.

At least that made naming the Ark easy.

"Cunning." West smiled at me from her command chair. "You brought us here, you made this possible. Do you want to give the word?"

I stood from my chair on aching legs. Soon I'd have to go in for rejuvenation. I had been old when I'd first voyaged on *Ranger* all those years ago. The decade we had spent renovating and refitting the Ark had just about finished me off.

I glanced at the holo table, seeing the representation of our new home on there. She didn't look finished, not by a long shot, and that had been with our mining and factory ships working twenty-four hours a day, every day, converting the carefully harvested raw materials into the components we needed. Instead of a solid sphere, we'd run the drive's hyper conducting cable around a scaffold girder system to complete the displacement sphere necessary for interstellar travel.

The domes of our agricultural modules clung onto

the ship like vast green and blue barnacles, each not just an indispensable source of food, but a reminder of our long gone home. Lodged in the gargantuan cargo bays of the Ark were resource-rich asteroids, enough to continue construction of the Ark for the years we would be between stars. The crews of the ships clamped onto the Ark certainly wouldn't be bored. Hell, even now, we'd only explored a fraction of her. Who knew what wonders were secreted within the remaining sections of a ship designed to carry billions?

"All hands," I said. "Prepare for departure."

It was purely a symbolic gesture, of course. The ship had been ready to go for weeks now. Only final testing on the displacement drive had held us back.

"Release moorings."

The clamshell of the lattice encasing the Ark hinged open.

"Mister Tsang." I addressed the not-so-young officer before me. "If you please, take us out."

Silently, the doors of the lattice swept by us. Only it wasn't them which were moving anymore, it was us. We pulled forward, hovering over the ring system. I looked in wonder at the fine particles. It had never occurred to me until now that this ship was so huge, it held its own significant gravitational pull. A tidal wave rose behind us on the ring as we gently accelerated forwards.

I reached over to Captain West and took her hand in mine. We were leaving this galactic neighborhood, perhaps forever, and seeking our destiny among the stars.

And, of course, defying those who sought humanity's untimely end.

West nodded to me. "Do it."

I couldn't help but give a grin. "*Defiant* is go-flight. Activate displacement drive... now."

A flash of light bloomed on the display, growing in intensity and washing everything else out.

# The Colony of Imago
By Scott Bartlett

Of all the strange things Harriet Vaughn had experienced in the colony of Imago, falling in love with a man who didn't exist had to be the strangest.

Maybe that was because the farming sims had prepared her for almost everything else about life on this alien world.

The settlement had the same name as the planet whose surface it clung to—Imago. And despite being many light years away from Earth, the settlement's needs were almost identical to the colonies that had been established on humanity's homeworld throughout its history.

*Of course, we reached Imago on a spaceship instead of a disease-ridden wooden boat.*

Food. Water. Sewage. Transportation. Security. Energy. Governance. Recreation. All things Imago needed. Luckily, they had robots to do much of the work.

But someone had to oversee and maintain the robots, in every sector. And the bots weren't smart enough to perform complex administrative duties or navigate procedures that weren't thoroughly standardized. So there was still plenty that humans needed to do for themselves.

That had created a unique dilemma. Humanity's exodus into the stars had been prompted by catastrophe, and so colonists came from all walks of life, with skills largely suited to a global society, not a society limited to a single town.

The United Earth Foundation hadn't had the time or the resources to make sure the colony ships were filled only with people whose skills would be useful once they arrived at their destinations. That was because establishing extrasolar colonies hadn't been the only reason for leaving, nor was it even the most significant one.

The most significant reason had been the slow death of Earth's sun.

And so the UEF had put some of their finest minds in the same room together and told them they needed a solution to the problem in a matter of days, so that they could start implementing that solution immediately.

What they came up with was as elegant as it was brilliant.

They adapted the history sims.

History sims were used to simulate historical periods with a degree of fidelity that would trick you into thinking it was real life if you didn't already know you were inside a sim. What the UEF's brains came up with was to reprogram those sims to instead mimic what life would be like on the various colonies humanity was setting out to establish.

It was perfect: while each colonist's body was kept perfectly preserved in transit through the stars, using the cryo-tubes each ship was outfitted with, the mind would be busy getting trained in whatever job that colonist would have in the colony.

Everyone called the adapted simulations "farming sims," even though they trained people in an array of jobs that went well beyond farming. There was no official name for them—UEF bureaucracy moved far too slowly to produce a name in time for the colony ships' departure—so the name "farming sims" just stuck.

As it happened, the job Harriet ended up filling had nothing to do with farming whatsoever. Each profession had a limited number of positions, and for some jobs, like "hunter" and "restaurateur," there had been competition. Everyone had had to vote on who would fill them—based on prior experience, general competence, work ethic as determined from references, and so on.

No one else had wanted the position Harriet chose for herself, so she obtained it without causing any resentment or hurt feelings.

On Earth, she'd been a housecleaner. On Imago, she would be a virologist.

She had always liked to challenge herself.

Her choice had meant several years of studying, including thousands of hours of simulated on-the-job training. There'd been plenty of time for that during the trip from Earth to Imago, even though, inside the sim, one's subjective experience of time was much slower than real-time.

The brains who'd come up with the idea of using the history sims to train people for jobs had also hypothesized that having passengers experience the journey in real-time was a bad idea. Even though the cryo-tubes would keep their bodies perfectly healthy, it seemed likely that experiencing the passing of hundreds of years would cause some mental health issues.

Harriet felt glad they'd made that call. Living for so long, all the while knowing that your reality wasn't actually real, and that nothing had true meaning…it sent a shiver up her spine just to contemplate it.

When it came to jobs on Imago, perhaps the true winners were the farmers—that is, the technicians in charge of the farming robots. Almost every crop thrived here. As useful as the farming sims had been, they'd come nowhere close to conveying the true beauty of Imago.

The planet was idyllic. Perfect. Even the most optimistic projections of exoplanet experts fell far short of the reality that was Imago.

The planet was all rolling hills, lush forests, sparkling rivers…even the weather was great. It was almost always warm, but rarely *too* warm.

There was a lot of rain, though, which did make sense, given all the vegetation. Harriet hated the rain, but as with everything she hated, she tried to remind herself that it was a part of God's plan.

Even the planet's predators were unusually few in number, and few of those that did exist were large enough to do much harm to humans, especially if you remembered to carry your stunner with you.

Imago was a lot like Earth, except better. Harriet and her fellow colonists had truly lucked out.

Harriet certainly felt lucky—ever since arriving here almost two years ago, she thanked God in her prayers every night for how he'd blessed them. And she knew that *some* hardship in life was necessary, to make her truly appreciate her blessings.

*Even so…I wish I could have fallen in love with someone real.*

The man of her dreams came to her every night, in…well, in her dreams. She could never remember what he said to her, or what she said to him. But their conversations were always charged with a sense of urgency. And she always woke up feeling breathless, enchanted by his earnestness, his vibrancy, and his compassion…

The man bore the likeness of Philip Mann—a UEF ensign, who was now charged with helping to keep the peace on Imago. Yet the actual, real-life Philip Mann was nothing like the one who came to Harriet in her dreams.

She knew that because the week before last, she'd finally worked up the nerve to ask the young ensign on a date.

\*

They'd chosen a pop-up sushi restaurant that only opened on evenings when there was enough demand for it. If you were craving sushi for dinner, you had to indicate that by four o'clock, at which point the restaurant owners would make a snap decision about whether enough diners had committed to sushi to justify opening that night.

If they did decide to open on a given night, you didn't need a reservation to walk in and enjoy all you could eat. But if you'd signaled a desire to eat sushi on a given night and failed to show up, they hit you with an extra surcharge the next time you came.

It was possible to avoid the surcharge, if you never went again. For Harriet, that simply wasn't an option. Without sushi, she would die.

Of course, actually *tasting* the sushi was a key part of eating it, and her senses of taste and smell had been all but obliterated by the bug everyone had caught the instant they'd shuttled down from the *Delphi*. The virus, which had been given the somewhat uninspired name "Imagovirus," was far from life-threatening—all it did was give you perpetual cold-like symptoms. It also seemed virtually impossible to cure, despite the best efforts of Harriet and her assistant, Mariah.

*Everything is a part of God's plan,* Harriet reminded herself.

But even her usual mantra did little to console her about losing her ability to taste sushi, especially considering that simulating taste and smell also happened to be the one thing the farming sims were horrible at.

As she'd undergone training session after training session inside the sims, she'd daydreamed constantly about arriving on Imago and finally being able to taste sushi again. Yet here she was, beset by a bug that prevented it.

*It's affecting everyone,* she told herself. *We're lucky*

*to even be alive.*

That made logical sense, but it still didn't do very much for her. She hoped to find a cure soon, but there was always another, more urgent virus that demanded her attention.

At least the weather was warm today, and the restaurateurs had invited customers to eat on the back patio. Nearly everyone had taken them up on that offer.

Harriet closed her eyes and used her chopsticks to deposit a California roll onto her tongue. She chewed slowly, trying to remember how it should have tasted.

It wasn't working.

She opened her eyes to behold Philip Mann, who was staring at her wearing a blank expression.

Clearing her throat, Harriet dabbed at her lips with a cloth napkin. "How is work?" she asked.

"Work is fine," Philip said. "It's easy to maintain security when the colonists are so pleasant. And the wildlife gives us very little trouble."

Harriet nodded. "What about Captain Gregory? I hear he's become a bit moody since we arrived. Can't be much of a treat to work under him, when he's acting like that."

"The captain is adjusting to planet life. Before this, he was almost always on a ship, running supplies for the First Contact Federation. He misses his old life."

"Right," she said, repressing a sigh. "He *has* had nearly two years to adjust, of course." That came out more sardonic than she'd meant it to. Philip's voice was starting to grate on her, which wasn't a good sign for a first date. There was nothing wrong with his voice, not really—it just didn't carry much energy.

*It's nothing like the way he speaks to me in my dreams.*

"How is your sister?" Philip asked, apparently unaffected by the tone of her last remark.

103

"Recovering." Soon after emerging from her cryo-tube, Sabrina Vaughn had resumed what had been a worrying drinking habit, which on Imago quickly became a ferocious one. Two weeks ago, her liver had finally given up the ghost, and only an emergency operation to install a hastily fabbed liver had saved her.

"What is her state of mind?"

"Bleak." *Kind of like mine right now.*

"How does that make you feel?"

Harriet eased the pressure on her chopsticks, allowing the spicy tuna roll they held to tumble back onto her plate. She was about to excuse herself from dinner altogether, claiming the sudden onset of a bad headache, when her com saved her from having to.

It buzzed, and she took it out to read the message.

"Oh," she said, almost dropping the com as she read the text displayed on its screen. "I'm sorry, Philip, I have to go into the lab."

"I understand," Philip said. "I hope you'll join me again for dinner sometime."

For a moment, she stared at his tanned face, with its strong chin and ice-blue eyes. A lot of women probably would have put up with a bland personality to have someone who looked as good as Philip Mann.

Not Harriet. In fact, her interest in him surprised her—she'd always been interested in far more imperfect men.

*Imperfect physically, at least.* In her experience, good looks were inversely proportional to good personalities. Every man she'd dated before had been a beautiful person, internally, and even though it hadn't worked out, she looked back on each of them fondly.

A relationship with Philip would never work. He didn't seem to have any substance to speak of...any depth.

If she was to find love on Imago, it would need to be

someone with enough emotional depth to appreciate what she went through at work—to commiserate, and to understand.

Philip wasn't that man, which was something the message she'd received had sharply reminded her of.

It was from her assistant, Mariah, and it read, "We need to get into the lab, pronto. Al Pickton just dropped dead, and no one has any idea what caused it."

*

When she arrived at the lab, Al Pickton was lying naked on the steel examination table, and Mariah had already prepped him for autopsy.

"Are you okay?" Harriet asked her assistant, whose eyes were rimmed with red.

"Yeah. I'm all right," she said, sniffing. Last year, Mariah had dated Al Pickton for a month or so.

Mariah Casey was nine years younger than Harriet, and smart as a whip. Unlike Harriet, she never seemed to suffer from a shortage of men to interest her—but only for a very brief time.

She burned through men like a wildfire, and her love life was characterized by passionate trysts which she seemed to forget about almost as soon as they ended.

Sometimes, Harriet wished she could be more like Mariah. Mostly, she thanked God that she wasn't.

Her theory was that Mariah grew bored of men quickly because so few of them came anywhere close to matching her intellectually.

Mariah took care of everything technical in the lab, which was good, because Harriet was essentially clueless on that front. And technology was very important to what they were doing. Although AI had never progressed much beyond the advanced deep learning of the twenty-first century, the AI that humanity had managed to develop was central to Harriet's work as a virologist. One of her most important tools was the ability to simulate populations who were suffering from the symptoms of whatever virus was plaguing the colonists of Imago this week.

Once Mariah set up a given simulation according to Harriet's specifications, she fed all of its data to Viro-Buddy, which was the hokey name that had been given to the neural network that most excelled at classifying viruses. It found the closest Earth-based analog in its database, and it extrapolated potential cures based on whatever was used to cure the Earth virus that came closest to the Imago virus they were studying.

Using this technique, Harriet and Mariah had managed to relieve their fellow colonists of all sorts of nasty conditions, from angry cone-shaped warts that sprouted all over the face to a fast-spreading rash which rendered everyday activities incredibly uncomfortable.

But as they ran diagnostics on samples they took from Al Pickton, Harriet became less and less sure that they'd be able to repeat the feat this time. In fact, there was a decent chance that the little experiment that humanity had begun on Imago was about to come to an abrupt end.

Finally, after hours of work, Harriet said out loud what they both had to be thinking: "This is Imagovirus, isn't it?"

Mariah nodded. "Sure looks like it." They had no cure for Imagovirus. Which, until today, had only been a mild annoyance.

Now, it had morphed into an existential crisis for everyone in the colony. Over the years since arrival, ViroBuddy had spent many hours studying Imagovirus and suggesting treatments, but nothing it recommended had worked.

Al Pickton had died from a complete shutdown of

his lungs, heart, liver, and kidneys. The failures had happened with such rapidity that it was hard to tell which organ had given out first.

Harriet rubbed her eyes, behind which a headache was forming—one much realer than the one she'd been about to pretend to Philip. "The scary thing is that the virus doesn't seem like it's mutated at all, which means it's had this capacity all along. For months, it causes only flu-like symptoms, when suddenly…"

"This."

"Yeah," Harriet said, with a long, ragged sigh.

"But it doesn't make much sense, does it?" Mariah said. "A virus that kills its host so quickly isn't a very successful virus. How can that help its life cycle? If it kills everyone on Imago, where does it go next?"

Harriet pressed her lips together. "That's something we'll need to find out. Fast."

*

The very next day, Rudolph Green followed Al Pickton in keeling over without any warning.

Except Green didn't die right away. Only his lungs had given out, and a pair of paramedics who'd happened to be operating in the area had managed to get him on a ventilator before he suffocated. Harriet was notified immediately, and she rushed to the hospital to see Rudolph.

By the time she got there, he was already dead. Her shoulders slumped when the receptionist gave her the news.

"Do you want to examine him now, Ms. Vaughn?" the receptionist asked. "Or should I have him brought to your lab?"

*Well, I can definitely stop rushing to see him.* Interviewing Green while he'd still been alive had been the truly promising prospect. Still, studying him so soon after death could yield something. "I'll see him now."

She collected all the data she could from Green, and then she requested that his body be brought to her lab and placed in the refrigeration unit there.

On the way out of the hospital, Harriet ran into Theodore Yates in the hallway. She caught him by the wrist as he attempted to sidle past her in the corridor, avoiding eye contact.

"Theo. Were you visiting Sabrina?" Theo had dated Harriet's sister for a couple months after the *Delphi* had arrived at Imago, and he still kept close tabs on Sabrina. He was a creep, in Harriet's opinion.

"Uh…" Theo cleared his throat, his eyes darting.

"You did something for her, didn't you?"

He sniffed.

"You tweaked her sim," Harriet said. It wasn't a question. While Theo had a reputation for being a careless jerk, he was Imago's resident expert on the history sims, which made him the *de facto* expert on the farming sims.

"She wanted the alcohol to have a stronger effect," he rasped at last. "I see it as progress, Harriet. Simulated livers don't give out."

"I see it as enabling. Don't tweak her sim again until you check with me first. Do you understand me?"

"I understand that you can *piss off*," he said, apparently having found his guts somewhere. With that, he stormed toward the hospital's main entrance.

Harriet glared at his retreating back. It never failed to amaze her how much gall Theo Yates could muster sometimes. He certainly didn't have a good reason for having any self-confidence.

*He's a toothpick-shaped coward.* And mostly, he acted like one, though every now and then a wave of superiority would wash over him, and for the rest of the conversation it was like he'd suddenly remembered he was secretly God Emperor of the Universe.

She found Sabrina awake, her eyes rimmed with redness, probably from crying.

"I want you to get Theo to reverse what he did to your sim," Harriet said.

"Hello to you too," Sabrina answered, grimacing.

"Did you hear what I just said?"

"Yeah."

"And?"

Her sister smiled, though the expression didn't contain an ounce of happiness. "You can shove your ultimatums up your ass. You don't rule me, Harriet. You don't make the law. I'm allowed to do anything I want with my sim."

"He's enabling you. After enough simulated booze, you'll want the real stuff again. I know you, Sabrina. Way better than he does."

"You don't know me at all."

Harriet glared at her sister for a moment, before she managed to rein in her emotions. *This isn't getting us anywhere.* She drew a breath and took the seat next to the bed, trying not to let her shoulders slump again.

"Maybe you're right," Harriet said, her voice much softer. "Maybe I don't know you."

"You don't."

"Why are you like this, Sabrina? Why can't you make the most of what we've been given here?"

"What have we been given?"

"A chance," Harriet said. "A fresh start."

"And who gave that to us? God?"

Harriet inclined her head. "All gifts come from God."

"Bullshit. The war gave us this, Harriet. And in exchange, it took Earth, along with everyone we knew."

Slowly, Harriet shook her head. "Our friends are probably still alive out there. They were all assigned to colony ships. We saw a lot of them off ourselves, didn't we? And Cathy and Brian saw us off."

"The most important word you just used is *probably.* We don't actually know, do we? And we may never know. That's just it. We're separated by so much distance that no one will know if something catastrophic happens. Not until it's way too late, anyway. We've been scattered across tens of thousands of light years. We went from having the net—from being able to contact anyone we wanted instantly—to *this.* We might as well be a different species from our friends, now. Future generations probably *will* belong to different species, for all intents and purposes. If they survive."

Harriet's gaze drifted from Sabrina's to settle on the blank hospital wall, oppressive in its sterile whiteness.

"The sims are what I have to get by, now," her sister went on. "I know I can't drink in real life anymore. I know it was an atrocious waste of the fabber, to replace a liver because I couldn't stop myself. So I'm *going* to keep drinking in the sims, Harriet. It's all I have."

"I get it," Harriet said.

With that, she stood and left the room.

As was usually the case, her conversation with Sabrina had left her feeling depressed. But it had also given her an idea. If Sabrina could tweak her sim, what was stopping Harriet from tweaking her dreams?

Harriet considered herself deeply religious, and she'd always been fascinated by passages from the Bible that depicted God's use of dreams to communicate important messages to his followers.

*God told Jacob that Jesus was the gate to heaven. He showed Joseph the future. He promised Solomon wisdom and power...*

Why couldn't he use a dream to lend Harriet guidance about what she should do about Imagovirus?

In one sense, it seemed crazy, and it would probably

sound crazy to anyone to whom she said it loud. But Harriet was getting desperate, and she had always believed that God watched out for his children, especially in times of crisis. To Harriet, humanity's attempts to survive out here in the cold reaches of space definitely qualified as a time of crisis.

She had a passing interest in lucid dreaming, and she knew it was possible to train yourself to have them regularly. But the increased control and retention that came with lucid dreaming had never been quite enough to motivate her to learn how to do it.

Now, she *was* motivated. With lucid dreaming, she could lend structure to her recurring dream, and in it, she could do whatever she willed.

Yes, a part of her longed to kiss the version of Philip who existed only in her dreams, and to feel his arms around her. But even more, she wanted to remember what they spoke about when she woke up.

*God is giving me these dreams for a reason.*

She planned to find out what that reason was.

*

Between seeking a cure for Imagovirus and teaching herself to lucid dream, Harriet's every waking moment was full.

In the lab, she and Mariah did manage to hit upon a plausible life cycle for Imagovirus. It seemed that its strategy was to kill off an entire population and then go dormant, except that the virus persisted even after it killed its host. It survived in a sort of stasis, much as humans did inside cryo-tubes.

Over the ensuing years, the host's body biodegraded, and the virus remained in the earth, to eventually be taken up by plants through their roots. Once that happened, the plants themselves became infected, and so did whatever animal ate the plants.

That ingestion by animals was also when Imagovirus did its mutating, which it did rapidly, over and over, until it hit upon a form that allowed it to spread quickly through the population of whatever species it had infected.

At first, the virus caused only flu-like symptoms. Then, suddenly...

Death.

The life cycle of Imagovirus was one of death, and it explained why the planet's animal population was so sparse. Harriet had no idea when the virus had first evolved, but it represented a slow-moving apocalypse for all macroscopic life on Imago.

Discovering Imagovirus' life cycle ended up doing nothing for their efforts to find a cure. More and more people died, and Harriet and Mariah remained powerless to stop it, despite the increasingly early mornings and late nights they were putting in at the lab.

Luckily, Harriet quickly found that the techniques she used to train herself to lucid dream could be fit fairly easily into even the busiest of lives.

Imago's net archives had all the information she needed. Each colony ship had been given a compressed download of almost the entirety of Earth's net—a repository of virtually all human knowledge, sent into the stars in hundreds of directions.

To begin, Harriet started a dream journal, and each morning after waking she spent five minutes scribbling her dreams inside it. This was a technique meant to increase her dream retention. It began to work within a week, which made her marvel at the fact that she'd never managed to keep a dream journal before.

*If I'd known it had been this easy...*

Another technique involved checking to see whether she still had the ability to affect a room's light levels. It was next to impossible to adjust the light level in a dream, and so the moment she tried a switch and it didn't work, she'd know she was dreaming.

Whenever she entered or exited a room now, she hit the light switches to make sure they were still working. That had the potential to cause some social friction, which became clear when she went to her dentist for a checkup. The occupants of the waiting room immediately voiced their displeasure at what she'd done, loudly, and she was warned not to do it again on her way out.

She managed to restrain herself, but only barely. For full effectiveness, she figured it was important to test the lights in *every* room. That way, she would start to do so whenever she dreamed, too.

Or that she needed to change a light bulb.

Either way, she uncovered plenty of ways to teach herself to lucid dream, and she implemented them all. She constantly checked digital time displays to see whether she could properly read them, and during her scant breaks, she brought up pages from the net archives at random, to make sure their text was stable. Shifting, unreadable text was another sign of being inside a dream.

In the meantime, more and more colonists were dropping dead from Imagovirus. By now, it had cut short twenty-six lives, and Harriet shuddered to think of what would happen to the colony if she or Mariah were next. Every sniffle sent a jolt of fear through her body.

At last, after weeks of frustrated efforts, she gave up. She woke up after yet another night of no lucid dreams—at least, none that she could remember—and cursed as she sat up in bed.

*I'm terrible at this.*

She'd also begun to realize how ridiculous it was, to remain so focused on her dreams when people were dying in real life. Even though it took up very little of her time, it was demanding more and more of her cognition, and it was time for her to stop.

*God isn't trying to speak to me. I'm not special. And the only way I'm going to help the people of Imago is to focus completely on my work.*

She stumbled out of bed, threw on a t-shirt, and left the bedroom to begin her morning routine, which began with drinking the coffee she'd programmed her coffee maker to start brewing for her just before she woke.

When she entered the kitchen, there was no coffee smell.

There was, however, someone sitting at her kitchen table.

It was Ensign Philip Mann.

"Philip...what are you doing here?"

His face had a haggard look, as though he'd been feeling just as frustrated as she had. Before answering, he paused for several seconds.

"I'm doing the same thing I've done dozens of times before," he said, speaking with great deliberation. "If only I could manage to make it *work*."

With a hand that trembled slightly, she reached toward the light switch to her left.

When she hit it, nothing happened.

*I'm dreaming!*

To make sure, she walked to the washroom that led off from the kitchen and tried that light as well. Still nothing.

Excitement welled up inside her, and she willed herself to calm down. Of the handful of lucid dreams she'd ever had in her life, at least half of them had been ruined by getting so excited she woke up.

"Philip," she said, "things are different tonight."

Again, he paused before speaking, and when he spoke, he did so rather slowly. "You've said similar things before," he said. "But you never remember our conversations afterward and you take no action."

Harriet tilted her head to the side. *Action?*

"You don't understand," she said. "I *know* that I'm dreaming. I'm lucid dreaming!"

"Hmm," he said, though not before pausing once more. He narrowed his eyes a little. "Well, that *is* new." He still sounded skeptical, though.

More importantly, he sounded nothing like the Philip Mann of her waking life. This Philip's voice was resonant with emotion, hinting at an inner life so rich and deep it might be bottomless.

This was the Philip she loved.

Taking a seat across from him, she stared him right in the eyes. "This *is* different, Philip. Now, tell me— what did you mean when you said I haven't taken any action? Action on what?"

He drew a ragged breath, running a rough hand over a stubbled cheek. "Escaping," he said after a time.

"Escaping?" she repeated, shaking her head. "Escaping what? And why are you pausing before everything you say?"

After pausing again, Philip answered, with the air of someone explaining something for the hundredth time. "Our realities aren't completely in sync, Harriet. Speaking to you through your dreams is the only way we can talk at all. The simulation runs at a fraction of the speed of reality, rendering any conversation I'd try to have with you inside it so slow as to be meaningless. But dreams are almost ideal. Since humans don't dream in real-time, but several times faster than that, we can actually talk here."

Harriet wondered whether her eyes were as wide as they felt. "I'm sorry, Philip, but I'm completely lost, here. Simulation? What are you talking about?"

"The farming sims. You're still inside one of the farming sims. Still in cryo."

Her chest clenched, and she struggled to relax, to maintain the dream. Philip's words had caused her to experience shock and disbelief in equal measure. "So if what you're saying is true…we haven't really arrived at Imago?"

"Oh, we've arrived," the ensign said, with a tiny, bitter smile. "We're in orbit over Imago right now. Except the exoplanet experts got this one wrong. It's not the verdant utopia they thought it was. It's a barren rock with a poisonous atmosphere."

Now it was Harriet's turn to pause, and when she finally found her voice again, she stuttered: "H-how long ago did we arrive?"

As he answered her, even his bitter ghost of a smile fell away. "Years. The UEF only gave us enough fuel for a one-way trip, Harriet. We've been here for years and years."

*

"That's impossible," she said, getting abruptly to her feet. The motion knocked her chair over, but in an instant later it was upright again, even though she hadn't picked it off the floor.

*Just like it would in a dream.*

"This isn't real," she said. "It's a dream. A nightmare. And you're nothing more than a dream character trying to scare me."

"I wish that were true," Philip said. "Truly, I do. But it's all too real. And I'm real. I'm lying in a bed on the *Delphi* right now, with my head inside a sim unit I managed to obtain. Just as I have dozens of times before, trying to get through to you as you dream."

"Why me, then? Why are you contacting me?"

"Because we spoke a few times during the actual farming sims, back when I was also still inside them.

When we were still in transit from Earth. We chatted enough that I learned you're probably the most religious person of all the colonists. Being that devout, I figured I'd have the best chance approaching you through your dreams. I figured you were the most likely to attribute enough significance to them that you'd take a closer look."

"I went on a date with you a few weeks ago. You didn't mention any of this. In fact, you didn't say anything that was the least bit important or relevant."

"That's because that wasn't really me. The sims aren't very good at mimicking human consciousness— you were talking to a glorified chatbot. Same goes for the crew of the *Delphi* and some of the FCF members. Haven't you noticed them all acting pretty aloof since you arrived? Like they refuse to engage?"

"Yes," she admitted.

"That's because they *can't* engage. Not like a human could. The only way to cover up their limited intellect is to give them distant, formal personalities."

Harriet blinked, still fighting to steady her breathing. When she spoke again, her words came out almost as slowly as Philip's: "Imagovirus…this is why Imagovirus prevents us from tasting or smelling properly, isn't it?"

Philip nodded. "The virus is a fiction, used to cover up the fact you're still in a sim."

"Who else is still trapped here?"

"Almost all the civilian colonists were left in cryo. The ship automatically revived the captain and crew first, as it was programmed to do, to ensure an orderly revival of the other passengers. But the captain overrode the second part."

Harriet shook her head. "All this time, I thought Imagovirus was killing us. But it isn't real." She said it again, so softly that her voice was barely audible, even to her: "It isn't real."

That brought a drawn-out exhalation from Philip. "I'm afraid it *is* killing colonists, Harriet—in a sense. A very real sense."

"What do you mean?"

His lips were tight. "At first, keeping the colonists in cryo was strictly about conserving resources. Without an arable planet to exploit, there were only enough supplies to sustain the crew and a couple squads' worth of FCF marines."

"Wait," Harriet said. She was still trying to poke holes in Philip's story, because she really didn't want to believe it. "Why didn't the captain just send out a distress signal and have the crew go back into their cryotubes to wait for rescue?"

"Because we have no cryotechnician aboard. Before leaving Enceladus, there was a limited number of those to go around, and not every ship was assigned one."

"Great," Harriet murmured. To safely enter cryostasis, you needed a specialist. Otherwise, the most optimistic estimates put the probability of death at well over ninety percent. "You said *almost* all the colonists are still in cryo. Who else was revived?"

"No one…no one else was revived."

"Yet not everyone is still in cryo?"

Philip's facial features were strained, taut. "This is what I meant when I said Imagovirus truly is killing colonists. It's also what made me decide to start trying to contact you. A few years after we arrived in orbit over Imago, our organ fabber broke down, and a few months after that, the first mate was diagnosed with lung cancer. By the time the ship doctor detected the cancer, it had already spread to both lungs, and the only way to save him was to replace them."

It took only a moment for the meaning behind Philip's words to sink in. "The captain ordered one of the colonists' lungs to be removed," she said.

"Yes."

"And everyone just went along with that?"

"No, actually. The captain called a general meeting, where he asked to hear how everyone felt about what he'd done. He ordered everyone to speak their minds. By the time it was my turn, I sensed that something was going on, and I lied, saying I was fine with it. Once everyone had spoken, a squad of marines drew their sidearms and shot everyone who'd objected to the captain's actions."

*

Harriet and Philip had left her house to walk the streets of Imago, which were empty and eerily quiet.

Everything looked just as it did in real life—except her waking life wasn't real either, was it? "Real life" was just as false as this dream. If Philip's words were true, the dream was actually the realer of the two, in a sense.

"So every colonist that dies in the sim is having their organs harvested in real life."

Philip nodded. "The captain justifies it by insisting the colonists wouldn't survive without their captain and crew, and so this is the only way to ensure the survival of the maximum number of colonists possible—by killing some of them to keep the crew alive."

For some reason, hearing the captain's logic made Harriet feel even more nauseated than she already had. "Whose lungs did they take?"

"A man named Pat O'Malley. Did you know him?"

"No," she said, shaking her head. "But…" Heat flashed down her back, and her vision blurred for a moment. "It's so unfair. So *cowardly*."

Philip nodded again. "They decide who dies by lottery. I've been so terrified that you would be chosen."

Harriet studied his expression closely. "Why? You

think there's something I can do to fix this, don't you? Something from inside the sim."

"Yes. That's the main reason I was scared…" Philip cleared his throat. "To the sim's occupants, they made Pat O'Malley's death look like an accident—an untimely fall down the stairs. But as more people got sick in real life, and the need for organs accelerated, they decided they needed a cause of death that looked less suspicious. Hence, Imagovirus. They'll take more organs if they're not stopped, Harriet. They'll kill more people. Our medical supplies on the *Delphi* are limited. People are aging, and a closed-in ship is the perfect environment for disease to spread, as I'm sure you know. The demand for organs is ramping up. So more colonists will die."

"What's the end game for Gregory? Does he think the UEF will look kindly on what he's done? Or the FCF, for that matter?"

Philip gave a slight shrug. "The captain's determined to survive until someone answers our distress call, and we have to assume the crewmembers he didn't kill are of the same mind. I expect Captain Gregory will have some sort of story cooked up to feed to whoever arrives, and he'll delete all evidence of what he's done. When the *Delphi* is rescued, any colonists who didn't have their organs harvested will be none the wiser, because this sim is preventing them from finding out what's really happening. Unless someone brings them back to reality."

"I'm guessing that's where I come in."

Philip didn't answer. Instead, he drew to a stop in front of Theodore Yates's house, and Harriet stopped, too. Philip turned toward her, eyebrows raised.

"Why are we stopping here?" she said. "Does Theo have something to do with all this?"

"He's the only civilian who's aware that he's still in a farming sim. The captain guaranteed him that his organs would never be taken—so long as he does what he's told, and never reveals the truth to the other colonists."

"But what does the captain need Theo for?" As far as Harriet knew, the man was completely useless.

Except he did have *one* use.

"He maintains the sim from within," Philip said. "Makes sure everything is kept consistent and believable. But most importantly, he watches everyone—makes sure no one has figured out the truth."

"How does he make sure of that?"

"Admin powers. Theodore Yates has the ability to spy on anyone, at any time. If someone starts acting like they know about the simulation, it's Yates's job to notify the captain."

That notion sent shivers down Harriet's spine. "Wouldn't it be easier for him to do that if he was outside the sim?"

"Actually, no. The sims were designed to prevent external monitoring, for privacy reasons. Only an admin can do it, from inside. Sure, you could pore over the code to figure out what's going on from outside it, but it's much easier to just have someone on the inside reporting to you."

"So Theo's job is to be Big Brother for the sim."

"Not just that. He's also the one that kills people inside the sim, and makes sure their deaths look realistic."

That caused a coldness to spread through Harriet. The idea that Theo had always had such power, over her and others.

*To think I gave him so much flak about my sister, when he could have signed my death warrant at any time…*

True, killing her in the sim wouldn't have been her actual death, but if she'd happened to unexpectedly wake from it, she felt pretty sure that she'd become next in

121

line for having her organs taken.

"How am I going to do this alone, Philip? How can I be expected to bring an end to the sim *and* retake the *Delphi* from the captain and his murderers?"

"You need to sneak inside Theo's house somehow and access the terminal he uses to oversee the sim. I'm not clear on what your options will be from there, but it seems like that's your best chance to escape."

Harriet didn't think the phrase "your best chance" imparted much in the way of comfort. But then, nothing about this was very comforting. "If I manage to revive my real body from cryo—what then?"

"You'll need to immediately revive Andrew Ferdinand."

"The man the UEF sent as governor of Imago? He hasn't already been revived?"

"No. The Andrew Ferdinand you see governing the colony in the sim is the actual Andrew Ferdinand—not some chatbot like the thing that's impersonating me. Captain Gregory knew that if he revived Ferdinand, the governor's authority would challenge his own. Technically, we're still on Gregory's ship and not in Ferdinand's colony, but Ferdinand has in his possession emergency codes that will shut down the colony ship and turn complete control over to him. If he inputs those codes, he can trap the captain and his crew wherever they are. From there, we can deal with them as we see fit—order them to disarm themselves and give themselves up for arrest, if they ever want to be let out. Threaten to turn off life support in whatever section we've trapped them in. We'll have options."

"And it starts with breaking into Theodore Yates's house, while hoping he doesn't use his digital superpowers to quash me."

A smile quirked the corner of Philip's lip. "I wouldn't have thought to put it quite that way. But yes."

"Hey, how hard can it be?"

"Pretty hard. But you can do it, Harriet. I...I look forward to meeting you in real life." His hardened soldier's veneer had softened into an expression that was much warmer.

She offered him a small smile, and she knew the mission he'd given her wasn't the only reason for her accelerating heartbeat. "I look forward to meeting you, Philip."

*

When Harriet woke, she remembered everything Philip had told her.

What was more, as crazy as it seemed, she believed it. All of it. Just as God had sometimes sent his angel to deliver messages of hope, she believed that God had sent her Philip, whether he knew it or not.

Unfortunately, his message did seem pretty crazy, and she knew it would sound even crazier if she tried to explain it to Mariah. It would make her assistant think that the pressure of seeking a cure for Imagovirus had finally driven her over the edge.

And yet, for the plan she had in mind to work, she needed Mariah.

So she lied.

"I think I have a lead on a cure," she said halfway through the morning after her dream—after she'd worked out the kinks from the fib she planned to tell.

"Seriously?" Mariah said, looking up at her through eyes underscored by dark patches.

*We're both so tired.* And yet, in Mariah's eyes shone hope. *I just pray that she's right to have that.*

"Well...I think I have a lead on a lead. If that makes any sense. It involves Theo Yates."

"Yates?" Mariah screwed up her face. "What could

he possibly have to offer us?"

"It's his hobby to tinker around with sim tech, and from the way he's been talking lately, I think he's made a breakthrough that would improve it by leaps and bound. He refuses to do anything but talk around it, but from his bragging I think it's something big. And I think it could help us improve ViroBuddy enough to get a better handle on the Imagovirus."

"Okay. So let's ask him to give it to us."

"He won't. He can't stand me."

"That's irrelevant, isn't it? This isn't about you, it's about saving the colony."

"I'm afraid he may very well be that petty. Even if he does give it to us, I think he'll want something in return—something involving my sister. I'm not willing to use her as a bargaining chip, Mariah. She's fragile enough as it is." Harriet hoped her indignation was coming across as authentic.

"All right," Mariah said, shaking her head. "All right. So, what do we do?"

"I think I can get him to leave his house. When he does, we break in, hack into his terminal, and copy its hard drive onto a com to sneak back here with it."

"This is getting a bit bizarre, Harriet."

*You have no idea.* "I know. But I really can't think of another way. Things get bizarre when you're trying to get any good out of someone like Theo Yates."

"All right," Mariah said. "If you really think this could lead to a cure…"

Twenty minutes later, Mariah was hiding in an alley between another residence and one of the colony's two general stores while Harriet rang Theo's buzzer.

He opened the door, squinting out at her. "Harriet?"

"Theo. I have a favor to ask."

A smile slithered across the creep's face. "*Really?* That's fascinating. Do you want me to move even farther away from your sister? Maybe you want me to leave the colony altogether, to live in a tent in the woods?"

"No...the opposite, actually. I've decided that if tweaking her sim will make Sabrina happy, then I'm fine with it. She's been having trouble with it, but she refuses to contact you after I...well, after I scolded you at the hospital. She's mortified that I might have scared you away."

"I see. This *is* unexpected. So what are you asking, exactly?"

"I'm asking you to go to the hospital and help her calibrate her sim the way she wants."

"I did that already."

Harriet shrugged. "She says it isn't working properly."

"Strange." Theo cocked his head to one side. "Sims don't normally glitch after *I* set them up. But I'll have a look."

"Thank you, Theo." She tried to give him a genuine-looking smile, but she was worried her disgust for him was showing through.

"If I do this...I want you to know that I've been considering asking your sister out again. If I do this, I want you to stay out of my way. In fact, I want your blessing."

"You have it," Harriet said immediately. "No problem." If all went well, this reality would end soon, and Theo would be in the *Delphi*'s brig, so she had no problem agreeing to what would hopefully be a very temporary arrangement.

"Perfect. I'll head right over."

"Thank you so much, Theo. I can't tell you what it means to me."

He held her gaze for a few moments longer, scrutinizing her, and for a moment, she was worried that he'd begun to cotton on to what she was doing. Then, that creepy smile broke onto his face again.

"Not a problem." He shut the door without another word.

With that, Harriet walked casually down the street— until she judged she was far enough away. Then, she circled back around to join Mariah in the alleyway.

They watched Theo's door for several minutes, each of which felt like an hour. At last, he left his house, carrying a suitcase that no doubt held whatever equipment he expected he'd need.

Once Theo disappeared down the street, Harriet dashed toward his front door, motioning for Mariah to follow.

The door was locked, but when they skirted the house they found a window he'd left open, which the back patio gave them easy access to.

They both climbed in.

"Oh my God," Mariah said, who'd entered first.

When Harriet joined her, she saw the reason for that reaction: the place was a total mess. Between dishes, clothes, takeout boxes, used tissues, and other unhygienic miscellany, there were almost no surfaces not covered with something.

Mariah's left hand was pressed to her forehead. "This could take forever, if we have to sift through all this junk."

"I doubt we'll have to. He must use his terminal a lot, so we probably won't have to dig for it."

But a cursory search of two floors yielded nothing. Harriet was about to start overturning mounds of garbage when Mariah noticed a door they hadn't tried yet. When they did, it opened onto a set of stairs, which led down to a finished basement with a single room.

They found the room just as dirty as the upstairs, if not dirtier, but its focal point was Theo's terminal— uncovered by anything, just as Harriet had predicted.

Gingerly, Mariah lowered herself onto the office

chair in front of it, which was also uncovered, other than a sweat-stained t-shirt hanging over the back.

Blinking, Mariah looked from the terminal's screen to Harriet. "No hacking required, looks like. He's left himself logged in."

Nodding slowly, Harriet said, "Mariah, there's something I haven't been totally honest about."

Her assistant's eyebrows climbed toward her hair. "Oh?"

"I don't actually think Theo made a breakthrough that can help us. I needed to access his terminal for a different reason—one I would have had a lot of trouble explaining without us actually being here in front of it."

Mariah hesitated only for a few seconds. "What is it?"

They didn't have much time, so Harriet gave her as condensed a version as possible of what Philip Mann had revealed. She told her about the ensign visiting her in the dream, the discovery that Imago was really a lifeless rock, and how Captain Gregory and his crew were keeping the colonists in cryo while taking their organs to survive.

While Harriet spoke as quickly as she could, the expression on Mariah's face went from perplexed to skeptical, and then to a little angry.

But at last, Harriet finished. "I know this sounds crazy, and you're probably feeling pretty pissed off right now that I talked you into coming here for a reason that seems so insane. But please—do me the favor of at least verifying what I'm saying. Have a look on Theo's terminal and see what you find."

Scowling, now, Mariah turned back to the screen in silence, clicking around the terminal gingerly, as though unsure why she was bothering to comply. But then, when she ran a scan for all the programs installed on the terminal, she hit upon sim management software that had clearly been set apart from other such programs on Theo's machine.

"That has to be it," Harriet said. "Open it."

When Mariah did, an interface popped up with a long list of colonist names, as well as locations throughout the colony.

Mariah clicked on her own name, and it showed an overhead view of her and Harriet in Theo's basement, as though the upper floors had been torn away and they were looking at themselves from the sky.

Even from where she was standing at Mariah's side, Harriet could see her eyes widen.

Mariah clicked on Sabrina Vaughn's name, and it showed her sitting up in her hospital bed.

Next, she clicked on an icon that bore a sun shining through white clouds, and when she did, a list of weather conditions popped up.

When she clicked "thunderstorm," a rumble sounded from outside, and even though they were downstairs, they could hear rain pelting the windows above.

"Okay," Mariah said, her voice barely above a whisper. "I believe you now."

At that moment, they heard the front door open overhead.

Following that, Theodore Yates's thin voice called out:

"Who's down there?" he demanded.

*

Harriet and Mariah shared wide-eyed glances, and then Harriet steeled herself.

*This is no time to freeze up.*

"I'll go upstairs and try to stall him," she whispered. "You see if there's anything that can be done from here." She nodded at the terminal.

Mariah nodded back, planting her fingers on the keyboard, where they flew.

For her part, Harriet forced herself to raise her foot to the first stair, and then the next.

Theo didn't come down to meet her. Instead, she found him standing near the front door, his stance signaling wariness. When he saw Harriet, his eyes narrowed.

"Theo," she said, trying to sound as placating as she could, though her voice wavered a little. She decided to go with the same fiction she'd originally concocted for Mariah. "I can explain. This is about my work in trying to find a cure for Imagovirus. It—"

"Bullshit," Theo said. "Someone got to you, didn't they? We have a traitor on the *Delphi*. Someone *told* you."

She tried to feign ignorance. "The *Delphi*? The *Delphi*'s in orbit with no one on it, acting as a communications—"

But Theo took a menacing step forward. "I started to worry a little, when you began to work so hard on curing Imagovirus. Because there *is* no cure—not in this reality—and I thought you might find that odd. But no. You can't have figured things out this quickly. Someone got to you."

Knowing the game was up, Harriet was about to lunge at Theo when a pistol materialized in his grip.

"I knew something was up as soon as you encouraged me to visit Sabrina. That's not you at all. And then the sudden thunderstorm…" He shook his head. "Doesn't matter. I don't like to be the one to do this, but you've forced my hand. Say hello to Captain Gregory for me."

Except, Theo remained perfectly still, and he didn't fire. Tilting her head sideways, Harriet studied him.

"Harriet!" Mariah called from downstairs. "*Get out of the way!*"

Immediately, she sidestepped—just in time. The pistol fired, and the bullet zipped down the hall, through the kitchen, and out the back window.

Then, Harriet saw that Theo *was* actually moving, but with incredible slowness. With the speed of glaciers, his hand began to lower, and his face took on the beginnings of a rictus of rage.

"Get down here!" Mariah yelled.

Harriet wasn't accustomed to taking orders from her assistant, but these were special circumstances. She scurried down the stairs to join her at the terminal.

"That gunshot will attract people," she said when she reached Mariah. "They won't understand what we're doing—they'll think we lost it and broke into Theo's house."

"They'll also find Theo moving at the same speed my last boyfriend used to get out of bed." Mariah shrugged. "Anyway. It looks like Theo controlled who departed the sim from here. You mentioned that any FCF members we see in the colony are actually low-functioning automatons. To avoid having too many of those walking around, Theo was obviously killing anyone who'd been chosen to have their organs taken. From what I've been able to glean, he's been crafting each death to make it look natural and logical to the other colonists—like he did with Imagovirus. But there's also a feature here that just straight-up kills people. We don't know for sure that dying in the sim is what triggers an exit from the cryo-tube. It could be that escaping requires an extra step, maybe taken by someone aboard the *Delphi*. But if that's true, we're screwed anyway, unless you can get in touch with your dream friend again, and I doubt we have time for that."

"So we have to try this," Harriet said. "It's our only hope."

"Just to be clear, boss—are you asking me to kill

you?"

"I'm telling you it's your job to kill me, as my assistant."

"That's what I thought you were saying." Mariah clicked through the interface, until an angry scarlet rectangle labeled KILL appeared. Below it was a drop-down list, and after Mariah found Harriet's name and clicked it, she hovered the cursor over the blood-red button. She shot Harriet a glance with raised eyebrows.

"Wait," Harriet said. "You have to kill Andrew Ferdinand too."

"You're telling me to kill the governor?"

"Yes."

"Is that part of my job, too?"

Harriet grimaced. "He has emergency codes that we'll need to take over the *Delphi.*"

"If you say so." Mariah switched Harriet's name to Ferdinand's, and she clicked KILL. "That's him dead. Ready for your turn?"

Pressing her lips together and clenching her fists, Harriet nodded.

Mariah clicked the button. Harriet crumpled to the floor, her consciousness fleeing.

\*

The bottom of her cryo-tube unsealed, emptying all its liquid through the grate built into the deck below. Next, padded robotic arms gripped Harriet by her hips and armpits, lowering her gently to the same grate.

Even though she wore a durable rubber bikini meant to provide a modicum of decency, leaving one's cryo-tube was meant to be a private affair, and typically colonists were revived one by one, to allow them to dress before rejoining the others who'd exited their tubes.

But as Harriet stared through the haze of her returning vision, battling immense grogginess, the steel cold against her elbows and knees, she became aware of another's presence.

"Governor Ferdinand?" she croaked.

"Negative," a reedy voice rasped—a voice that shook in a way that came only with advanced age or illness. "Though it makes sense that you'd think so. It appears he was an important part of your plan, which explains why he's currently kneeling below his own cryotube, coughing and sputtering."

Harriet looked to her right, where she saw confirmation of the voice's words: the well-muscled, mostly naked Andrew Ferdinand was indeed on his hands and knees beneath his own tube.

Next, with a great effort of will, she managed to lift her gaze to the owner of the voice.

It took her a long time to recognize him. He had aged greatly, far more than she'd been expecting, and he resembled old photos of people who'd surpassed one hundred years naturally, before the invention of life extension technology.

He also held a pistol—one that closely resembled the gun Theo had tried to use on her.

"*Your* organs will come in handy," Captain Gregory said. "But I can't let Andrew Ferdinand live long enough to harvest his. He's too great a flight risk outside his cryo-tube."

With the labored movements of old age, Gregory pushed himself off the cryo-tube he'd been leaning against and began walking toward Ferdinand, the hand that held the pistol raising toward the governor.

Cryotechnicians strongly recommended waiting at least an hour after revival from cryo before engaging in activity that could be considered strenuous.

Harriet figured that tackling the captain of the *Delphi* from behind probably qualified. But she couldn't exactly afford to wait.

Gathering her strength and her will, she surged upward from the floor, connecting with the captain's hunched back and wrapping her arms around his torso.

Gregory staggered forward, but Harriet maintained her grip, pinning his arms at his sides, trying to bring him down.

The captain kept his feet. Now, Harriet was mostly using him for support to remain standing herself, and her grasp was quickly weakening.

Still inside her loosening embrace, Gregory turned, and he managed to raise his pistol's muzzle to her abdomen. He fired.

Incredible pain radiated out from the bullet wound instantly. She fell back, but her arms remained around the captain, and this time, her backward momentum was enough to bring him down.

Something broke inside the captain as they landed, likely a rib, and he cried out.

Harriet fumbled at his grip, and she managed to pry his gun from age-weakened fingers. That done, she raised it to his skull.

The gun roared, and Gregory's head acquired a small, round hole where the bullet entered. His full weight came down on her then, causing her to cry out. When Gregory's head lolled sideways, it revealed a much larger, much messier exit wound.

Andrew Ferdinand crawled over to her. "Ms...Ms. Vaughn, isn't it?"

"Yes. Hello, Governor."

"You've shot the captain!"

"Killed him, if I'm not mistaken."

"So you have," Ferdinand said, fingering Gregory's neck, presumably for a pulse. "There's a lot that's odd about this situation."

"I'll explain everything later. But for now, the most

salient information is that the captain and crew have kept the colonists trapped inside the farming sims while they harvest our organs, one by one. You need to use your emergency override codes to take control of the *Delphi* and trap everyone who's awake wherever they are on the ship."

"All right, then," Ferdinand said haltingly.

"After that, if you'd be so kind as to help me to sick bay…"

"Yes. Of course."

With that, everything went dark for Harriet—almost as though she was dying for the second time that day.

*

She woke in a bed in sick bay, with IV tubes sprouting from her arms and heart rate monitors clipped to her fingertips.

From the bed beside hers, an elderly man smiled at her, his head nestled on a pillow.

"Hello," she said, her voice coming out as a rasp, just as it had in the moments after she'd exited her cryotube.

"Hi there."

"Is…is everything all right?" Harriet asked. "With the *Delphi*, and with the colonists?"

"It's as all right as it can be. The colonists have been revived, and the crewmembers were apprehended, along with the FCF marines that enabled their crimes."

"Good." Then, something made her study the old man next to her intently. She stared hard into his ice-blue eyes, and finally she stammered, "P-Philip?"

He nodded slightly, his head never leaving the pillow, and his smile turning down only a notch. "Ensign Philip Mann, at your service."

"You're…you're so *old*."

"True."

"In my dream, you looked in your late thirties!"

"It's how I wished to appear to you. The ship's supply of life extension drugs ran out a long time ago, and we lost our appearance of youth. The colonists' organs have been the only thing allowing the crew to stave off death. I didn't want to tell you that. I never wanted you to see me like this, because now this is how you'll remember me. But it was unavoidable."

"Remember you?" Harriet repeated. "Are you going somewhere?"

"I'm dying, Harriet. Dying slowly, for months now. The same period I've been trying to contact you."

"So, you...you lived almost your entire life while doing nothing about the captain's crimes."

"Yes. But telling you that probably wouldn't have endeared me to you, and it was important that you trusted me. If you didn't, you might not have acted."

"I guess not," she said, her heart racing—but not for the reason it had raced during her dream conversations with Philip. Now it raced with anxiety, and even a little fear.

"There's something else I didn't tell you. I'm dying of cancer, which has spread from my stomach to the rest of my body. But before it spread..." Philip grimaced, and a single tear leaked from his right eye, sliding sideways down his wrinkled face. "Before it spread, I accepted a stomach transplant from one of the colonists. So I'm just as damned as the captain was."

"Philip..." she whispered.

"This is my death bed, Harriet, and it's only here that I began to atone for what I've done. I requested a sim unit be brought to me, and the captain granted my request. Why wouldn't he? I'd never given him a reason to mistrust me before. And I used that sim unit to contact you, to arrange all this. To put a stop to what was happening."

"What next, then, Philip?" Harriet said, her voice cracking. She was crying too, now.

"The rest is up to you and the other colonists. How you'll conduct yourselves. How you'll spend your time remaining aboard the *Delphi*. A distress message truly was sent to the nearest known colony, and if it arrived safely, and the colonists there heeded its plea, then they should arrive for you within a few years at most." He smiled, though this time, the expression looked far more forlorn. "The rest is up to you."

"I loved you, Philip," she said, even though she knew it probably sounded crazy—falling in love with a man who'd appeared to her only in her dreams. *But it was real, wasn't it?*

"And I loved you, Harriet. I still love you."

"I don't love you anymore," she said, shaking her head against her own pillow. "You're as much a murderer as the rest of them."

"Yes," he said, and closed his eyes, turning away from her.

Two weeks later, Philip died. By then Harriet was feeling well enough to attend his funeral, though she still needed Mariah's help to get around. When Philip's metal coffin was jettisoned into space, Harriet wept again.

A few weeks after that, she rejoined Mariah, this time in the *Delphi*'s lab. It was much tinier than the simulated one they'd shared for what had felt like years, but had really been decades. There was still plenty for them to do. The *Delphi* was the perfect incubator for disease, which was a large part of why cryo-tubes were necessary for interstellar journeys. But after the indomitable challenge of Imagovirus, they tackled each shipboard illness with methodical determination, and they defeated them all.

Harriet often thought about Philip—the old version

as well as the young, in equal measure. In large part, she owed her life to him. They all did.

And yet, he'd been monstrous, too. Fortunately for them, his monstrosity had been contained enough for him to do the right thing, in the very end, after dozens had already been killed.

She missed him, despite all that. Or maybe she just missed what she'd thought he was, once.

She and Andrew Ferdinand ended up dating a few times, but by the time the rescue ship arrived, they'd mutually decided to end it.

That was just as well, because the rescue ship had two cryotechnicians, and the colonists were once again placed in cryo for the journey.

Given the ordeal they'd gone through, they were offered the option of opting out of the farming sims while they were en route to the planet that would become their new home.

But Harriet chose to enter the sim once again. After all, what little real-world agency the sim had allowed her *had* saved her life. If she'd been totally unconscious, then she could very well have died instead of fighting through to the real world.

Besides, the colony of Somnus already had two virologists, and they didn't need any more. So Harriet would need to learn a new trade.

*Perhaps I'll choose farming this time.*

That would likely prove a lot less stressful. Somnus was said to be ideal for human habitation—a utopia, basically.

Almost every crop thrived there.

# Spiderfall

By Scott Moon

Eva took another step toward the launch bay, stopped, and put her hands on her hips. A strand of her diamond-blue hair floated in her large helmet. She ignored it, but accepted the soothing effect of its nearly inaudible song. The hair of her people looked like silk, but was as coarse and musical as a violin bow across the strings of life.

She wasn't the only colonist considering the launch bay opening. Fifteen meters wide and ten meters high, it was large enough to accommodate one shuttle at a time. With her left hand, she reached up to check the neck of her environmental suit. The alloy bands protecting the seals looked and felt new. The helmet visor was so clear she could believe it wasn't there.

She dropped her hands, but hipped them a second later.

"Nervous?" Jax asked from her left.

Eva had grown up with the woman, who was one year older, then attended the ad hoc Exploration Fleet Academy her father designed post-exodus. Like most of her crew, she had spent most of her adult life on one starship or another.

Jax would always be Eva's rival. Despite her superior age, Jax had always lived in Eva's shadow. Jax was human, and an average human at that. She didn't have the snow-white skin and diamond-blue hair of Eva's people.

Ten years after the Empyrean war, they'd grown into

a deeper friendship and a harder rivalry. The reason wasn't obvious or distinct. Raised together by nannies, bodyguards, and teachers, neither of them knew any other way to interact.

Jax stood taller, with the more robust form of an earth-born human. She had larger breasts and curvier hips. Her hair was blonde or chestnut, depending on how strong the ship lighting was at the moment. Eva had overheard enough of the men on the colony ship talking about Jax to know that the young woman was attractive. Depending on the narrator, she was a hot-blooded nymphomaniac or an ice-cold sex machine.

The same men who claimed to have slept with her also said she was a force of nature who never admitted to being wrong. Hot or cold, but always fierce, she intimidated the crew easily.

Eva smiled. She didn't look back. It was better if her friend and rival didn't see her expression. Eva suspected Jax was still looking for her first kiss.

"Of course I'm nervous. Planetfalls are dangerous."

"Then why are we making one? We don't have resources for this type of thing. The orbital survey of this rock doesn't suggest it'll be a fun place to live, even if we can survive here."

"I already gave the order. We're going down to check it out. You don't have to come if you don't want to." Eva paused. "Have we had communication with the fleet?"

Jax made a negative sound. "What do you think?"

They stared down on the stratosphere of the planet as pilots and mechanics reviewed checklists on the two shuttles she had selected for the mission. The same routine had been followed prior to pumping the launch bay atmosphere into storage containers. Everyone wore their environmental suits. This part was easy. Eva felt safe even with butterflies dancing in her stomach. On the planet, gravity would make the suits cumbersome and stifling until they were sure it was safe to breathe the air.

"I think I'd like to know what happened to our comm system," Eva said, knowing exactly what went wrong with it but hoping nobody else did.

This close to the planet, everything looked huge. She saw continents and oceans that were mostly icefields, but had potential at least to support life. Jax stood beside her now. There was no way to know if she was appreciating the stunning panorama for what it was. Her second in command had no nervous habits to betray her.

The rest of Eva's team waited several steps behind. Montgomery was a former soldier in charge of security. Carter was both a soldier and a fighter pilot jock, who would complain loudly about the boredom of landing the clunky but safe shuttle. Amanda, Carter's co-pilot, was an equally renowned veteran of the war against Empyrean.

All three were human, probably more loyal to Eva than her own people — none of whom had volunteered for this mission. She suspected they still resented not being included in her father's colony ship, wherever it had headed.

"That's another reason we shouldn't be taking unnecessary risks. If we get down there and need help, no one is coming to save our asses. My recommendation stands. Maintain an orbit and work on the communication problem."

"I'm aware of your recommendation, Jax. I also know that if I don't put my feet on a planet soon, I'm going to go crazy. Same for the crew."

"Sure. Maybe. But there are others who don't agree."

Eva popped the knuckles of her gloves and exhaled forcefully, suddenly frustrated and impatient. "They don't have to agree. My father gave *me* command of this ship, not them."

"Are we missing our daddy?"

Eva turned and faced her. The wrap-around helmet visor did nothing to stop the power of her eyes as she stared into the human woman's face.

Her father had nearly died when the assassin Pyr rescued them. Never affectionate in the first place, he'd become cold and distant after the ordeal. Eva felt like he blamed her for the loss of the *Impregnable* and his fall from grace.

Powerful leaders in the UEF would never forgive him for failing to fight off Empyrean's Astrals and the assassin Pyr. They gave him command of the smallest fleet, then sent him to the farthest reaches of space.

"I'm sorry," Jax said.

Eva turned and walked toward the first shuttle, summoning the crew with one hand. Montgomery and Carter led others to the shuttle she would be taking. Jax grumbled, but took her team to the second shuttle.

She brooded as the crew conducted final checks and prepared for launch.

Engines came online. The flight control officer gave the green light and the shuttle floated from the bay. Small steering jets oriented them toward their destination and let physics do its work.

She felt the increasing effect of gravity take hold. Atmosphere buffeted the vessel. Her eyes watched the spectacular approach of the planet, but her heart and mind braced for death.

She thought of Pyr in the chaotic battle the nearly immortal assassin had waged against Empyrean's shock troops, to give Eva and these few colonists another chance at life. The woman had been evil, someone who made a bargain with the devil so that Eva's people could survive.

She locked the memories away. This mission would be dangerous despite the lack of murderous enemies sent by a star-god bent on genocide. Surveys from orbit indicated the planet was habitable, but what a computer thought possible and what flesh-and-blood mortals could tolerate were two different things.

"How's your suit?" Montgomery asked.

She smiled. He was probably ten years older than her and far too nice. In her old life she might have flirted — maybe cornered him in private and jumped him — but romance was the last thing on her mind now. She had to lead this expedition and start a new civilization. That was all a colony was, after all.

Tall and lean by human standards, his complexion was darker than some but lighter than others. He kept his hair in a buzz cut and hadn't removed the scar below his left eye from, to hear him tell it, a training accident. He could be loud and forceful, but generally defied the macho soldier stereotype.

"How are we doing, Carter?" she asked.

The ship bumped hard several times as the atmosphere thickened.

"I'm getting a lot more crosswind than I thought, but nothing too bad," Carter said.

Eva waited for his tough-guy sarcasm, but it didn't come. She moved to the cockpit and saw him fighting the controls, veins popping out on his arms as he muscled the ship onto its proper vector. Amanda sat in the co-pilot seat, her hand resting easily on her double stick, ready to take over if needed. Eva found herself fascinated with Amanda's light touch and the way she moved with each twitch and jerk of the controls connected to Carter's double stick.

Carter spoke without looking at either of them. "Strap in, Eva, or go back to the crash couches. Cockpit rules."

Eva slipped into a seat and secured the five point harness.

Ice fields rushed upward. Gravity pulled on her body as Carter banked into his final approach for the landing. The rocky plateau that had been designated for their touchdown looked small. Under other circumstances, she would have been fascinated with the swirling patterns of the volcanic rock set against a white background.

She glanced out the window, marveling at the peculiar sensation. For years she had been used to looking at video screens and simulations made to imitate a window. Several hundred meters to the right, the second shuttle made its descent. Plumes of moisture spread out from the wingtips.

"Is that normal?" she asked.

Amanda shrugged. "No matter what our scientists tell you, surveys from orbit are educated guesses."

Eva nodded to herself. That was the argument she had used on the crew.

Amanda keyed up the intercom. "All crew and passengers, brace for landing. Touchdown in thirty seconds."

Eva saw it coming, but the impact startled her. The restraints slammed against her. Spots danced in her eyes. A memory of burning ship parts tumbling through space came and went in a heartbeat.

"Not so hard," Amanda said.

Carter laughed.

Eva slowed her breathing as Carter and Amanda conducted one system check after another. She had been a passenger on enough ships to know that everything they did was part of a checklist. The rhythm of their voices was soothing and routine.

She checked her own gear and went to the back of the ship, where a ramp was lowered to the surface. Montgomery and two of his security force went first, spreading out into a semicircle with their weapons ready. She waited patiently.

"Secure," Montgomery said.

Eva strode down the ramp at a leisurely pace, looking at the planet that might become their home. She touched the left side of her helmet and spoke on a private link to Jax. "Status report."

"We're down," Jax said. "My security team is linking up with Montgomery and his people. This landing strip is small, so we should have a perimeter set very quickly."

"First impressions?" Eva asked.

"It's cold. I don't like the wind or the ice. However, I did see some open caves on the way down that seem to be full of vegetation... or slime. Hard to say."

Eva checked the ship and the security team, then moved toward Jax. Together, they walked to the edge of the plateau and looked down into an expansive canyon. Far below, she thought she could see flowing water. Tall green grass flowed around it.

She waited for Jax to comment on the scene.

The moment grew as Jax seemed reluctant to admit she had been wrong. This planet was a place where humans could live. Eva touched the left side of her helmet again and called to her science officer, Doctor Arno Peterson. "I'd like to start conserving our stored air as soon as possible."

Peterson's distinct accent lilted through her earpiece. "One hour, Eva, then I give you the all clear."

"Ten minutes," Eva said, staring at indistinct movement near the river several hundred meters below.

"Thirty minutes. Far too abrupt, but for you, done," he said.

"Ten minutes," she repeated.

"Thirty. Minutes."

She was satisfied with thirty minutes, but ignored him until she could almost feel him growing uncomfortable.

"Ten minutes, under protest," Peterson said.

"That should be the motto for this mission," Eva said. "Make it happen."

A tour of the flat and solitary space she had chosen for planetfall brought her to a chasm. A wall of solid ice stood a few meters out of reach, towering high enough to cast her team in mild shadow. Through gaps, she saw a webwork of dark green vines and dripping water. A smear of gravel marked one section of the glacier-like wall.

"Are those vines or excrement?" Jax said. "The green stuff looks chewed up and compacted."

Eva looked closer and thought of a cheese grater or meat grinder, pushing out processed food.

Something moved.

She jerked her vision to one of the cave openings ten feet above her and across the chasm.

"Shit!" Montgomery said. "Jackson and O'Brien, get your asses over here. We've got alien contact." He moved closer to Eva and guided her back several steps. Shouldering his rifle, he visually searched for whatever had moved.

Eva left her sidearm in her leg holster and concentrated on examining the curious creatures. "Ice spiders?"

"They look dead, almost mechanical," Montgomery said.

Jax holstered her pistol. "I think you're looking at their false eyes. Wait until one of them opens a mouth. I think all of their sense organs are in there."

"Damn, that's disgusting," Jackson, one of the security team, said.

"Give me a threat assessment, Montgomery," Eva said.

"They're not large — the biggest is less than half a meter across, including the legs — and they're just looking at us. Hard to see if they have teeth or claws. Call me

145

crazy, but I think they could jump the chasm if they wanted to eat our faces, but they haven't. I put them in the 'avoid them because they're creepy' category," he said.

"Doctor Peterson, I need you at the perimeter as soon as you wrap up your assessment of the breathable atmosphere," Eva said.

He came quickly, cutting his evaluation of the air's quality down to less than ten minutes. "I must have more data to decide if they are predators or prey."

"Everyone is prey or predator to something," Jax said.

Doctor Peterson gave her an annoyed look, then turned his back to her as he faced Eva. "The air we can breathe. Radiation levels we can survive. But staying here is no good. The plateau is unstable."

"How unstable?"

"We are lucky not to be at the bottom of the ravine," he said. "When we take off, you will see. The shuttle thrusters will collapse everything."

"What about our first contact species?" Eva asked, nodding at the eerily curious creatures covering the ice wall.

"They will be unaffected. This is their environment. They will be accustomed to avalanches," Peterson said.

Eva nodded. "Jax, I suggest we move to site number two. Do you concur?"

Jax hesitated, then studied the crawling ice spiders on the face of the glacier. "We should return to the *Legacy*. Send down drones and analyze what data we can gather from orbit. We need authorization from Fleet command to start a colony, anyway."

Eva shook her head. "We don't have enough fuel to go up and down from the surface."

"That's what I said before we came down," Jax said.

"We'll move to site number two. Instruct the pilots

to use caution when lifting off," she said.

Montgomery took charge as though fighting a battle. "Attention all security teams, this is Montgomery. Hold your positions and monitor the alien contact. Non-security personnel, collapse back to the ship immediately."

Eva and Jax returned to their respective shuttles. The science teams collected samples and moved with urgency. Moments after they came up the ramp, the security teams clambered on board.

Montgomery banged his fist three times against the inside of the cargo bay. "Last man," he called out.

Eva hurried to the cockpit and strapped in.

"How are we doing, Amanda?"

"Five by five. Ready for liftoff. Steady as she goes. We don't want to destroy this scenic paradise."

Eva watched Carter slide the double throttles forward and felt the ship lift into the air. The roaring engines vibrated everything in the ship.

"I can try for gentle, but there's a limit. It takes a lot of force to get up. This planet is basically the same gravity as Earth."

"Understood," Eva said. "Pull up a monitor. I want a better look at what we're leaving behind."

She watched plumes of smoke in debris blasting from the landing site. Moments later, the entire wall of ice started to come down. It collapsed like an avalanche, but there was something strange about it.

Eva connected with Jax on her private command link. "Are you seeing what I'm seeing?"

"Roger that. I'm kind of glad we're not still down there."

Eva watched as what had appeared to be a glacier wall disintegrated. Thousands upon thousands of the strange spider creatures un-linked from each other and crumbled like living gravel towards the bottom of the canyon. Larger creatures exploded from the river grass and fled the avalanche. What followed seemed to be a feeding frenzy, but that might have been her imagination. With all the debris in the air and the exhaust from the ship engines, there was no way to monitor what happened in the canyon floor.

"Doctor Peterson, I'm forwarding you a video for your analysis. Please make recommendations for a future contact with this species of alien."

She returned her attention to the view screens and the sky above the harsh and beautiful planet. This was the correct planet. The message she had received from Pyr had scared the hell out of her. There had been times she'd thought it was merely a nightmare.

With the nearly immortal assassin, she knew there would always be danger. She owed the woman her life. Everyone on this expedition, whether they knew it or not, owed Pyr their future. It was only right they came to answer her call.

*

Eva locked eyes with Montgomery.

"Why are we here?" he asked. "The real reason."

She wanted to answer, maybe even abandon her plan and hide in her room wrapped in his arms. The fantasy evaporated quickly. The way he'd talked to Jax since the first landing suggested they had something going.

And she couldn't turn back now.

"The next displacement drive jump will use all of our fuel," she said, keeping her voice low as the landing party erected survival tents near the ships. "This delightful rock has resources. In time, we can assemble refineries and refuel."

Situated on a dry river bed, the location felt both scenic and vulnerable, with mountains and glacier fields surrounding them. Memories of the spider avalanche caused her to shudder. She looked up for the hundredth time for anything that might come rushing down on them.

"Everyone knows the risk. Jax isn't wrong about the rest of the crew. Nearly half are adamantly opposed to exploring this planet. No one wants to live here. Even your people, who like the cold, are afraid to come down," Montgomery said. "And that was before the Spider-lanche."

"You're not wrong," she said. "How do you think *this* conversation would go at the next system capable of supporting a colony? Oops, this place is a death trap without the natural resources to refuel. Let's leave... wait, we can't."

Montgomery clenched his jaw, then rubbed his forehead with his non-gun hand.

"Walk with me," Eva said. The light of two powerful moons and a dense star field illuminated their progress. Creatures cried out warnings in the night. Others sang repetitively musical songs. Wind brushed the tops of surprisingly Earth-like trees, or what looked like evergreens. Doctor Peterson had sternly advised all personnel, even the armed security teams, to avoid the forest. And large bodies of water. And caves. And basically anything farther than a hundred meters from the ships.

"How much do you know about me and my father?" she asked, passing one hand through her hair to gather it behind her shoulder and silence the nearly subliminal music it made.

He walked a few steps before answering. "Your father was the security director for the *Impregnable* and saved the president of the UEF from assassins and Astral strike teams."

Eva shrugged and rolled her gaze to one side. She'd made the mistake of criticizing her father in public before. His people, basically all the survivors of the *Impregnable* and its support fleet, were fanatically loyal to him. Her father was a man who did his duty even at the expense of his own family.

"What do you know about Pyr?"

Montgomery's stare was hard. She was glad, in a way, because it showed the soldier he really was. He was a gentleman, nice to children and old ladies, but a warrior at heart. She thought she was going to need some of his higher-level skills before this was over.

"Pyr was sent by Empyrean to kill the president, and tried to use me to get to my father. But you know my father; he did his duty. Pyr took me and was fleeing the system," Eva said.

"Then she came back and fought the Astral shock troops. That much I know. It's cited in the academy as the negative effects of infighting. The 'evil consumes itself' argument."

"Do you believe that argument?"

He didn't answer.

She continued.

"We don't have to get into the details, but it's safe to say that for whatever reason, Pyr used the power Empyrean gave her against the Astrals and killed a lot of them. That's why we were able to escape."

There was a long silence as they stood at the edge of the too-small clearing.

"Why are you talking about this?" Montgomery asked.

"I just think about it sometimes," Eva said. She looked around. "What's your assessment of this site?"

"It's no better than the first one. There's not enough arable land to start even a small colony, and I don't like being at the bottom of this valley."

She looked at her feet for a second, then met his gaze. "Should we quit? Give up?"

Jaw clenched, he took a moment to calm himself. "In the morning we can finish up and move to the last site."

"That's going to go over well," Eva said. "I need your support."

*

Eva hurried toward the science team and their discovery. Jackson and O'Brien stood with them, weapons ready.

"What do we have?" Eva asked.

"Just evidence of advanced civilization. And by this I mean they used tools. Quarried stone to make the shrine or whatever it is," Dr. Peterson said.

"Who found it?" Eva asked.

"Jackson and O'Brien," Dr. Peterson said.

"We were on patrol, ma'am," Jackson said.

Eva studied the writing on the stone, but not for long. "Continue your patrol. Brief Montgomery and let him decide how many people he wants searching this area."

Jackson and O'Brien moved away from the alien monument.

"I should like to question them," Dr. Peterson said.

"You make discovery sound like a crime," she said, kneeling close to the five-by-ten structure. Only twenty centimeters high, it looked solemn and grim. "Grave marker?"

"Maybe," he said. "The markings appear religious or at least primitive. I would caution our less scientific members against jumping at conclusions. This is as likely to be a well-cap as a gravestone."

"Could it also be a door or a hatch?"

Dr. Peterson swallowed and looked around for the security team.

Montgomery and Jax arrived fifteen minutes later.

She studied them, not sure what was off, but something was different between them. His face was flushed with color and she seemed unusually content.

"Jackson called me with an update. I doubled the patrol. What do we have?" Montgomery asked, looking at the flat structure instead of making eye contact.

Eva waved him toward the stone.

Jax stood back, hesitated, then came forward as well.

The structure that Jackson and O'Brien had discovered was obviously manufactured by a sentient race. Someone or something had quarried the stone, crafted it, and engraved it with a combination of symbols and hieroglyphics. There were complex patterns of dots that everyone agreed was a numerical construct.

"You, perhaps, are right, Eva. It is a tomb or shrine," Dr. Peterson said.

Eva barely heard him as she realized what had changed between Jax and Montgomery.

She spoke to Peterson without looking at him. "Run every test you can without damaging it, Arno. If there are sentient creatures on this planet, I don't want to alienate them by destroying their sacred places."

The silence that followed was awkward. Jax provided updates on the survey teams, and Montgomery advised that the area was secure and he was rotating his personnel to keep them fresh. Eva barely paid attention.

She watched the narrow valley. Her sense of dread increased. The first location had been identical to the description Pyr sent her two years ago. This narrow valley with the mountains that felt like prison walls was not the right place. It couldn't be.

Images of the spider ice wall collapsing caused her to shudder. Jax and Montgomery stopped in mid-conversation and turned to watch her.

The earpiece of her radio, now that she no longer had to wear a helmet in the cold but rich atmosphere, chimed a priority alert. "Identify and report."

"It's Jackson again, ma'am," the voice said. Atmospheric disturbances affected the transmission. "We found something, but I'm not sure everyone needs to see it."

"You're a security officer. Can you tell me if it's a risk to the other people on the mission?"

"You better see for yourself, ma'am." Jackson started to say something and then stopped. She could imagine him hesitating and looking around, hoping O'Brien would back him up in what he was about to say. "Maybe you should bring Montgomery. I don't know if she's dangerous. She looks dead, but I'm not good with cryosleep technology. Just don't bring the doctor."

Eva had a pretty good idea why Jackson didn't want her to bring Arno Peterson. "Why shouldn't I bring the doctor?"

There was a long pause.

"Pyr killed his family."

"What are you saying, Jackson?"

"Can you just come, ma'am?"

Eva excused herself from the science team and moved away. She leaned against a rock, clasped her hands together, and lowered her head. Fear, relief, and self-doubt ran through her like a nebula. A few moments later she braced herself and went to see if Jackson and O'Brien had found the savior and the doom of her race.

Without her helmet on, she had to pull the tablet from the utility pouch and follow the navigational prompts. She checked it frequently as she climbed the narrow trail. The steps were a product of erosion, and the trail itself was unlikely to have been caused by animals. The only thing she had seen clearly on this planet were the spider creatures that didn't seem like the type to follow such a limited causeway.

Larger creatures had been lurking in the grass below the first landing site, but she hadn't been able to see them well. The size had been difficult to estimate. She thought they looked something like whale cows. Once they started to move, they had been very fast to escape the avalanche.

The trail twisted back on itself and soon she felt like she was climbing straight up. "What made you come all the way up here?" she asked over the radio.

O'Brien answered. "Standard procedure. This path led to an overwatch. It wouldn't do to have a sniper or some other threat above us."

Eva found them standing around some type of escape pod or cryosleep chamber. It was difficult to say what the power source was, but it was strong. There was no ice or other moisture within a meter of the coffin-like pod. She couldn't hear mechanical buzzing as she might from a human-made device.

She told the two security officers to step back. They hesitated, but complied with their weapons ready. She couldn't hear what they were saying on their security link, but thought they were probably telling Montgomery what she was doing.

A sleeping version of herself looked up through the composite glass. The escape pod was alien technology. Not surprising because as a servant of Empyrean, Pyr had access to any of the conquered civilizations in the galaxy.

Eva looked down on the blue hair and milk-white skin. The woman had her eyes closed and didn't seem to be breathing. Her lips were dark and red, almost the color of rust or dried blood. She lacked the softness of Eva's form. Pyr was an assassin and a warrior. Thousands of years ago, when Empyrean had first come to their home world, Pyr had made some type of bargain to spare a small sample of their people. In return, she had become the Hand of Empyrean, enforcing the godlike creature's will across the galaxy, usually by assassination.

"Montgomery," Eva said into her radio. She didn't have to turn away, because the connection was wired into the bone structure of her jawline. The sensation had been strange when she'd first started using it, but now it was like second nature. Sometimes she wondered if they weren't becoming part of the same shared consciousness. Access to her team was so easy, it was like they were part of a machine designed to serve a greater purpose.

"I'm on my way, Eva."

"Don't bring Dr. Peterson," Eva warned.

"Jackson and O'Brien said something to that effect. I have Jax with me," he said. Audible static caused him to seem farther away than he was.

"Eva, are you okay? I know what you're thinking."

"You don't know what I'm thinking, Montgomery. Just get up here."

She stared at the tomb of Pyr and controlled her emotions. The woman had saved her life and destroyed her home in the same day. The nearly immortal assassin had almost abandoned her father and her people in the human allies to their fate, while keeping Eva as her slave prodigy.

Then, when it was done, she disappeared for almost ten years. Now, with the life pod exposed to the atmosphere of this strange planet, Eva knew that she hadn't been dreaming. The confirmation of her decisions should have been reassuring, but wasn't.

Montgomery and Jax arrived and looked at the device in mute fascination. Eva watched them and evaluated their body language. Several times they glanced at each other, then back at the cryosleep pod with the Hand of Empyrean imprisoned within.

Jax approached Eva. "Did you know she would be here?"

Eva nodded.

Jax stepped back and crossed her arms over her abdomen. She hugged herself and looked away.

Montgomery looked up from his work, checking the display screen on his hand scanner several times. "There's an energy signal that doesn't belong here. We have to assume this life bond has power and that abomination within is alive."

Eva watched. His reaction confirmed what she had expected of him. "You fought against her."

His face filled with color as his head dipped in acknowledgment. His eyes never left hers. "She killed a lot of people before she came after your father and the president. I knew people who had been tracking her."

"I imagine they're dead," Eva said. Sadness filled her soul, but she concealed her emotions.

"Is this the reason we're here?" he asked.

Eva gathered her thoughts before she answered, aware that everyone was watching, including the security team now standing at the edge of the trail. Jax, always her rival, looked at her in a horrified new light.

"She told me this world would support us, and that the next would be our death if we chose to go there. I don't love her. She terrifies me even in dreams. That doesn't change the fact that she's seen everything in the galaxy. There are worse options than listening to her advice."

Montgomery glared at her and Jax shook her head.

"We're here. We can't leave until we build industry capable of processing raw materials into fuel," Eva said.

Dark storm clouds passed overhead. Montgomery took a step closer to Eva. He motioned back toward the cryosleep pod. "Are you going to wake her up?"

"Why would I?"

*

156

Over the next several days, the rest of the colonists were brought down from the ship. The third landing site proved to be well-suited to the needs of a basic colony. Montgomery kept a guard on the tomb of Pyr. Survey teams decided there were significant mineral deposits in the canyons below the ice spiders. Plans were made to collect geological samples.

When cloud cover cleared, the FCF *Legacy* discovered there were grasslands to the east that extended for thousands of miles, without variation.

"Not sure what lives there," Jax said to the department heads and team leaders assembled in the long mess hall tent. "The grass is estimated to be three meters tall. That's probably good news, because it means it's possible for larger, more advanced life forms to live in this biosphere."

"After the spiders, nothing will surprise me," Amanda said.

"Thanks for jinxing us," Carter said.

Several conversations broke out. Eva watched the colonists talk and wondered when they would get around to discussing Pyr. Most were content to speculate about the shrines and ancient ruins already located. Was there sentient life here? If not, what happened to them?

Eva couldn't help but feel sad. She had brought them here and could think of nothing more to do for them. Spiderfall, as they were calling the planet, had plenty of resources. In time, this place could be a permanent settlement, or a way station where fuel and other materials were gathered.

She waited until the double moons were full and she could barely see the dense cloud fields beyond them. The trail to Pyr's tomb was colder than the rest of the planet, lonely in ways she couldn't explain. The guard gave her a nod when she stepped into the small clearing.

Heat from the pod kept ice back in a perfect circle.

"Take a walk, O'Brien," she said.

"Ma'am," he said, stepping to the head of the trail where he could see her without violating her privacy.

Eva leaned her head against the clear shell. She relaxed, but sleep eluded her. Pyr's words were like her own thoughts, never heard, seen, or felt... not exactly.

"Why did you bring us here?" Eva asked.

Wind brushed over the mountain tops and through the pass below the isolated plateau. Night clouds drifted toward unknowable destinations.

Eva waited, content with the silence.

"I begin to make amends," Pyr said.

"You can never return what you've taken from so many people," Eva said, or thought.

"I may be of some use to you and your people. Sooner than you think, unfortunately," Pyr said.

"Should I open your cryosleep pod?"

"Not yet."

# Colony: Earth

By Robert M. Campbell

## 1

John Smith was born at home on April 5th, 2263, in the abandoned town of Westfield, Vermont. His mother Jane and father Paul had help with the delivery from the Grants, their only neighbors for fifty miles. Samuel Grant was an older gentleman who'd been a farm veterinarian all his life. His wife Mildred, also his assistant helping to run the business, was blind in one eye from falling off a horse in her more sporting years.

The delivery was, by all accounts, perfect, and little John came into the world with a strong set of lungs and a keenness to root stronger than some foals, according to Sam.

The Grants stayed the night while Jane slept with her new baby, and Paul watched over them with a glass of whiskey and some tobacco in a pipe he'd found in the neighbors' house after burying the owners, the Hawkes. He'd found them dead, together in the living room, the shotgun still in old man Hawkes' hands.

That was last winter just as the last of the food supplies were running out.

*

John grew up in the long winters of Vermont. His earliest memories were of him and his father on long drives through the barren empty wastelands of New England in the short summer months. The orange sun cast its warm light on them through the scrawny trees. Scavenging became harder and harder as the years passed. The short growing season meant they had to augment the larders from nearby villages and then from further into the remnants of cities, never into the populated ones. One summer, they ventured north across the border into Canada and found a small town along the highway named Cornwall. They'd been turned away by men with pitchforks and shotguns and told never to come back. The highways were covered with derelict cars and farm equipment. Disabled robot trucks were stripped down for parts and positioned across the highway left as barricades.

He wasn't allowed into the stores when he was younger. He and his mother would have to wait in the truck, hunched down in the back as Paul sneaked in, bag over his shoulder and a revolver in his hand. John had never heard him fire the gun, but one summer in '67 he'd come running out of the store with a man chasing after him. The image indelibly printed on John's four-year-old mind of the scrawny, hairy scavenger running after his father, mom screaming beside him at the vehicle to start and it not listening to her because she wasn't in the control seat. Paul reached the truck door ahead of the scavenger, dove inside and ordered the car to back up and give him manual control. The rest of the day they drove in silence as far as they could.

John could see his father'd been shaken by the encounter.

They were able to grow some corn and root vegetables for the winter. Turnips, carrots and parsnips. Squash and pumpkins further out, while they still had enough light to feed them. They had a hay field and some goats

160

and an old dairy cow named Bessie who passed away in '68. That year was the last time John had eaten beef. That was also the last year they'd had a dog. John remembered the hurt as his father took Sally out back into the field and put her down. The gunshot still rang in his ears.

It was hard living, but it was good too. His mom used to read to him whenever she could. She taught him the Bible and they had a good collection of printed books in the house. They had the whole library on their tablet. Sometimes, he'd wander into a room and catch his mom watching something on the handheld screen, voices on low volume.

"What's that?" he might have asked.

"Oh, nothing. Just something from before," she'd say.

From before everyone had left, and those left behind had rioted and burned their own cities, was what she meant.

He knew she wasn't exactly telling him the truth. "Can I see?"

"No, you're too little. Maybe next year," she would say, then ask him if he wanted to help her make cookies, and the screen would be forgotten.

*

Those early memories of his mother's videos were young John Smith's first suggestion that there was more out there in the world.

One winter night, they huddled around the fire for warmth. He was maybe twelve. The stars sparkled overhead and a sea of distant particles swam in the night sky. In the north, sheets of green and purple rippled across the ionosphere from the constant solar winds.

"Where is everybody?" John asked his father.

"What do you mean?" Mom and dad exchanged glances.

"You know, everybody else? Not just the scavs, but you know, people." He paused and poked at the fire with a stick raising sparks. "Where are the other kids?"

He could see the hurt look on his mother's face then, but she tried to hide it.

"There ain't any, son. They've all gone," his father said, closing the screen to the fireplace.

"But where? Can't we go there too?"

"No."

"Paul," his mother said. "He's old enough to know. He needs to know."

His father looked at her hard then. He wasn't a violent man, but he was stern; he had good reason to be. He got up and went into the other room and came back with the tablet. They never used it at night, always fearful of running down the batteries. It was used sparingly, charged up on the house's power system of solar panels and wind generators. They'd already lost one cell and hadn't been able to replace it, the house no longer storing the charge it once could.

"It happened thirteen years ago. A year before you were even born. A great evil came to our solar system. They said they were stars, like our sun, but they had minds of their own. They came here to destroy us."

John listened to his father tell the tale of Empyrean and his offspring. The battles of Jupiter and Mars. The blasts of fire from the sun and the many millions of lives that were lost in the great searing that broke the orbitals and left the sky in ruins. Huge tracts of Earth had been scorched in the violence, with incredible losses of life.

"And then they left. Our sun is dying, John. It's lost a tenth of what it was and it's going to lose more. They don't know how long it'll take, but it's going to die. So everybody got onto these space ships and they left the earth. Went out there among the stars to find new homes."

They were quiet for a long time after that.

"Dad? Why'd you stay?"

His mom smiled at him then and took his hand and answered for both of them. "Because this is our home."

2

Fifteen.

John was on a hunt with his father, walking through the pine forest through ferns and fallen needles. Their feet sank into the soft earth, still wet from the rains of the past weeks. It was approaching dawn, the sky beginning to brighten into what passed for days. The winds and rains were near constant this summer. They'd barely seen the sun, and the crops were struggling.

"You think we'll get any heat this year?" John asked.

"Hush."

A crack and then silence and they peered through the trees, crouching low. Paul nodded to his son, and he raised his .308 and quietly released the safety on the hammer. John sighted through the scope, the young buck turned and looked towards him through the trees, and he squeezed the trigger. Birds flew from their roosts into the trees above as the shot rang out through the woods.

The buck staggered and fell and the two men ran towards it, jumping over fallen logs and through bushes to reach their quarry. The buck, on its side, struggled and kicked once and then lay still, breath bubbling out of its mouth and nose. A red ring grew on its neck.

"Good kill, son. Let's get to work."

"He's pretty scrawny. Only ten points." John safetied his rifle. No need to waste a bullet now.

"We'll have steak tonight." His father grinned.

They spread out and began gutting the animal on the

ground. Father and son passed a metal cup, drinking the blood.

A sound like tearing fabric and then a loud explosion knocked them on their backs. John looked up to see a blazing light crashing through the sky above, tail of fire ripping the clouds apart in a burning torrent. A nearby tree exploded, sending a shower of splinters and needles at them just as an even louder blast erupted down in the gully below.

"You all right?"

John's father was over him, checking for injuries. His ears were ringing. "I'm OK. You?"

Paul nodded and looked through the trees below. The tops of the trees were smoking.

John stood up and ran to the edge of the clearing. "What was that? Meteor?" He stopped himself before calling it an angel. He'd read more about space in the intervening years since talking to his mother on that cold, frozen night outside. None of the books in their libraries had anything about the cloud of debris orbiting earth and moon since the war, but he'd made inferences.

"I don't think so. Let's get our deer back home and we can come and check it out."

"I'm going down there." John jumped down the side of the hill, skittering on his side, gloved hand bracing him. He was halfway down the hill when he realized he'd forgotten his rifle.

His father called after him. "John! Wait!"

They ran forward, crashing through the brush along the smoking trail of smoldering pine tops, the wake of destruction widening as they neared the wreckage, half buried under a furrow of dirt and uprooted trees.

It was big. John slowed and approached the black-ened chunk of space debris jutting out of the ground more cautiously. It looked like the corner of a pyramid, standing almost as tall as the neighboring pines. The corner appeared reinforced, still shiny and obviously made of sterner metal than the rest. Triangular vents decorated the surface near the corners, hissing smoke. The whole thing was crackling and pinging as the metal cooled after its violent re-entry.

"Don't get any closer, John. Get down."

John looked at his father, who stepped past him, rifle to his shoulder pointed at the triangular craft. He wondered whether it was a satellite or something that could carry people, when one of the vents lit up brighter than the day and made a coughing sound. Paul staggered backwards and fell on his ass. His gun fell beside him.

"Dad!" John scurried to him and his father waved him away. His face and clothes were blackened and smoking, hair singed.

Another hiss from the fallen construct and the whole side nearest them gave way, dropping down to reveal a complex nest of compartments, densely-packed triangular spaces containing intricate machinery and storage and components neither of them could fathom. In the center, a larger pyramidal volume contained three inhabitants. A gigantic shape reared up and staggered to the edge on two legs. It raised a metal-clad arm and reached out with a three-fingered claw before toppling out, suspended by cables and hoses.

"What do we do?" John asked his father, who coughed and staggered to his feet. He picked up his gun and raised it at the metal monstrosity in front of them. He approached, cautiously, circling in.

"There's two others up there. They ain't movin'," John said as his father stepped up what passed for a ramp to the dangling alien before them. He stuck his gun into the thing's head or helmet or whatever it was and poked it. The thing raised the arm again, fingers spread.

"I think it's hurt," John said, coming up behind his father. The thing was massive. Had to be over nine feet tall and probably half as wide. The helmet was set deep in the shoulders, no neck visible. The tiny visor offered no visibility to whatever may be inside. "Is it a... a robot?"

"Don't think so. There's somethin' in there."

"We should get it out."

Paul lowered the gun and put the butt on the ground beside him. "Might kill it if we open it up."

John considered this. "I'll call Doc Grant."

"You better run. Get your ma to help with the deer."

3

It was months before the creature showed any signs of recovery. One morning, they went to check in the barn and their goat, Ralph, had been ripped apart. Blood and fur were on the huge, three-fingered hands of the alien and around its wide mouth.

Doc Grant had found broken bones and was worried about internal injuries when they'd brought the thing in here. They'd needed to use the tractor with it's trailer to move *it* back to the farm. We called it an "it" because Doc Grant didn't know if they had male and female, and couldn't tell from his examinations that he'd performed when it was unconscious.

"Best I can do is hope for the best, I guess. I'm more worried about those burns on your face and chest, Paul."

"I'll be fine, Sam," his father had said. In the following weeks, the skin had peeled and left behind black spots on his face and neck where the alien craft had burned him. His eyebrows never grew back.

They survived that winter with only half the goat's milk (yes, Ralph was a girl), but the fall hunting season had been bountiful, with four deer and a freezer full of rabbits.

John watched the alien whenever he got the chance.

166

He'd sneak into the barn after chores and watch it sleeping. It spent a lot of time curled up in the straw and blankets they'd left for it. It slept so deeply they couldn't tell if it was breathing or not. Doc Grant thought it might be a kind of hibernation.

"You might not want to be around when it wakes up," he'd advised. "It's going to be hungry."

*

"Ma?"

"Yes, John."

"Is our guest an angel?"

John was joking, prodding his mother about her oft-repeated story about the lights flitting about in the night sky.

She became angry then. Her normally smooth brow bunched up and her eyes blazed. "You must never suggest such a thing! That beast is no angel. It is a devil and will be the death of us."

John stuttered an apology but his mother wouldn't hear it.

"I forbid you from seeing it. Don't think I don't know about you sneaking into the barn. I know what you're doing and I forbid it! Go to your room!"

This confused John, but he was determined to learn everything he could about the devil that lived in their barn. He went to bed that night with the tablet under his covers, researching the bear-like aliens until long after lights out.

They were called the Kyooli and had come to Earth with one of Empyrean's daughter stars. They flew in small, non-displacement-capable ships in triads; the first group was captured aboard the FCF-097 *Morrison* during the battle of the Fifteenth Fleet around Jupiter. They were unable to learn much about the race after that encounter, but a small group had been taken to a refuge in Montana, where they were allowed to remain under strict supervision by UEF scientists and xenobiologists, before those all left for other parts of the galaxy.

*

John was over in the stand of scraggly pines, chopping wood, when his father hobbled over to him, calling his name.

He set his axe down and waited for his father to approach. The winter had been hard on his father and his leg was permanently stiff now, the knee wouldn't bend. He walked with a cane he had spent the winter carving and finishing.

"John. Come to the barn. Our guest is waking up."

John beamed and had to hold back from jogging ahead of his father, instead helping him through the field of stumps. Their heavy rubber boots squelched in the spring mud.

When they arrived at the barn, they found the alien sitting up, gnawing on a frozen deer haunch, gripping the leg in its claws and chewing on it with big white teeth.

The smell in the barn was incredible.

It took a moment for the beast to notice them standing there and with a final ripping crunch, it set the bone down on the straw beside it and stared at them.

John stepped forward and raised a hand. "Hi," he said to it.

The creature raised its hand in a mirrored gesture, three fingers outstretched into the points of a triangle. A low growl from deep inside the alien's barrel chest served as acknowledgement.

John stepped closer. "We had to cut you out of your suit," he said, feeling he needed to say something. "It was hard going, but we got you out of it. Too bad there isn't much left, but we were able to save the helmet." He strode over and heard a gasp from his mother as he approached. He hadn't heard her enter, but when he turned to see, she was already gone. "It's over here," he said, pointing.

The beast turned. Its mostly hairless head sat atop a pair of broad shoulders. The skin hung off it like that of a sumo wrestler. There was muscle underneath that thick hide, but it was buried under layers of insulation. John reached into the straw and dug out the helmet and held it out in front of him like an offering.

The creature took it, turning it around in his hands. For a moment it looked at John, their eyes meeting, and he saw something in them. Something like hate.

The beast flung the helmet from his hand and it crashed into the wall of the barn with a deafening bang like a gunshot. It picked up the venison and resumed gnawing, the crunch of bones signaling the end of their meeting.

*

Recovery was slow for the alien. It had suffered some severe injuries in the crash. It was weeks before it got up and moved around on its own. John visited it every day, slopping out the barn with a shovel and piling fresh hay into the stall. He wore a bandana around his face and made a big production of it, like he used to do with their horse. The beast's hair grew back, in clumps at first, gradually covering it in a short gray-brown pelt.

"PHeee-ew! That's a big one, right there," he might say, pointing his shovel at a pile. Their guest was well-behaved. It had a corner it used and would do its best to cover it up with straw. It didn't help much with the smell.

"You think this stuff'll make good fertilizer, or are you guys too different for that? Maybe I'll get you to poop in a field and see what grows," he joked. The creature didn't seem to mind.

One day he found the creature standing up. It was using an old barn board as a crutch. The heavy timber would have been too big for John to lift himself, but this thing…

"Hey, you're up."

"*Keeyownli.*"

"Hey! You can talk!" John scratched his chin, wondering what the creature wanted. "I'm John," he said deliberately, while pointing to himself. He had to start somewhere. "John."

The beast tilted its head at him. It pointed, three fingers combined to form a single sharp spear, the long arm pushing the claw into John's chest. *"Garn,"* it rumbled. Then it pointed at itself. *"Keeyownli."* Or something that sounded a lot like that.

"You mean Kyooli? That's you, right? Your people? Kyooli?"

The creature made a face that looked like a grimace.

"John." He pointed at himself. "Human." He held his arms out and waved his hands around in a gesture he hoped encapsulated his entire person. "Human."

The creature stood up straight. *"Grawrn,"* it boomed. Hands like spades waved in front of it. *"Keeyownli."*

John laughed. "All right. Grawrn!" He pointed at the alien and he could've sworn the creature smiled at him.

*

It was slow going. Grawrn didn't use a lot of words, but listened to John the whole time he spoke. Sometimes, Grawrn would point at things in the barn and John would give them names. "Hook." "Shovel." "Tackle." "Bridle." He'd do his best to show him what they were for, but some things, like the old horse bits, didn't make a lot of sense without a subject for demonstration.

One afternoon during one of these sessions, Grawrn drew a round triangle on the dirt floor and pointed a shovel at it. *"Kreeeowon,"* it said. John was beginning to think of the alien as a "he," but he didn't want to assume too much. They weren't really that familiar yet.

"I don't understand," John said, shaking his head.

Grawrn carefully added more pieces to the triangle with its claw. Three round sections. One of them, an oval, extended outward from the triangular shape.

"Is that your ship?"

*"Kreeowon,"* it growled at him.

"OK. We can go see it." John stood up. "I'll show you where it is."

*

John was quiet on their way to the ship. He hadn't been back to it since they'd recovered the alien. Grawrn. He remembered the state they'd left the fallen ship in. Side opened, his two broken companions still belted into the ship in their suits. John had a sinking feeling as they approached that he had done a terrible thing bringing his friend here, but he couldn't warn him–it, he reminded himself. There wasn't anything he could do for the dead aliens – Kyooli, he reminded himself. They were a people.

They approached the vessel in silence. Grawrn lowered his head and sniffed the air. Its small ears retracted, then stood up on its head, listening, twitching in the cool air.

The ship was dirty now. The pyramid was covered in dead leaves and damp from rain and the year's snow,

171

stained where the water had run down the entrance to the ground. John hung back as Grawrn approached, still tasting the air, mouth opened and panting. Grawrn's heavy feet squelched in the soft earth, raising water. With a heave, the big alien dropped the timber it used as a walking stick and lumbered forward into the ship's opening. It rushed up the ramp and dropped to its knees in front of the two aliens in their suits, still strapped into their seats, vines creeping up their legs from the forest floor.

Grawrn dropped to his knees and let out a howl unlike anything John had ever heard before, the sound echoing off the hill through the trees. Birds flew from their branches into the sky as the sound rang through the forest. Not sure what to do, John stepped up behind the big alien and put a hand on the coarse brown hide of its back. The big head turned back with glistening black eyes and John gave it a hug, wrapping his arms around its head. "I'm sorry," he said. "We should have shown you sooner. I didn't know what to do."

The big alien pushed John away and climbed inside. It began undoing the restraints and hauled the first of the aliens out, then the other, laying them down on the opened side of the ship. Then Grawrn removed their helmets. It sat between them for a long time after that, in silence, the insects chirping and birds singing all around them. John sat down on a fallen tree and waited.

After a long while, Grawrn heaved its bulk up and crawled inside the cramped ship and began rummaging around, opening panels and compartments. It gathered up equipment John couldn't make sense of from appearance and arranged it neatly on the floor amongst the dirt and leaves. It found a harness and put it on over its shoulders and began strapping equipment into it. Finally, it pulled out a wrapped implement over six feet long and strapped it to its back. One last look and a stabbing motion into one of the compartments and the ship lit up inside. The lights turned red and Grawrn stepped out, picked up the timber and began lumbering up the hill. It paused and turned, making sure John was following, then motioned with a clawed hand for John to hurry up.

Clambering now, stepping over the fallen tree trunks and sliding in the scree, he heard a whine increasing in pitch behind him. John felt a grip on his arm and was hauled up the embankment and dropped on his back behind some trees, just as the ship lit up in a white-hot fireball. The rush of air on his skin was like a hot wind followed by a cold whoosh as the fire was snuffed out. He flopped himself over and crawled over to the edge of the tree trunk and looked down at the crater. Nothing remained of the alien ship. Grawrn was looking at him, crouched on one knee. Then one of its ears twitched and it turned its head.

"What is–" then he heard it too: Men shouting over mechanical crunches. A woman's shriek.

Grawrn crept forward, quieter than John would have thought possible given the creature's bulk. John crouch-walked behind the alien through the trees, wishing he'd brought his .308. "Wait," John hissed. "They could be dangerous. Raiders."

Grawrn held a hand back behind it, signaling for John to stay back, then pulled the bundle off its back and began unwrapping a huge double-ended spear with blades on each end the size of small swords. The sword staff made a humming sound in the alien's claws as it crept forward.

"Bring the tractor 'round," one of the men hollered. "I want to see what that explosion was."

Another mechanical crunching sound and John saw four large wheels rip through the smaller trees at the forest's edge, black metal box sitting atop the big-wheeled chassis, carrying a man and a woman in the seats up front. It reared up on its back wheels and slammed into the woods, breaking trees in half. Beyond, John could see their barn was on fire, black smoke curling up into the sky. The homestead's doors were hanging open and men and women came out of it, their arms full.

"No..." John whispered as Grawrn rose up to its full height. Three meters of brown and black muscle rose and stepped out of the copse of trees towards the man who'd called for the tractor. The man opened his mouth, maybe to scream as he saw Grawrn stalking towards him, the man's mind unable to register what he was looking at. With a whoosh Grawn brought the sword spear around and down, splitting the man in half, both pieces slowly falling beside one another about a central mass of gore.

Grawrn stalked forward towards the men and women coming out of the farmhouse. One of the women screamed, then a man opened fire with a pistol. The short pops sounded like a .22 to John. He heard sounds like tree bark snapping as the bullets bounced off Grawrn's shoulders and chest, and then it dropped its head and charged forward, powerful legs pumping, clawed feet tearing trenches in the soft ground as it barreled down on the intruders and swung the staff through them, the humming sound getting louder as it ripped through three bodies in one stroke.

Grawrn bellowed in rage and the remaining raiders ran over one another to get to their vehicle, now desperately trying to back out of the woods and turn around. The driver revved the tractor's engine and smoke billowed out of the pipes sticking out of the sides. Then the wheels dug in and it churned mud and dirt, John watching as it picked up speed and wobbled towards Grawrn, standing its ground in front of the house. The tractor must have weighed five tons, heavy metal and huge antique combustion engine atop an over-built chassis. John watched in horror as it approached. "No!"

Grawrn swung the blade and it hummed through the front wheel, through the frame into the engine block, and stuck there. The machine dropped down onto the broken wheel, collapsing like a falling barn as Grawrn crawled up the wheel with its claws, onto the smoking engine and into the front compartment where two terrified humans met a horrible end.

4

The days after the invasion of the homestead were a hazy blur in John's mind. Somehow, he and Grawrn had decided to set out together; whether at his own insistence or Grawrn's urging, he wasn't sure. He just knew they had to leave. Packing had been hasty and not clearly thought out. On the road, there were items he missed. The home's tablet, for instance. They'd over-packed on guns and ammunition, his bow and two quivers full of arrows. There wasn't a lot of food to bring, most of it in freezers and rifled through by the raiders during their search of the house. Instead his pack was full of his hunting clothes, a parka, hats and gloves and socks.

They'd been two days onto the Long Trail when he realized they had no flashlights, no matches, no axe. He'd had a little cry that night as they sat chewing dry ration bars and a cold tin of beans.

Grawrn didn't seem to need much, fortunately, but couldn't live off its stores indefinitely, John figured. They'd have to hunt and he'd have to build a fire somehow. Maybe build a drying hut to cure some meat. They'd make it.

It took them three weeks to reach the Ithiel Falls along the Lamoille River. They followed that to Johnson, an abandoned village straddling the Long Trail and West Settlement. They scoured the town and found more supplies they could use. John found a hatchet he liked in one of the houses. He added an axe with a decent blade to his collection of tools. He found flints and matches and lighters and some of them even worked. It was getting late in the summer and the trees were beginning to yellow in places. Fall was coming early. Earlier every year, his father used to say. The orange sun was still warm and the mosquitos attacked them at dusk, making it hard to wear anything comfortable in the heat.

They stayed in Johnson for the night and heard the roar of machines as the sun started to set. Grawrn gripped his sword staff to its chest, ears flicking at the sounds as they huddled inside what used to be a church. The roof was partially collapsed and exposing the sky. Machines roared over shouts and calls as the vehicles rolled through the town. John could hear destruction as they tore down houses, scavenging for anything of value. John slept fitfully that night with his .308 against his chest, until eventually he was awakened to the sound of crackling and yelling. Smoke crept under the door to the church; they'd barricaded it with pews and lumber from inside the building. When the raiders had been unable to break in, they'd set the church on fire, with John and Grawrn inside.

John hacked at the floor with his axe and Grawrn jumped in to help, tearing floor boards up with its claws. They crawled underneath the building and huddled there in the crawlspace as the fire licked up the walls outside, smoke filling the tiny space under the floors. They crept underneath, Grawrn barely able to fit in the cramped space, flattening itself out against the dirt and dragging itself forward to the edge of the wall. A flimsy lattice of partially rotten wood was all that separated them from the outside, but they could still see lights flashing as the raiders circled the buildings and razed the town of anything useful.

Eventually, the scavengers got bored and John and

the alien snuck out to the river and made their way into the woods again.

"We can't go to the towns. It's too dangerous," John said. "We have what we need now."

"Good," Grawrn growled in reply. "It junk."

After two days, they woke up one morning and John heard the snort of a deer, the breaking of branches. He crept up and shot it with his .308. A twelve point buck. Grawrn watched him clean the animal with interest, occasionally licking its lips. John passed it a cup of blood and together they drank.

"Good," Grawrn said.

"Good," John agreed, wiping his face with the back of his arm.

They ate meat that night, over a fire. Grawrn was upset when John set his steak on the flames and reached in and pulled the meat off with its claws. "Not good," Grawrn said in its gruff voice.

"Fire makes it good," John said, quoting his father.

"Not for Grawrn," it said, tearing off a hunk of meat and chewing happily.

"Hey, Grawrn, I've been meaning to ask you something."

"What?"

"Are you a…" John wasn't really sure how he was going to explain this, but had to try, for his own curiosity. "Um, are you a man Kyooli, or a woman? Something else?"

Grawrn looked at him funny, chewing its meat slowly.

"Like, man, like me, or woman. Like… Like my mother. Was."

"Mother." Grawrn considered.

"So… you're a woman? Female?" John cut a chunk of meat and chewed on it, then put it back on the rocks near the fire. "That explains why you pee sitting down."

Grawrn ignored this and picked up a leg and bit into it with a crunch. Finally it said, "No." And that was that.

*

As fall deepened and the days grew shorter, they set up camp at the base of Mount Mansfield in an abandoned log cabin at the end of an old service road. John had a hard time finding deer that fall and as the nights grew longer, he was worried about how much food they'd have for the long dark months that followed. Grawrn was an eating machine, going through a hundred pounds of meat and bone in a few days. It was an alarming pace, and John was beginning to suspect something was wrong.

"You OK?" John asked.

Grawrn looked up from a deer shank, blood around its snout. "OK," then resumed eating, cracking and crunching into the bone and sucking out the marrow.

"I'm going hunting again tomorrow, but we need to spend some time getting ready for winter. We need a lot of wood and I could use your help."

"Me help."

"OK."

The next day, John came back from checking his traps with a few rabbits and some purslane for greens, and found Grawrn sitting on a pile of wood, polishing its sword staff. The blades gleamed blue in the afternoon sun. The nearest stand of trees had a large hole cut into them, branches and leaves and pine needles scattered on the ground where the trees used to stand.

"Enough tree?" Grawrn asked, noticing John coming towards it.

"It's a good start. Thanks, bud." John slapped Grawrn on the shoulder as he walked past, hanging the rabbits on a hook outside the door.

"Small meat. Need big."

"That's all we got today," John said. He turned and saw Grawrn reach up and pluck the rabbits off the hook and begin tearing into them.

"Hey! That was supposed to be our dinner."

Grawrn grunted and ate all three in barely a minute, wiping its muzzle on the back of a brownish arm, hoarking up some fur. "Need more."

"What the hell, man? Maybe you should go hunting for yourself."

Grawrn stood up, slung the sword staff over its shoulder and stalked into the woods.

John made a meal out of some leftovers, managing something resembling chili with venison heart and some scraps of tenderloin he had in the cooler. After the red sun went down, he began to worry. He slept alone on a ratty old mattress without a fire, unwilling to draw any attention to their little cabin in the woods.

The next day, he got up and went hunting. Carrying his .308 at dawn, he crept into the woods, sniffing the cool air, scent of pine needles and decaying leaves in his nose. The sound of a bubbling brook was interrupted by a splash and John sneaked forward, body low, close to the ground. He peered through a bush.

Grawrn stood in the stream, waist deep, a big trout flapping in its jaws. It crunched down and ate half of the fish, then lunged forward, displacing a huge wave and coming up with another fish in its jaws. John watched the brute for a moment before crawling out of the bushes into view. "Hey!" he called.

Grawrn turned and roared, head scanning along the bank of the stream before locking eyes with John. The big alien lumbered forward, water streaming off of its thick hide, leaving an oily slick on its thin coat of fur. John thought the alien looked something like an over-sized otter just then, but couldn't read the alien's intentions as it came towards him.

"I said, 'hey'!" John repeated, and he saw a glimmer of recognition in Grawrn's eyes. "Did you forget who I was?" John realized he was still clutching his gun in his hands and lowered the barrel, pointing it down at the ground.

Grawrn dropped down onto its claws and bumped its head into John's chest, almost bowling him over.

"What the hell?" John laughed and gave his friend a scratch behind its small, round ears. "I guess I'm not hunting this morning. You've scared off everything for miles around."

"Fish." Grawrn pointed with a claw at the bank of the stream at a small pile of trout, the topmost still flopping in the air.

"Well done, bud." He gave the big alien another scratch and he could've sworn he heard it purr.

*

Winter came early.

The first snows fell in late October. The increased altitude in the hills meant colder weather. The clouds from the north rolled down and they were snowed-in by mid-November. Huge squalls rushed over the mountain and swirled, dropping blizzard after blizzard upon their small cabin.

Grawrn was sleeping more and more and eating less. Which was good, because John was worried about their supply. By December, Grawrn had fallen into a deep sleep and wouldn't wake up, leaving John alone to fend for himself. On snow days, he'd stay inside for the most part, keeping the fire going and cooking soups and stews with the leftover meat they kept frozen in the box outside. Clear days, when the orange sun crept low into the clear blue sky and the air from his breath froze in the wind, he'd stalk into the forest to check his traps.

At night, the coyotes howled in the hills around them.

John had some books he'd found on their way here. He particularly liked *The Hobbit* and read it cover to cover twice that winter, once aloud to Grawrn while it slept. Another book, *Catcher in the Rye*, he didn't enjoy, though. He made a point of seeking out more books after the winter was over. He drew a lot. A collection of pencils and papers kept him busy, first drawing pictures of their old homestead from memory, trying to get the details of the barn and house right. Then the trees, then landscapes around the cabin.

At night sometimes, when it was cold and still, John would sneak outside the cabin and look up at the twinkling stars and flashing debris orbiting in the sky. Green and purple aurorae rolled in sheets across the night sky as the sun shed more of its skin.

Inside, he'd read to the sleeping alien. John didn't know if it could hear him when it was like this, but it gave him something to do. The adventures of the scheming dwarves in the mountains took on a deeper meaning to John, hunkered down in the lee of Mount Mansfield.

By February, John realized he hadn't spoken to anyone in five months and wondered if he'd gone crazy. He stared at Grawrn's sleeping form on the floor, back barely rising and falling with its deep breathing and felt a surge of resentment. "Wake up!" he yelled over and over, eventually breaking down in tears.

By late March, John had stopped bothering with the fires. He chewed birch bark and dried service berries he found in the forest, left by the birds. He returned to the cabin one late afternoon after foraging and found the door open. More accurately, the door had been ripped off the frame and was lying on the slushy ground. John approached cautiously, gun in his hands, when a roar from the side surprised him and Grawrn barreled out of the woods straight at him, bounding on all fours.

"Grawrn!" was all he had time to say before the beast was upon him, pinning him to the soft ground. A snarl of teeth and claws and John thought he was going to die. "It's me! John!" he yelled, while trying to protect his face.

He heard a grunt and felt a hot breath on his face that smelled of piss and old musk and then the alien jumped away, crashing into the woods. John sat up and gathered his rifle. A gash on his arm from one of Grawrn's teeth bled through his shirt. He got up, covered in muck and snow, and limped into the cabin cradling his arm.

5

Spring came late. Another big snowfall kept John and Grawrn stuck in their cabin for another month before they dared set out on the trail again. The birds were coming back and they were seeing more animals in the forest. Scrawny deer on the verge of starvation scavenged for any sign of edibles. The streams thawed and the fish made their way to the spawning pools.

Grawrn was ravenous. Its skin hung loosely from its frame as it stalked through the forest hunting for food. John watched as it stood in an icy stream, scooping fish out of the pools straight into its mouth. After watching this for two days, John left Grawrn to its business and went off hunting alone, eventually bagging a scrawny deer.

He was cleaning the animal, almost ready to start butchering it, when Grawrn loped out of the trees and sank to its knees, hoisting a hind leg to its face. John continued working in silence until the sounds of feeding settled into a slow crunching as it cracked the bones.

"You feel better?"

Crunch. "Yes."

"You almost took my arm off. I thought you were going to eat me."

Silence. "I am sorry."

John looked at the creature, the leg bone in its three-fingered claws.

"I. We hungry after long sleep. Have to…" Grawrn trailed off, looking for the word.

"Eat?"

"Fill. On *Keeyown* we not long sleep. Only space." Grawrn resumed crunching on its bone, a loud crack as it split open.

"You hibernate during space travel?"

"Yes." Grawrn slurped some marrow out of the bone and lapped it up.

"What do you do when you wake up?"

"Special feeding animals make trip. Used to. Before star came."

The star. The evil that swarmed into the solar system and destroyed their sun. Destroyed the orbitals and their ships and forced everyone off the planet. The devils. "Did it talk to you? The star?"

"No. But did others."

"What did it say to them? Why did it do it?"

Grawrn thought for a long time, sucking the marrow out of its bone. It was silent for so long John didn't think it was going to answer him. "Star hungry."

*

For months they traveled through the Green Mountains and down through New England. John avoided the eastern seaboard and the population centers of the northeastern United States. They crossed the I-80. The old interstate highway was littered with abandoned long-haul trucks and the occasional burnt-out passenger vehicle.

183

The riots after the lotteries left a lot of damage to the streets as people struggled to get to the local uplift centers that would carry the new colonists into space. Those left behind dispersed. Half of the eastern seaboard was left with nowhere to go and a government in collapse. New York City and most of the coastline down to the Carolinas was a ragged scar. The interior didn't fare much better.

They moved away from the ruins of New York but chanced a look into Allentown, Pennsylvania. The abandoned city was littered with debris and garbage as the inhabitants either fled or barricaded themselves inside. Those who stayed tended to be of a self-reliant type. Those who stayed in the remaining cities were there because they had no other choice. No other idea how to survive. The ones who were there now were running out of things to eat. The planet's broken infrastructure separated people who used to be neighbors and turned them against one another. The transition government had failed and splintered, until all that remained were a few struggling city-states.

Still, there were a lot of useful tools and materials in the cities that didn't get scorched and it wasn't hard to find places that hadn't been stripped if you were willing to take the chance to venture inside.

It had been a couple of years since John had gone scavenging with his father. He felt a pang thinking about him as they walked down the interstate into the outskirts of the city. Brown and gray stone buildings gave way to taller concrete and glass further in. The old manufacturing centers downtown had been replaced first by commercial areas, then tech centers, and ultimately a mix of downtown residential as the population bled out from Philadelphia and New York.

"So empty," Grawrn observed, peering inside an old abandoned textile mill. The brown bricks were crumbling and the glass was blown out of every window. "Where people?"

"All gone. Other places, I guess." John marveled at the old mill. He'd never seen anything resembling an industrial structure before. The worn and weathered old sign painted on the front wall read, "K. N. Moritz and Yeung."

John's feet hurt and he was desperate for some new socks and underwear. He'd take an all-new set of hiking clothes if he could find them. They had a lot of land to cover if they were going to get to Montana and Grawrn's people. His plan for this year was just to reach the warmer weather of West Virginia before winter, and they weren't even halfway before his socks had given out, then his boots.

The textile mill turned out to be a bust. He knew the old Walmarts and Costcos would be gutted by the scavengers, so they risked going deeper into the city. "The good stuff is in people's homes," he recited, explaining what his father had told him on their outings years before. "Houses are easy pickings, but most get turned over pretty quick. You'll find the best stuff in old apartment buildings and places with security systems still in place. We'll need tools to get inside, though."

"I have tools." Grawrn said, shrugging to make his sword staff swing around under his arm.

"Yeah, that should do."

They scoured the outer apartment buildings, finding many had already been picked clean. Further in, they were able to put together a few things that would keep John warm and dry. "Best to layer. You can always take stuff off if you get too hot," John said, holding up a wool sweater.

"Cans?" Grawrn asked, holding up a tin of tomatoes.

"Sure! Everything you can find. Check the dates, though."

Grawrn grunted and began filling bags with old canned goods and dried food they found in the cupboards. It poked open a tin with one claw and took a sniff, turning up its lips around its teeth. "This junk."

*

Loaded down with their packs, on the southwestern outskirts of Allentown, they encountered a man in a truck. They'd been hiking alongside the I-78, planning to head off towards Reading, when they saw the old electric Toyota weaving through the empty road towards them.

"Hide!" John yelled, trying to push Grawrn off the road towards a stand of maples as the truck rolled up.

"You got a bear trouble?" the man asked.

John stared at him and Grawrn stood up and waved a three clawed hand.

"Oh, I see. Yer one o' them 'coolies,' ain't you. Never met one of you before. Hello there."

"Hi," Grawrn said with a low rumble.

"Where you two headed? Quite a load you got there."

John stepped up and peered into the truck. "Montana."

"That's pretty far." The man scratched his chin. "I'm headed back into Allentown, but I can give you a lift to Reading if y'like. Some good folk down there, might be able to hook you up with a ride."

John looked at his friend and shrugged. "What do you think?"

"I tired of walking."

"All right," John said, lifting his gun fractionally under his arm. "You ain't tryin' anything funny, are you?"

The man laughed. "I'm just offerin' you a lift. You don't want it, I can be on my way."

"No, wait! I'm sorry." John realized this was the first person he'd met outside of Doc Grant and his wife who weren't his family. "I just... We accept your generous offer, kind sir."

The man laughed again. "Climb aboard. Your friend here's gonna have to ride in back." He jerked a thumb at the box. "Make yerself comfortable, friend. Don't mind the parts."

Grawrn climbed in and crouched down in what appeared to be old electronics and engine parts.

"What're you doin' with those?" John asked as he got into the passenger seat after tossing his extra bags and rifle into the back with Grawrn. He kept his knife on his belt just in case.

"Oh, I build radios, computers and old engines. Anything I can put together out of old parts. You need something?" The man turned the truck around and they accelerated down the road, dodging potholes and debris. The trees flashed past. John looked out the back window to see Grawrn squinting into the wind, ears pressed back into its head.

"A radio?"

"Sure. Come in handy. There's a whole network of ham operators out there. Most reliable way to keep in touch with folk now that everything's fallin' apart."

"No kiddin'," John said, all smiles. "Sure, mister. I'd love one."

The man smiled again, his grey whiskers sticking out and his eyes scrunching up. "All right, we'll see if you've got anything to trade for it. Policy, y'know? I'll cut you a good deal, though." He winked at John. "Take that bear off your hands."

"What?"

The driver chuckled. "Just a thought. Y'know they ain't real popular with most people."

John looked at the man. "Why not?"

The man gripped the wheel tighter. "Back in the war, they killed a lot of good people. Herschef Colony on Ganymede got wiped out. No survivors. Bunch of the Fifteenth Fleet was destroyed. The *Saratoga*..." He cleared his throat. "Tens of thousands of people died up there. Men, women and kids."

"It wasn't their fault. That star thing destroyed their homeworld and turned the Kyoolies into slaves. They weren't even aware what was happening."

"That may be, but most folk don't see it that way. They ain't people."

"Look, maybe you better let us out here." He looked back at Grawrn, still enjoying the wind in its face.

"Suit yerself. Might want to stay out of sight. Never know what people'd do."

"Yeah. Sure. Thanks."

The man pulled over and came to a stop on the side of the road near an abandoned recharging station covered in weeds. Grawrn climbed down, look of confusion on its face, surprised they'd stopped so soon.

"I'll still take that radio if you got one." John said as he climbed out of the cab.

The man got out and rummaged around in back and pulled out a small silver radio with a chrome antenna. "This oughta work for you. You'll need a solar panel to charge it, but it's also got a crank on the back you can turn."

John was amazed. "And I can talk to people on this?"

"Oh, sure." The man scratched his belly. "Won't get great range with that little amp, but it'll get you a couple hundred miles or so on a good day. You want further, that'll cost ya." He grinned.

"Wow, thanks. What'll you take for it? I got some canned tomatoes, peas and beans..."

"Ah, you can have it. I don't need any of those old

cans. Probably kill you with botulism anyway." He looked at Grawrn. "You better keep your eyes open. People won't take kindly to an alien with an open carry."

"I will," Grawrn replied.

"Take care, you two."

"Thanks for the lift," John said.

6

They traveled southwest for weeks, skirting highways and the outskirts of abandoned settlements and towns. Sometimes they came near communities that were obviously still occupied. Buzzing drones and still-functional electric vehicles whizzed past on the roads.

The man in the truck had said people wouldn't understand Grawrn. Implied they might attempt violence. John knew what Grawrn was capable of if provoked, but a mob of people would probably kill it. John was determined to get his friend to Montana. To safety so it could be with its own.

At night when they camped, John played with the radio, turning the dial, listening for signs of life. Distant squawks and chirps signaled the existence of something out there, but he couldn't make out any voices. On a whim one cool cloudy night, he tried transmitting. He didn't know what frequency he should be using, so he just picked one at random and pushed the "Talk" button.

"Hi. This is John. Anyone out there?" He spoke into the little hole labeled "mic" and waited. "I'm out here, we are traveling and could use a place to stay. We're going to Montana. Anybody out there wants to help me and my friend, we'd be much obliged." He clicked off and waited. No reply came that night.

*

They traveled for weeks. Every day, John would hand-crank the radio as they walked, building a charge in the battery. Every night he'd try a variation on the same words. He began to worry the man had given him a dud.

They were straddling the border between West Virginia and Virginia high up in the Appalachian Mountains, walking the Blue and Gray Trail they'd hooked onto from a town called Brandywine, when they came to a peak with a squat stone tower. Old camp sites where people had made fires were still there. A worn metal circle in the ground declared it a US Coast and Geodetic Installation named High Knob Hill.

"Seems like a good place to set up," John said, and began pitching his tent. First the tarp, then the stakes. The cloudy sky was taking on a chill as they approached September. "We're gonna have to start thinking about where we're going to settle for winter soon," he said absent-mindedly, as Grawrn piled some wood into a circle.

"Not want sleep yet."

"I know. But in a couple months it'll be winter again."

"Sure."

After they'd eaten some beans and dried meat, they sat around the fire. John was sitting on Grawrn's crossed legs like he was in an enormous chair. It was warm and the fire was making him sleepy.

"You never said if you were a boy or a girl Kyooli," John said through a yawn.

"Not exactly same. I *nyartleth*. Raise young *Kyoolitan*."

"What's a *Kyoolitan?* Like, children?"

"Almost. Some become children. Some do not. Like animal. *Nyartleth* make *Kyooli* from *Kyoolitan*."

"Er, what makes these Kyoolitan?"

"Boy and girl Kyooli."

"And you're… different?"

190

"Third."

John grimaced. "So, are you a he or a she?"

"Third."

John's radio crackled and a voice interrupted them. "Hello. Is John there?"

John tumbled out of Grawrn's lap and rolled onto his blanket, grabbing the radio. He stabbed the talk button. "Hello? Hello, this is John. Are you there?"

Static, then the voice. "Hello, John. My name is Pierre. If you can hear me, you are getting closer. I would like to offer my assistance in your journey if you could do me a small favor." He spoke with a slight accent John couldn't place. It sounded different to his ears. Fancy.

John looked at Grawrn and they shrugged. "What kind of favor?"

A pause. The fire crackled. Then, "I could use your assistance rescuing me."

*

They ventured southwest through the mountains towards Roanoke, not really knowing what to expect. For days they traveled, alongside the 617, through the thick trees and brush. It was barely a road anymore, winding through the hills of West Virginia, the blacktop cracked and pitted, sometimes with trees growing out of the middle of the road. They descended the hills, hiking the trails in the cold and wet fall weather. The trees changed, dropping their leaves all at once. They woke up one morning to find they'd been covered in a light snow. They left the highway and descended the mountains south and east as Pierre had instructed.

They'd been walking through the barren trees, John complaining about the sores on his feet, when a buzzing caught their attention. A small hexcopter buzzed past then circled and came back, whirring above the treetops.

John and Grawrn did their best to hide, but the drone found them and hovered there, blowing leaves at them, blinking a light.

"Hello? Are you John and his traveling companion? It's me, Pierre. I'm not far now." The voice was projected by speaker, but he spoke normally.

"You better not be trying anything funny," John yelled over the roar of the rotors, hefting his gun at the small hexcopter, cameras and various unidentifiable bits of hardware hung underneath.

"I wouldn't dream of it. Now if you'd follow me, please, I only have limited range in this vehicle."

Grawrn growled at it and they set off down the mountainside.

After a rushed descent, they crossed an old road and passed through neglected fields; coarse hay and weeds impeded John's progress, so he walked behind Grawrn, who hewed a path with its sword staff. Eventually, they came to the bank of a river, cold water rushing from the mountains around a bend. "I'm over here," the copter said to them, rain steaming off its rotors, then sped away.

"Wait!" John yelled and they resumed their pursuit.

The hexcopter dove on over a high chain metal fence, razor wire running along the top. Warning signs hung from the fence, their messages faded and worn almost to the point of unrecognizability. Grawrn shrugged and hacked a hole through the links like it was nothing more than an old bed sheet. They crossed through the field towards some squat concrete buildings. Cracked blacktop roads criss-crossed through the empty facility. A blackened aircraft tower stood, if only barely.

"Not much further," their aerial companion instructed, and led them to the edge of the river and stopped, hovering. "I'm down here." The drone spun in the air and shone a beam down the side of the river embankment.

John and Grawrn crept up to the edge and peered down.

A grey capsule supported on orange inflatable pontoons bobbed at the edge, a red light blinking on the pointed peak. It was maybe six feet across and half as tall.

"You're in that thing?" John asked.

"In a manner of speaking, I suppose. Hurry now, before I'm swept away on the current."

John shimmied down the embankment; Grawrn slid on its butt, then stood up in hip deep water. Claws punched into one of the pontoons and it deflated, partially sinking. "Now not float," it said.

"Good, good, you'll need some ropes. See those tow hooks on my canopy?"

John crept around the edge. "Where's the door on this thing? How do we get you out?"

The drone touched down and balanced precariously on edge of the river. "I can't get out. That is me." The light on the drone blinked, lighting up a patch on the capsule in green laser light that read. "HMCS-HALIFAX. COMPOD. 0001. PROPERTY UEF/FCF. EARTH."

*

They spent the night securing the pod in the cold rain. The little hexcopter guided them into the complex of buildings to a supply shed where they found ropes and, to John's complete delight, a seemingly endless supply of all-weather gear. Boots, clothing, jackets, parkas, hats, helmets, all in huge abundance. All in army green, perfectly preserved. John replaced his worn hiking garb with all-new fatigues and a camouflaged water-repellant parka. He completed the ensemble with a woolen hat and yellow goggles. Grawrn struggled to get its head through one of the parkas, but it only barely covered its shoulders like a scarf.

"Once I'm secured properly, I can point you to a vehicle you can use to transport me to my new housing," Pierre informed them as they tied off the ropes around a sturdy tree on the bank of the river. They were covered in mud, but John didn't care. He was used to it and had a limitless supply of fresh clothes to choose from.

He smiled at Grawrn, who yawned at him, blinking behind its own pair of yellow goggles strapped around its head.

"All tied," Grawrn said as it pulled on the heavy nylon rope, watching the tree bend.

"Good. Now follow me up to the hangar. There's an all-terrain vehicle we can use."

They worked through the night, not caring about the cold or even noticing as the rain turned to snow. John was fascinated by the talking space pod and kept asking him questions as they worked. "How did you get here in this river?"

"A bit of luck, actually. I was reactivated sometime after the evacuation. I think an emergency system in the facility I was being housed in turned me on when it flooded. I'd have been trapped if it weren't for the self-inflating pontoons I was equipped with in the event I suffered a water landing." It talked a lot, which suited John just fine.

"Where were you?"

"A former naval facility outside of Norfolk. It had been a test facility for the FCF. All abandoned now, of course. Nobody in the FCF or UEF stayed behind after the evacuation," the drone said as they winched the pod out on the end of their line. The transport's electric motor whined as it pulled the heavy pod up the bank. The buzzing hexcopter supervised beside them.

"Figures," John said, spitting into the mud.

The pod came up over the edge of the bank, covered in mud. They continued hauling, and winching the thing up onto the back of a flatbed trailer, the ramp lowered. John tied another set of lines to it through the rings and used the winches on the trailer to pull it up, then locked it down with strapping. He patted the side of the pod and climbed into the driver's side of the APV. The interior looked like some of the pictures he'd seen of the automated tractors he'd looked up online on his parents' tablet.

A pang of remorse hit him in the gut thinking about them, but he pushed it down. He wasn't done yet.

Grawrn climbed into the back of the APV and the suspension bounced as it got settled.

"Where to now?" John asked.

"I can direct you to a bunker where you can get cleaned up and have something to eat. Sadly, I doubt the accommodations are top-of-the-line. This base wasn't exactly designed for comfort," Pierre said through the APV's radio system.

"What is this place, anyway?"

"It used to be the Radford Surface Ammunition and Vehicle Plant. It was never properly decommissioned, however."

"Good thing for us." John smiled at Grawrn and held up a hand for a high five.

Grawrn gave him three.

7

The journey west was considerably easier. Pierre told them what they needed to do. They moved his capsule onto the back of a Consolidated General M2078 Mobile Assault Platform. It had the connectors needed to power the capsule seemingly indefinitely, and enough space inside to accommodate John and Grawrn in something close to comfort. They loaded it up and set out on four smart tracks that tore up the countryside with ease. The nuclear power plant didn't require charging or any maintenance that John could see. Pierre assured him he could take care of it.

They tracked back north, through the Midwest. Grawrn stayed awake throughout the trip. They ate K-rations out of the stores and sat and talked.

"So, what kind of name is 'Grawrn', anyway?" John asked.

"I thought you wanted me to repeat what you said," the bear-like alien said over a mouthful of peanut butter. "Never bothered to fix."

"Really? What's your real name?"

"Doesn't matter. I am Grawrn now. Family." The bear smiled and deployed a tongue, licking the sticky peanut butter off its lips.

"Grawrn?" Pierre asked. "I still don't understand how we should refer to you. In the third."

Grawrn tilted its head. "I am third."

"Yes, but are you a 'he', a 'she', an 'it'?"

Grawrn shrugged and stuck its muzzle back into the jar of peanut butter, tongue scooping out the last of its contents.

"I kinda think he's a he, but he says he's a 'mother'. A *nyartleth*," John tried to explain.

"I am not familiar with that term," Pierre admitted. "The Kyooli arrived while I was still deactivated. We will see if we can shed a little light on the matter once we arrive in Montana."

"Agreed," John said.

*

It took them nearly a month to reach their destination. The blighted interior of the country provided little food or shelter, so they remained inside the M2078 MAP for most of the trip. One day, during a particularly intense blizzard in Nebraska, John asked Pierre about what he was.

"So, what were you doin' there? Why were you... I dunno. Shut down?"

"I think I'd seen something my superiors didn't particularly care for," he explained gently. "An alien race capable of manipulating and controlling humans through their endocrine systems." He fell silent for a moment, as if remembering.

"You were in space?"

"Oh yes. I was the Ship's Assistant aboard the displacement ship, HMCS *Halifax*. An FCF vessel under the joint forces of Canada, the United States, Japan and Mexico. We ... I lost them all. All hands..."

"Holy... How'd you get home?"

"An automated communications drone carried me in this capsule back to Sol system. I was recovered by the FCF *Dumont* near Jupiter and brought back here."

Grawrn spoke, crouched low in the back of the gun control pod near the rail gun's auto-loader. "Is hard. Remembering. Seeing your friends and family die."

John looked at his friend with sadness. "Yes," he agreed. "It stays with you."

"We mustn't let that deter us, though, eh?" Pierre said with what sounded like renewed enthusiasm through the tank's onboard speaker system. "We will perservere. We have a great deal of work ahead of us. Meeting the Kyooli in Montana, then, I hear, there are cities to the south of us. Caracas, Venezuela and Bogota in Colombia have been taking people from North America. Refugees, I suppose."

"What'll we do down there?" John snorted at the

implausibility of it.

"Help the people. There's work being done at the launch facility in French Guyana. We need to clear the skies so we can reclaim space and return to orbit. It will take years. Decades, really, but we can do it."

"Then what?" Grawrn asked. "What is point?"

"Rejoin our friends and families. Up there." They couldn't see it from inside, but Pierre raised the forward turret and pointed his gun skyward in the howling blizzard outside. "We still have thousands of years before our sun expands into a red giant. Plenty of time to reboot the Earth and civilization."

\*

That was a long time ago. Those first memories of meeting Grawrn and Pierre in my old country home back in Vermont. I'm an old man now, but I still remember those summers in Montana with Grawrn and hir people. They didn't really accept hir at first, accused hir of going "native," I guess. We won them over eventually, though.

Pierre was true to his word. He helped us get there and waited around, even fired his gun a few times at the raiders stupid enough to try to attack the clade. We stayed there a few years before we got the wanderlust again and decided to take Pierre up on his offer to go south.

It was a hard road, but it got warmer as we moved south through Chihuahua and the Durango. The M2078 was a capable platform and it held up well, only breaking some edges on one of its tracks.

Bogota was unimaginable. A vast city sprawling under the mountains. People of all types and colors lived there under a tacit agreement to get along. Sure, there was still crime and occasionally violence, but the people sorted it out. It was the last best place on the western land masses. Florida all the way up to the Carolinas was wiped out by floods and covered in ocean. The Gulf of Mexico invaded the midlands. California and Baja were gone. And that was just North America. In the east, old Africa was scarred, cut in half from the Ivory Coast right through to Tanzania. Two continents now, North and South Africa.

Northern Asia didn't fare well. The freeze came across the Arctic and turned Russia down through Mongolia to ice. Rumors of domes in China around some of their cities turned out to be true. They maintained a lot of their tech and had begun helping with the cleanup of our skies.

I never did make it into space, but I did get to see a rocket launch out of the Deux Branches facility that Pierre and I helped build.

In the end, I settled down. Met a nice girl named Lupe from Argentina and had a couple kids. Now we've got four grandkids, at last count. We have a nice plot out in the forest, grow some cassava and have a few cows. It's not easy, but we love it.

Grawrn even came out to visit with some of hir little Kyoolitans. They're like puppies, all floppy and enthusiastic, but haven't developed their big-boy brains yet. Grawrn nursed them into full-fledged baby Kyoolis out there on the farm and we watched 'em grow into the most amazing people together. They live with us on the farm and we've promised we'll all go up to Montana to visit one day.

Pierre's too busy to hang out much anymore. He's too busy overseeing the Orbital Reclamation Project. The junk in orbit was getting too shredded up to let anything get through, so the first batch of launches were literally designed to explode and punch holes in the debris. He says he's on a one-hundred-year time-scale, but we're already able to get some satellites up there.

He's promised he'll take us to Montana when the time's right.

To the inhabitants of New Skaarsgard, this is John Smith, Mayor of Camp Pedro, Planet Earth, signing off.

End transmission.

# Howl

By Scarlett R. Algee

"Are you sure this is a good idea?"

Grace Morgan sits on the edge of her waiting cryo tube, studiously ignoring the scowling UEF security officer looming over her. Instead, she looks over his shoulder, out the viewport, where she can see the first hab dome going up panel by fabricated panel. *We should have brought a better fabber*, she thinks, then reminds herself, *but one's coming.* Still, not bad for three weeks of work.

She meets the officer's gaze and smiles a little. "It's a perfectly good idea, Mr. Straley. I haven't had a decent night's sleep since we left Enceladus, and that's been eighteen Earth years ago, if I have to remind you. Somebody had to ensure the rest of you woke up properly, so I think I've earned a week or two to rejuvenate." Grace knows she could have gone into cryo with the rest of them, of course, trusted the bulk of the journey to autopilot or at least a copilot, but she's never liked to rely on a ship's computer that heavily—or other people. Too many little things can happen. "Look. I landed thirty people on this planet—"

"In a snowdrift," Straley answers sourly.

She shrugs. "It's winter in this hemisphere. Couldn't be helped. Besides, most of it melted as we set down, but that's not the point. Thirty people. Take me out of the equation, and you and your little crew, and the Ebisawa girl…"

Straley looks down the row of cryo tubes, and Grace

can't help following his gaze. There's only one tube in this module still occupied, by the nine-year-old daughter of one of the hydroengineers. Grace hadn't liked bringing a child along—she should have been on the colony ship with the rest of her family, still nearly half a year out—but the girl's father is necessary to getting the water processing systems started, and a berth for his daughter with the advance team had been one of his sign-on conditions. A ragged teddy bear sits atop the tube, a slump of pastel fluff that might have once been purple, with a ratty pink ribbon around its neck.

"Anyway." Grace brings Straley's attention back; the thin line of his mouth has softened a little. "Take the seven of us out of the equation, and that only leaves twenty-three people who need looking out for. Four point six apiece. I know the UEF probably still wishes *Lansing* would've had room for more than five of you, but I'm sure you can all keep the scientists and engineers fed and rested and reasonably entertained. The two biggest known predators on this planet are a two-meter bony shark and something like a hawk with scales, it shouldn't be a problem."

Grace takes another peek out the viewport: snowing again, windy. "Give it about five months, when Shackleton's twenty-five thousand appointed colonists show up with seed stock and starter plants and embryos and breeding fauna. Everything from krill and plankton to penguins and leopard seals, even polar bears and caribou...they'll be bringing species that didn't even live together on Earth. God knows what that'll do to the local ecology. At that point you might actually have your work cut out for you, but at least it'll be summer and you'll have a few hundred extra hands. Now if you really don't mind, I'd like to catch up on my sleep—"

The comm unit on Straley's belt chimes. He sighs, still glaring at her, and thumbs it. "Yeah."

"Hey, boss? Is the old bitch down yet?"

Straley makes a choking noise. Harry Pierce: his second in command, as if that means anything with a security complement so small. Grace recognizes the New England nasality in the man's voice and sits up straighter. "Well. I've been called worse things."

"Captain, I'm sorry, he's—"

"A little rough around the edges, like all of you. Lighten up, Nick." She grins, rocking on her perch; eighteen years out of cryo means she's got twenty years on him easily, surely that warrants a first-name basis. She plucks the comm from Straley's unresisting grasp. "Harry. This is the old bitch herself, what can I do for you?"

"I. Um." Pierce goes dead silent for three seconds. "Ma'am."

"Indeed." Grace glances down at the cryo tube longingly. The damned thing is starting to look almost comfortable. "Get on with it, please."

"Um. Right." Another tick of silence. "We've found a ship, Captain." Pierce clears his throat. "What's left of her. Pretty sure she's FCF, but she's torn up pretty bad."

Straley's eyebrows go up. Grace gapes at the device in her hand. A First Contact-era ship on this snowball, where the survey's never shown there's anything here to make contact with? "How far out are you?"

"About five klicks, almost due southeast," Pierce answers. "We're clearing her off now."

"Right. Suiting up and on my way." She slaps the comm into Nick Straley's hand and hops to her feet. "And I was looking forward to that nap."

*

Straley tromps away as soon as he's stopped the crawler. The vehicle's temperature sensors give an external reading of minus sixty Celsius. Grace pulls the hood of her parka up as she steps out onto a patch of refrozen snow; the cleats in the soles of her boots engage on contact, nipping into the ice beneath the snow crust with a faint crunch. She takes a deep breath and immediately regrets it; Shackleton is a colder planet than Earth, even when it's not the middle of winter, and the frigid air bites at the back of her throat. She reaches into the neck of her parka for the soft-rolled collar of her smart suit, and stretches the material up over her nose and mouth; still, the exhalations she makes through the fabric escape as smoke.

Then she looks up and her eyes refocus. "...My God."

The FCF ship lies atop a ridge of icy rock at a slight angle, strangely flat-bottomed, her outer and inner airlock doors completely retracted, her belly ripped open. Some of the outer hull plating along the tear has crumpled; some has ripped off, edges sticking up out of the wind-drifted snow, pitted and rust-eaten and lichen-covered. Straley's little security team and a few of the outpost technicians are picking their way into the ship or across its surface; Grace can't help being reminded of a gutted whale carcass mobbed by starving seagulls.

"Impressive spectacle, isn't it?"

Grace turns. The voice belongs to a thin woman bearing UEF insignia—one of Straley's, then, pale and blonde and bare-headed. She has to wrack her brain for the name; too much of what's happened since her own ship *Lansing* had left Enceladus has become a blur. "Anders, right? Jessica?"

"You remember me." Jessica Anders grins, picks up a handful of sugar-fine snow in an ungloved hand and lets it drift through her fingers. "You have no idea how glad I am to stretch my legs properly."

No hood, no mask, no gloves. The smart suits ame-

204

liorate the worst of the cold, but the tech still has its limits. Jessica hasn't seemed to notice yet, and Grace frowns. "Aren't you at least a little cold?"

"Oh, not really. I grew up in Iceland, I'm accustomed to the great frozen north. Besides, the gloves get in the way." Jessica pulls her face mask up—humoring her, Grace guesses. "My last job before being assigned to you and *Lansing* was evacuating the American researchers from their Antarctic bases. The ones that would leave. Most of them wanted to stay just to see how fast a billion years of ice would melt as Sol started changing." Jessica smiles and pulls her hood forward, stuffing her hair into it. "Believe me, I got used to the cold fast. This, this isn't so bad."

She bends over, and Grace, looking down, realizes the younger woman is standing over something. It takes her a second to differentiate the sleek white-cased rectangles from the snow surrounding them. "Tablets?"

"Tablets," Jessica confirms. She holds one out: the screen is spiderwebbed with large cracks that are full of ice crystals. "Harry's brought eight out, and he says there are a few more aboard, but they're all like this."

Completely unusable. Dammit. Well, it would have been foolish to hope otherwise, after more than a century. Grace scans the length of the fatally wounded ship. Snow's piled high around the nose and tail; she can't see any markings. "Any idea of who she is?"

"*Aurora*, I think." Jessica pauses in pulling on her gloves to gnaw a fingernail. "That's what Harry called her; he found the data recorders too, but they're just like these old tablets—frozen over and dead as hell. Still, it'll give the eggheads something to play with."

"Yeah." Grace watches the bustle of activity for a few more seconds. Like *Lansing*, *Aurora* had been a modular ship, at least from appearances; unlike *Lansing*, separated into its constituent parts to set up their outpost,

*Aurora* is still in one piece, except for that awful rip. "Any signs of the crew? Bodies inside?"

Jessica shakes her head. "Haven't been in there yet." She scans the people, waves at one woman, then raises her hands to her mouth. "Signy? Signy! Captain's here!"

A plump, short woman detaches herself from a small knot of people and trots over, her boots churning up the powder-dry snow into little plumes that scatter like salt. "Captain Morgan? I didn't think we'd see you up and about for a while."

"Dr. Sigurson." Good: her name comes readily. Grace smiles wryly, more than a little relieved. "Oh, I couldn't miss the action." She steps away from Jessica, who's picking through the sync cables still attached to some of the tablets, swearing when they snap apart in her hands. "So. What do you think happened here?"

"Captain, I'm a doctor, not a technician." Signy doesn't quite grin at her own joke, but the protective fabric stretched across her lower face ripples faintly. "If I had to guess? Some sort of critical failure. Harry says the landing gear didn't deploy, it's still locked in. Whatever happened, they came down hard, and I doubt this was their intended destination." She pushes her fingers into the hood of her parka, toying with a lock of dark red hair, then beckons for Grace to follow her to the dead ship. "None of the modules seem to have retained power at all. Nothing works, even though the mods should've had fission batteries of their own. Cryo's smashed to hell, must've taken a direct hit, but three tubes are still intact. They have bodies in them, although…"

They've reached a slanted piece of rusty steel grating that leads up to the airlock doors. Grace eyes it dubiously; icicles hang from the edges of some of the openings, while others stud the earth visible underneath, broken off by the pressure of footsteps. She steps up onto the edge and it bends a little under her weight. Grace looks down at Signy, who's not following her. "Although?"

"That's it. Just three." It's Harry Pierce who answers, leaning out the airlock, reaching for her hand. "Watch your step, Captain, it's not too sturdy. Sorry about earlier."

Grace leans up and grabs his wrist. He leans back, letting her use him as leverage. At the edge of the doors, a fragment of grating snaps off under her foot. "Don't mention it. Thanks." She steps through the open doors and adds, "What do you mean, 'just three'?"

"What Signy said," Pierce answers. He doesn't let go of her hand till they're through the inner doors, which are crumpled at the top; he has to duck to clear them. The deck plating is rucked up under their feet in a half-meter-wide corrugation that runs both fore and aft, but grows more pronounced as it traces rearward. "Don't step on that, it's not stable. Anyway, Signy's right, we've only found three bodies. And I know this tub had more people than that, she'd have been kitted out to the teeth."

"Of course." Grace studies the dislodged plating. "Which way?"

"Cryo?" Pierce nods aftward. "Back there, but you'll have to go through the hab mod and there's stuff thrown all over, and that's *if* you can get through, you're taller than Signy. It's not pretty." He grimaces. "Galley was on the lower deck, which was smashed clean flat, and if anybody was in the engine room, well, there's nothing to find anyway. We'll have to get a drone or a bot in, scan for…whatever you'd look for."

There's a clank from a forward compartment, and Pierce turns toward it. "Shout if you need us. Watch where you put your feet."

*

207

It's too quiet.

That's a foolish thing to notice, but it's what sticks out in Grace's mind as she picks her way along the damaged deck into *Aurora*'s hab module. Pierce had been right about the mess: bits of plating; scrap metal of all kinds, bent and twisted; bits of weather-smoothed glass. The rust stains under her feet tell her the precipitation's been inside more than a few times. Some of the racks have collapsed entirely, torn from the walls; a few hang listlessly by their drooping supports, as if waiting for a stout wind to finish the job. She knows that Pierce is still within the ship, and probably Straley, too, but she can't hear voices at all, or even the wind that should be whistling through: just her own uncertain footsteps, and the creaks and groans of the wounded metal.

In any case, one of them had had the sense to bring in a string of LEDs—tiny bulbs, but at least she's not stumbling along in complete dark. Something yellowish catches her eye on the floor: a piece of discarded fabric, maybe a shirt once, now moldy and bile-colored. Grace picks it up tentatively; it falls apart in her hand. Another broken tablet lies propped against one crazily-angled fallen rack. It doesn't disintegrate at her touch, but the cracks in the screen and casing are wide and mossy.

There were people here. That much is obvious from what's left behind: this tablet; scattered heaps of clothing rotted by a century of freeze-thaw cycles; too-faded photographs in shattered frames; a half-melted mess of wires and plastic that might have once been a music player. *Aurora* had a crew. Even assuming the worst, they have to be here somewhere. There should be more proof of people. Bodies. *Something*. She counts the racks. Twelve. *Aurora* had room for twelve.

Grace tucks the tablet under one arm and trudges onward.

*

The doorway leading into cryo is crumpled at the bottom by the spreading impact ridge, and bent inward at one side. The ceiling is far too low, as if a ton of snow has shoved it inward. Maybe it has; Pierce had made the observation that Grace was taller than Signy. Trying to duck through the doorway and simultaneously avoid the unstable plating that rises from the deck like a new mountain range, Grace has a new appreciation for his remark.

She shoves the aging tablet into her suit to keep it from crumbling further. Finally, after a sideways wriggle that her hips don't appreciate, Grace is in the cryo chamber. The LEDs continue here; Signy must have dropped a few when she'd come in. Not enough for Grace's preference, but the cool bluish light lets her see the worst of the damage. Twelve tubes, four along each of three walls. The room should be humming, the cryo mod's fission battery should be good for another century or more, but all Grace hears is her own quickened breathing and the snap of cold-brittle acrylic shards with almost every step. The floor is littered with the stuff; five of the twelve tubes are utterly ruined, exploded from the landing impact, and two more have great cracks and holes in their lids; even if they could be removed, they'd never be used again.

That leaves five tubes reasonably whole, and as Grace crunches toward them, she notices a slight upward incline to the floor. *Aurora*'s landing had been a little off-center, and she grits her teeth against the sudden illusory feeling that the deck's tilting under her. She reaches the nearest cryo tube and latches onto it.

The lid is scored by long thin marks that don't penetrate the surface, super-sized versions of a cat's impatient scratching. Curious, Grace peels off one glove and runs her fingers over the icy acrylic: the scratches have left palpable ridges in the material at several angles, and spreading her fingers to fit the marks suggests that whatever clawed at this lid had paws as wide as her hands. Grace tugs her glove back on hurriedly and shakes her head. The surveys say there's not a known predator on this planet with dimensions like that. It must be a fault in the lid, or another effect of exposure to the elements.

She finds the three occupied tubes Signy had mentioned, but there's very little inside them now. Skeletons in rotting uniforms, wisps of hair still stuck to their skulls, resting in beds of cracked, murky sediment. Grace looks away and pulls her mask back down, grateful that the air is only chill and faintly metallic, grateful that these tubes are completely sealed.

"Please say you're not thinking of opening that." Grace turns around; Nick Straley is standing in the doorway, gripping the crooked frame; he has to stoop to lean through, and the posture makes him look ridiculously outsized for the space. "Captain? Why don't you come forward and look at the command deck? At least we'll have room to stand up straight."

Grace coughs at another frigid lungful, nods jerkily, and starts to pick her way to him. The cold makes her throat burn, but it's almost welcome. Finally she gets her breath back. "...Have you found any of the crew up there?"

"No." He reaches out to help her through, stiff and unsmiling. "No. It's the damnedest thing."

"Nick, come o—" Grace stumbles getting back through the ruined doorway, and only Straley's grip on her arm keeps her upright. She scowls. "Come on. If there aren't bodies inside, there have to be graves outside. Have you seen signs of scavenging? Predation? In this climate, we should at least be finding bones."

Straley just shrugs and leads her along. "Could be graves. We've thought of that. There might have been survivors for a while. But that'll take equipping a drone or two with ground-penetrating radar, maybe infrared. Magnetometry, if you want to look for evidence of survival." They're back alongside the gaping airlock now, Straley guiding Grace's steps away from the wrecked deck plating; a strong gust blows in granulated snow that sticks to the metal, and she covers her nose and mouth again, grateful to have her parka's hood around her face. "But the fact of the matter is, we've got two hab domes, an agridome, and a water processor to finish in the next four months, and the techs are already asking if we can cannibalize this thing for materials. So doing anything else is kind of low on the list of priorities."

"True enough." Grace has to admit it stings a little, listening to this man tell her their mission, but... "You're right. We can remove the ship, mark the site, and have it excavated when the colony's running. I'm not here to play archaeologist."

She walks past him into *Aurora*'s command module. The deck is less damaged here, though she still looks down before making a step, and the tilt she'd felt in cryo is definitely not her imagination. One workstation is toppled, another wobbles when she walks near it, and the captain's chair is decidedly askew. There's a faint scent in the air here that she hadn't noticed elsewhere and needs a moment to identify: mold. "Cozy." Another small stack of tablets fills the lopsided seat, and she takes out the one she'd found and adds it to the pile. "Relatively speaking."

"Grace, look, I don't like it either." It's the first time since they'd met on Enceladus that Straley's called her anything but 'Captain,' and Grace frowns. "Something went wrong here. Really wrong. Whatever made *Aurora* crash here, it sure as hell wasn't some urge to say hi to the locals. That's what worries me. What's here on Shackleton, what's in this system, that we don't know about? The sun—" Straley pauses, biting his lip. "The sun here's got three other planets. Only this one was part of the survey."

She crosses her arms, scowling. "You think we have hostile neighbors?"

"I don't know what to think—oh, what the hell." Straley's been picking at the pile of tablets, chipping bits of plastic off their brittle casings. Now he lifts the stack and paws beneath it, pulling out a battered, blackened metal box. "Harry must've found this, whatever it is."

He fumbles with its tiny latch. Jessica had been right; the gloves get in the way. Grace pulls hers off and takes the box from his hands, wincing at the burn of frozen metal. Peeling her fingertips carefully from its scarred surface, she tugs at the latch. It snaps loose in her grip, and the lid follows, falling completely off. "…Well."

Straley glances down. "All that for a book?"

"Yeah." Grace gathers the pieces of the box and deposits them next to the tablets. The book it had held is the size of her palm, thick coarse paper bound in flaking hand-sewn brown leather. "This looks like a diary." She opens it with care, grimacing at how the binding crackles and begins to split, but the flyleaf inscription is still legible, written in large neat letters. "Captain Victoria Jeffress, FCF 2039E *Aurora*, August sixth, twenty-one eighty-five."

She half expects Straley to hold out a hand and claim the thing as UEF property, but he only leans on the back of the captain's seat and studies her. "Think that'll have your answers?"

He holds up the box and lid. Grace lays the little book back inside, pulls her gloves back on, and takes the box back, clamping it shut with both hands. "I think it's a start."

"Good. What do I tell the techies about the ship?"

Grace hesitates. She doesn't like the idea of *Aurora* being picked over like a chicken carcass, but the old ship will never be safe or spaceworthy again. Another gust comes through the airlock, this time with a whistle behind it, and *Aurora*'s hull groans, shuddering with the audible scrape of rock on steel. It's time to go.

"Get someone to open up the way into the cryo chamber," she says. "I want those remains removed so they can be buried properly when the soil thaws. If that means removing the tubes too, I want it done." Grace starts back toward the airlock, trying to ignore the rising noise of the wind and the faint judder coming through the soles of her boots. "If they do that first, then they can scavenge the rest." She catches Straley's arm and pulls him round to face her. "Tell them to start tomorrow."

*

After seeing the wreck of *Aurora* up close, Grace has a fresh appreciation for *Lansing*, even if her own ship was split into its separate components nineteen days ago. Sure, the hab module—detached from *Lansing*'s other independently-powered modular elements and set somewhat to one side, for some illusion of privacy—is just as cramped as it ever was, and she really just prefers to sleep in her command chair because the thing reclines, but it's warm and dry, nothing's covered in mold or littered with glass or rotting away, and most importantly, no one's *dead*.

One of Grace's eyelids twitches. Probably just as well she's not going into cryo anytime soon. Those images will need a while to go away.

*Lansing*'s command module has become the core of the outpost, the structure everything else is centered around. The viewscreen's a five-way security monitor now, displaying high-definition video from the cameras set up thus far: one inside her own mod, one inside the hab, one at each of the current construction sites, one watching over the tiny outpost as a whole. She guesses they'll have to add one to monitor *Aurora* now; even with just thirty people, there's bound to be at least one good fight over whose projects get which parts. She leans back in her seat and eyes each of the views: silent, dark, still, except for the thick blowing snow in every exterior frame. The only area she doesn't have eyes on is the detached cargo module Signy Sigurson's using as clinic, surgery, lab and living quarters. The doctor has some setup of her own; she'd been quite firm about patient confidentiality.

*As if anything that happens here stays secret long.* Grace turns her attention to the frail brown book she'd retrieved from *Aurora*. Captain Jeffress's diary: she's been gently turning it over in her hands for ten minutes, tracing the seams in the old leather. Now she opens it carefully. The binding crackles but stays intact.

*6 August 2185*

*We launch in six hours and Bill's just handed me this, now that everything's stowed away and I'll have to shove it inside my suit. Says he had it made last month when we visited Northern California. I love the man, but I can't imagine what he was thinking. I'm an FCF captain out to make contact with alien worlds and he thinks I'll have time to write anything by hand? Has he ever even* seen *my handwriting?*

Grace chuckles. Vicki Jeffress's handwriting is angular, but does have a certain half-formed looseness to the letters that suggests it wasn't exactly a skill she used much. It makes her wonder about her own handwriting, neglected for decades. She turns the page.

*Maybe I'll start writing in this thing once we're properly under way. It really is sweet of him. Right now I have more important things to do. Signing off.*

The next page is a list of names, with Victoria Jeffress and Bill Brady at the top. Grace scans the rest, some catching her eye: Dezmon Riley, Kordelja Czakja. Ten in all, rather than the full twelve Aurora could accommodate. She wonders which three are the skeletons in the cryo tubes.

She turns a page, then another. Nothing else has the exuberance of the first entry; instead, the diary becomes a maintenance log, sparsely updated. The only thing she learns is that their original destination had been the outermost planet in the Mu Arae system.

More pages, mostly undated, increasingly blank, as if Captain Jeffress had got bored of the 'diarist' idea quickly. Then one page reads 17 February 2186, and the script is sharp-edged with anger: *If Riley and Carter don't stop squabbling over Kordelja, I'm putting them both out the airlock. She's not even interested. I'm putting all non-essentials in cryo for the duration because I'm sick of having to deal with this.*

The very next page says, *Cryo plans suspended. Bill's found an anomaly. He says it's coming toward us. I'm afraid it's the Star.*

Grace puts a finger in the diary and lays it in her lap. Empyrean. She should have known. It all comes back to Empyrean; hell, the rogue sun-killing star is the reason humanity's fleeing Earth by the millions, the reason she and the crew of *Lansing* have set up here on Shackleton to receive a loaded colony ship.

She opens the diary again and turns a page.

*oh god it's following us*

The next three pages are blank. When the writing resumes, it's much looser than before, shaky, almost child-like.

*I don't know where we are. I don't know what day it is. I haven't slept. I think I have a concussion. I think it's bad.*

*O'Leary and Losnedahl are dead. They have to be. They were strapped in down below when we came down, and the lower deck pancaked when we hit the ridge. We're not getting life signs from down there. Riley died this morning from his head injuries. Sarai and Kordelja have multiple internals, and probably won't last the night. We'll have to put them in the cryo tubes. Brandeis has a broken leg. Carter and Smada seem okay except for bruising, but I have a concussion and Bill's got broken ribs, and Kordelja is our doctor. I don't know what we're going to do. We're losing heat.*

*Or was that yesterday? Nothing's clear anymore.*

*There's a large blank space, and then the handwriting resumes. It's a little tighter, a little clearer.*

*This is my fault. That's clear.*

*The Star caught us by surprise when we entered this quadrant. I thought we could evade it through displacement. I didn't expect it to follow us, or make the displacement drive stop responding. When we snapped back into normal space, we were already burning hard for the ground.*

*I couldn't stop it. I couldn't stop it.*

*I can still hear the hull ripping screaming*

The writing ends there. Grace takes a deep breath. She knows full well what the war was like; she'd lost family members on the warship *Resolute*, and they'd died looking Empyrean in the face. In the days of first contact, when the mere mention of "the Star" had practically been a proclamation of death...no wonder Captain Jeffress had panicked. Just the name makes Grace's own heart race now.

She flips back through the pages, trying to put full

names to *Aurora*'s known dead. Dezmon Riley, Kordelja Czakja, Sarai Cooper: they're the skeletons in the cryo tubes. Vincent O'Leary and Craig Losnedahl, crushed when *Aurora* had fallen out of the sky. Grace can only hope it was instantaneous.

*Beep.*

The noise makes her remember her headset, stuffed into her seat's storage pouch; it's beeping insistently. A glance at the viewscreen shows incoming audio, so she fumbles the headset out and on and opens the channel. "Morgan."

"Goddammit, Grace, do I have to freeze to death out here?"

Nick Straley. Grace swears under her breath and slaps down the button that opens the outer door. A few seconds later the inner opens with a chime, and Straley stumbles through, flinging his arms to shake off the snow. "Jesus Christ, woman." He makes his way to the crash couch and drops heavily, pulling off his gloves and throwing his hood back, yanking the stretchy fabric of his face mask down and letting it snap into a rolled collar around his neck. "Stuff only works so far."

"Nick, what were you doing out there?" She studies the split screens; all the external sensors are still reporting gustier winds and heavier snow. "There's a storm coming in."

"Thought I'd take one last look around." His hands and face are pale; he scrubs his fingers through his cropped sandy hair, making it bristle. "Minus eighty-three out there, probably falling. These smart suits are only good to seventy-five below, and then you start feeling the cold damn fast." Straley shivers. "Please say you have coffee."

"Of course." Grace scrambles from her seat; he's shaking too badly to fetch it himself. One of the perks of being captain, once they'd come solidly aground, is that

217

no one had objected when she'd lifted a coffeemaker from the galley. She checks the water, dumps ground coffee into the filter, punches a button, and in twenty seconds has steaming black brew in a thick-walled recycler-friendly cup. Straley takes it with both hands, and Grace turns back to her console to nudge the temperature up a little. "You'll be warm in a minute, Nick, catch your breath."

For a few seconds he just pants between sips of coffee. Then he spots the book. "Learned anything?"

"Empyrean," she says flatly. "*Aurora* crashed because they were running from Empyrean."

Straley stares at her, then shakes his head. "Shit. Again."

"Pretty much." Grace's headset beeps again, right as the viewscreen pops up another 'incoming audio' message. "Nick, is anyone else out? Harry or Jessica?"

"Jess, maybe, she's a snow bunny." Straley gets up stiffly, comes to the screen, taps the option to route the audio through the speakers. "Who's there?"

"I-i-it's D-Don. Ebisawa." The engineer's teeth are chattering audibly. "L-let me in, p-please."

"What in the world," Straley mutters, but Grace is already punching Ebisawa in.

Ebisawa doesn't stumble, though his safety goggles are completely fogged. He's dressed just as thickly as Straley is, but the little exposed flesh she can see has a bluish cast. Grace ushers the man into a seat; a corner of her screen shows an outside temperature of minus one hundred Celsius, and a fast drop. They've already surpassed Earth's coldest recorded temperature. She just makes another coffee for Ebisawa. "Is there a reason my crew's trying to freeze themselves to death tonight?"

"N-no ma'am." Ebisawa takes the goggles off and drinks steadily for a few seconds, and some of the grayness leaves his face. "I've been g-going over the water processor plans at the site, m-making tweaks for the next phase of construction..." He drains the cup—Grace takes it back—and the steadiness is back in his voice. "I lost track of time, and of how cold the weather's getting. But I had an idea for *Aurora* I wanted to run by you."

Grace hands him a fresh dose of coffee and holds her hand out for Straley's cup. He shakes his head, watching Ebisawa. "We're listening."

The lanky engineer fidgets. "I understand there are some remains to remove before we can salvage the ship for fabrication."

Word travels fast. Straley scowls. Grace just nods. "That's right. Go on."

"I thought we could spare enough material to fab some ossuaries," Ebisawa says. At their combined blank looks, he fiddles with his slowly clearing goggles and adds, "Bone boxes, though that's a little oversimplified." He traces dimensions in the air with his hands. "About seventy-five centimeters long and twenty-five centimeters high, since we're dealing with skeletal remains. It's perfectly respectable, it makes storage and burial easier since we're waiting for a thaw, and you don't have to remove the cryo tubes."

"Because you want to scrap those too," Straley guesses.

"It's not like we'll be using them." Grace has to admit, the idea makes sense. It could be weeks or longer before the weather warms enough to make standard burials possible. "All right, Don. You have my approval to go ahead. You can start tomorrow, provided we're not mid-blizzard."

"Thank you, Captain. It struck me as a good idea." Ebisawa doesn't get up yet; he has his fingers laced around his cup and a hesitant set to his mouth. "There's...I have a request, if you don't mind hearing it."

Grace glances at Straley; the security chief is just watching intently. "All right, let's have it."

"After the remains are removed…" Ebisawa gnaws his lip. "I want to wake up my daughter."

"Don—"

"No," Straley says flatly. "No. Not happening. That's not in the agreement, Ebisawa, and we've got enough to do here without a kid running around—"

Ebisawa holds up a hand. "Just hear me out, please."

"You signed a contract," Straley begins.

"Nick." Grace sighs. She's tired and headachy and doesn't need an argument. "Just listen to the man. Don, you'd better make a good case."

"It's the ship. *Aurora*. I want Kiana to see the ship." Ebisawa lowers his head. "I know, I know, she's supposed to stay in cryo till her mom gets here. But *Aurora* will be scrap by then and I want her to see it intact. From the outside; I wouldn't take her in."

"Hell you wouldn't," Straley growls.

"She'd be suited up properly. I can tether her to me if I have to." Ebisawa's pleading now. "Kiana's nine, Captain Morgan, she won't just run off. Please. Just give us this one thing. I'll put her right back under afterward, if that'll make everybody happy. I just want her to see that other people were here."

Grace studies him. A child at large is still a risk in Shackleton's weather, unless she holds him to the tether idea. "Nick?"

Straley frowns, shaking his head. "Your call. Not mine."

Of course. He'd told her on the first day, her job was to give the orders, his was to save people from themselves, but now he's putting all the responsibility on her. Grace musters a smile. "Since you'll have other people on hand, and if you're serious about the tethering…it should be fine. Provided the weather's okay. Go get some sleep, Don, we'll see in the morning."

Ebisawa jumps to his feet. "It'll be fine, Captain, I'll take perfect care of her. Thank you. Thank you." He puts his goggles on and pulls his suit tight around himself, and when Grace opens the door, letting in a swirl of snow, he makes a run straight for the hab module.

"You're making a mistake," Straley says darkly, leaning back across the crash couch.

Grace rolls her eyes and settles back in her chair. "Think of it as a chance to prove yourself." She looks back. "…You're not sleeping there."

"Stop me. All the people who could throw me out are on my side."

"Fine. Fine." All Grace wants to do is stretch out in her chair and pass out for a few hours, not argue over space she can afford to share. "But if you snore you're going right out in the snow."

\*

The first thing that's gone up at *Aurora*'s site this morning is indeed an exterior camera, though Grace, parked in front of her new six-view monitor, doesn't see or hear much more than blowing snow and groaning wind, interspersed with occasional gust-torn shouts. It's distracting enough to make her turn off the audio.

Don Ebisawa had apparently gone sleepless last night, because he'd shown up at Signy's door right at sunrise with his newly-crafted ossuaries, ready to clear *Aurora*'s cryo tubes. Bleary-eyed and full of coffee, Grace had dutifully accompanied them back to the crash site, back into the ship's half-destroyed cryo mod, helping Ebisawa open the tubes while Signy, in surgeon's mask and an extra layer of gloving, had removed the skeletons piece by piece. It had been a silent and remarkably scentless affair: with the decay processes long

221

completed, the only odor released in opening the pods was a thick dusty one like powdered chalk. Signy had worked quickly, saying they could be reverent later.

Almost immediately afterward, Signy was waking Ebisawa's daughter; he'd been adamant about Grace keeping her word. Toweled off and dried, stuffed into a tiny smart suit, Kiana Ebisawa's only answer to Grace's greeting had been a tiny squeaked "Hi," as the girl blinked owlishly, still half-asleep, one hand wrapped around her father's arm and the other clutching her disheveled teddy bear. She'd been a shy child even in her family's presence, back on Enceladus, and being surrounded by strangers on a brand-new planet hasn't changed that.

She'd gone out to *Aurora* tethered, as promised, clipped to her father's suit like a puppy by six feet of thin steel chain.

Well. Don had been as good as his word. Back in the command center, Grace turns up the heat and makes a fresh batch of coffee. She's still not quite happy with having Kiana awake and about, or with Don's promise to keep her off the fractured ship, but she's mostly still occupied with whatever had happened to the rest of *Aurora*'s crew. She has to flip through a lot of blank pages in Vicki Jeffress's diary to find the next entry, and some of the blanks slip out in her hands; after a century of subnormal temperatures, the book's breaking down in the warmth.

*19 March 2186*

*Somehow we've maintained power to the forward section, though only at sixty percent. Thank God the atmosphere on this planet is breathable.*

*I've healed. Bill's healing. Something like spring is coming, or at least the snow is starting to melt and the air's warmer, and the others have been out exploring in the slush. Yesterday Brandeis and Smada found a stand of woody plants, like young conifers. Carter broke the ice skin over a pond and caught some kind of fish— large, bony, with mouths full of sieving teeth, like relics from prehistoric Earth. Scooped them right from the water with his hands. The bony plates had to be snapped off with knives, bit by bit, but we cooked them over a fire of conifer twigs and the flesh, once free of the bones, was clean and salty. The most pristine air humans have probably ever breathed, and we're already polluting it…but none of us are sick yet, so I think we can say that the fish are safely edible. Brandeis wants to try one of the hawks next. He calls them hawks: bird analogues with beaks and talons, but leathery, scaly skins instead of feathers. They'll flap away if you get to within a few inches, and they seem to be silent, but you can get quite close. Bill's tablet still works, so he's using it to take pictures.*

*We've started naming things, I guess. Bill's named the sun McMurdo, he says officially, and he's calling the planet Shackleton, though intrepid Antarctic explorers we're definitely not. I just want to find out where we really are, how far the Star pushed us off course, and whether we've got power to blast a message back to Earth. It's a pretty planet, in a bleak sort of way, rocky under the snow, and with flowering mosses starting to peek through the melt, but it's not home. It's not going to be home. The supplies we do have are going to run out soon.*

Grace sips her coffee. "And a hundred years later, here we are. Welcome home." But the thought nags at her: half of *Aurora*'s crew survived the impact that killed five people and crippled the ship. What about the five that had made it? They can't still be alive with no access to longevity treatments, so where are the graves,

223

the signs of even temporarily settlement? She turns a page—carefully—and scowls into her coffee.

*Seventy-two light years.*

*Our course was for Mu Arae, just less than fifty light years from Earth, with an advanced civilization rumored on one of the outer planets. But when the displacement drive malfunctioned and spit us out, we'd crossed one and a half times that distance...in some direction. Bill says this system is an unknown, it doesn't match anything in the catalog. Nobody on Earth has an idea in hell where we are. I can't even guess if they're looking.*

*I don't want to stay here. I don't. We're hearing noises at night, since the thaw started. Yips and howls, like a coyote pack is nearby, though we haven't found any animal tracks yet. We can't get the airlock doors to close now, so we've started barricading them at night with the crates we've salvaged from our cargo. But the noises are closer tonight than before, and I don't think a hundred kilos of dry rations is going to keep anything out long—*

Grace's console lights up with a whoop. Emergency message. Shit. She drops the book and cranks up the channel audio, filling the space with the noise of wailing wind. "Nick?" She screams it. "Jessica? Harry? Is anyone there?"

"Grace!" It's Nick Straley. He's breathing heavily, coughing; in the background, just audibly, someone's screaming. "She's gone! The kid! Something got the kid!"

*

"You said you'd take care of her, Don! What the hell happened?"

Grace doesn't mean for the words to come out as a scream, but they do, ringing around the tiny confines of

Signy's makeshift medical office. Don Ebisawa just huddles in his chair, wrist still dangling the length of steel chain; the carabiner at the free end now holds only a torn piece of Kiana's suit and the loop it had been clipped to. "I didn't do anything! I didn't let go, she didn't run—we were standing alongside the stern of the ship, I was trying to get her to come in close out of the snow." His shoulders heave; his breaths are quick and shuddery. "She loved it. She was dancing in it. Then the line went taut and I thought she was playing—I couldn't see for all the snow blowing around—and something growled and it went slack, and I—I—"

He puts his face in his hands. "That's enough," Signy snaps. She's sewing up a gash in Straley's cheek. "From both of you."

"He's right. About the growl," Pierce says. "I heard that, even with the wind."

"I saw it. Something." Straley takes advantage of a break in the suturing to talk. The blood that had been frozen down his face when he'd come back into camp is thawed now, running freely from the two gashes Signy hasn't stitched yet. They look disturbingly like the scratch marks Grace had seen on *Aurora*'s clawed cryo tube. "White, maybe gray, ran on four legs. I was bent down and it just knocked the hell out of me, I didn't know it had—"

Signy puts a gloved hand over his mouth. "Shut up and be still."

"We couldn't see," Jessica interjects. "It's not Don's fault, we couldn't see anything either."

"Right. Everybody out." Signy's got her 'I'm in charge' voice on. "Nick, sit down and let me sew up your goddamned face. Dr. Ebisawa, you stay, I have something to give you. The rest—out. Let me work. Then we'll plan."

\*

Twenty minutes later, Signy's striding into the command center with both men in tow, Straley grimacing beneath his layers of bandaging and Ebisawa looking distinctly woozy. She has a mini-tablet in her hand. "Captain. We can find her. We can find her right now."

Grace has been sitting with Pierce and Jessica, just waiting, trying not to talk about animal attacks and hypothermia, but Signy's pronouncement brings her to her feet. "How?"

"Transmitting microchip," Signy says. "I put so many of the blasted things in colonists' kids on Enceladus, I damned nearly went blind. Don't remember chipping Kiana, but I checked my records and found her name and frequency, so..." She waves the tablet. "We can start back at the crash site. As long as I have this, I can track her."

Jessica whoops. Grace sinks back into her seat, feeling suddenly boneless. Is it really going to be this easy? "Harry, Jessica, what kind of weapons do you have? Pistols? Rifles? Whatever did this, there might be more."

"Both. Plasma," Straley answers for them. "You're not leaving me here to sit on my ass. Get up, Grace, we've got a crawler to load."

Signy guides Ebisawa into a seat and squeezes his arm. "Just sit tight, Don. Try to rest. We're getting your little girl back."

\*

The crawler makes slow progress in the driving snow, but Signy's tracking app picks up a signal half a kilometer past *Aurora*, a regular little *click* that gets louder and faster as they get closer to its source. Grace glances around at the three UEF officers and can't help asking:

226

"Shouldn't we have picked up the rest of your team?"

"Crocker and Haskins?" Straley shakes his head; a little blood oozes out from under a bandage. He lets it lie. "Overkill. Their job's keeping eyes on the construction sites and the scientists. You saw how fast the word got out about *Aurora*—the sooner we can get the girl back before too many people notice she's gone, the less panic we have on our hands." He manages a scowl. "Damn, Signy, drive faster, I want to get to this brat before she's last week's lunch."

"Not there yet." But the tones from Signy's tablet are picking up speed, and in another half kilometer they're a constant trill. She slows the crawler, squints through the windshield. "Visual's no good, too much snow cover, but she's close. Let me switch to geolocation."

The tones die, and for a second she studies the screen, then cuts the crawler's engine. "Right. Got a fix on her. Looks like six hundred meters. Come on, everybody out."

*

Signy's tracking leads them to the sloped mouth of a cave, partially obscured by snow. Almost gleefully she shoves her tablet into a pocket and bends to scoop the snow away by hand. "Looks like we'll have to crawl part of the way, it's so angular," she says. "Jess, you're thin, you can go first."

But they've barely started their single-file trek into the cave mouth—more a downward-sloping tunnel—when Jessica stops. "I hear something."

Pierce makes a doubtful noise. "I don't."

"Guys, wait." Grace cocks her head, straining; the tunnel walls have swallowed any sound from outside. Then she gets it: a faint cry like a high-pitched bark.

227

"No, I hear it too. Come on. We need to hurry."

What she thinks, but doesn't say, is *yips and howls*.

\*

They see the light before they reach the end of the tunnel: wavering, flickering, distinctly blue.

Jessica makes it out first, then the others, finding they can stand now. They're in a roughly round cavern, stalactites and stalagmites showing the passage of the water that had hewn it out, but the source of the blue light isn't water; it's a bioluminescent pool in the cavern floor.

"Pretty," Signy quips, "and here I am without a sample kit." More tunnels branch off from this room, arching upward or downward, and the pool's shimmering glow doesn't reach far past its edge. In that near darkness, something moves.

Pierce draws his pistol at once. Signy just calls out, "Kiana? Honey, is that you? We've come to res—"

A hunched shape shuffles closer to the pool, into view, and Signy's voice dies in her throat, because this…*creature*…isn't Kiana Ebisawa.

Not entirely. Not anymore.

"Jesus Christ," Straley breathes. The thing—Kiana—inches closer. Her clothing is gone, only a few scraps of suit remaining around her waist; her skin is chalk-white and waxy-looking, the paleness broken here and there by splotches of her natural pigment. Only her face is mostly unchanged, though one eye has gone purple instead of brown and a single fang has broken through her lower lip. She eyes them listlessly and hobbles closer still, bent in a kangaroo-rat posture, still clutching her tattered teddy bear with hands gone long and clawed.

"The pool," Signy begins, "it must be something in

the pool—Kiana? Did you drink the water? Talk to me, baby."

"Stop wasting time," Straley snaps. "Jess, grab her and let's go—"

Kiana lifts her head and chitters.

Almost immediately, a larger, paler creature slinks out of one of the tunnels on all fours, hissing and growling. Pierce shoves Grace out of the way and lifts his pistol to put a smoking wound in the thing's rump; it shrills, bares its fangs, and starts to back up the cavern wall before whirling and breaking for its tunnel.

More yips. "Get the kid," Straley demands, "now!"

Kiana just sits. Jessica goes to her, takes her spindly arms and tries to pull her along. Grace, looking over Pierce's shoulder, sees a flash of lanky white. "Jessica, move!"

Another animal charges out of the upward-turned tunnel, yipping and snarling. It gathers its limbs and lunges—

Pierce grabs his plasma rifle and puts a hole in its chest. Grace flinches away from the sing of the weapon and topples onto her side, watching in seeming slow motion as the creature's extended body plunges into the glowing pool. Jessica, struggling with Kiana, turns just in time to catch the luminous splash full in the face.

Her screams are thin and high.

*

They're crowded, again, in Signy's clinic, minus what's left of Kiana Ebisawa; the changeling girl had been locked into the back of the crawler, trussed and heavily sedated. No one's had the heart yet to tell her father.

Jessica's screams had become whimpers by the time they'd reached the outpost, her eyes swollen shut, her face blooming with spreading chalky patches. Under anesthesia, she's quiet altogether; and though Harry Pierce is first on his feet when Signy emerges, grim-faced and bloody, he's not the one she beckons to. "Captain? May I have a word?"

Past the inner door, the cargo module housing Signy's practice is partitioned with half-walls of corrugated metal. Jessica's out of sight behind one of them, though a beeping monitor betrays her presence. Signy waves Grace into a chair and starts stripping off her bloody scrubs, stuffing them into a large biohazard bin. "Well. She'll live."

Grace swallows nervously. "Will she be all right?"

"Eventually, with some scarring." Signy pulls on a fresh scrub top and takes her own seat. "I'd need a pure sample to be completely sure, but my guess is that the stuff in that pool is some kind of potent mutagenic bacterial soup. I had to do the same surgery on Jessica I'd do for skin cancer—just peel the layers away until I hit clean flesh. It's a pretty apt comparison. Instant tumor. Her eyes..." Signy pauses. "You can't peel layers off a person's eyes."

"Can she see?" Grace asks.

"I won't know until she's awake. But the swelling's gone down, that's a good sign." Signy huffs out a long breath. "That's all I know right now. I wanted you to hear it first; you'd better let me break it to Harry."

Grace nods, standing slowly. "What about Kiana?"

The doctor's quiet a long moment. "My guess is that she ingested the liquid, or those creatures tried to immerse her in it. Given the uneven coloring, I assume the latter. It seems to work fast—Jessica got off lucky."

Grace guesses that's true, after a fashion. "What are you telling Don?"

"When they're both awake? The truth." Signy waves at the door. "Now shoo."

*

*21 March 2186*

*There are intelligent predators here.*

*They're the creatures we've been hearing at night. Bill calls them howlers. Carter's given up his favorite fishing spot since he saw one there two nights ago. He said it stood on all fours, thigh-high to a man, white with purple eyes, looking like a skinned dog with a fish in its mouth.*

*It wouldn't run from him, so he ran from it.*

*30 March*

*Sidereal year's 378 days here. I don't know why I'm using Earth terms. We'll never see Earth again with this ship.*

*Bill's gone.*

*After Carter's sighting, Bill took Brandeis to go howler-hunting. He wanted to catch one, study it. That's been six days ago, and I hear the howls all the time now, and sometimes I think they're screams. If they were all right they'd be back by now.*

*Smada's taken to huddling on the floor, mumbling to himself. Last night I caught him trying to pull down the barricades. Let them in. He wants to let them in.*

*I'm tired. Tired of failing, tired of this place. I want to go home. I want my husband back.*

*Our power's starting to fail. If I'm going to send that message out to Earth—to anyone—I have to do it now. I have to try. I owe Bill that much.*

Grace squints and rubs her eyes. The book's binding has split completely in two, and loose pages keep falling out. Only one more page bears any writing.

*31 March*

*Message sent. Howling's closer. Nothing to do now. Signing off.*

Grace stares at the words for long seconds before

they sink in.

"Message received," she whispers hoarsely. "The message was received. Somehow it got through. And here we are a hundred years later, about to colonize a planet we know by the name Bill Baker gave it, facing the very things that probably killed him, and nobody told us. Nobody told us at all."

She drops the book. "Son of a *bitch*."

*

It's been three days.

Jessica's up and about now, though she's tight-lipped and heavily bandaged. She can see after all, though her eyes have turned a deep wine color, sclerae and irises together; when they leak, which is often, her tears are transparent and red.

Don Ebisawa is hiding in his quarters; his work on the water processing system has been taken over by his subordinates. Signy's rearranged her partitions to form a sturdily-walled quarantine area for Kiana, who's still sluggish and unresponsive at the best of times and snappily aggressive at the worst. Signy's keeping her sedated out of an abundance of caution, though her very presence in the camp has got half the crew sleeping in the cryo module instead of the hab.

Grace walks through both tonight, understanding the appeal of a bed with a lid, even though it can't possibly be comfortable. She certainly doesn't understand how some people manage to share one. Her own desire to go into dreamless cryosleep seems like a lifetime ago now. In fact, only Signy, with her new drone-acquired mutagen sample and her stash of snakes and feeder mice she's somehow kept in cold storage all this time, appears to have any joy in doing anything.

When she's spent enough time in her tiny room in

the hab mod to bathe and change, Grace pulls her smart suit back on and trudges back to her command post. Straley's not there, which faintly worries her—there have been howler sightings nightly since they've brought Kiana back, but he insists on the nightly patrol—but Don Ebisawa is, which somehow worries her more. He's thinner than he'd been four days ago, and practically colorless.

"Don." Grace puts a pleasantness she doesn't feel into her voice, and goes for the coffeemaker. "I'm glad to see you up, I've been worried about you. Please. Sit."

"I can't stay." His voice is colorless too, papery. "Captain, I don't think I can do this."

Grace takes her seat. "What do you mean?"

"Kiana." He sways, runs a hand over his face, and drops onto the crash couch with a thud. "It's…it's just so much, everyone here's afraid of her, afraid of *me*, it's hurting the production quotas we need for the colony, and…" His shoulders quiver. "I go to see her every day and she doesn't respond, she doesn't recognize me. She has full fangs now, did Dr. Sigurson tell you? She tried to bite me tonight."

No. No, Signy hadn't told her that. Grace frowns, because she feels as though crying is the only alternative. She has to make all of this work, somehow. "Don, what do you want to do?"

"Take her back. Let her go." He doesn't hesitate at all. "Captain, I still love Kiana. She's still my baby, even if she doesn't know it. But I can't be a father to her like this, and I can't risk endangering anyone else. I couldn't forgive myself if she hurt someone." His eyes are glittery. "Please. Let's take her back."

Back to that cavern? Back to those beasts, to keep being changed, to be made one of them? He's serious; he's actually serious. "Don, please," Grace offers soothingly. "You're overwrought. You need to get some rest."

She won't let him get a word in to protest. "Go sleep. I insist. We'll talk in the morning."

It's a long time after he's left before Grace has calmed down enough to attempt sleep herself, and the next thing she knows is Straley shaking her awake. "Grace. Get up. The kid's gone again."

Her eyes snap open wide. "Kiana? Nick, what happened? How did she get out?"

Straley laughs grimly. "Her old man. Her old man did it. Broke into the clinic while Signy was at the hab dome site, dragged her out, put her on a fucking leash and fucking gave her to Harry to 'take back'." He reaches down and yanks her upright. "We need Signy's tracker. We have to find them."

\*

They don't need Signy's tracker, because they don't have to go that far.

Something, some kind of hunch about animal instinct, makes Grace drive the crawler back toward the cave, back toward *Aurora*, and in the ship's now fragmented shadow they find Pierce.

He'd come this way on foot, apparently, in the warmer early-morning lull in the wind and snow. Grace bends over his body—torn, skin and suit, from throat to belly, still faintly steaming in a swath of bloody, refreezing slush—and wonders why. Had he meant to take Kiana out just so far and turn her loose, trusting her to find her own way?

Pierce's eyes are wide open, his face a rictus of shocked agony, tiny crystals of ice beginning to form on his lashes. Straley looks once and turns away, coughing, retching. Jessica sinks to her knees in the crimson mess and takes his face between her hands, whining, dotting his forehead with her own sticky red tears.

There's no sign of the girl, no sign of any leash.

*Fine*, Grace thinks. *Fine. Let her go. Let this be the end of it.* "Jessica? Honey? Let's take him home."

\*

"I shouldn't show you this. I shouldn't even have them. But there's cryostorage for lab animals, so." Signy's reconfigured her space yet again. Her clinic's two beds are occupied—one by Harry Pierce, thick dark sheets drawn over his body; the other by Jessica, still restless even under heavy sedation, who'd screamed until her throat bled. She leads Grace past them, to the back of the module, without a second look.

She's set up two tables and a series of glass tanks. It's close and dim, musty-smelling, and in the containers on one table, small things rustle. But Signy is occupied with the second table, and turns on a lamp with a weak blue light. "I've been testing the mutagen on some of my rats, by injection." She reaches into one tank with a gloved hand and draws out a little pale form that's curled and stiff in her palm. "You see most of the effects. You don't get the odd eye color, but there's the claw growth, the fur loss, the pigment change." Signy lays the rat down and indicates two others, similarly changed. "The results repeat."

Grace swallows bile. "Why are you doing this?"

"Getting to that." Signy turns to face her, leaning on the table. "I've found out a few things. These are just the ones I haven't dissected yet. Outward changes are consistent. Inward changes, organs and so on, are minimal—a heart's a heart and a stomach's a stomach. But there are two *big* exceptions. One," the doctor ticks off the points on her fingers, "there's a wholescale and almost immediate destruction of frontal cerebral mass."

"So you're saying it destroys higher brain function."

235

"Insofar as rats have that," Signy agrees. "Of course, we still don't really know if Kiana was directly submerged in the mutagen or if she ingested it, but some of her behavior—the sluggishness, the aggression, the lack of speech—points to some degree of cerebral damage."

Maybe putting the girl down when they'd seen her changed state would have been better for everyone. Grace would at least still have a UEF officer alive. "What's the other thing?"

Signy looks back at her container of euthanized rats. "The mutagen destroys adult reproductive capability. Gonads, gamete production, the works. It's still intact in the juvenile, but changed."

Grace can feel her stomach knotting. "Signy, I don't like where this is going."

"Neither do I, Captain. Especially not now." Signy motions to a second tank that's covered by a green surgical drape. "I have to be practical, you know. I breed the rats for the snakes. Feeders. Two days ago I injected a four-week-old female rat with the mutagen, waited out the changes—it took a few hours—and put her in the tank with one of my corn snakes."

"Wanting to see what would happen when the snake ate it?" Grace guesses.

"Eh, maybe partially. Mostly I wanted to see how the new aggressive tendencies in the rat manifested in the presence of another species. I got…surprised." Signy removes the towel. "Look."

"What am I—oh my God, Signy." Grace bends for a closer look. The corn snake is dead, lying on its back in a convulsive curl, its underbelly ripped straight open and its abdomen empty. But the rat is nestled high in an opposite corner of the container, hanging from the glass in a cocoon-like sac that seems to have extruded from her own flesh; underneath her, at the tank's bottom, a small pyramid of tiny soft-pink spheres has gathered.

Grace fights back a gag, turning away. "Those are—those are *eggs*."

"Yes."

"*How?*"

Signy drops the towel back in place. "I don't know, and that scares the hell out of me. Acquisition of genetic material by ingestion shouldn't be possible. It sure as *hell* shouldn't be possible with an unrelated species. That rat wasn't even mature enough to breed." She pulls her gloves off with a snap and grabs for a fresh pair. "I'm disposing of all this as soon as I've tended to Harry. Straight into the incinerator. Dammit, he was too good for what happened to him. They were engaged, you know? Harry and Jessica. They didn't deserve this."

She reaches out bare-handed and takes Grace by the shoulders. "Find Kiana, Captain Morgan. I don't think you'll have to look far, but *find that girl*. Find her and end this. Before we have an even bigger problem."

*

"Are you kidding? Are you fucking kidding? Of course I want to go after that little bitch," Straley growls. "But not directly, not like before. I want eyes on the scene before I even think of sending *people* back into that hellhole."

Straley's taken over Grace's command chair, hunched over her console, programming a drone to detect the transmissions from Kiana's microchip. She puts a hand on his shoulder. "Nick. She's still a nine-year-old girl and it's not her fault."

"Yeah, well, according to Signy's crackpot theory, your nine-year-old *ate* Harry to get his DNA." Straley shakes her off, pecking in commands, getting a green light when the drone comes online. "She's not a little girl now, Grace. She's—call me monster or asshole or whatever—she's a threat. If Harry'd shot her on sight in that cavern and we'd picked off the stragglers instead of trying to drag her back here, we'd all be a whole lot safer right now."

He slumps in the seat with a heavy exhalation; the fight's temporarily burned out of him. "Harry was my friend, Grace."

"I know, Nick."

"He didn't deserve that."

"I know that too." Grace's throat is tight, but her eyes stay resolutely dry. She touches Straley's shoulder again and this time, he allows it. "Better give us the camera view."

"Right, right." Straley inputs a command; he types with two fingers. "Launch in three."

Grace counts off three seconds. On the viewscreen, camera link established, the drone whirs to life, rotors spinning up as it begins to lift and head southeast. The camera shows the snowy ground rapidly falling away as the drone ascends. "Good job, Nick."

"It's what I'm for." He fine-tunes the drone's movements, so that *Aurora*'s visible—increasingly bare, now that lights have been set up for round-the-clock dis-assembly—but carefully skirting the place where Harry Pierce had died, keeping that bloodstained patch of earth and snow out of view. "Shouldn't we be messaging someone about this?"

Grace is silent a moment. She'd considered that, and done the calculations. "*Aurora* tried it. Got a message through. It was ignored." She watches the ground race past beneath the drone, its flight path changing a little as Straley corrects for the wind. "What would we say, Nick? That we're failing and can't handle it? We can't even turn back the colonists now, they won't have the resources to go elsewhere on such short notice."

"Hold it, hold it." Straley's talking more to himself,

but Grace falls silent. "Coming up on the cave. Look, you can see the tracks the crawler left."

Grace looks, and frowns. So close. She remembers the day she'd landed *Lansing,* and how the depth of the snow had taken her by surprise, but no one had anticipated how near disaster could lie. "Take her down carefully."

At the cave's mouth, the drone skims the ground. Its camera picks up a clump of wet snow. Straley sucks in his breath. "Good thing we're using a mini. This'll be tricky."

"You've got it." Grace rubs the back of his neck. "Wait. Where's the signal from her transmitter?"

"Where's the—fuck." Straley stops the drone in place, just centimeters inside the tunnel. He puts the little device through a few turns to dislodge the snow, then pecks in another command that sends a quick chirping noise through the speakers. "Audio was off. Good catch."

Grace keeps her eyes on the screen. The tunnel's getting lighter and the light has that familiar sick cerulean hue; they're close. "You're welcome."

The drone keeps descending, with a few careful maneuvers from Straley. The signal from Kiana's transmitter chip has gotten stronger on audio, its chirp nearly constant. Suddenly free of the entry tunnel, the drone glides into the cavern with the glowing pool, its camera suddenly swamped with the quivering blue light, and Grace grabs Straley's arm. "There she is, Nick, stop the drone."

"Jesus Christ." Straley types a command hurriedly. "Let's hold that."

The drone hovers, unnoticed. Above the pool, Kiana Ebisawa hangs suspended from the cavern ceiling, enclosed in a cocoon of glistening, weirdly fleshy material. Only her head and shoulders are free, her arms lying limp along the curves of her prison, her eyes closed, her altered face utterly expressionless.

A commotion at the bottom of the cocoon, a ripple of the wet leathery bindings, draws the attention of one of the adults. Exactly what's going on is blocked from view as the creature moves between the girl and the drone's camera; but then it crawls quickly away, bearing something small and ovoid in its mouth, trailing strings of mucus. The object is carried toward the wall of the cavern, out of easy sight.

"Zoom out and turn," Grace orders.

Straley inputs another command, and the view widens. The light provided by the mutagen pool falls off sharply past its glowing edges, but there's enough ambience to track the pale howler's trek up one wall, where it deposits its sticky burden with a care that looks like reverence. The camera pans along the sides of the cavern: still dark, but pebbled-looking now instead of smooth, studded with myriad squashed spheres that gleam damply. "Grace, tell me what the hell I'm looking at?"

Grace doesn't answer right away. She's thinking of Signy's rat, the eviscerated snake, the tiny globules clustered in the corner of a glass tank.

"Eggs, Nick," she says quietly. "She's laying eggs."

"Jesus fuck. Signy wasn't kidding. She really wasn't." Straley's staring at the screen with his mouth open. He realizes it and shakes his head quickly, and moves the view back to Kiana. His bandages are off, and the scarring claw marks on his cheek are livid in the blue light spilling from the pool and transmitted by the camera. "What do we do? There's got to be...hell, I don't know, hundreds of those...*eggs* already. Thousands, maybe. We don't know how fast these things will grow, Grace. We can't handle thousands."

There's a thread of panic in his voice, of incomprehension. Grace glances away. In her mind's eye she can still see Harry Pierce's opened body: the pain and terror frozen in his eyes, the ice forming on his lashes, Jessica's crimson tears freezing down the ruin of her face.

"Get our people. Signy. Jessica…and Kiana's father." Grace takes a deep breath. "She has to die. Everything in that cave has to die."

\*

Grace swivels a little in her seat and watches her little gathering: Signy on her feet, Straley sitting flat on the floor, Jessica and Ebisawa sullenly quiet, in different ways, on the crash couch. "I know what we have to do."

"Of course you do." Ebisawa glares at her, then glances away. A muscle in his jaw twitches. "You have to kill my daughter. Do you think I haven't thought of that?" He looks back at her just as she's about to protest, and waves her silent. His expression has softened, or he's steeling himself into neutrality. "Captain. I'm not angry about it. Not at you. I've seen the footage now, I've heard Dr. Sigurson's explanation of what's happening, and…Kiana's suffering. She has to be. This is no way for my little girl to exist. ..and she's still my little girl. Please, let's do what we can. Even if that means the worst. I can—" His face contorts for a second, Jessica gripping his arm. "I can live with the consequences."

That's a reaction Grace didn't expect, and the anguish on his face is heartbreaking. "I don't want any more loss of life, Don," she sighs. "No more death, no more injury. We've had enough. So I'm not looking at a direct manned attack. I want to weaponize the drones."

"I don't like that idea." Signy lounges against one of the unused workstations, elbows resting on its surface, chin on her crossed wrists. "It's admirable, Captain, but I don't think it's tenable."

"Yeah, no." Straley stretches a little but doesn't

241

move. He's gray with tiredness, and his pallor makes his scars stand out. "Think, Grace. They're microdrones. Even our biggest ones are minis. Topography, reconnaissance, some weather observations, that's all good. But we saw drones on Earth get taken out by birds all the time. What if these 'howlers' notice a drone and think it's food? Besides, they get battered to hell when the wind's not dead calm, what makes you think they'll handle a payload even if we can spread our resources that thin? I'm with Signy. We need maximum effect with minimum effort."

Jessica sits up. "What if we seal off the cavern?"

"How?" Grace demands. "Explosives? We're supposed to save those for starting mining operations and blasting ice cores."

"Not the mining explosives." Jessica shakes her head. "We—the UEF team—we were sent with an ordnance allowance. It's still in storage"—she looks questioningly at Straley, who grimly nods—"and it's not much, but we have grenades and sticky bombs, maybe some C4. It was all packed as rescue material, you can free people from rock falls and crawler accidents if you're really careful, but there's no reason it wouldn't work the other way." She gives Grace a faint, twisted smile. "Sorry for the secrecy, Captain. You weren't told because you didn't need to know."

Of course. "Still. Collapse the cavern," Grace muses. "But we only know one entry point. What if there are others? This damned planet could be cobwebbed with these things."

"It's probably not." Signy straightens up. "Remember the drone I used to fetch my sample? I kept the camera on, and there were bones at the bottom of the pool. Human bones, clean ones. That's the rest of *Aurora*'s crew right there. Has to be." She brushes hair from her face. "I'm not speculating on how the howlers started.

242

Maybe some quadruped that's extinct now tried to drink from the pool and fell in, like a tar pit. But I think they're an anomaly here. They can't have large numbers, the mutagen makes adult reproduction impossible. I think they attacked the remnants of *Aurora*'s crew because they were hunting a breeding juvenile"—Don Ebisawa winces audibly—"and maybe they've been dormant until now." She stops, pinking faintly. "Enough with the speculating. Jessica's right. Destroy the queen, destroy the eggs, collapse the entrance. We can hold any stragglers at bay until we have greater numbers."

"That's good," Straley interjects, "it's solid. But we'll need boots on the ground to plant all that."

Jessica's smile fades. Her bruise-purple eyes leak sluggish red. "Two pairs right here. That's enough."

She means herself and...Ebisawa? Grace hauls herself upright. "Jessica..."

"I don't take orders from you, Captain Morgan, you can't stop me." Jessica tucks one arm around Ebisawa's trembling shoulders, and the man sits up straighter. "I know what I have in mind. I know it means no coming back. But neither of us has anything to lose. I've already lost Harry, and Don..." She trails off a second, voice unsteady. "Don will get to be with his daughter again."

Grace bites her tongue. Signy and Straley are both quiet, watching her, while she wants to rail at the injustice and can't find the words. Jessica's right. Sacrifices have to be made now to keep everyone else safe later.

She finds her voice. "When do you want to go?"

Jessica studies the feeds on the viewscreens. The sun's just come over the horizon, and once again, the wind's fallen calm. "Right now. Let's do it right now."

*

The last thing Jessica does, after putting on her smart

suit and shouldering her plasma rifle, is pull her hood and hair back from her face with one hand, and start peeling off her bandages with the other. "It doesn't matter," she says to Signy's grimace of protest. The skin beneath the stained gauze is red and raw, the cut-down layers clearly visible through the remaining transparent dressings. Along her cheekbones and her forehead, so is the bone. She pulls her hood up. "It doesn't matter at all."

Jessica hugs Straley—"Keep everybody in line, boss"—but shakes hands with Grace. "Captain Morgan, I'm wired for audio, to a point, so keep a channel open. But no cameras. Not inside. We'll set up something external for you, maybe it'll work."

She looks Ebisawa over, claps him approvingly on the shoulder. "Let's go."

\*

Jessica keeps almost perfect radio silence for six kilometers, breaking it only with fragments over the hum of the crawler: "Turn here." "No, left." "Watch that rock." Then the crawler's engine spools down in a low descending tone, and she speaks up. "Captain? We're here."

Grace blinks hard at the sound of her voice. "Reading you."

"Turning off to set up now."

Silence again, ticks of it. Grace stands in front of the viewscreen, too fidgety to sit. It's too easy to imagine Jessica and Don creeping into that entryway, trying to maneuver in that dark narrow space to plant bombs and wires and a timed detonation device. "...I hope Jessica's doing the work."

She hadn't meant to speak, but there it is. Straley eyes her sidelong, shifts position beside her so their shoulders touch. "So do I. Deep breath, Grace."

Is she breathing? She's breathing. "I can't believe they're doing this. I can't believe I said yes to it."

"You didn't say yes. You just didn't say no," he points out, drawing a deep breath of his own. "So. Is the old bitch still taking a cryo nap after this?"

It's a joke, Grace knows, but it stings. God, how selfish she'd almost been. "And be able to look all of you in the face afterward? I can't. I feel like I'll never sleep again."

There's fuzz on the open channel. "Set up," Jessica says, and she's breathless. "I—no, Don, I'm fine, it's just blood in my eye. Captain? Okay. We're going in. Don, watch your step."

Their movements crunch and scrape. Pebbles slide. Ebisawa swears almost inaudibly. "Bad time to be claustrophobic."

Jessica winces. "Keep moving or I'll shove you."

"Going. Going—oh God. God, there's light."

Ebisawa sounds awestricken. Grace can hear a change in the crunching noises; they must be in the cavern, pulling themselves upright. She manages a whisper: "Jessica?"

"We're here." Jessica's equally quiet. "My God, they're everywhere, these things are *everywhere*—"

"Kiana!" Ebisawa's voice flutes, breaks. "Daddy's here, baby, Daddy's h—"

"Don, no," Grace whispers, and something hisses. A second, a third. Four. Five. Six. Growling. Claws on stone. Yip. Yip. Yip.

Howl.

"Captain." Jessica's voice is overshadowed by the thrum of her plasma rifle powering up. "I'm cutting the audio now. External video goes live in five seconds. Detonation in sixty. Take care of the boss for me. Don, let's move."

"Jessica," Grace begins, but the link is already severed.

*

A new window pops up on the viewscreen almost at once, displacing the view of the camp itself, showing the opening of the cave at a little distance. "Fifty-five seconds," Straley says.

"Don't." Grace curls her hands into fists. "I hope they're going for the eggs first. The eggs and the girl. I hope Don doesn't try to kill her himself."

"Forty."

*I hope it's quick. Quick and painless.*

"Thirty." The countdown's in the corner of the frame. Straley's begun to shake a little. "Twenty-five."

Grace wraps her hands around the edge of her seat and shoves her nails in. She pummels the fabric. "Nick, stop. Please. Stop."

"Five seconds," Straley whispers. "Three seconds. One—"

The ground heaves as rock and snow launch silently into the air. The rumble hits almost immediately, pitching and rolling the floor underneath them, making Grace grab for the back of her seat, making Straley grab for her. Workstation screens topple and shatter; LED housings drop from the ceiling and crack. The view from *Aurora* goes dark. Outside the cave, the view convulses wildly, grayed by a cloud of dust and vapor; when it finally clears, the image is half black, canted at an acute angle.

"Turn it off, Nick." The rubble clogging the cave mouth judders and shifts as it begins to settle, dust and smoke wisping out of gaps between the fallen stones. The screen goes dark and Grace blinks, puts a hand to her face, realizes it's wet. When had she started crying?

Why can't she stop? "What have I done? What have *we* done?"

"Grace. Grace, don't." Straley's voice is thin and cracking. "We all did what we had to, all right?" He wipes her eyes with his thumbs, with his fingers. He has gun calluses. Of course he does. "We're safe. We're safe."

Outside, Grace can hear shouts and screams. Someone beats at her outer door. She pulls away from Straley, but then reaches out for his hand, catches his wrist instead. *A memorial*, she thinks, *we'll put a memorial out there. For everyone*. "For now."

"We're safe," he still insists. "We have twenty-five thousand people coming, remember? Five hundred will be armed UEF staff." Straley shifts out of her grip, closes her hand in his own. "If anything crawls out of that cave, we'll be ready for it. We'll have to be."

Grace lets him squeeze her hand. His fingertips are still wet with her tears.

# A Time and a Space
By Nathan Hystad

Clark Thompson stared out the window in his stuffy office, seeing the looming yellow dwarf hanging in the sky like a reminder of what used to be. He rubbed his temples, hoping it might give him a moment of reprieve from the constant pounding these meetings caused.

"Ambassador Thompson, these are serious issues. If we don't do something about it, the crops might be ruined for the foreseeable future," the man prattled on once again. This was his fourth visit this week, complaining that the team in charge of pesticide distribution was holding out on him, because he didn't grease their wheels. Bribery and non-compliance were against the colony protocol, but Clark could hardly bring himself to care at that moment.

His gaze flicked back to the sky, the bright yellow star in the cloudless sky of a new planet called New Skarsgaard. He'd served with the First Contact Federation (FCF) Admiral when Sol was invaded some twenty years ago, and the least he could do, was honor the dead man by naming a planet after him. His sacrifice had allowed them to explore in relative peace.

"Are you going to do anything about it?" the farmer asked, voice rising to an almost inaudible pitch.

Clark shifted his focus from the past to his present. He was in charge of this world, this colony, and the people needed a leader. He just wished it wasn't him.

"Yes. I'll be sure to discuss this with Henry this afternoon. I'm sorry it hasn't been resolved sooner. My apologies." He stood and extended his hand, letting the man know the meeting was over.

"Thank you, sir." He shook and left in a hurry, as if lingering might leave time for Clark to change his mind.

He opened his desk tablet and took a sip of coffee from the newest crop, admiring the people's tenacity. Sixteen years on a strange world, and they already had coffee, beer, and chocolate: everything needed to survive the perils of being on a colony planet.

His screen flashed through messages from all the department heads: one looking to discuss the school curriculum, then something about a clogged sewer drain pipe, and a fence that one of the local herbivores had chewed through, letting the goats out.

With a flick of his wrist, he slid to an old screen he forgot he'd left open. Images of his wife appeared before him, her red hair glistening in the sun. A sun that was now dying. Earth's sun. Before he would let himself get sucked into that mindset again, he closed the tab, and a video he'd brought up the night before sat unplayed.

"Play," he said aloud, and his old professor's voice chimed in over some graphics on the class's smart board.

*"I know it's all confusing at this point, but by the end of the course, you will have a much better understanding of the wormhole. Research teams have recently started exploring the constructs of a wormhole, and we expect to have working models in a couple of decades. They're really just energy folding space and time,"* his old professor's voice said through the desk tablet.

*"Can we hypothesize, then, that with enough understanding of the wormhole, we could potentially isolate one from the other?"* an eerily familiar voice asked from behind the camera. He'd been so young and ambitious back then, so full of questions.

*"Mr. Thompson, are you asking if time travel can be real?"*

*"I suppose. If you can fold space, then perhaps it's*

*possible to only fold time,"* his own voice answered.

*"Yes. I do believe we will find it can be done. But I imagine it will be centuries before we understand it enough to create a viable working practice. Don't forget, your first..."* The professor's voice trailed off as Clark muted the screen.

He brought the picture album up again, and stared into his wife's eyes.

"Jeanie, hold all my meetings. I'll be back in the morning," he said into his tablet.

Checking the colony maps, he confirmed where the wormhole generator was sitting gathering dust. He was going to solve the problem he'd posed in that class thirty years ago. He was going to isolate time from space.


*Two years later*


New Skarsgaard stretched out below him: a beautiful small planet, teeming with growth and life. He knew he'd be able to see the colony if he zoomed in enough on his viewscreen, but for the time being, he wanted to enjoy it as it had been before they'd come to the world. Resplendent in its untouched surface. No pollution, no wars scorching its surface, just nature at its finest.

A light alarm broke him from his daydreaming, letting him know the generator was charged and ready for another test. The device was smaller than he'd thought possible years ago, about a quarter the size of his small transport vessel. It sat attached to the space station they left above the planet. Usually a team of two rotated in and out of it, but Clark had sent them all packing while he worked on his experiments, though it had been a battle with FCF Officer O'Sullivan. He'd eventually won out, and had given O'Sullivan his ambassador title while he was indisposed, pissing off all the department heads, but he didn't care. He was so close to his answer. It would be any day now, he could feel it.

He keyed in the next parameters, a 0.001 variance to the last test, and in a gut instinct, he went against his constant stabilizer percentage, lowering that by the same amount. He couldn't explain it, but he knew something was different before he tapped the blue *Confirm* square on the tablet. The generator whirred and the blue-white glow of the tiny wormhole swirled in space five thousand meters away. It was so beautiful. Every single time he felt in awe of the destructive and unstable folds in space. He often reminded himself that even though it was astonishing, it was also deadly under almost every circumstance.

Another press on the tablet, and a tiny probe flew toward the dancing maw of the wormhole. He couldn't see the small sensor out there, but it blipped softly as it neared its destination. Soon the blip ceased to exist as it travelled through the opening and into somewhere else...*somewhen* else, if he finally had it right. The wormhole stayed stable, and Clark took a deep breath to contain his excitement. After playing with the controls, the blip came back, slowly moving toward him.

His now trembling hands moved quickly, accelerating the probe and sending the readings the short distance so he could analyze them.

Images of New Skarsgaard appeared on his screen. He zoomed to where their colony was situated. Nothing but trees and lakes covered the area. Clark stood up and quickly sat back down as his head swam. He'd done it! He'd damn well done it! His fingers ached to set course for the swirling light, but it wasn't big enough for his ship, or safe to do so. It could become unstable at any moment, but he'd done it. All of the work to climb the ladder, becoming a UEF leader, and then ambassador of a colony, all paled in comparison to what he'd just accomplished.

They'd all want to understand it, and to duplicate it for their own wants, but he couldn't tell them. It wasn't for them, or for humanity; it was for him. For his wife.

Her picture smiled at him from his secondary screen, her image forever static over the past two years as he worked tirelessly.

More data streamed from the probe into his database and he inputted the information into his program, comparing variances with time differences. He'd have to make the wormhole a little bigger for his ship to fit through, and he needed it to fold time just enough. Twenty-two years, specifically.

*

"What do you mean, you're leaving?" O'Sullivan barked at him from behind Clark's own desk. Clark looked around the messy office, and for a moment felt a pain at seeing the disarray his replacement had left it in. It was fine. It was no longer his, so he let it go.

"Just let me get my things out of the desk, and I'll be long gone. You can have full control of this colony just like all you FCF-types wanted." Clark normally considered himself a quiet, subdued type, not one to get riled up by confrontation, but this arrogant man brought out the worst in him.

"You listen here. You were given the charge of leading us, and you were doing a fine job. What is this obsession you have? You spend the last two years up in space tinkering with a damned wormhole, that's never going to bring you anywhere but *dead*." O'Sullivan was almost yelling at that point.

"Anywhen…" Clark mumbled.

"Anywhen? What the hell does that mean? You're a strange man. You think you can just take one of our ships and leave? Along with the WHGEN?" He was referring to the wormhole generator, the one that had been sitting unused for over a decade before Clark chose to find it.

"You wouldn't understand, and I don't expect you to. Just give me my stuff, and I'll be leaving. I don't need your consent. Technically I'm still in charge here." Clark heard his own voice get gruff, and his fingernails were digging into his palms so hard he thought he could feel a drop of blood fall off his left hand.

"Listen. I don't have your things. I gave them to maintenance last year. You weren't coming back, and I needed the space," O'Sullivan said.

Clark strode over there, causing the FCF man to hop out of his seat. He pulled on the right desk drawer and slid it open. It was full of useless trinkets: paperweights, rubber bands, and things they just didn't need in the twenty-third century.

"Where is it?" Clark yelled, his pulse racing as he thought about the memories stored in there. His wife's hairbrush, her diary…their wedding vows, written on napkins from the lounge of the hotel they were married at. They had been nervous and sloppy drunk the night before, leaving the vows to the last minute because they assured one another they could speak from the heart at the moment. Turned out after five glasses of Ganymede red, and an empty stomach, they decided they'd better be prepared. The results were almost sad, but hilarious. He treasured those memories, and always kept the napkins close. Now they were missing.

"I told you, maintenance…" He was cut short as Clark threw a right hook at him, catching the larger man off guard, and O'Sullivan almost fell on his back from the impact, but he caught himself, clutching his jaw.

Clark's hand burned in pain from the punch, and he held it to his chest, backing out of the room.

"Get the hell out of here, Thompson! You're nuts! She's gone, and you and your wormhole can't change that!" O'Sullivan yelled across the office.

Clark paused, feeling the words wash over him. Instead of letting them anger him even more, he took them and let himself use them as motivation. The man was wrong about everything. He would change the past, and then his present.

*

The FCF Type-Four transport vessel was comfortable and spacious enough for a crew of eleven, and a decent amount of storage. He only needed some clothing, food rations, and medical supplies, so it almost echoed like an empty room in a new house. He'd spent enough time on board the FCF vessels that he knew he could handle a trip like this, but doing it all himself caused him more than a little anxiety. He was a scientist and a UEF ambassador, not a pilot or engineer, and he'd initially thought he could convince someone to come back and help him.

The bridge was nice with just him there, and he almost laughed at the luxury of the newest ships. The original First Contact vessels had mostly been welded-together metal, function over fashion. This many years later, with more than just military types flying in them, they were as pretty as they were efficient.

When he'd poked around the FCF and any others for crew potentials, he got nothing but cold shoulders, no doubt at the orders of O'Sullivan. Clark had waited against his hopes until he had a full grasp of the ship, and this had delayed him by a month while he read schematics, took training simulations, and learned the inside-out of the cryo-tubes. The trip back was six Earth years, but in the cryo, he would hardly age.

The wormhole generator was clasped to the ship, and would be enclosed by the displacement drive's sphere shield. Moving the ship out a few thousand kilometers from New Skarsgaard with his plasma drives, he calculated his anchor, and set the coordinates into the computer. Two hours after arriving in orbit, he was heading FTL toward his old home, nervous about being alone for the trip, and excited about what was to come.

With any luck, he wouldn't be alone on the trip back. Instead of slipping right into the sleep chamber, Clark decided to run the numbers a few more times, and make sure his wormhole would work. He watched his screen countless times, as the calculations showed a swirling blue-white simulation with the exact amount of hours it was folding. When he was confident his values were all right, he finally let himself think about heading into the tubes for the long journey.

As he strapped himself in, and set the instructions, the worry something would go wrong in transit struck him hard. If it did, he might be stuck somewhere. It was doubtful he would be able to fix anything seriously wrong. Perhaps he would be able to use the generator to get from point A to B more easily. He should have considered using the wormhole for the trip from New Skarsgaard to Earth. But he didn't have time for that. And since he wasn't aging on the trip, and it didn't matter when he arrived, since he was heading to a particular point in time, it only made sense to take the six-year journey the tried and tested way. Even when the wormholes had been used during the war for fast travel, their behaviour was sporadic and unreliable.

No. Clark knew he was taking the right course of action. Once out of his fleet suit, and into his beige shorts, he slipped into the tube, closing the hatch behind him. The soft plush lining felt comfortable against his skin, and he pretended he was just going to sleep in a high-end hotel back in D.C. With the press of a button the air felt lighter, and his eyes closed slowly. He knew they would open in a blink, and he would be near Earth once again.

The scene played out like a vintage movie, cast on the back of his eyelids. It was the same memory he'd seen every time he closed his eyes for the last fifteen years.

*Long Island, the least likely spot for the colony transport pick-up to Clark, but he wasn't in charge of the logistics. From there they would meet at Enceladus with the other lottery winners for their specific colony. Of course, most of the people heading to Clark's colony were hand-selected for their skills in one area or another, and with them their families, so the actual random lottery process was much smaller than the UEF was advertising. Clark felt of two minds about it, because they needed those skilled workers and minds to succeed, but he did want everyone on Earth to have a fair shot at life after the sun went Red giant.*

*From Long Island, they could meet from most hubs of the USA, by land, air, or water, so it made sense, but there were just too many people there for Clark to feel comfortable. He would have preferred the fields at Kentucky, where they were from. His wife, Madeline, clutched his hand as the small transport vessel lowered toward the large concrete shipping harbor along the ocean. People were lined up against the fences for what appeared to be forever, when he'd looked as they were a thousand meters up. They appeared to be yelling and pushed against the chain link; armed guards created a semi-circle around the dignitaries that would be leaving in this first batch to Saturn's moon.*

*Madeline looked out the window and he could tell she was afraid. Afraid of the crowds, but more afraid of leaving Earth for a life so far away.*

*"I'm sorry, Maddy," Clark said.*

*"For what?" she asked, turning to look him in the eyes. She always had the most beautiful eyes. Hazel with a ring of dark green around them.*

*"For spending more time trying to climb a ladder than spending time with you. For not giving you a family and a white picket fence." His eyes were welling up.*

*"It wouldn't have done any good anyway." She waved to the dimming sun in the sky. "Clark, I've always known you were driven, and I wouldn't have been with you if I wanted a different life. I love you, and always will."*

*"You'll work side by side with me at our new home. You can oversee the gardens, and we'll have dinner together every night," Clark promised.*

*She squeezed his hand one last time as the transport softly landed on the ground.*

*The doors opened, and they took their few personal items off; the rest of their stuff would be on the equipment vessels arriving before them. They were greeted with a cacophony of yelling, and Clark felt his pulse pick up. It was akin to the feeling of a tornado sweeping through Kentucky farmland on a hot summer night, dark skies and strong winds, right before it all came to a sudden calm.*

*Loudspeakers were booming across the open space, about the lies of the UEF and the fact the lottery was a sham. The fences were rocking back and forth, and in moments they were down in sections. Floods of people poured through and were running across the concrete pad toward Clark and Madeline. The guards moved forward, guns raised, and a few of them tossed gas canisters at the impending mob.*

*"We have to get out of here!" Clark yelled at his wife, grabbing his bag and her hand. Laser fire erupted*

around them, and now he knew the rioters weren't empty handed. The larger vessel sat near the water line, some one hundred meters from them, and that fifteen seconds would feel like a long run. His legs pumped as he tried to close the distance, and he turned around as he was half way there, only to see his wife going back to the small ship.

"Maddy! Get over here!" he yelled, but she couldn't hear him over the noise.

He tossed his bags down, and ran back for her. Laser fire was everywhere, and defense drones hummed around the sky above them, shooting people down. It was pure chaos. Madeline had dropped her pack. That was why she was so far behind. She'd gone back for it.

He saw her grab the pack, and the rioters closed in around her.

"No! Maddy, come to my voice!" he yelled, still running for her.

Overhead, drones were picking off targets, and they saw the group around his wife. Her ID chip was undoubtedly being scrambled by being around so many bodies. They opened fire, and ten people instantly fell to the ground.

They peeled away from her like a banana, and Clark saw her standing there, unscathed for a second, people all around her on the ground. Then she fell alongside them.

He was at her side, stumbling over corpses to get there. The guards were there, dragging him away. She had a burn on her forehead where the beam had hit. Clean death, as the drones were programmed to do. His heart melted, and he screamed like he'd never screamed before. He cried out in anguish, as they dragged him away from the remaining rioters, and into the transport vessel. He hadn't even realized he'd grabbed her pack, until days later, when he'd finally stopped moaning and *crying. In it were their napkins with their drunken vows on them, a diary, and her hairbrush.*

He blinked his eyes as consciousness slowly came back to him. The memory was so vivid he almost spat, to get the taste of iron and laser fire out of his mouth, but it all came back to him. Alarms softly chimed to let him know his heart rate was too high, and he breathed it out, like he'd done so many times before going to sleep.

He was back, or at least he hoped he'd made it without incident. It honestly felt like he'd just settled into the tube, but he knew it had been years by the cyro-clock readouts embedded in the chamber's glass viewscreen. Amazingly, his body wasn't more than just a little stiff as he got out of the cryo-tube. The lights softly flicked on, slowly getting brighter over a few minutes, allowing his eyes time to adjust.

He didn't need to check his location to confirm where he was. The sun hung in space, dimmer and more ominous than he could have imagined. On the way to a Red giant but still a couple centuries or so from being critical, though it was unlikely anyone on Earth could still be alive. Or maybe they'd found a way. He wouldn't put it past the resilience of humans to find a way to survive and perhaps even thrive. It would have to be much colder there now, so he imagined anyone still there would have emigrated to the equator, looking for solace.

Guilt that he hadn't just come back and got another round of colonists came back for an instant, but the UEF had been right. There was hardly enough for any of the colonies to ensure the people they brought with them would be fed, let alone thousands upon thousands more. He knew there should have been a better way, but they'd never expected the war to happen.

Earth looked sad as well. Continents had been destroyed, and half of what used to be Africa was now under water. He sat there, head pounding as he considered checking to see if he could find signs of people, but he stopped himself. He wasn't there for them. He was there for her, and soon he would be *then* for her.

Not wanting to waste a minute, he confirmed the wormhole generator was undamaged from the transit. It was inside the shield of the ship's sphere displacement drive, so there should have been no way for anything to pierce it, but the scientist in him had to ensure safety first. He stared toward the sun, remembering the day he saw it shooting flares off to defend Sol's invasion. That felt like a lifetime ago.

The computer chimed; the diagnostic scan was complete, and the generator was ready to go. The past few years were culminating to this moment, and he slowly keyed in the parameters. The blue-white swirl appeared a thousand feet away, and he took a snap-shot with the ship's cameras to mark the occasion. Earth and the sun lingered behind the beautiful maw of the time hole.

Wanting to just fly through it, he almost set course, and did just that; but instead, he took the precaution of sending his probe through first. He sat, nervously sweating as it entered and returned through the opening, and when he saw the shots back of the lush green and blue planet, and bright hot sun, he knew he'd done it. Clark's hands shook excitedly as he moved the ship in front of the wormhole. From there it was daunting and gorgeous. He entered slowly, his ship rocking back and forth for a few moments before settling back down, as he crossed through the small fold.

Just like nothing happened, the ship's viewscreen showed Clark something he'd never thought possible a few years before. A healthy sun, and Earth as it had been.

He'd made it.

The ship's time equipment couldn't adjust for the

movement backward, so he could only hope he was indeed in the right time, or on the right Earth for that matter. The idea that a wormhole could travel through other dimensions was more than a theory according to reports he'd heard during the war. A crew had come from an alternate Sol to help find the location of their ultimate enemy, Empyrean. He prayed his calculations were accurate.

Since he was in an FCF Type-Four transport vessel, he would raise no eyebrows as long as the identification number was valid, which he knew it to be. He brought the generator with him, wishing he could leave it, but fearful that someone would take it or worse while he was back on the surface of Earth. He couldn't risk that.

The quick trip down to Earth was exhilarating. It was never as much an oasis as some societies had hoped, but it was a far stretch from the brutality of the world pre-United Earth Foundation, before the threat of interstellar wars and alien invasions. They as a race had been petty and selfish, bickering about religion, borders, and so much that didn't benefit the race as a whole. Religion still existed, but finally humans could be humans, and put their energy into something bigger than their small planet. Of course, that level of enlightenment had been cut short when the war came.

He passed through the atmosphere, his ship jiggling at the change of pressure, but stabilizing quickly. He flew high in the sky, over Canada, lowering as he was over Indianapolis. The rolling pastures that gave his old home the *Bluegrass State* nickname spread in front of him, and he swallowed hard, fighting back the emotion of being there... of being then.

There was a large transport landing area near the university where she worked. He'd picked this time for selfish reasons. His other self, the one from that time, was working hard in Washington. He was part of the colony transition team, and it had been weeks since he'd been home to Madeline. If he was going to convince his wife to come with him, he knew that doing so at a time when he knew she was angry with the present 'him' would bode in his favor. It felt underhanded, and he hated doing it this way, but what choice did he have?

It was three years before the invasion. From the displacement travel, he would appear about 15 years older than he was... forty-eight to her thirty-two. Once landed, he noticed there were no other space vessels in the landing pad, and he knew this would only draw attention to himself. He rushed out, half-running to the automated taxi pods. He stood at a blue one, and saw his reflection in the mirrored glass. When did he become such an old man? He felt like he was in the prime of his life, but the grey in his hair and the wrinkles around his eyes begged to differ. She would be repulsed by him; maybe even think him some lunatic, and not Clark at all.

With great trepidation, he held his thumb to the device, knowing his print would get him access to the UEF's account, and he was let in the travel pod. After saying his destination out loud, the vehicle began moving, and Clark looked out the window longingly. He'd come to love his home on New Skarsgaard, but Kentucky would always be his real home.

The trip was fast, the roadways designed for multiple layers and efficiency; traffic jams were a thing of the past. Soon the pod was pulling over, and Clark saw the beautiful grounds of the university. She spent her lunches eating outside in the gardens, and he was right on time as planned.

The pod zoomed away, leaving a nervous Clark standing there, alone on the sidewalk. He could do this. He'd traversed space, then time, to make it here. Talking to his wife should be no problem, but it was. He hadn't seen her since that day. The day she was killed, and he was ushered away screaming. The day it all ended for him. He started walking with purpose. That was the wrong way to look at it. There was no then or later, only now.

Clark's confidence grew with each step, and by the time he reached the gardens, he was so sure it would go well… until he spotted her. She was sitting on the bench he'd seen her at so many times before, but not enough times as well. He saw the lonely look on her face as she ate her lunch, no doubt a sandwich, since cooking for one wasn't much fun. His gut felt like he'd been punched, and he almost doubled over at the pain. Maybe he didn't deserve her. Maybe he should go find the younger version of him, and make sure she got put on a colony ship without him. He stood there, worrying and wondering when he heard a voice calling his name.

"Clark? Honey, is that you?" Her voice sounded like an angel, and he couldn't help but run to her. She was standing now, squinting at him, and he stumbled over his feet and almost fell as he approached her. He recovered and soon she was spinning in his arms, tears of joy and fear spilling down his face. She was laughing, until he stopped and set her down. Her hand instinctively went for his face, but it paused in the air just short of his cheek, and her jaw dropped.

"Clark?" she squeaked. "What happened?"

"It's me, Maddy," Clark said, knowing he was the only one she let call her by that name. "Let's sit down."

He took her hand and led her back to the bench she'd been sitting at. "I have so much to tell you, and it's going to sound a little crazy."

"Are you really him?" She reached for her purse, perhaps thinking to call her husband who would be in Washington right then. He took her hand in his, and nodded.

"It's me, the Clark you know, but older. Your husband… well *me*, is in Washington where he told you he is. This is going to be hard to believe. Earth is invaded. Ships come from far away… slave races of an evil sentient star, and they almost destroy us. Our sun on some level protected us, but by doing so, sacrificed itself. The project your husband is now working on, the secret one… is the UEF and FCF working on building hundreds of massive colony ships which we use to branch off to other worlds, and save humanity." He stopped, knowing he was giving too much too fast.

Madeline was in shock; her face had gone ghost white. "Wait, what happens? Why are you here, then?"

Clark was almost surprised by how quickly she recovered from the news and how her always overly intelligent brain comprehended that something must have gone wrong for him to be back.

He'd considered this part over and over during the past couple years at the colony, as he sat in the station above the strange planet, working tirelessly on the wormhole generator. Looking into her eyes, he knew he had no choice but to tell the whole truth.

"It was a mess. The riots were spreading. So many people were being left behind, and they knew the lottery the UEF kept spouting about was a glorified joke. They brought who they wanted to before random selections, and even those were never random. Most people were never considered; the top ten percent after the shoe-ins were then placed under a lottery. Word got out." Madeline held his hand, and looked deep into his eyes as he went on. "They ripped down the fence, and had guns. The drones were there to protect, and when you went back for your pack, the people surrounded you. The drones opened fire, and you didn't make it." He choked on his words. "They pulled me to the ship and I left. I left you there on the ground in a pile of other bodies. They dragged me from you," he said, breaking down once again. She held him close, and he felt how much he'd missed her through every bone in his body. "I never gave up on us."

Pulling free she held his face in her hands. "How did you ever make it back to me?"

"I'll tell you on the way," he said, seeing a few ships fly overhead. His gut was telling him it was time to go.

"To where?" she asked, standing when he did.

"To our ship, then to our new home, New Skarsgaard," he said.

"New Skars...wait, I can't leave Clark. I can't just leave my life here!"

All the worry this would happen rushed into Clark, and he felt light-headed. He had to convince her. He needed her. "Your husband will be fine. I lived, and traveled through time to give you a new life. Maddy, I'm so sorry for all the times I took you for granted. I focused so much on my stupid career trying to climb the UEF ladder that I never gave you the love you deserved."

"Oh Clark, I knew you were driven when I married you. For the most part, I'm happy." She stopped, and looked at him closely. "You've always allowed me to do my own thing, too. I just wish we could spend more time together."

"*We* can," he said quietly.

She shook her head. "Maybe I can change what happens, save the world."

"But it's already happened. Don't you see?" he asked. "Just come with me to the ship. I'll show you images of my new home. Decide for yourself." Another FCF patrol crossed the sky above them, and though Clark doubted they would have an inkling of who he was, their presence put an unease in his mind.

"You've been through so much. My Clark has never had that look that I see in your eyes." She held his hand as they walked to the transport pods. "It's a sadness like none I've ever witnessed."

This hurt him, but he understood. "I'm your Clark, too."

"I know… this is all just so complicated."

An automated taxi pod arrived and Clark wondered if it was the same one that had brought him there. They headed back down the road, and Clark felt a fool for not even asking Madeline if she wanted to stop at home and grab some things. But he knew that would be presumptuous, and they could always do that if she decided to go along with him.

As they approached the vessel's landing pad, he knew something was wrong. Sirens were going off in the distance, and though it was the middle of the day, a massive flare erupted from the sun, slowly cascading from high in the sky, eastward toward the outer solar system. It was huge.

This wasn't supposed to be happening. When was he?

"What's the date? What's the date?" he asked.

She told him, and it had to be wrong.

"This can't be. I was sure I had it right." He must have screwed up the wormhole. He'd come back to invasion day. Of all the odds, this was his bad luck.

An officer arrived on an air-bike, sirens blasting. "Sir, we need all ships brought to Washington now," he said, scanning the ship with a handheld tablet. "This must be some sort of glitch; this ship is already there." He stepped back, hand lowering to his side. He scanned Clark and Madeline. "And you, Mr. Thompson, have just been flown to *Glory* by the Admiral's orders."

Clark pushed the worry aside, and exuded every bit of snooty United Earth Foundation Ambassador he had in him. "And just who in the hell do you think you are? Flying over here while we're being attacked, and ques-

266

tioning why *I'm* here? Do you think I don't know Blair asked for me? Do you think I don't know about the impeding attacks? Get the hell out of my face, son, before I get you thrown into the front end of Carter Hayes' squadron where the heaviest action will undoubtedly be!"

The man shrunk a good three inches, and stepped back apologetically. "We need to go now, Maddy," he urged.

There they stood on a massive concrete slab in the middle of a warm Kentucky day, the sun had just sealed its fate, and Earth was about to be half destroyed. Pandemonium would follow.

She ran alongside him, her fears pouring out of her beautiful face in a grimace and tears. Her home was about to be destroyed, and Clark had come with a mad tale of time-travel. He couldn't imagine what toll that took on her.

The loading ramp lowered for them, and they crossed over the small area in a few strides heading into the small vessel. Madeline looked around, breathing heavily, and Clark realized it had been years since the younger him had taken her anywhere on an FCF ship. The last time was their honeymoon, when they'd headed on a cryo-trip to Saturn's moon. Now those same moons were about to become the base for a mass-exodus of the colony vessel process.

"Welcome aboard, First Officer Thompson," he said and saluted her. She laughed aloud and his heart melted. He still couldn't believe she was there with him, on that ship, and they could go back to their new home. A safe world.

"Aye aye, Captain." She laughed again, but he could see the reservations in her face. Her life was there; her *real* husband was, too.

Clark hesitated, almost asking her if she really wanted to do it, but held back and lifted the ship into the air. Soon they were heading through the atmosphere into the darkness of space, Earth behind him for the last time in his life.

"Clark, we'll be okay then?" Madeline asked, eyes wide as they soared on their plasma drives.

"We'll be better than okay, Maddy. We'll be together."

The space around Earth was filling up, ships everywhere, and Clark knew he had to get out of there or be somehow trapped in the coming storm. FCF war vessels loomed nearby and he scooted under them, ignoring the messages coming through his comm-system.

A ship roared by, and he recognized it as *Glory*, the very same ship his other self was on at that moment. He felt goosebumps race across his body at the paradox, and it only urged him to accelerate the drive.

They traveled that way for an hour, until space was nothing but a calm black vacuum. They talked back and forth about things, mostly Clark filling her in on the war, and then the colony trip. He skipped over his loneliness, and told her about setting up the terraforming machines on a breathable planet. It really only needed a nudge to get the atmosphere to accept them, but not hurt any local wildlife. He described in detail the plant life, which she would be the most interested in, since she came from a long line of green thumbs. He couldn't wait to show her the trees there. Some of them were three hundred feet tall with roots just as long, and he could almost picture her face light up at the sight of its grandeur.

"I think that's far enough out of the way. We should have a clear path now," he said, showing her the wormhole generator screen. She'd taken intro physics at the University of Kentucky as well, so she grasped most of the concepts with ease, though her field of study was botany. The day she told him she was to be a professor at UK was one of the best days of his life.

The generator vibrated gently outside of their ship, being towed around like a trailer in space. Worried about the error he'd made getting to the past, he triple checked his figures before starting the wormhole up, and when it began to appear, they both laughed, and hugged.

"I just have to send a probe through first, and then we are good to go, if all the signs are accurate on the other side. Shouldn't be more than a few minutes," he said, and she stood closer and kissed him. It had been so many years for him, but he felt the familiarity and kissed her back passionately. In a minute the wormhole was forgotten, and their clothes were in piles on the bridge floor.

Soon Clark lay on the deck, with Madeline's head resting on his chest.

"Clark, I love you. I'm so glad you came for me. I thought *this,*" she waved her hand between the two of them, "would feel strange, but it felt just right."

And it had.

Alarms blared and Clark jumped to his feet to see red ship icons appearing on the tablet before him. "Where the hell are those coming from?" He zoomed through his viewscreen and figured it out quickly. Wormholes were opening in the distance, ships entering Sol through them. "I should have known! We were flanked from both sides by the enemy and a plasma ship…" He was cut off at the sight of the massive solar-flaring triangle ship entering space near them. It was huge and coming directly in line to his wormhole.

"We have to go now!" Clark yelled.

"What about the probe? You didn't test it yet!" Madeline shouted back, while trying to toss her clothing back on.

He didn't wait, just fired the plasma drive up and rushed to the opening. Klaxons shrieked, as the huge ship was on a collision course with them. Everything slowed and Clark breathed as they flew at full speed. Five... breath... four... breath... three... breath... two... one. The ship was in his viewscreen and it looked like he was about to collide with a star, when they passed through the wormhole. He cut it off seconds later, and whooped as his sensors showed it closing with no ships following him through.

"Hot damn, we did it!" He spun her around and they celebrated being alive, and together. Until he remembered he was naked. He'd have to leave that part out when he told the guys back at the colony.

Zooming in on the image of the sun, he saw it was much dimmer, like the sun he'd seen when he first arrived in-system. He was confident he was in the right time.

The displacement drive was charging and the coordinates were set, and once fully clothed again, Clark and his wife had dinner together at the table, eating travel rations that were almost as tasty as her old home cooking. He felt like they were on a date again, and he even found some jazz to play on the vessel's speakers while they finished up the last of their bites.

The displacement drive announced it was ready to engage, and he triple checked the anchor in the Skarsgaard system, and hit the keys.

"Give us six years, and we'll be home," he said, squeezing her hand.

She looked nervous, but said with no tremors in her voice, "I look forward to it."

*

Once again, Clark shook the blurry vision away and squinted at the dim lights. They'd made it back home, and he couldn't have been happier. Turning to his side,

270

he saw the cryo-tube beside him opening up and the lights coming on much like his. This was Madeline's first trip being put under, and he hoped she took it better than his first one. He'd had a headache for weeks.

"Are you okay, Maddy?" he asked, concern heavy in his voice.

"Just a bit of a headache. Nothing some water and time won't heal." Her voice, while groggy, had an air of excitement in it.

Once out, they dressed in FCF uniforms and Clark checked their coordinates. Everything looked fine, and soon they were closing in on New Skarsgaard. Clark wasn't sure what would happen, but he hoped O'Sullivan would keep the ambassador role, and he and Madeline could just live and be active members of the community and workforce.

"It's so beautiful," she said staring at the image of the planet through the viewscreen. The lush greens and blues were evident from their vantage point. Clark saw their continent, and zoomed the screens in to show her the colony.

"What the hell?" Clark gasped, looking for signs of their structures. "Was it a storm?" He tracked the area and could see no indication that any human had ever been down there. His chrono readings still showed a continuation of his first time from leaving, but that was only accurate to the ship's timeline.

"I must have had the wrong parameters, just like when I folded time to Earth to get you." Clark stood, thinking hard.

"Or it folded us into another dimension," Madeline whispered.

It was possible, and Clark realized he'd been dealing in things he probably had no right to mess with, but he had managed to get his wife, and at that moment that was all that mattered.

"So do we go down and wait for them to show up?" he asked, imagining young Clark arriving to find old Clark with his thought-to-be dead wife. It wasn't ideal.

"You said there were dozens of habitable colony planets, right? Let's roll the dice and find the closest one. What's another trip in cryo?" she asked, and he laughed and warmed at that.

"I'm so glad you're here. Let's go find our new home," Clark said, and in an hour, they were back asleep and heading outward, into the space beyond.

# The Light of Distant Earth

By Tim C. Taylor

1

I could begin my story with *Homo sapiens*, my distant ancestors, spreading their relentless fingers of colonization over the virgin lands of an earlier Earth, one warming after an ice age.

Except they weren't virgin lands those ancient explorers colonized. Someone had been there before.

Well, hominids. Not *people*, perhaps. At least not in the strictest sense, but some things don't change. The same is true of Safe Haven, or whatever you choose to call this place.

We were here before you.

But it will be your destiny to thrive on the land we readied for you, just as those early people thrived on distant Earth.

Guess I'm rambling again. It's the terminal meds. They're keeping me going a little longer, until I've finished my final task, but they burn my concentration. Time is short. For me. I pray not for you.

So I'll jump forward a million years from our distant ancestors. Jump in space too, and welcome you to a moment on Haven-Three Colony on the edge of the Orion Spur, where we had been chased by a remorseless doom.

I could tell you the date and time, but it would mean

nothing to you. It meant everything to us, though.

It was the day officially named Earth Death, but many of us called it Death Day One, because even then we knew a worse day would follow in a few decades.

*Captain, I don't wish to hurry you...*

Yeah, yeah. Stop gassing and say what you have to while you still can. Okay, I got it. But in order for them to understand the horror of Earth Death, I first have to explain the Blight.

2

We fled Earth's destruction in sorrow, but also hope.

I think we humans are at our best when faced with adversity, and what challenge could be worse than losing our home to the vengeful stellar being, Empyrean? Stubbornness drove us on as much as anger, desperation, and cold strategic planning. We had no choice. Empyrean forced us to grow, to spread ourselves amongst the stars or perish in the attempt.

We were the Haven Mission, the farthest flung of the First Contact Fleet. Out here, toward the tip of the local spiral arm, the stars are younger, and the youngest that were yet old enough to possess habitable planets were thought to be in the Cone Nebula. Perhaps here, the strategy teams had reasoned, the anger of the ancient stellar beings would carry less weight. All we wanted was to live with the stars in peace. At least, until we grew strong enough to demand their respect.

Hope breeds endemically amongst our species. We had scarcely begun our immense journey before many of us pointed to our destination at the rimward edge of the spiral arm, and looked to the gulf that lay beyond. If malign forces, still barely understood, had caused us to flee the Solar System, perhaps one day we would also be forced first from the arm and then the galaxy itself.

We did move far beyond our destination, but not in the way those dreamers imagined.

The Blight wouldn't let us.

At first, no one could agree whether the Blight was a disease amongst the stars, or a form of attack. Until it was too late, we had never even guessed that stars were living beings. Perhaps the Blight was yet more evidence of our ignorance?

Stored as I was in a deep-cryo compartment, I never saw the birth of the Haven-One Colony around 15 Monocerotis in the Cone Nebula, or Bridge-C as the colonists named it. It was a running joke amongst the fleet that when we explored Bridge-C's candidate habitable planets, we would discover wide, sandy beaches and perfect ski slopes. Turned out, that wasn't far off the truth for the world of Haven-One, but only after many centuries waiting in cryo sleep while the terraformers detoxified the atmosphere.

I never saw its death either, over a thousand years later. At the time, I was thirty light years away in a star system we called Bastion, working lengthy, stim-extended shifts piloting intra-system mining craft amongst the Kuiper objects that fed the establishment of the Haven-Two Colony.

Forty years previously, a Haven-One observatory had noticed an unexplained cool patch in Bridge-C, and named it the Blight. It was an anomaly – nothing more – and was logged and forgotten. And even though the Blight slowly grew over the following years, most of the colonists were unaware of its existence.

Without warning, it started spreading exponentially.

By then, there were over seven million souls on Haven-One. As a precaution, some of the children and a handful of adults were evacuated to an old Explorer-class ship, *Intrepid*. But the old ship could only berth 8,000.

The children had barely boarded when Bridge-C was suddenly wrenched out of its natural sequence. A billion years ahead of schedule, it underwent a helium flash that was inexplicably channeled out in a concentrated disc across the plane of the ecliptic. It was like the Reaper's scythe slicing through the planets. As its helium ash fused into carbon, the star emitted thousands of years' worth of energy output in just a few seconds – and its atmosphere opened up like a dragon's maw to let the energy flare out unimpeded.

Planetary atmospheres vaporized above molten crusts. The shockwave's photon pressure was so immense that the burning planets were even nudged out of their orbits. Haven-One died in milliseconds, and *Intrepid* was lost seconds later as it prepared to displace out of the system.

When scout ships returned to inspect the scoured system, they found the star once more at peace, back in its main sequence. Having rid itself of the biological infestation amongst its chattel planets, the star was now content. That was the interpretation many placed on the loss of Haven-One, and although the First Contact Fleet and the United Earth Foundation cruelly punished anyone voicing such defeatist sentiment, it was hard to counter the assumption that the Haven Mission was doomed.

Haven-Two was next, fifty years later, and by then the light had reached us from more stellar flares coming in from ever-closer neighbors. It was as if a line of beaters was deliberately driving us against the rimward edge of the Orion Spur, forcing us out into the immense, lifeless wastes that separated Orion from the Perseus Arm. I was in command of one of the five remaining colony vessels, and I argued that our displacement drives had enough range to take us back coreward, to reunite with the survivors of other FCF missions. But no one could tell whether the Blight was also spreading coreward. Maybe if we retraced our journey back toward the dead Earth, all we would find were other glowing embers that had once been planets. We just couldn't tell. Not without journeying there in person.

We had traveled so far, and lightspeed communications were too slow and the other colony fleets too distant. We were alone. Only our colony ships could return and warn the rest of humanity, but could we spare one of our surviving fleet of five for the nine-hundred-year round trip?

Then something changed. One of my crew detected an impossible radio transmission. Jimmy Khan, his name was, and for a while I thought he might have saved our mission. I gave him a team of people whose discretion I could trust, and they confirmed that Jimmy had heard something. A beacon of hope. From the very edge of the spiral arm, where no FCF craft had ever visited, we were receiving a garbled message. It was too corrupted to decipher quickly, but its encoding was unmistakable.

Out there at the rimward edge, from a system outside the Cone Nebula, someone was transmitting Morse code.

## 3

*Talking of messages... I need to move you on, Captain. You were going to explain Death Day, remember?*

Death Day. Yes... The second Death Day. Is that what I was talking about? Termination Day – yes, I remember hoping that, with the end of the world finally here, the United Earth Foundation would have mercy on a harmless old fool, and allow me to meet my doom with vacuum beneath my legs on my old command. The truth was that I was only able to take the elevator into orbit and the auto-shuttle to *Spirit of Endurance* because no one cared enough to stop me.

Someone *had* noticed my return, though. "Welcome aboard, Captain Acualla," greeted my old cryo officer, Lieutenant Parker. "It's good to have you back."

I frowned at Parker's crisp salute and tried to interpret the sparkle of mischief in his eyes that he couldn't prevent spreading to his mouth. Who the hell could grin like that when all life would be obliterated from Haven-Three in less than an hour?

I returned the salute, grudgingly. This was the man who had planted the idea in my head of meeting my end on my old ship. I supposed I owed him a little respect – but not much. "You're an idiot, Parker. Always were prone to flights of fancy. For a start, this is Termination Day. There won't be a tomorrow. If I'm back, then it's not for long. More importantly, I'm not anyone's captain. After my criminal act during the previous Death Day, I was cashiered and then jailed, remember?"

"Negative, sir. You are still an FCF captain."

Sincerity hardened Parker's words to such an extent that I regarded him properly for the first time. He wore the uniform of a UEF functionary, and the sight twisted my insides with guilt. The United Earth Foundation had used me and my unpatriotic misdemeanor on Deck 13c as an excuse to disband the First Contact Fleet throughout the system. The spacers couldn't be trusted, they reasoned. They were probably right.

"Say again?"

"Captain, you were never discharged because the UEF pen pushers were in too much of a rush to shut down the Fleet. You were never transferred to the UEF, nor discharged. You're the only member of FCF personnel left in the system."

"I don't give a damn, mister. It makes no difference. Unless you're expecting me to pilot this crate across the wastes to the Perseus Arm?"

"Not *exactly*, sir."

I might have been a miserable jerk, back in those final days–

*What's to say you aren't now?*

Whoever programmed you was *definitely* a jerk.

*I rest my case.*

If you're deliberately irritating me as a ploy to keep
me talking, it's ... it's probably working, but please
don't distract me. This is difficult enough as it is. Where
was I? Parker. Lieutenant Parker – or rather former Lieutenant Parker of the FCF, and now extra-planetary
maintenance team manager for the UEF – was up to
something. But his poker face wouldn't yield to my scru-
tiny, so I gave up and hurried over to the CIC, where the
others were waiting to join me in the countdown to our
extinction. Despite the dust and the UEF vandalism, I
could tell someone had kept essential systems well maintained, because–

*Hurry up! Sorry, but that's not important to your
audience. Get to the events on the CIC.*

Shut up. I'm getting there.

*Captain Acualla, you don't have much time.*

Okay. I get it. Yada yada death cults and the sorrow
that laced every look, every word on the planet and off it
in our final days. The end of everything and everybody.
We were convinced these were the last moments of the
entire human race. Making illicit love on a sun-dappled
riverbank, Beethoven, the first people on Mars, wine and
beer at a patio barbecue, the ultimate sacrifice paid by
generations in the world wars, and blockbuster movies –
it all ended here and now with us. You'll have to imagine all that because I don't have time to tell you. Termination Day was upon us. It was our turn. The Blight had
finally come to Haven-Three and the UEF plan was to
hold hands and sing songs around a campfire until the
wavefront hit and we turned instantly to plasma.

*Spirit of Endurance* still had its seed banks, terraformers and displacement drive. We could have had one more throw of the dice, except the UEF command had declared it was game over, and taken the dice away. The decision was cowardly, but even I have to admit it wasn't made easily.

Taken in by the signal emanating from the rimward star that we named Beacon, the Haven Mission Senior Council gambled all on Haven-Three being our last, best chance. We sunk everything into making this colony work, and the first signs had looked good. Beacon-Five had a breathable atmosphere and temperate climate. Within weeks, the pathfinder colonists were on the ground, working.

By then, we survivors of the Haven Mission had acquired hard-won experience of colony building. With a grim determination, we constructed floating agri-islands in a tenth of the time we had spent on Haven-One. We had developed a ruthlessness too, and who could blame us after the way the galaxy had treated us? Instead of treading lightly on the new planet's ecology, we brutally tore down mountains and cut off whole ice shelfs to feed our need for raw materials. And all the while, *Spirit of Endurance* was on the mind of every colonist. If the Blight reached us on Haven-Three, the ship could become a lifeboat, but only for a few. Who would live and who die?

Knowledge of the signal – the very reason we were here – had been heavily suppressed by the UEF, who became more dictatorial with every passing month. Maybe they had a right to be. Before the Earth Death day, there had been a botched attempt by frightened colonists to seize my ship, the reason why my left hand is prosthetic. A permanent state of emergency was declared throughout Haven-Three, all in an attempt to keep a lid on the pressure cooker of a doomed colony while the authorities pieced the garbled message back together.

But when they did, the message we had placed so much store upon – the reason the star had been named Beacon – turned out to be a warning about the Blight. It told us a few details we didn't already know, but not nearly enough to defeat the oncoming threat.

The UEF kept the secret of the mystery signal to the end, but they no longer pretended we had hope. Haven-Three took a collective vow to limit its people's suffering. There would be no further colony mission. No false optimism. There would be no more children. It became the greatest of society's taboos: to bring a life into the world, knowing it would be cruelly cut short. Only a tiny number of malcontents were selfish enough to break this prohibition.

And that was why I was no longer a captain. I presumed the daughter I had fathered so scandalously was still alive somewhere down on the planet below. She would have been nineteen, but she would never make twenty.

Such a tragic waste!

Haven-Three had started strongly, but then gave up the fight. We made ourselves comfortable and waited for death.

*Captain... the CIC?*

We had learned a lot about the Blight by the end; all of it useless. But we did know enough by Termination Day to put a timer on the screens of my old ship's CIC as we counted down to our end.

At eighteen minutes and two seconds, one of the young UEF-uniformed crew announced, "Incoming transmissions. Multiple signals, they're coming from Beacon... *From the star.*"

I had strapped myself into the command orb. I don't know why; it just felt the most comfortable place. But when the signals came through, many nervous faces on that deck naturally looked to the command position for direction. And, despite the years that had passed, it felt natural to give it.

"You," I said to the girl who had spoken. "Can you run the *Spirit*'s core systems?"

She blinked. "Ah, yes, Captain. Mr. Parker taught us basic operations so we could demonstrate them to tourists."

"Tourists!" God, I hated what the UEF had done. "Never mind. What's your name?"

"Schraeve, sir."

"Well, Schraeve, I'm making you my communications officer. Find out what the hell these transmissions are. Everyone else, you're working for Schraeve now. Do what she says. Now, where the hell is Parker?"

My old officer was nowhere to be seen. There were only a handful of kids and a few old dignitaries trying to ignore this interruption to their deaths.

"Sir, transmissions are coming from science probes positioned very close to the sun."

I had to nod at Schraeve to continue.

"It's not just sensor data, there is a distributed AI analyzing the data and piggybacking its conclusions in real time onto the raw feed. It's... Oh. There is a virtual watermark. It's HOPE."

"Shut it down," I growled. "Bloodsucking shits."

The Movement for Humanity, or HOPE as everyone was calling it by that time, was one of the many death cults and fringe movements that challenged the UEF's lockdown on dissent. HOPE was the most hated, because it preyed on the despair of its victims to screw them out of every credit they had.

"Belay that!" shouted Parker, who jetted into CIC with a grin on his face and a thruster unit on his back. "By God," he said, "we've actually done it!"

Before I could ask what *it* was, Schraeve reported unauthorized boats entering the main hanger. We were being boarded!

I remember glancing up at the countdown.

Whatever the hell was going on, it would all be over in sixteen minutes and forty-two seconds.

4

Cameras in the hangar bay showed it unexpectedly filled by two GP-13 shuttles coming in hot, rear ends first. GP-13s were bruisers, designed for heavy haulage of big, dumb objects. I thought the crazy pilots were going to wreck the ship, and we would die a spacer's death in hard vacuum, but they slowed their approach with a perfect thruster burst that did no more damage than scorching the hanger deck. I gave a low whistle. That was one helluva piloting display.

My missing left hand itched as I looked up from the hangar feed and watched for the guns I expected to be drawn on me in the CIC. But everyone here was as surprised by this boarding as me. All except for one person.

"Mr Parker, explain yourself!"

"We're carrying on the FCF mission," Parker replied with a worrying tone of wonderment. "We just brought in additional seed banks, robot landers, terraformers, and 827 colonists. And what's more, the sensor probes we scattered around the sun have just given us the data that will one day beat the Blight."

"Who are *we*?" I asked grimly, praying that they weren't the boneheads I thought they were.

"The Movement for Humanity. Commonly known as HOPE."

They *were* said boneheads. Crap! I sighed, regretting ever coming up here. Then I remembered that it had initially been Parker's idea and all became clear. "And I suppose you want me to pilot my ship to a new colony site?"

"We can override the controls if need be. But, yes, we prefer you in command."

Should I play along? I watched the boarders scurrying out of the shuttles. The equipment they brought, and the probes around Beacon that had brought back the data that had gotten Parker so excited – to do all that under the nose of the United Earth Foundation must have cost trillions. And every credit had been screwed out of brainwashed cult members.

I didn't care about those dumb cultists now. It was the children of the people down there in the hangar I was thinking of. The ones not yet conceived. It wasn't fair to bring false hope into a doomed world, as I had done with my own daughter.

So I decided to stall. We had only minutes left, barely enough time to spool up the displacement drive. "I won't do it," I told him. "Dammit, Parker. It's the end of the world and you're forcing me to admit the UEF were right all along. I'm not going to displace *Spirit of Endurance* out of here."

"I'm not asking you to. I'm asking you to pilot through the wormhole."

"Are you completely nuts? Every signal given off by that thing says that it's faulty. It's not even the right color, and the probes sent through thirty years ago didn't survive to send back a test signal."

"You're wrong," said a young female voice over a general ship-wide comm channel. "The probes *did* survive. I found their transmission. I heard them report back."

"Who is this?" I snapped in irritation.

"Dad. It's me."

*Dad!* My memory of the next few seconds is totally blank. I imagine I was flapping my mouth like a landed fish.

"Dad?" she prompted.

"Why? Why didn't anyone else find the probes?"

"Because they weren't looking in the right place. I detected the signals transmitted from the moment the probes emerged from the far end of the wormhole, 651 light years away."

My mind described a downwardly spiraling orbit about the stunning implication of what she had just said.

The probes transmitted their data at lightspeed and they had flown through the wormhole thirty years ago. To reach Haven-Three from a distance of 651 light years, the probes must have sent their signals 621 years *before* they passed through the wormhole.

I had been a First Contact Fleet captain; I'd been taught all major theories and practice of space-time travel. If you took the mathematical models of faster-than-light travel and flipped them through a half turn, then you were no longer describing travel through *space*. As my old astro-navigation lecturer liked to tell us, FTL travel and time travel were the same thing; it was only the woefully limited human perspective that drew such a sharp distinction between them.

Unfortunately, I *was* a woefully limited human, and it took me several seconds to change my perspective. But when I did, it felt as if I'd been woken from the dead.

"All hands!" I announced across the ship. "Follow the arrows to the nearest acceleration station. We're getting out of here. Fast!"

5

"Sir, incoming transmission," said Schraeve. "Patching through."

Half the screens now showed a white-haired woman whose face pinched in fury at this disturbance to her impending demise. "What little prick is...? Oh, it's you,

Acualla. I might have guessed."

"Can't chat right now," I told the Governor of Haven-Three. "I'm a little busy."

"Power down! Now!"

I ignored her and checked the main status board. With the help of Parker and the kids, the *Spirit's* main thrust engines were already active, and the displacement drive was spooling up.

"I command all UEF craft in the system. I order you to desist, Acualla."

Displacement drive would be online in thirteen minutes... Thirty seconds *after* the Blight hit. I shut down every safety protocol I could find, and shaved fifty-five seconds off the jump preparations. It was gonna be hellishly tight, but we could do this.

"You're nothing better than a pirate," ranted the governor. "To think I argued against your execution. And this is how you betray the uniform you once wore."

The governor's words didn't bother me, but her contempt stung. I glared at her face. "I don't answer to you. I'm an officer in the First Contact Fleet. I report to the senior FCF officer in this system. Not to you."

"You're nothing but an administrative oversight. Who is this FCF officer you think you report to, anyway?"

"Me. I answer to myself. I'm in command of the Haven Mission fleet now, and I say the *Spirit of Endurance* is flying out of here, and there's not a damn thing you can do about it. Now get the hell off this channel. Acualla out."

6

Without needing my guidance, Schraeve cut the connection and the governor's features were replaced by the countdown, but it was no longer the countdown to our deaths. I couldn't help but grin. As dramatic farewells went, I thought mine had rated pretty high.

I was growing to like Schraeve. She reminded me of myself, thirty years younger. I could teach her to become a fine ship's officer.

"The wormhole, Dad. The wormhole."

I almost did as my daughter asked and changed course for the wormhole. I'd never been permitted to be a father – never even been allowed to see her or know her name – but just the way she said *Dad* sliced me to the core. It took the familiar hum of the spooling displacement drive to bring me to my senses.

"No," I told her. "We'll displace out, then you'll have plenty of time to analyze your data. We have enough fuel to return here later."

The problem with dramatic farewells, is the embarrassment when you realize it isn't goodbye after all.

Even before ship systems reported what was happening, I felt the displacement drive die.

"You little prick." The governor's face filled the big CIC screens once again. "Did you really think we hadn't thought of that?"

"Parker!" I said calmly. "Can we regain our drive?"

"No, sir. I'm seeing overrides surfacing at multiple levels. It would take days to free us."

"Change course," I ordered. "Make for the wormhole. Check you're strapped in tight, kids, because I'm about to bring this old crate to life."

Powerful attitude thrusters responded to my command gestures and brought the *Spirit's* nose around. Then I opened up the main engines, shaking the ship with a throb of urgency and sending someone tumbling across the deck to slam into a bulkhead. I ignored them and concentrated on the burn that would give us the vector we needed to thread through the wormhole.

Then our main engines also shut down.

"In your own way, you're almost admirable," said the governor. "But I can't let you go. Our colony made a pact that binds all of us. Your duty is to die with us, and I'll make damned sure you perform your duty this time."

Parker sighed in defeat. "She's right, sir. We are not getting main engines back this side of the Blight shockwave."

I ignored both of them. I was too busy running flight vector analysis in my head.

"Your outfit calls itself HOPE," I accused Parker. "Live up to your name! Attention, shuttle pilots in our hangar bay! Report your status."

"There's just one pilot, Dad. Me. I slaved the other boat to mine."

"Damn. Then I'll have to come down in person."

"What... what are you going to do?"

"Do? You're flying a GP-13 and you have to ask? I spent years flying one of those, towing endless Kuiper objects to supply the construction of Haven-Two."

"But what...? Oh, I see. Running diagnostics on towing systems now."

"Don't bother. If the towlines aren't working, we're dead anyway. We'll only get one chance at this. Prep both boats for flight and then disable the slave control. I'm coming down to pilot the other GP-13. Parker, I need your thruster pack. Now!"

7

I wasn't as mad as my daughter feared. The *Spirit of Endurance*'s subassemblies had been moved around the construction dock by an attendant fleet of tugs. And the *Spirit* had been pulled out of the yards by tugs before its first shakedown flight. Giving the old girl a tow wasn't strange at all. But to redirect an existing course and thread her through a wormhole with just a pair of GP-

288

13s… I guess you could call that a little *challenging*.

Me? I call it desperate.

The *Spirit* wasn't far off course. All she needed was a little nudging, but powerful though the GP-13s were, the *Spirit* carried a *lot* of momentum. To swing her around, we needed to constantly adjust our position, so we could maximize the change to her vector while keeping the towlines taut.

Burn.

Turn.

Burn.

Turn.

We repeated the procedure many times until I realized we'd overcooked it, and the *Spirit* was in danger of hitting the wormhole side on – which meant she would have such limited clearance that I didn't think we would get through.

As we shifted our GP-13s to counter the *Spirit*'s spin, I finally found time to ask the question I'd been burning to ask my daughter. "What's your name?"

"Hope."

"No, not your organization. *You*. What are *you* called?"

"That's my name too."

"You named yourself after their organization?"

"No. They named themselves after me."

I grinned. This girl would do me proud. "Let's pray you're named well, Hope, because we're going through. Detach towlines now!"

We broke free and looped back behind the larger ship, following the *Spirit of Endurance* through the swirling vortex of the wormhole.

The rip in space-time had hung, ignored, in the Beacon system for so long that I had forgotten how beautiful it was. And how deadly.

Flecks of light from the spontaneous creation of exotic matter punctuated the vortex, which appeared so deeply violet in my simple camera feed that it was barely visible against the darkness of space. And there, at the central aperture, was the endless tunnel, a darkness so profound that more than one wormhole-worshipping cult had declared them to be the divine portals God had reached through to touch the mortal universe.

Colony ships were the biggest ships ever constructed. *Spirit* wouldn't have much clearance, and she was coasting now.

This was going to be close.

*Spirit's* hull suddenly flared and I flung up my arms to shield my eyes. But the ship didn't blow. It was a reflection, I realized. The orbit of Beacon-Four's moon had taken it closer to the dying sun than its parent, and the Blight had caught it. Vaporized it.

We had just moments left to pass through.

Hope lit her main engines and flew her shuttle beneath the big ship. A heartbeat later, I followed her course. No good in the *Spirit* leaving without us.

We were in. The GP-13 seemed to stretch like rubber before snapping back to common sense and shooting down an endless tunnel that reached out before us. The walls of the tunnel were slightly translucent, enough for me to see heavily blue-shifted stars appearing to flee away from us, as if we were an abhorrence.

I swapped to the aft camera and saw the *Spirit* follow us down the tunnel. Saw its spin sending its nose on a slow collision course with the tunnel wall. Saw the coruscation as the ship brushed against the tunnel's sheath and bent like a demonic hound's chew toy.

I hailed my old ship, but I knew there would never be a response.

8

*Captain. Captain? Are you still with us? You have a duty to fulfill.*

I'm here. But I'm not a damned machine. You can't understand how these memories still gut me to the core. You can't know what it was like when we emerged out the end of the tunnel and boarded the *Spirit of Endurance.* We found it awash with floating corpses. There wasn't a mark on their bodies, not so much as a look of surprise. Hope and I conjectured that exotic ionizing radiation had wiped out many of the ship's primary automated systems. But the old colony ship was designed from the beginning with many levels of redundancy. Its crew was not.

It sounds so stupid now, but I kept thinking that if I poked the floating people, then they would crease up with laughter and reveal that it was all a prank. They looked frozen in the act of living, not like any corpses I had ever seen.

But I didn't dare touch them, because then I would know for sure that we were truly alone.

Eventually, numb with loss, we respectfully secured the dead in the cryo stores.

The ship drifted on.

With the colonists gone, and Haven-Three consumed in a fiery death, I wished away the universe outside the *Spirit's* hull. To even look upon the destination the ship had chanced across would have been a despicable act of disrespect, as if the death of everyone could ever be something from which we might *move beyond*.

On occasion my daughter and I spoke to each other, but we said nothing.

I spent most of my time in my old captain's stateroom, gazing into the stash of Earthlight I found there, probably recorded during Earth Death, the moment when, in a desperate act of rebellion, Katrine and I had brought a doomed life into a galaxy that wished humanity dead.

9

*Captain? Who was Katrine?*

All right! I'm getting there. My story didn't play out in strict chronological order, so I don't see why my telling of it should fit your linear straitjacket. Damned machine. You want the first Death Day. Earth Death. I'll give you that.

We'd fled the Earth's destruction at faster-than-light speeds.

But then we settled down to establish the Haven colonies, and the light from distant Earth began to catch us up.

Everyone on Haven-Three knew how to train a telescope back along our path to see the light Sol had sent out when she was still alive. Many were trapped by the sight, unable to do much else but stare endlessly at the dot of light. The Atlantic Ocean, the snowy peaks of the Himalayas, flocks of flamingos, elderly couples doing the crossword together over morning coffee, and the hopeful orbiting ships before the war came: all of these were encoded in a handful of photons buried within that dot. Those infinitesimal messengers connected us to an Earth that was still alive, still dreamed of a future.

Earthlight jewels were constructed to capture these precious final rays of light: gleaming translucent orbs with impenetrable black polyhedra at their centers in which the photons were suspended by a cunning mechanism I never fully understood – and please, God, let that not be a lie. To view the captured photons would be to destroy the jewel, but the knowledge that they held the light from distant Earth was all we needed.

The most ornate of the light jewels were reserved for

the end. Earth Death. The moment when the messenger photons carrying the news of Sol's death would finally reach us on the edge of the Orion Spur, and Sol's light would die. Or so the ritual suggested. In fact, the human eye couldn't detect any change in the quality of Sol's light on the day it died. But seen through more sophisticated devices, the light betrayed the move to fusing helium, to the inevitable swelling of the sun into a red giant that would burn the Earth to an airless cinder and possibly swallow it whole.

Sol's doom sounded the death knell for Haven-Three. I thought the UEF was mad. Earth Death should have been an alarm, a call to action, not a signal to give up and wait for the end. But the UEF grip was strong, and in the minds of the colonists, I was the one afflicted with madness. And a dangerous form of psychosis that threatened to blow the colony apart. No one could be allowed to dream of hope.

Perhaps they were right, but I couldn't give up – just wasn't made that way – and I wasn't alone. While the rest of my crew and self-invited dignitaries watched Sol's climactic death throes play out in real-time, holding hands in silence while sipping the early results of Haven-Three's viniculture, I was in the ammunition store on Deck 13c, expressing a mutual form of personal defiance at the galaxy with Ensign Katrine Thornsen. Nine months later, our daughter was born, but by then I was in jail, and so was Katrine. Haven-Three's two most reviled criminals. I still don't know whether Katrine died or went into hiding, but I could never find her again.

Those Earthlight jewels held a fragment of Sol and Earth within. After we passed through the wormhole, and stored away the dead, I lost track of time, captured by what lay inside the jewels. A few days passed, maybe more, until my daughter roused me. "It's time, Dad. We need to decide what we do next."

I expect I looked at her blankly. I don't recall.

"I've been working though the data from the probes we sent to analyze the Blight. Dad, we can beat it!"

I came out of my funk.

The cold patches the astronomy team on Haven-One had discovered turned out to be machines replicating across the coronal surface. The engines that triggered the helium flash were themselves triggered by a simple radio signal. Machines could be destroyed. Signals jammed. The Blight could be defeated. We couldn't yet strike at whoever had sent the deadly machines, but their first attack could be deflected. Maybe traced back to its source, to a target against which humanity could unleash its full capacity for destruction.

This new information wasn't salvation.

But it was *hope*.

"Dad, they're still there," said my Hope. "The people of Earth are still alive. Help them. Look!"

I glanced at the screen she was holding in position above my head. It was a dot, a G-Type main-sequence star.

"It's a real-time view of Sol," she said. "The wormhole has taken us back in time."

"I know." And I did, but I had been too numb to see the possibilities in this amazing journey.

"We've emerged 621 years in the past, still around Beacon, where in the future we will build Haven-Three."

"Earth's too distant. They won't be listening, can't hear us."

"We need to teach them about the Blight, warn them so they can prepare. Persuade them to *come here*."

I looked up my daughter's face, filled with an optimism that I couldn't share. "You mean, to lure them in with a tempting signal?"

"Exactly!"

"Like the one that drew us in from Haven-Two?"

I couldn't face those bright young eyes, so bewildered by my words. I looked away and confessed to the great secret that I had helped to keep. Haven-Three had been built on a lie. We had chased a signal, hoping for salvation, but found nothing but ghostly echoes.

"What did they use to broadcast this signal?" Hope asked.

I shrugged. "An ICT-7A comm unit. It's a standard FCF model optimized for interplanetary transmission, but can also be deployed as an interstellar relay."

"Do we have any on board?"

"Yes, I replied, my words slowing as my brain spooled up to process the implications. "We've got scores of them."

Her voice lowered to a whisper. "Did *we* send that message, Dad?"

"No!" I slapped the halo of Earthlight jewels from around my head. "Maybe there's a version of us down there right now, but it's not me and not you."

"Right!" she said. "We don't send that message, we'll send one that will *work* this time."

A pang of loss hit me without warning when I recognized that fierce determination in her eyes: that belief that she could take on the galaxy and win... and that I could, too. She was so much like her mother.

We gazed open mouthed into each other's eyes, and although no words were spoken, I had no doubt that we were communicating at a deep level, building upon the implications of what we had said.

"And to work, we need to warn Earth in good time," she said, grinning.

"Which we could do by lashing the ICT-7As together into a huge virtual array," I said with a smile that echoed hers. "We would push a clear message, narrow-beam it back to Earth."

"But before that we need to go through the wormhole again."

We both laughed, and added in unison. "And again."

10

Fuel and life support were not in short supply. We were, after all circling through a hoop if you saw our journeys through the wormhole in three-dimensional space.

But how far back should we go?

The question was taken out of our hands after our third transition through the wormhole. We emerged into a younger version of the Beacon system, but the wormhole no longer existed. Perhaps it hadn't been built yet. The mechanics didn't matter. We had ended up where we had started, 1,863 years in the past. It was time.

Time.

Time...

*Captain? Captain! Captain Acualla! You have to finish.*

Time. Oh, God, it's almost time. *It hurts!*

We built another colony for you. For you who find our signal and come here. Safe Haven, we called it. And you'd better be human, damn you, or I'll return from the afterlife and kick your butts.

Oh, we didn't build cities, floating agri-arcologies, hydropower generators or delicatessens. You'll have to do all that yourselves, but the terraformers and seed banks are doing their job. Over a hundred light years from Earth and you should find a lush Eden with a clean atmosphere, filled with things you can eat, but nothing that's going to eat *you*.

And up there in high orbit about the planet, we've parked asteroids and Kuiper objects to supply you with enough raw materials to get started. The rocks we flattened off as cubes are the key, as you've probably figured out by now. Each one... Ahhh...! Each... one has a

296

hardened data canister with everything we know on the Blight. And nestled beside each canister is an Earthlight jewel. Treasure it. Please. It's all that's left of the Earth we knew.

And… and one day, you'll chance across a GP-13 shuttle that suffered a pressure breach. If there's a desiccated corpse inside, treat her… treat her with respect, okay? She's not a damned archeological curiosity. You owe her.

And so do I.

Not long now…

We were… were going to narrowcast the answers to you. Give you instructions. But my daughter taught me something… to trust those who follow to know what to do. Which is why the canisters are paired with ICT-7a transceivers, massed to beam you a single word, encoded as dots and dashes.

Hope!

That's the word we sent you, because there may be a way out.

Hope!

And I know we won't be beaten.

Hope!

We're as stubborn as mules, and keep coming back no matter how many times we get knocked down. We're like rats, and cockroaches, and the moss that infiltrated my lawn long ago on Earth, no matter what treatment I put down, because we are all from Earth, and that's the way we are. We are going to spread ourselves across this galaxy – and beyond one day – because *that's what we do*. Captain Acualla, First Contact Fleet, out.

Unnggh! Sorry about the coughing. Did you manage to hear what I was saying?

*Yes, Captain. Loud and clear.*

Uhh. Eyesight's gone. Numbness spreading up my legs. If only it would reach my chest. Ahh! Because it

HURTS! So... is it working?

*The comm array is already transmitting your code-word, and I've been streaming the account you've been dictating to every other canister in the network, as instructed. You did good.*

Are they ready for ultra-long-term secure storage? All encryption and access codes disabled?

*Yes, Captain. Though, you needn't have bothered asking. I'm not some fucking UEF bureaucrat. I'm a First Contact Fleet Type-4 AI, and proud of it.*

Did I teach you to say that?

*Yes, sir.*

Guess I did something right, then. Unghh! Not long now... I shan't say goodbye. You're just a recording machine. A very – ahh! – important one, though. Hey! You're not still recording, are you?

# A Change of Plans
By Dennis E. Taylor

Coming out of cryo was worse than being seasick. Captain Henson groaned. He'd *been* seasick, back when there were things like sea cruises and vacations, and a comfortable, civilized planet to enjoy them on. The only saving grace was that this nausea would be over in a few minutes.

He reached up and pulled his eyelids apart, loath to wait for his tears to dissolve the gunk holding them together. The casket lid was up, and his First Officer, Katherine Rougeau, looked down at him. He turned his head carefully and checked his arm. The various catheters, needles, and sensing devices had already retracted into the wall of the cryo container.

Henson grinned up at her—tried to, anyway. He wasn't sure if his face was working properly yet. "Someday, Kat, I'll get out before you."

"In your dreams, sir." Her tone was light, but she looked away, and Henson noticed the concerned expression on her face.

"What's up, Commander?" This was only their third trip out, but the arrival was supposed to be routine. Normally, the ship A.I. would place the *Ouroboros* in a high orbit around the target planet, then begin waking up the crew.

Rougeau reached a hand down to help him out of the casket. She seemed to be able to shrug off the effects of cryo as easily as getting out of bed in the morning. Henson admitted to himself that he was far more average in that particular area.

He stepped out of the casket and paused to check the other units along the wall. More than half were already empty, and the rest were in the late stages of the revival process, according to the readouts at the feet of those units. Henson shivered, even though the temperature in the cryo room was only mildly lower than normal room temperature. Something about the low lighting, the grey and almost featureless equipment, and the acoustically enhanced quiet always made him feel like he was in a morgue.

He signaled Commander Rougeau to follow him as he made his way to the galley for the critical first cup of coffee.

"I checked status, Captain, as soon as I was up. We're in a solar orbit, just outside the habitable zone, rather than in a planetary orbit."

"What? Why?" Henson's eyes widened as he rounded on her. A.I.s didn't just decide to deviate from plan on a whim. Such change would only come with bad news attached.

The commander made a couple of false starts before responding. "The A.I. was unable to identify a habitable planet to orbit."

Henson spent the rest of the short walk in silence, and prepped his coffee while he worked through the possibilities. He took a slow sip before replying, "We have extra-solar planetary surveys going all the way back to the early 21$^{st}$, Kat. Every planet on the United Earth Foundation's target list has been tagged by at least two independent surveys. How is this possible?"

"I'm sorry, Captain, I didn't get that far. Came to get you instead."

"Right. Well, let's get to the bridge, and assemble the staff. First the facts, then the running around in panic."

\*

Captain Henson stared up at the monitor. The image showed a brilliant planet, with sunlight reflecting off a surface almost completely covered in ice. He rubbed his forehead, then swept his gaze around the bridge. The bridge staff, sitting at consoles which formed a horse-shoe shape around the Captain's chair, waited quietly for him to set the tone.

"Okay. Mr. Kumano, report please."

Jea Kumano, the planetary specialist, glanced at his tablet. "I started by checking the original surveys, sir. There were three that catalogued this system as having a habitable planet. Oxygen, good temperature range, chlorophyll lines, and so on. This was supposed to be about 95% Earthlike. One of the better ones."

"…Which is why Pan Quantum Corporation bought it," muttered one of the crew.

Rougeau turned in the direction of the comment. "Belay the politics. We all have our opinions about the PQ deal, but this is no time for it."

Henson waited a moment for any follow-on grumbling to subside, then gestured to Kumano. "So where's our paradise?"

The man made a face. "That's actually 36 Draconis IV on the monitor, Captain. Valhalla. The thing is, the surveys were done using conventional astronomical techniques, and this system is 77 light years from Earth. Sometime after that light left this system, the planet endured a global extinction event."

The room became quiet as the implications sank in. Kumano played with his tablet, and the image of the planet rotated and expanded. The magnified view showed a crater, clearly visible in outline through the glacial covering. "This is the most likely candidate. It's about 50% bigger than Chicxulub. I'm speculating, of course, but it looks pretty fresh, even through the ice. It would have raised enough dust cover to lower global temps over a significant period of time. And that probably put the planet past some climatological tipping point, which stabilized as this." He gestured up at the monitor.

*So Valhalla is having Fimbulwinter. How oddly appropriate.* Henson carefully kept his face neutral. A smile would be completely inappropriate, but his mental monologue was sometimes unable to limit itself. "Is it totally covered in ice?"

"No sir. There's a little open ground near the equator." Kumano glanced over at Sachs, and Henson turned to her.

Barb Sachs, the crew exobiologist, looked momentarily startled, as if she'd walked into her own surprise party. She recovered quickly. "Er, yes. A few patches of land have managed to stay ice-free, and some flora and fauna are surviving in those areas. Whether they're thriving or not, that's another question. This would have been a devastatingly quick change, and I'm sure it took down eighty to ninety percent of the biodiversity of the planet."

"So what's the status of the planet in regards to habitability?"

Sachs stared at the captain. "Sir, you can't seriously be thinking about dropping the colonists here anyway?"

Henson grimaced. "Ms. Sachs, you know the politics. And you know the situation back at Sol. If we come back with the PQ colonists still onboard, then Pan Quantum will either want their money back, or more likely they'll want priority on the next ship out to the next best planet. You remember the uproar the first time. Now imagine them muscling another group out of their assigned target. Maybe a group that your families are part of."

People looked at tablets, the monitor, anywhere except at each other. Pan Quantum Interplanetary had been the biggest corporation in the Solar System, and they'd traded all their assets for an early colony ship and a preferred target planet. The UEF had come close to being brought down by the backlash. In a life-or-death situation, line-crashers weren't well-regarded.

Henson continued. "We won't just push the colonists out the airlock without a thorough review, Barb. However, if the planet is still livable, it doesn't matter if it isn't the pastoral paradise that they were expecting. So, the question remains: can the colonists live there?"

Sachs poked at her tablet for a few moments, more likely stalling for time than actually looking anything up. She met the captain's gaze. "It'll be dicey, sir. We're talking about ten thousand people being dropped into an ecosystem that's very fragile and still adjusting. If they go native right away and try to live off the land, they'll crash the ecosystem for sure. That would be a death sentence for the entire colony."

"The colony supplies include enough rations for everyone for a year," Hertzog interjected. As the landing specialist, he would have the best idea of the colonists' supplies and capabilities. "But as a long-term thing..." He shook his head. "There's no leeway. They have to stretch supplies as long as possible while affecting the native biology as little as possible, while trying not to starve."

"There will be attrition," Sachs said.

"How much?"

Sachs closed her eyes and dropped her head. "Two to three thousand people, maybe, in the first five years."

*

"Oh, *hell* no!" Samuel Jacobs, the colony project manager, glared at Captain Henson. "You're talking about a death sentence for a large portion of our population, and

303

a life sentence in hell for the rest! This isn't colonization, this is abandonment."

"Mr. Jacobs, the UEF's terms of service are very
clear. We make no guarantees beyond the basics. Unless
it's completely unlivable, you get what you get. Every
single shipload of colonists that leaves Earth faces that
same risk."

"This isn't every single shipload, Captain. We paid
for this ship. We *literally* paid for this ship. We *literally*
helped build it. We could have just built our own entirely and gone off on our own—"

"—except that the UEF wouldn't have allocated a
planet to you—"

Jacobs glared at Henson, but otherwise ignored the
interruption. "—but we wanted to contribute to the overall effort. All the corporation asked in return was a good
planet for our employees. Now you're reneging on the
deal. But you'll happily keep the ship, won't you?"

"We aren't—" Henson bit back his response. Really,
this was going nowhere. "Mr. Jacobs, we've done what
you asked. We've delivered you to Valhalla. If we take
you back, we not only waste a thirty-year round trip out
of this ship's service life, but we will *literally*, since you
like that word so much, be sentencing one other group to
death. You know as well as I that we'll never get everyone out-system in time, even with twice the number of
ships. We estimated when we started the process that as
many as a quarter of the colonies would fail. Some of the
colonies are slated to go out to worlds that we *know*
aren't much, if any, better than this."

"That's supposed to make me feel good about the
situation? Those colonists would go out with equipment
suitable for the expected environment."

*Enough already.* Henson took a deep breath. "Mr.
Jacobs, there is no leeway and there are no options. If we
return you to Sol, I think I can guarantee that you will

die there. The UEF *will not* give you another shot. At most, you'll go to the end of the line, which is pretty much the same thing. So we'll be proceeding with the colonization of Valhalla. You can cooperate, or you can go down to the planet kicking and screaming. But either way, we'll be staying for three months to help with settlement, then we'll be returning to Earth."

Jacobs glared at Henson for a few more seconds, then seemed to deflate. "Fine, Captain. Let me get my specialists defrosted and we'll figure out what we can do."

\*

"Come." Henson looked up as Oscar Thorne, the Security Chief, walked in and stood at parade rest. Henson gestured to a chair and Thorne sat down.

The captain steepled his fingers. "Oscar, I have a security concern."

"The colonists?"

"Yes, frankly. Jacobs ran a multi-trillion-dollar empire—well, a portion of one, anyway. He's used to getting his way, he's no stranger to strategy, and he's probably in the habit of playing hardball. Should we be worried?"

Thorne frowned. "Well, they outnumber us ten thousand to fifty. Except that we won't be defrosting all of them at once, of course. We'll shuttle them down in small groups, so it shouldn't be a large risk. There are very few weapons on board anyway, and we have them all. We have the security clearances, we have control of the ship's systems... honestly, I'm not sure what they could do, short of some kind of brinksmanship threat with a bomb or something."

Henson shook his head. "No, even if they pulled off something like that, their only viable strategy would be to force us to ship them back to Enceladus. We'd have Federation Marshals waiting for them when they defrosted, and they'd all spend the rest of their lives in prison. Or more likely just get sent back to Earth, which would be a death sentence. Valhalla may not be much, but it's better than that."

"And that's the thing, isn't it?" Thorne sat back in his chair and crossed his arms. "These are all white-collar workers. Executives, managers, office personnel, technical people. They were prepared to land in a mild, Mediterranean climate, and ramp up at their leisure to something post-industrial. Instead, they'll be adapting to an ice-age climate, with limited access to resources and only the equipment they brought with them, and they'll be spending all their time scrabbling to stay alive."

"Thanks a bunch, Oscar." Henson rubbed the bridge of his nose with thumb and forefinger. "Just what I need, more guilt."

"It's a crappy situation, sir. We're like dandelions, tossing seeds into the wind, hoping some of them take, and knowing we'll lose some of them. It's a cold-blooded approach, but the only one available to the human race."

Henson nodded, silent. The Solar System was doomed. Anyone still there when the Sun started its final inflation phase would be dead. Earth would be seared and parboiled, then vaporized. At that point, the only hope for humanity would be the colonies that had already been established.

He knew that.

It didn't help.

He thought of his own family, already in cryo on Enceladus, queued up with their colony group for a chance at life on another planet. One more trip out and then he would retire and join them in the frozen wait. Then he would face the same risks as any other colonist.

The same risks that Jacobs was now facing.

*

The PQ representatives sat along one side of the conference table, the ship's officers along the other. It was an inevitable configuration, but still set the tone as one of confrontation.

*Well,* Henson thought, *that's probably what's on the menu anyway. Might as well get the ball rolling.* "How is progress, Mr. Jacobs?"

Jacobs leaned forward on his elbows, and interlaced his fingers. The body language projected earnestness, excitement, and supplication. Given the man's former occupation, Henson suspected it was a deliberate choice.

"As well as can be expected, for something we have no enthusiasm for," Jacobs said. "I have some alternatives I'd like to talk to you about, though, Captain. Ways that we can turn this into something more than a simple scrabble for survival."

"All right, Mr. Jacobs." *Really, I shouldn't be surprised.* Of course they'd have been looking for alternatives. But the overwhelming probability was that those alternatives would require something from the *Ouroboros* and her crew.

"We need a few extra months of your time. I mean, for the *Ouroboros* to hang around for a while. I estimate about one year beyond your expected departure date."

That might be acceptable. Barely. There would be an inquiry when they got back to Earth, but Henson could likely survive that.

"And we'll need to keep the ship's fab systems when you leave."

"You'll *what*?" Hertzog stood up, hands on the table, shock written on his face.

"And two of the ship's shuttles."

Hertzog collapsed back into his chair, speechless. His exaggerated eye roll was response enough.

"What's this in aid of, Mr. Jacobs?" Henson asked, interrupting the overacting.

Jacobs poked at his tablet and glanced towards Henson. "We need a head start to get industrial processes working. There's no way we'd be able to get anything going planetside with the equipment we brought—not through all that ice. Even if we luck out and find some rich ore, a half-dozen light-industry printers just won't be enough. But with your help, and the extra equipment, we can start an orbital manufacturing platform, using asteroid mining for our resources. This will allow us to get ahead of the game."

"Why don't you just ask for the entire ship?" Hertzog's face glowed red, and his snarl left no doubt of his opinion. Henson caught his eye and made a *calm down* motion.

"That would actually be ideal, Mr. Hertzog," Jacobs replied, ignoring the silent byplay. "The scenario I'm laying out is a minimum viable option for us, and still leaves us with considerable risk. But it at least allows the *Ouroboros* to leave under its own steam. It's a compromise."

Henson leaned forward and spread his hands on the table, body language that signaled putting all his cards on the table. No doubt Jacobs recognized the move. "Mr. Jacobs, I don't own this ship any more than you do. I can't make decisions to give away equipment that's necessary to the operation of the vessel. Equipment that will have to be replaced when we get back—assuming that it *can* be replaced—which will take the *Ouroboros* out of service for even longer than the one-year delay you're asking for." He shook his head. "We have too few ships, too few spare parts, a shortage of resources back home, and too many people to get out of the system before it becomes uninhabitable. Please stop acting as if you're just asking to borrow my pen. Anything we give you, in the form of time or equipment, worsens the odds of survival for some *other* colony group. This is very much a zero-sum game."

Jacobs looked to his left, and nodded to a man who had been introduced as Mark Andrews, the colony group's head of engineering. As Andrews began to poke at his own tablet, Jacobs said, "Well, we tried. Captain Henson, I would have preferred if we could have done this in a civilized, agreeable manner. I understand your points about the people back home. However, my concern is the here and now, and the people whose safety and future I'm charged with. As such, a compromise having failed, we will be taking control of the *Ouroboros*, and taking what we need."

There were gasps from the crew side of the table, and Thorne leaped to his feet, reaching for his sidearm. The buzz of the intercom cut through the tableau, followed immediately by Rougeau's voice. "Captain, this is the bridge. Our consoles have just gone dead and the A.I. is not responding. Please advise."

"Stand by, Commander." Henson looked at Jacobs. "Your work?"

Jacobs nodded. "No doubt you've prepared for a frontal assault or a suicide threat of some kind on our part. However, many of our people helped design and build the colony ships now owned by the UEF. We have some insider insights into control and operation." He smiled briefly at Henson. "We are now in a standoff situation. My people can't take complete control unfortunately, but your people can't operate the ship."

Thorne drew his sidearm. "We can start by taking out a few of the conspirators."

"Won't help," Jacobs replied, unperturbed. "First, we've made sure that none of our critical personnel are accessible to any of your people with weapons. They have their orders already, and are perfectly capable of carrying them out without guidance from the people in this room. And as soon as you start killing people, we start retaliating. Among other things, we have control of Environmentals."

"We will do everything we can to stop you." Henson found himself surprised at the steel in his voice, despite his intention to project calm.

"And you will succeed, if that is your intention, Captain. Central Engineering has physical security—we were unable to figure a way to gain control there. In a worst-case situation, you can force the reactor to go super-critical. And we can't defrost the colonists without your cooperation, at least for the moment. Or do much without the shuttles." Jacobs swept the room with his gaze. "But please understand, this is not a symmetrical situation. If we defeat you, or you surrender your ship, you still live. You might even be able to return to Earth someday, if the ship can be made spaceworthy again once we're done with it. On the other hand, if we're defeated or surrender, we will die. Understand that—being sent down to Valhalla under the conditions you have specified is a death sentence. You have nothing to threaten us with. It's death, or death."

He stood and gave a small smile. "No doubt you'll wish to discuss this amongst yourselves. I'll be available at any time for further negotiation. However, we'll begin our operations immediately, to the extent we're able." Jacobs nodded to the room, turned, and walked out, followed by the other PQ representatives.

Thorne safetied and holstered his weapon. "It would seem I was insufficiently devious. My apologies, Captain."

"Son of a bitch," Henson muttered. He gave himself a shake, then said into the air, "Did you get all that,

Commander?"

"Yes sir. We've done a quick audit. It's about what Jacobs said. We control engineering, cryo, C&C, and externals. They control or at least have denied us control of fabrication systems, environmentals, drive systems, A.I. systems, and astrogation."

Henson thought for a moment. "Contact Engineering. I want some of them in space suits at all times. They can work out the shift schedule. If they lose contact with the bridge, they should be prepared to blow the reactor."

"Sir…"

Henson returned Sachs' horrified stare. "Barb, right now there's nothing to stop them from just turning off our air and waiting for us to die. Or turning down the heat and waiting for us to surrender. We need a counter-threat for a proper détente. I don't believe it'll actually come to that. Jacobs could have gone that way immediately, had he wanted to."

He stood, looked at each of his officers. "Everyone take ten for pit stops and refills, then reconvene here. We're going to discuss strategies." He turned to look at the intercom panel. "Commander, I want you here for this. Delegate the bridge to Bertelli." Without waiting for a reply, he flicked off the intercom.

*

Henson looked around the conference table. This time, it was all bridge officers. A large pillow sat on the intercom panel, further weighted down with miscellaneous personal items. At Rougeau's perplexed look, Thorne explained, "We're up against programmers and technicians, Ma'am. Anything that's controlled by software is suspect. I'd like this discussion to be private."

"We'll need to be careful what we say when in range of an intercom, then. That's going to put a strain on things," Rougeau said.

"Bertelli's working on it," Thorne explained. "I'd put his tech skills up against anyone else, here or back at Sol. And he knows this boat at least as well as the PQ people."

"Okay," Henson interrupted. "What have we got? Commander, you had a discussion with Jacobs?"

"Yes, sir. As he pointed out, we're in a standoff right now, at least in the short term. Unfortunately for us, their backup plan is to start disassembling the *Ouroboros* for parts and materials. They can literally rebuild around us. Worst case, they could simply seal us in the sections we control, then ignore us."

Henson looked at Thorne. "What can we bring to bear if it comes down to a fight?"

"Captain, we're not a military vessel. Security has always been aimed at the drunken-crew level of problems rather than armed insurrection. We have perhaps a dozen handguns, and we're slightly outnumbered at the moment. If they get control of Cryo, that will change, of course."

"Can we launch the shuttles?" Sachs asked. Now that the initial excitement had worn off, Barbara Sachs seemed to be moving from terrified to outraged.

"No, we took them off remote access right away. Again, software." Henson gestured to her, palm up. "What did you have in mind?"

"Sir, whatever else they may want to do, if they can't get down to Valhalla, they're screwed. I was thinking we'd fly the shuttles out a kilometer and park them."

Thorne sighed. "The problem being that they're more likely to get control of them than not, which is why we took them off remote. Now, neither group can use them except by physically piloting them."

"And we have crew with spacesuits and weapons in control of the hangar deck."

"Fine," Henson said after a moment's thought. "So what are the obvious strategies? What can we do, what might they do?"

Thorne considered, his lips puckered in concentration. "They need the shuttles. As Sachs said, without those, no one is going anywhere." He nodded to Sachs. "So we need to not only defend it, but take steps to deny them the resource should they take the hangar."

"You mean blow them up."

"Or something. Doesn't have to be that dramatic. Maybe we can just remove some parts."

"Interesting thought," Rougeau said. "I'll talk to Engineering about options."

"What do we need?" Sachs asked.

"We need our ship back," Henson answered. "But specifically, even if we took back all systems, we still can't leave. We have to unload the colonists, and we can't do that without their cooperation."

"Maybe we should just do what they want and take them back to Earth," Kumano suggested. "The UEF can decide what to do from there."

Thorne shook his head. "That's no longer an option for them. As soon as they engaged in mutiny, they became criminals. Pirates, essentially. They'd know better than to agree to a return to Earth at this point—being dumped on Earth would be the *best* they could hope for. No, for better or worse, they're committed to settlement of Valhalla. The only question is how they're going to go about it, and whether we and the ship will survive the process."

"If they take apart the ship, we'll never get back. Our families—" Barb Sachs' eyes were wide and shiny with incipient tears.

"—won't know until they wake up at their destination that we never returned," Henson finished for her. Barb was retiring at the same time as Henson, and both their families were in the same colony group.

"Can't we at least talk to the colonists? Make an offer?"

Henson gave Sachs a small, sad smile. "Hey, we won't tell anyone if you let us go'?" He shook his head. "I wouldn't buy that. I doubt Jacobs would, either. And anyway, I already told him—truthfully—that a return to Earth for them would be one-way. Even before the mutiny."

Sachs looked at her hands, defeat written on her face.

Henson leaned forward. "I think Thorne is right. At this point, a standoff doesn't benefit us. They'll win in the long term. So let's work towards getting back to Earth, with or without the colonists still in cryo, and let the authorities work it out."

"Which means we need A.I. systems, drive systems, and astrogation. How do we take them back?"

"We don't," Thorne said. "Not in the way you mean, anyway. They don't physically control those systems, they've simply hijacked them in software. Or possibly by tapping into control systems somewhere, which is almost the same thing. We can fix that, given freedom to move about."

"What I'm hearing, then," Rougeau said, "is that we'll ultimately lose a standoff. They can wait us out and work around us until we starve, or we give up, or until they simply seal us off from the rest of the ship. We have to take steps, and soon, to take back the ship and head back to Earth."

Henson nodded. "That seems like the most sensible analysis." He turned to Thorne. "Let's talk tactics."

*

Captain Henson crept along the hallway, weapon in

hand. Never in his life had he visualized himself in a combat situation, and if there had been enough crew to go around, he'd have stayed on the bridge where a captain should be. But they'd have only one chance to pull this off, and no crew to spare.

A brilliant piece of detective work by Bertelli had pegged the location where the colonists had tapped into ship's systems—a small workshop in Fabrication Systems, used for forming opto-electronic components. It was the only reasonable point where the colonists would have been able to access and control the systems that they had taken, and it didn't include access to comms infrastructure. This would make their plan at least possible.

Preparations had been made, contingencies discussed. If they could take this location, then they could conceivably retake the entire ship.

Some cautious surfing of the monitoring systems had determined that most of the colonists were engaged in an attempt to cut into the Cryo area. Well, that made sense. Their whole strategy would center on waking as many of their own people as possible. A smaller group was attempting to gain entry to the hangar. That accounted for most of the colonists, and the rest were probably guarding the workshop.

Henson's strategy was simple. Two teams would attack each of the Cryo and hangar groups. They'd make a real attempt to capture the colonists, but their ultimate purpose was distraction. Before anything else, the crew needed to regain control of ship's systems, which meant taking the workshop.

That was up to Henson's team.

The captain looked down the hallway at the hatch to the workshop, dogged and shut. They would have to hope that the colonists would come out to rush to the aid of their colleagues. Otherwise, the team would completely lose the element of surprise—assuming they could even open the hatch from the outside. The hatches weren't lockable by design, but the colonists could have rigged something.

He checked his watch. The attacks on Cryo and the hangar should happen in less than ten seconds. He waited until five seconds, then held up five fingers, and counted down.

On zero, his earbud announced, "Going in. Team two, team three, execute."

After twenty excruciating seconds of silence, the earbud said, "Hangar deck, operation complete. Colonists are secured."

He reached for his *transmit* button. "Team two?"

"Not quite so good, sir," the earbud responded in Rougeau's voice. "Cryo group has some kind of what I think might be zip guns. Not terribly efficient, but probably lethal. And they seem to have a stockpile. I guess they've been busy with the fab system."

"Have they been using them, Commander?"

"Yes sir. No casualties, but we're pinned down. I think they're happy to simply hold us off."

"Then you're going to have to ratchet it up, Commander. Use lethal force—no more warning shots. A standoff doesn't benefit us. I want the Cryo group to call for help."

There was a moment's hesitation. No one on this crew was military. Some of them had never held weapons before. To be ordered to shoot to kill would take some mental gear-shifting.

Finally, "Yes, sir. Executing."

Again excruciating silence, this time for almost a minute. Then, the wheel on the workshop hatch began to spin. Henson and his group crept up and waited. The moment the hatch began to swing open, one of his crew grabbed and yanked. As a colonist fell through the door, still holding on, the assault group poured through with guns up.

The colonists were caught flat-footed. Gathered near the door with pipes and other makeshift weapons, they seemed stunned by the invasion. But then, these people weren't likely to be military either. This was a foreign situation for everyone, on both sides.

Henson gestured with his pistol. "Drop 'em. Do it now."

Slowly, carefully, the colonists crouched and placed their weapons on the floor.

Henson looked around, but couldn't see Jacobs. Well, it always would have been a roll of the dice. The colonists had been scattered in three different areas. Their leader could have been at any of them. This group was smaller than expected, though. He wondered if there was a fourth group that they had missed.

Henson gestured to one of the captured colonists. "You. Where's Jacobs?"

The man stared back, face a mask. "Henry Roberts. Circuit designer. Citizen Number 3411A CX3331 N102."

There was a chuckle from one of his team, and Henson allowed himself an eye-roll. "Oh, spare me. This isn't war, and you're criminals, not soldiers. And you're under arrest. So try to be realistic."

Roberts smiled, and Henson felt a sudden jolt of dread. Had he missed something? Had this been too—

At a shouted "Now!" from Roberts, the captured group dropped to the ground. At the same moment, more colonists burst out from behind equipment and furniture, pointing some kind of weapon—not zip guns, but something shorter and bulkier. His crew had been starting to relax once the action was seemingly over, and were now caught in their turn.

Henson brought his pistol around, hoping to give a

good accounting. But before he could even pull the trigger, he felt a sudden stab of pain in his chest. He looked down at two darts sticking out of his shirt, inches apart, trailed by long, thin wires. *Oh, hell.* There was a moment of unimaginable pain...

\*

Henson had never been tasered before, although he'd seen it done. Turned out it was every bit as painful as it appeared, both during and afterwards. He felt himself being lifted by the arms and placed on a surface. His limbs wouldn't obey him—attempts to move produced only painful twitches.

At least he wasn't dead, yet. But the assault had failed. They'd taken some colonists, which they would now have to put under guard, further stretching their resources. The colonists would mount another assault on cryo. This time they'd probably seal in the bridge crew first.

Either way, the crew of the *Ouroboros* had lost. They wouldn't return to Earth, he wouldn't ever go into cryo to be defrosted with his family on whatever distant planet they were assigned to. And his family would never know what had happened to him.

He felt himself being lifted again, then put down. A familiar smell, pinpricks on his arm. *Cryo? They're putting me in—*

\*

Coming out of cryo was, as it turned out, still worse than being tasered. Or maybe being put in cryo after being tasered was some perfect storm of discomfort. Henson lay still, trying to decide if death was preferable.

His internal monologue was interrupted by Commander Rougeau's voice. "You aren't even trying anymore."

Opening one eye to make focusing easier, Henson tried to smile. "I concede, Commander. You are the king, er, queen of cryo. Now, help me up?"

Rougeau grinned and reached down. Henson opened his other eye, attempted to focus on the hand, then gave up and let her handle the link-up.

Henson grunted with effort as he stepped out of the casket. "What happened after I was put in cryo?"

Rougeau shrugged. "We took a significant loss with your group being captured. There was simply no way to recover that I could see. I had a long talk with Jacobs after that. He showed me his plans and gave us some guarantees, and I decided to trust him, not that we had a lot of options. He put us all in cryo. Said it would be easier than guarding us, and anyway he knew we had family back home."

"They didn't disassemble the ship?"

"They didn't need to, sir, once we surrendered. With unrestricted access to the ship, fab system, and shuttles, they went with their Plan A."

"And?" he said, as he started for the galley.

"The project is far enough along that they no longer need the ship, sir. Jacobs gave orders to wake the crew, and we'll be able to leave as soon as we're all up to speed."

"How long?"

Rougeau didn't pretend to misunderstand. "Twelve years, five months. The UEF won't send anyone to investigate, of course. They don't have the resources. But by the time we get back, they'll have declared the *Ouroboros* lost and rescheduled colony groups."

"That's gonna suck for a lot of people."

"Well, yes, until we show up."

Henson sighed. "There will be an inquiry, of course.

I might lose my command."

"They'll lose more than you, then. I'll tell them to stick their job where the sun doesn't shine. I know several crew who've expressed similar sentiments."

"Thanks, Kat. I hope you don't have to make that choice." Henson shook himself and put his *captain* persona back on. "Have you inspected the colonists' work?"

Rougeau made a face. "I'm beginning to wonder if we put the wrong people in charge back at Sol. The Valhalla colonists are probably the most concentrated group of nerds, geniuses, and engineers that humanity has ever seen, and they've just finished a twelve-year stint with no bureaucratic oversight, no budget limitations, effectively infinite resources from asteroid mining to work with, and free rein to do whatever they want."

"And?"

"You'll have to see for yourself."

*

Henson was back in the captain's chair, surrounded by his bridge crew. He couldn't help contrasting today with the last time he'd been in this position. The monitor was showing a split screen, an O'Neill cylinder displayed on one side and a half-finished Bishop ring on the other.

"That thing is how big?"

Kumano turned to him. "The ring? Ten kilometers wide, two hundred kilometers in diameter. When it's done, it'll have over six thousand square kilometers of usable space, and a full one-gee equivalent at the rim. Meanwhile, it's a little crowded in the cylinder, but they wanted to have a habitat finished as quickly as possible so they could wake everyone up and have their specialists available."

Kumano worked his console and the view changed. "They've built a huge mirror at Valhalla's L2 point, which has increased solar heating by about thirty percent overall, since it's delivering sunlight twenty-four-seven. Er, well, twenty-nine and twelve minutes on Valhalla, I guess."

Hertzog threw up his hands in a gesture of surrender. "I wonder if there needs to be a re-think of the way colonies are planned and supplied. Our dump-and-run policy might get more raw numbers out there, but probably reduces long-term odds of survival."

Henson gazed at Hertzog for a moment in silence, then sighed. "Not our decision, Mr. Hertzog. We'll bring it up, of course. Assuming it doesn't come out in the interrogation." He turned to the Communications Officer. "Ms. Chen, please connect me with Mr. Jacobs."

It took only a moment—no doubt Jacobs had been expecting the call. His face popped up on the overhead monitor, looking visibly older than the last time Henson had seen him. That was yesterday for Henson, but twelve years ago for Jacobs.

"Ah, Captain Henson. Getting ready to return to Earth?"

"Yes, sir. You look like you're in fine shape. And thank you for—well…" *For not disposing of us.*

Jacobs made a moue of disapproval, as if he'd read the thought. "We're not barbarians, Captain. We only needed time to bootstrap. We gain little by keeping the ship at this point, and the karmic hit would taint us for generations. I'd rather begin this adventure on a proud note. Also…"

Henson raised an eyebrow, content to let Jacobs continue at his own pace.

"Captain, I know we're technically space pirates from a legal point of view. But if the UEF can get past that minor issue—well, this will be the first time that a ship returns with information on a confirmed successful colony. If they want to send more ships this way, we'll

321

have room for them. And jobs."

The captain stared, speechless. It was a virtual certainty that the UEF would jump at the chance, and with good reason. This would be better odds than some random planet only known by examination from light years away.

Henson nodded. "Thank you, Mr. Jacobs. I'll convey that to them. I think they'll make the right choice. Goodbye, and good luck."

"And you, Captain. And the people of Earth."

Henson nodded to Chen, who ended the connection. He looked around the bridge, then again at the monitor, which had switched to the view of the planet, still shrouded in ice. *But not for long.*

Humanity would survive. Even if all the other colonies failed, this one would carry the human race. Despite the way it had all gone down, Henson felt a moment of pride at the thought.

Maybe he could get his family's colony redirected here. It seemed a better bet than rolling the dice on an unknown destination.

Henson turned back to his staff. "Helm, take her out. Let's go home."

## About the Authors

### Felix R Savage Biography

Felix R. Savage writes hard science fiction, space opera, and comedic science fiction. He woke up one day to learn that he was a New York Times and USA Today bestselling author, but he continues to keep a low profile, and never stops watching out for any sign the lizard people have found him.

Download THREE free stories from Felix's science fiction worlds here: www.felixrsavage.com/free-books/

### Jasper T. Scott Biography

**SUBSCRIBE to the author's mailing list** and get two FREE Books with collectively over 5,000 Amazon reviews and an average of 4+ stars out of five.
http://files.jaspertscott.com/mailinglist.html

www.jaspertscott.com/

### Amy DuBoff Biography

Amy has always loved science fiction in all its forms, including books, movies, shows, and games. If it involves outer space, even better! As a full-time author based in Oregon, Amy primarily writes character-driven science fiction and science-fantasy with broad scope and cool tech. She recently completed the seven-volume Cadicle space opera series, a multi-generational epic with adventure, political intrigue, romance, and telekinetic abilities. When she's not writing, Amy enjoys traveling the world with her husband, wine tasting, binge-watching TV series, and playing epic strategy board games.

http://www/amyduboff.com

**Ian Whates Biography**

Ian Whates is a writer and editor of science fiction, fantasy, and occasionally horror. He is the author of seven novels (four space opera and three urban fantasy with steampunk overtones), the co-author of two more (military SF), has seen sixty-odd of his short stories published in a variety of venues, and is responsible for editing around thirty anthologies. His work has been shortlisted for the Philip K Dick Award and twice for BSFA Awards. His novel Pelquin's Comet, first in the Dark Angels sequence, was an Amazon UK #1 best seller, and his work has been translated into Spanish, German, Hungarian, Czech and Greek. Ian served a term as a director of SFWA (the Science Fiction Writers of America) and is a director of the BSFA (the British Science Fiction Association) an organisation he chaired for five years. In 2006 Ian founded multiple award-winning independent publisher NewCon Press by accident.

www.newconpress.co.uk


**Ralph Kern Biography**

Ralph Kern, a frequent contributor to the Explorations anthology series, has released three novels to date; Un-fathomed, which was acquired by Audible Studios for production, Endeavour and Erebus.

For as long as I can remember I've always enjoyed science fiction, especially the grand masters of the genre, Arthur C Clarke, Stephen Baxter, Alistair Reynolds and many more before deciding to try my hand.

I hold a degree in Aerospace Technology and won the opportunity to work in Milan on the design of a satellite with the European Space Agency, gained a Pilot's License (which led to the best weekend job going - taking Air Cadets flying in a motor gliders) and for a year was an officer cadet in the Territorial Army.

After all that, I had a quarter life crisis and decided that I would succumb to the kid in me and follow a career in chasing bad guys and joined the Police. That led to a huge hole in my life though, the desire to think about what I consider 'the big issues', a desire I'm addressing with my writing.

Nowadays, I've calmed down a bit and enjoy spending time traveling, seeing what the world has to offer, scuba diving, long distance running and writing, of course. www.scifiexplorations.com

### Scott Bartlett Biography
Scott Bartlett is an SF author whose most recent series combine space opera and military SF - The Ixan Prophecies trilogy (Book 1 is *Supercarrier*) and the Mech Wars series (Book 1 is *Powered*). Both series are set in the same universe.

If you like your sci-fi packed with action and interwoven with alien mysteries, you can **get 2 free books** from the Ixan Prophecies universe when you join Scott's mailing list: http://scottplots.com/traitor-giveaway

### Scott Moon Biography
Scott Moon started reading and writing science fiction and fantasy at an early age. He spent several summers of all night Advanced Dungeons and Dragons gaming be-

fore joining his first garage band and running off to Hollywood, CA to attend the Musician's Institute. Always a dreamer, it was the writing muse that always screamed loudest.

Years later he is still writing, still dreaming, and connecting with authors and readers through the Keystroke Medium YouTube show and Podcast (www.keystrokemedium.com). Examples of his speculative fiction projects include The Chronicles of Kin Roland (military science fiction / adventure) and the Son of a Dragonslayer trilogy (urban fantasy / horror / adventure) available in different formats on Amazon and other fine distributors.

http://www.scottmoonwriter.com/

Subscribe to his newsletter here.
http://www.subscribepage.com/h0a7o5

**Robert M. Campbell Biography**
Robert M. Campbell hails from the east coast of Canada, having recently returned to New Brunswick after extended stays in Toronto and Ottawa. An early love of astronomy and technology eventually led him to a career in software engineering. Robert studied Computer Science and Anthropology at Acadia University in Nova Scotia.

After twenty years working in the aerospace, government and open source software sectors, he has written his first science fiction novels, Trajectory Book 1 and

Book 2 – the first instalments of a projected six in the New Providence Series. Seedfall: New Providence Series Book 3 is out now.

Robert and his wife Deb live on their small hobby farm on the river where they focus on writing and art.

http://robcee.net/

Sign up for his newsletter at http://eepurl.com/cauWDz

**Scarlett R. Algee Biography**

Scarlett R. Algee's work has appeared in (among others) Sanitarium Magazine, The Sirens Call, Body Parts Magazine, and the recent anthologies Zen of the Dead and Lupine Lunes; she was also the copy editor of Explorations: First Contact. She lives in the wilds of Tennessee with a beagle and an uncertain number of cats.

https://scarlettralgee.wordpress.com/

**Nathan Hystad Biography**

Nathan is the Explorations series creator and editor, with 'A Time and a Space' marking his first full short story foray into the collections. He hails from Alberta, Canada, where he runs Woodbridge Press and works hard at writing his own books. His debut novel The Event, a modern day invasion SciFi Adventure, is being released early 2018. Sign up to his newsletter from his website link below for details!

www.nathanhystad.com

www.scifiexplorations.com

## Tim C. Taylor Biography

The author of military science fiction and space opera series, including 'The Human Legion' and 'Revenge Squad', Tim C. Taylor lives with his family in an ancient village in England. When he was a young and impressionable boy, between 1977 and 1978, several mind-altering things happened to him all at once: 2000AD, Star Wars, Blake's 7, and Dungeons & Dragons. Consequently, he now writes science fiction novels for a living. For exclusive free eBooks, swag competitions and much more, join the Legion at humanlegion.com.

## Dennis E Taylor Biography

Dennis E. Taylor is an avid SF reader, computer programmer, snowboarder, and runner. He lives in the Lower Mainland of British Columbia. After far too many years as a wage slave, he has retired and taken up writing full-time and sleeping in.

http://dennisetaylor.org/

32954091R00195

Printed in Poland
by Amazon Fulfillment
Poland Sp. z o.o., Wrocław